SCHRÖDINGER'S
CATERPILLAR

Zane Stumpo

Published in 2012 by FeedARead.com Publishing –
Arts Council funded

Copyright © Zane Stumpo.

Cover design and illustrations by the author.

A CIP catalogue record for this title is available from
the British Library.

All characters in this novel are fictitious and any
resemblance to real persons or events is strictly
coincidental. Apart from the doppelgangers, obviously.

Chapter 1

The caterpillar appears on a Tuesday morning at thirteen minutes past eight, clinging to one of the few remaining green leaves on Graham Paint's dying houseplants - although it takes a further nine minutes for it to unleash a quantum event which shatters the universe apart.

It appears to Graham, that is. In fact it has been lurking in his kitchen for a while, waiting for him to pad downstairs on the cream berber carpeting which flows through his semi like a great flood of muesli.

The caterpillar is big and sap green, with a very silly face drawn on its pulsating bottom. Its head is hidden away at the pointy end. But on its great verdant bum it has two eyes drawn with what looks like black felt-tipped pen. The eyes are coloured in with bright orange, while the pupils, again outlined in black, have pale blue centres. They are unfeasibly badly drawn. Why? you might ask. Do caterpillar predators have absolutely no artistic taste, no sense of irony, no grasp of when someone is totally taking the piss?

Clearly not. If natural selection can create creationists, then it can manage a caterpillar with a face on its arse.

The houseplants are Kerri's responsibility. 'Responsibility!!' Graham might have thought, if the caterpillar hadn't distracted him. That's a laugh, he would have muttered mirthlessly to himself under his breath. But he doesn't think any of this, because of the laughable green caricature clinging to his plants. Graham guesses that evolution has given it a rear end which, to a bird, looks like the head of a snake. So that's what birds think snakes look like.

Catapulting it out the window into the bushes on the end of a spoon would be temporarily satisfying, but ultimately not as rewarding as identifying it, classifying it, and learning of its habits and lifestyle. Pate, his colleague at work, is bound to know about caterpillars. Pate knows all about this sort of stuff, and also about everything else (except fashion sense and avoiding being irritating).

But first, Graham needs to get himself to the office.

And already, with all this staring at a drawing of a bird's worst nightmare created by Richard Dawkins or God or somebody, Graham will be at least two minutes, possibly three, late for work.

He picks up a big matchbox, empties the matches into the drawer which houses the string, pencils, playing cards, old spectacles, and bits of things which belong to things and scoops up the badly drawn caterpillar into the box. He will show it to Pate and relieve his itchy curiosity with the backscratcher of knowledge.

Graham thinks that Pate can provide him with answers. But the familiar pattern of his day has been disturbed in ways he cannot begin to understand. By putting the caterpillar in a matchbox, he has just changed his life forever. Or till it ends. Whichever comes first.

Graham puts the matchbox down on the granite worktop and switches on the kettle. He's not going to let a caterpillar disturb his morning routine. But a quick mental calculation tells him he's going to have to dress twelve percent faster than usual. Even Kerri's puzzling absence makes little difference, other than the lack of chainsaw noise in the bedroom as he rushes upstairs to grab a tie. Sometimes at this point there's a sudden choking sound as his wardrobe rummaging wakes her and she tries to inhale her own brains. This is generally followed by a plaintive wheedle...

"Grey?"

She calls him this, thinking it endearing. (Wrongly).

"Graaaey?"

Grey Paint. Sounds attractive. Fortunately this morning there's no bleat from the bed, and no need to explain that he doesn't have time to make her a cup of tea. He scans the ties. That one won't go with his shirt, that would clash horribly, that's gross, that screams 1978. He holds up 'won't go' and '1978', and puts '1978' back.

Charging back downstairs into the kitchen he pauses in the act of tying his tie to pour hot water into a cafetière. He pulls the long end through (tie) and plunges. A sploot of coffee fires upwards and lands on his shirt.

"Shit!" he hisses sibilantly. He's yet to master any other sort of hiss.

Then he remembers he's alone in the house, apart from a large green caterpillar with staring orange eyes (with cobalt blue pupils) drawn on its bum. It probably has only a rudimentary grasp of English vernacular.

"Arse!!" he yells.

"Shite!!!"

The extra 'e' adds at least an order of magnitude to the Richter Scale of sweariness. It feels much more efficacious. The sheer joy of the lengthened vowel releases his soaring heart like, like... ...well it reminds him of a hunting hawk thrown skywards. (Did I remember to point out that Graham can be quite a prat at times?) He looks at the stain on his shirt (his only shirt - how the hell is he supposed to work out how the washing machine starts? He tried a wash three days ago and his shirts are still gazing wrinkly at him through the glass as the machine absolutely refuses to negotiate for their release. He knows they are gazing wrinkly. They have wrinks in them). He looks at the stain on his shirt and comes back down to earth. Or more strictly speaking, berber.

"Bum," he mutters.

Graham dabs at the hot coffee on his shirt (Ow!) with some kitchen roll from the pine wall dispenser, then adjusts his tie to make the wide bit sit a little higher on his chest. That should hide the stain from most angles. Even if he had another shirt or could swap a hostage with the washing machine he wouldn't have time to change and still catch the 8.21 bus. He grabs his suit jacket from the chair where it has spent the night (Wouldn't that just piss her off if she knew about it! Ha!), adjusts his tie sideways, picks up his briefcase and opens the glass-panelled front door. Then dives back into the kitchen and grabs the matchbox, thrusts it into his jacket pocket, and skids back outside.

It takes him two minutes and forty seven seconds to make his way to the bus-stop - down the concrete slab path with chippings on either side, past his 4 x 4 gleaming on the drive. (Might as well look good even if you can't actually afford to drive it, park it or tax it. He could do a SORN certificate and formally take it off the road. But then he'd be stuffed for the seven mile trip to Tesco and the bottle bank. Oh well.) Out through the squeaky clanky gate, along the pavement past the other really quite similar houses (although Graham's has definitely got an extra couple of feet of garden which will be great when kids come along) up to the end of the avenue, left at the pillar box and down the street to the main road where the bus stops.

Normally.

Today he does it in 2.39. Strange how striding along like the clappers till your breath is laboured and your brow glistens only saves you eight seconds.

The bus shelter is empty.

"Shite!"

Again Graham allows himself an 'e', but fortunately he only thinks the word. Because he thinks it jolly loud. In his head he yells and screams it until it echoes back and forth between the double glazing and privet hedges.

The problem is this. There are normally between four and seven people at the stop when the bus arrives. The arithmetic mean is about 5.3, or was last time he kept a diary. So the chances of arriving at the stop seconds before the bus is due and finding nobody else there are about the same as finding eleven people waiting. In fact the probability that there are fewer than 0.3 people standing there (by chance) is 5% or less. Reckons Graham. So there's a 95% chance that he's just missed the bus. He calculates. Because he's like that.

Graham wonders how ordinary people without the benefit of an education and without lively enquiring intellects ever muddle their way through their sadly uncalibrated lives.

He peers up the street to the left where the bus would have headed.

No bus.

Then again, it only takes seventeen seconds give or take two or three to get to the trees at the end of the road and vanish, so he might have missed it by eighteen seconds and never know.

Now this presents Graham with a quandary.

Option 1: He can stay where he is and hope both the bus and its usual passengers are late. (He calls this Bus Not Been.) He'll be first in the queue (if one materialises) and can jump on board and grab the best seat available. But if the situation is actually Bus Been he could be standing here at the stop for ten minutes and will definitely be late for work.

However (Option 2) he can set off up the road and past the trees at the end and stride on another couple of hundred yards to the traffic lights near the shops. This allows him a choice of an additional bus (the number 19 which converges at that point with his usual 13). Graham's analytical brain tells him that Option 2 (Walk) gives him more choices of bus and a decent chance that he'll only be four or five minutes late. Whereas Option 1 (Stay) is a gamble. It's his only chance of arriving on time – but the downside is greater too. (See Example 1 at the end of the book.)

Take a chance and go for broke by staying put? Or opt for the mathematically correct way of minimising his lateness? What will he choose?

Kerri would know the answer. As she would put it -

"You're a wimp, Grey. You always imagine the worst that could happen and go out of your way to avoid it. Why don't you just trust your luck some time and take a sodding chance?"

"You loser," she would add, in case he'd missed the point.

Which is why Graham, after dithering like a small boy needing a wee, sets off up the road at a brisk pace, glancing back nervously over his shoulder every few paces at the empty bus stop.

At least he thinks it's empty.

Then he's not so sure. Is that someone inside the shelter up at the far end? A few yards further, glance back, and now there's a woman approaching with a wailing kid pulling at the buggy she's trying to push.

A few more yards, look back, and the bloke he knows from Number 11 strides up, looking up the road and down at his watch. By now the figure at the head of the queue is fidgeting from side to side.

Graham isn't quite trotting as he passes the trees, but he would be disqualified from a walking race. Assuming they'd let him take part in a grey suit in the first place. And let him walk while trying to look backwards, which could be construed as potentially dangerous.

Then as a schoolgirl runs towards the stop the bus sweeps into view, and pulls up smartly, herding all its standing passengers forward in a neighbourly huddle.

By a more mysterious mathematical law than the ones Graham has computed (The Law of Sod) he is

9

exactly halfway between the two bus stops. He dithers backwards and forwards, then starts to run up the road towards the traffic lights. If the woman has problems with the buggy, and drops her change, and the schoolgirl's pass has expired, and if the traffic lights stick on red, then he might, just...

But the Mysterious Mathematical Law also decrees that everyone has the right change and gets on in a trice, perhaps even a bice, if such a thing exists. One might imagine it would be two thirds of a trice. And in seconds (about seventeen you'll recall) the bus is cruising past where Graham stands, panting and defeated. Graham, not the bus. The bus is barely out of breath. Graham glares at the passengers, many of whom look like they're trying to stifle a monumental fit of the giggles. The schoolgirl covers her face with her hands as she sees Graham gasping and forlorn. The mother of wailing children purses her mouth as if she's holding her breath underwater.

Then Graham gets the shock of his life. A shock which could hardly be surpassed if he lived many lives.

A man is sitting in his favourite window seat, halfway up the bus.

The man wears a dark grey business suit.

He has a tie like Graham's, knotted so the small end is longer than the big end.

It really, really doesn't go with his shirt.

The man looks exactly like Graham, except Graham would never wear an expression like that - one of insufferable smugness.

It's uncanny. The man's eyes meet Graham's, and widen in amazement.

Doppelgraham nervously fingers his tie, revealing a brown stain on the shirt beneath. As the bus sweeps past, the man looks down at Graham's shirt. So does Graham. The two men sport identical Rorschach coffee tests. What the men see in these shapes is unambiguous.

Doppelgraham will get to the office on time.

And Graham, as usual, is stuffed. But precisely how stuffed he is, he doesn't yet begin to comprehend…

Chapter 2

Graham works in an open-plan office in a six storey building. Lifts, stairs and toilets are down the middle, dividing the office into two main areas. Each toilet block has two doors - one opening on to one side of the office, and the other, naturally enough, on to the other. Graham runs up the stairs to his floor and darts on to the wrong side of the building, then into the Gents, barely pausing to smack the button on the hand drier before emerging moments later by the door on the correct side. He applies the brakes and skids to a leisurely pace as he emerges, shaking the last few imaginary droplets from his hands, with an expression on his face consistent with the sort of chap who arrives at work on time, then takes a few minutes to freshen up and look his best before stepping forth to grace his more flustered colleagues with his presence.

"Fuck off, Grey," calls one of the herd.

"Sorry?"

"Think our heads button up the back?"

At the far end of the office Mr Edgar looks up. Mr Edgar is Graham's boss.

"I beg your pardon?" Graham persists to his streetwise colleague.

But all heads are down, working studiously.

"And I've asked you before not to call me Grey."

Edgar gestures with his head for Graham to join him. Graham quickly but neatly puts down his briefcase and smartly walks up to the end of the office where Edgar holds court. As Edgar opens his mouth to speak Graham jumps in. (So to speak).

"I'm terribly sorry I was just a little late this morning. Slight argument with a cafetière..."

"Are you having a laugh?"

"No sir! I just meant that - "

"I want these calls brought up to date."

And Edgar throws a folder of documents on the desk in front of Graham.

The company Graham works for is a small mendacious firm of management consultants. They specialise in tormenting clients who suffer from a fear of technology. EDITsolutions was set up by Simon Edgar when he left his previous employers, a large consultancy from whom he stole every technique, database and contact that he could lay his hands on. He was bound on departure by a "no competition" contract forbidding him to work in the same field or approach any of his previous employer's clients. There are two reasons why he wasn't taken to court when he set up a rival to his old company. The first is that the firm he was leaving had of course been set up by someone who had ripped off another firm previously and didn't want too much attention drawn to the nature and origins of their highly vaunted skills. The second is that any consultant there worth his or her salt was also planning their own exit, ripping off what they could, in order to set up in competition themselves.

The firm is called EDIT to incorporate the name Edgar and Information Technology. The originality and imagination shown in this choice is a fine metaphor for the knowledge and skill the company offers its clients. The word 'solutions' was added with a small 's' and no space because this implies, right up front, no whacking about the foliage, that EDITsolutions is contemporary, hip and brimming with street cred. Not as in credibility. More like the credulity of its potential clients. And these clients need solutions (with a small 's') because they have Problems (with a capital 'P'). And every other company created since 1994 has the word "solutions" in its name. Simon Edgar suspects it's mandatory - probably some ruling at Companies House. Simon wonders why all the best names, like Google, seem to have been taken years ago.

EDITsolutions offers a very reasonably priced company risk audit. For a ridiculously small fee the consultants will look at a company's computer system and assess its efficiency and security. The report which is then produced is detailed and voluminous. In fact downright weighty. EDITsolutions will always print it out rather than supply it on a CD just to let the client see, and feel, just how heavy and important it is. It then sits threateningly on the CEO's desk, since it is too massive to risk on a shelf.

When the CEO dares to open it he will wish he hadn't. His system is vulnerable to attack! His whole company is compromised! Legions of crazed hackers, snoopers, spies and (let's face it) - buggers - are sniffing round his drives, cables and airwaves. They can pick up signals from an innocent-looking wire and read every keystroke typed in to any computer. If the company uses any wireless technology then it is as good as dead already. Not just Wi-Fi, but wireless keyboards, wireless mice - everything is sending out signals to the mysterious ranks of fifteen year olds with backward baseball caps at this very minute cruising up and down the street, laptops whirring, in the back seats of cars with darkened windows and Eastern European number plates.

By this time, sweat is dripping from the CEO's brow on to the tome he is glued to (probably something to do with the solutions). He riffles and ruffles increasingly desperately until, big surprise, he falls upon the Recommendations section. By now he is really stuck. Firewalls, ASCII passwords, Interference Robustness, Worms, Trojans, and WEP 40/128-bit Hex - surely voodoo! Even Derren Brown at his most Machiavellian couldn't create so many spine-tingling assaults on the nervous psyche.

Fortunately a Solution is at hand (which will be why he can't put the report down) in the form of EDITsolutions! Thank God he's found them, and clearly in the very nick of time!! And yes, there in the covering letter they say they hope he found the report useful, and if there's anything further EDITsolutions can do to implement countermeasures, they'd be delighted to help.

The CEO didn't rise to his exalted position without understanding the benefits of delegation. (And his dad ran the company for forty years first, which may have helped too.) So he picks up the phone to the company's in-house IT specialist, and suggests he should come and have a look at The Report. The IT specialist is actually a guy in HR who once worked in a mobile phone shop, but not to worry - outside help is at hand. (HR is of course Personnel. Remember Personnel? That's the department that looked after staff when they were people and not resources.) And not surprisingly the IT guy won't take long to recommend to the boss that

EDITsolutions should be brought in to weave their magic and save the day.

That's when the fun really starts.

And the massive bills.

And the reign of terror.

Because EDITsolutions should really be called We Are The Virus You Dread Ltd.

"But surely that report is pretty impressive?"

Be quiet!!! You are only the reader, and convention doesn't allow you to ask naive questions during a book!

"But..."

Enough!!!

"B..."

Hey!!!!

Oh, all right. I'll explain.

The report is an old and trusted friend. Simon Edgar copied it on to a CD when he left his previous job. That company nicked it from someone else. Every so often someone finds a new scary threat and edits it in, for a laugh.

The client company's name is substituted every time using Find and Change. The original client was probably Laker Airways or Sinclair Cars.

It would all add up.

And Graham is profoundly sick of the whole thing.

His life is a crock of shit.

My life is a crock of shit, he thinks.

"My life is a crock of shit," he says.

Although he may have just thought it, and thought some apostrophes as well.

'My life is a crock of shit' is what he thinks. All the time.

And he wishes beyond anything that he could do something to change it.

Chapter 3

Where had we got to? I knew you'd make me lose the plot.

So don't fidget.

I mean it.

Right. Simon Edgar had just thrown the folder down in front of Graham. So Graham scurries back to his desk and takes a look. Graham is one of the shock troops who leap in through the breach in the company's defences once they have been exposed to The Report. (Long echo fades away...) His job is to start unpicking the computer system, discovering all the while that things are MUCH MUCH WORSE than initially seemed to be the case.

Graham removes the laptop from his briefcase. He soon has it booted up and logs on to his emails. There are four new messages flagged as unread. He quickly checks them. Nothing that can't wait.

Des at the next desk turns to study him. Des is a prat. His hair has migrated south for the winter and now nests under his nose.

"That was a bit of a bold wind-up, Grey me old son."

"Sorry?"

"The bit about being late."

"I realise nobody round here seems to pay too much attention to punctuality, but it's all about respect really. Is my time worth more than yours?"

Des looks at him with bafflement written all over his face. Although from this angle you can only see flem. Baf is round the back, and ent is hidden behind his right ear.

Graham can't abide unexplained details, non sequiturs and loose ends. (Either. Remember he can't stand lack of punctuality. Keep up!) So he feels obliged to fill the silence by volunteering more information.

"It was only a few minutes. But I believe in pulling my weight. So after this morning's unavoidable delay..."

"You weren't late."

"Well I was actually, because if you check my watch against the clock up there you'll find that when I spoke to Mr Edgar - "

"You'd already been in half an hour before that."

"Pshaw." (I hope we can agree on that spelling.)

"You came striding in, said Hi! to Edgar, then made a couple of calls and breezed out again."

"Don't be ridiculous. Anyway, how would you know? You're never in at that time."

"I started at eight because I'm knocking off early this afternoon to get the car's emissions checked."

"How did I look?"

"Same as usual. Well maybe not as confused, now you ask."

Graham looks stunned. He had been planning to rattle through his expenses and shoot out again to see the client he is currently advising, in order to rack up more chargeable hours. But now he doesn't know what the hell's going on.

Graham has consternation written all over his face. From this angle you can only see a stern countenance, and from where Des is sitting it seems like a con. But if Graham were to turn his head a fraction, we would see that the nation awaits...

Chapter 4

Graham has been working with his current client for four months. Emission Solutions Ltd are a waste disposal firm. They manage waste segregation, into recyclable categories like plastics, glass and paper. They collect it in gaily coloured plastic wheelie bins. They help firms to meet their environmental targets. Then they chuck it all in a landfill. Now they're targeting the motorist. The market for fleecing drivers was already pretty saturated, so they had to work out a new angle. Fortunately cars pollute the planet too. And that's where Emission Solutions comes in.

Their approach is almost the same as EDITsolutions. Find something scary that the customer doesn't understand. Crank it up from scary to terrifying, under the guise of providing helpful advice. Charge top dollar to make the fear go away. But find something new to frighten them next time.

So it's a bit odd they didn't see through the sales pitch from the consultants. It was almost their own script.

As Graham sits in his office trying to work out his next move, Emission Solutions is already open for the day and preparing to greet a new customer. A middle-aged lady drives her vast Sports Utility Vehicle onto the forecourt. You know the kind - outside dimensions the size of a Transit van, while inside the four seats are squashed into a space slightly smaller than a Mini.

A highly trained specialist mechanic waves the lady into the garage and directs her up on to the ramp. Fortunately she decides to drive rather than walk up, concerned that otherwise the man will hoist her up into the air and look up her skirt. She drives forward on to the ramp, pulls on the handbrake, steps out of the door and abseils ten feet down to the ground. The ramp hasn't been lifted yet. That's just the way they design SUVs.

The man leaves the vehicle running and presses the button to hoist it aloft.

"Nasty noise from your exhaust there," he volunteers as a conversational gambit.

" $\mathit{2zzzzzzw}$," he adds.

That's the word I'll use for a sharp intake of breath. 'Pssst' means 'Hey look over here' and 'Shhhh' means 'Be quiet', but nobody's ever cracked 'Sharp intake of breath'.

So " $\mathit{2zzzzzzw}$ " it is.

"The bolts are corroded. Makes it difficult to take out the middle section. Now you don't want to damage that bit at the front. That's the catalytic converter, and if that gets knackered we're talking silly money.

" $\mathit{2zzzzzzw}$.

"I mean, really silly money. We can try to take out the middle section, but it'll take a few hours for labour, and it might not work. But we're happy to have a go... Might be better to take off the whole rear assembly - then it's a simple job - see those bolts are fine there. So if you want it done by tea-time, then... By the way, you didn't really drive here on those tyres, did you?"

Emission Solutions have taken the market to new levels. They have an incredibly sophisticated computer to check your car. If you don't pay for the privilege of using it then there's no telling what might happen...

Failed MOT, obviously.

The imminent death of yourself, your family and loved ones. Not just from bits skidding, leaking, breaking, exploding or bursting into flames. But creeping hidden assassins - armed with poison fumes, airborne toxins, insidious cancerous chemicals.

Mass fatalities within a twenty mile radius of anywhere you drive.

And, of course, the destruction of the planet.

"Fortunately we've got just the Solution. It's a machine that we stick up your exhaust pipe and connect to a computer. We tune your thingy. And you'll soon be right as rain."

This all strikes a gynaecological chord which is finely calculated to bring a clammy sweat to the middle-aged lady's brow.

"I'm not too sure about that rear suspension either - that can be as bad as worn tyres..."

But despite their polished scare tactics, Emission Solutions still didn't see themselves in the mirror when the consultants came to call. So now Graham is already well underway with the programme of installing a complex new computer system which will require constant attention from EDITsolutions to keep running. The new system has Spyware monitoring and virus detection at system, server, drive, partition, folder, application and document levels. You can't open a file without the file being taken into a dark room, having a light shone in its eyes, being deprived of sleep, made to assume uncomfortable and strangely deviant positions and having electrodes attached to its testicles. Unless it's a girl file, in which case it is placed in a dormitory and told that it's not really very attractive and will probably never find another file to share a folder with.

This process guarantees that each computer is free of viruses and other nasties. It also takes forever. The system grinds to a halt, wheezing and coughing over tasks that ran faster on the old machines ten years ago.

Fortunately there is a Solution. Since the computer spends most of its processing power constantly examining its own entrails you have to get a much faster computer. A wonderful, modern beast with the very latest operating system. On which none of your old programs will run. So you then have to update all your software. And the new software allows you to download security updates every few days off the web. Which opens up the risk of infection.

Fortunately there is a Solution. EDITsolutions will offer you a maintenance contract which keeps the computers just about chugging along, and which also keeps your company in thrall to their ministrations for all eternity.

Chapter 4 again

Got carried away a bit there. Let's restart Chapter 4.

Graham has been working with his current client for four months. He's become a familiar face. Trusted, liked even, because his work doesn't clash or compete with anything done by the staff. From Ron down to the cleaners, everyone confides in Graham. The costs of having a full-time consultant are pretty scary, but compared to the digital Armageddon which would be unleashed otherwise, and the financial meltdown which would follow, the cost seems bearable.

So when Doppelgraham strides confidently across the yard he's greeted with cheery banter from the lads in the service bays.

"Throw up on your shirt then?"

"Pity you missed the tie."

Doppelgraham studies their greasy overalls.

"What's the difference between Hugo Boss and a pair of manky overalls? No, I didn't think you knew."

He ducks the greasy rag which is thrown at his head and pushes the revolving door to the office reception area.

"Hi Dorothy!"

"Hi Graham! Another day, another dollar!"

He smiles and strides confidently through to the office which has been set aside for his use. There he removes the laptop from his briefcase. He soon has it booted up and logs on to his emails. At first he is surprised to see no new messages. Then he realises that there are four at the top of the list which he hasn't seen before. They bear today's date. Yet despite the fact that he's never seen them before they're marked as having been read. He glances up at the clock. It's seven minutes past nine, and they've all arrived in the past hour or so. How the hell could someone read his emails before he sees them? And if it was some crazed hacker why wouldn't he just mark them as unread again to cover his tracks?

Doppelgraham has concern written all over his face. Although from this angle you would only notice once. Which contrasts oddly with the notion that he is Graham's double, or Doppelganger.

Doppelgraham shrugs off his frown and logs off. He picks up the phone and dials a three digit number.

"Peggy? Can I have a word with Ron, please?

"Hi Ron. Yes, no rest for the wicked, yup. Ha ha. Look, have you got a moment? I've been thinking of a way we might be able to simplify things here, and save you a bit of cash. Yeah, I'll be right up."

Doppelgraham hangs up. He is thoughtful as he closes the lid of his laptop and heads purposefully out of his office towards the stairs.

Chapter 5 at last

Graham picks up the phone and dials Emission Solutions.

"Hi Dorothy! ...another dollar, yes. Look have I..."

He tails off as he realises the idiocy of what he is about to ask. 'Have I already seen you this morning?' How stupid would that sound? Or 'Have you seen someone who looks exactly like me?' Paranoid and alarming.

"Did I..."

No better.

Dorothy saves him.

"I thought you'd gone upstairs to see Ron? How come you're on an outside line?"

"I'm on my mobile." No need to reveal he's not in the office, and some mysterious clone is wandering about their premises.

"Ah, of course. Stop by on your way down, will you? I've got some mail here for you."

"Sure thing."

Ten minutes later, Graham is in a cab heading for Emission Solutions. No buses now - he's on the client's tab. Most of his colleagues get private hire cars to take them to work at the client's expense, but Graham thinks that's going a bit far. He tells the cab to stop at the end of the road, pays the driver and collects a receipt, and the couple of blank ones he gets along with it which he will fill in with different coloured pens in his own time, some with his right hand and some with his left, to vary the handwriting.

He can't work out how to get in without being spotted, because Dorothy's desk commands a broad view of the yard and visitor car park. Someone identical to him must already be in there, and he can't raise awkward questions by arriving twice. Instead he looks for another way in. He enters the yard of the furniture warehouse in the next industrial unit, then sidles up the path which leads round the building to the wheelie bins at the back. There he peers through the metal fence and scraggly bushes to the upstairs floor of Emission Solutions, where Ron's office is sited. It's a modest location, but it does enjoy an uninterrupted view of the girls' playing field at the back of the industrial units. By craning his neck Graham manages to spot Ron at his desk. He can make out the pine-effect plywood veneer covering the walls and the calendar which extols the virtues of silicon spray lubricants for the motor trade. Ironic, really, considering the shape of the women holding each canister aloft.

Graham ducks as Ron walks to the window and stands observing the fifth and sixth form girls playing hockey, their gymslips tucked into their knickers to allow their sinuous limbs full freedom.

"Didn't know Ron was into hockey," thinks Graham.

Idiot.

Graham stretches his neck forward again to see what Ron is up to. Ron turns away from the window and stands there for a while. It looks like he's talking to someone. Graham steps up on to a couple of pallets which lie behind the wheelie bins. Sure enough, there's someone else in there with Ron. They're engaged in conversation. Ron walks away from the window towards the far side of the office to consult a planning chart. As he does this, the other figure moves towards the window to enjoy the view. Graham sees a dark business suit, but can't quite make out the face. The tie looks familiar, though. His darkest suspicions are confirmed. It's Dopplegraham - his unwanted double. Graham cranes further forward to see through the bushes. He is distracted by the girlish shrieking from the field nearby. Then his foot slips from the pallet, and as he tries to grab the fence and bushes to save himself an awkwardly protruding piece of wire catches the front of his trousers.

Doppelgraham is in full flow, outlining his plans so that even Ron can follow, making good use of the planning chart. Doppelgraham is a little distracted by the fact that the "Today" plastic sticker is still on the ninth of February. A better indicator of the present is how far into the year the slightly grubby finger marks have reached. "Why do I still get the crappy little businesses?" Doppelgraham asks himself silently. (Answers on a postcard...) "Why don't I get the consultancy jobs with the big multinationals who can really afford to bleed money?"

Then, as he's about to bring his speech to an irresistible conclusion, he's distracted even further. He steps up to the window to get a better view of the hockey match. (How the hell does Ron ever get any work done?) Then he notices a policewoman following a furniture security guard down the side of the warehouse, under the CCTV camera on the corner of the roof. They step over to some wheelie bins. Then, remarkably, they pull a man out of the bushes. He is

29

alarmed, dishevelled. His shirt protrudes from the front of his trousers. He waves his arms (or tries to, against the grip of the law), revealing a familiar coffee stain on his shirt. Good God Almighty! thinks Doppelgraham. It's the man who stared at me when I was on the bus this morning. The panting, wide-eyed apparition who gave him such a start. Now he seems to have been arrested while ogling a girl's hockey match, with his flies undone. Despite the fact that he is a squirming pervert and I am clearly a decent sort of chap we look identical! Oh my God! My whole reputation could be in jeopardy if there's some self-abusing loser trying to impersonate me.

Blurting a sudden apology, Doppelgraham turns away from the window, past a surprised Ron, and heads out of the office and downstairs.

Ron scurries over to the window. At the side of the warehouse a policewoman is leading a man in a suit away up the path and out of sight, holding him firmly but at arm's length to avoid contamination.

Graham must have witnessed something, realises Ron. He must have gone to help. Of course Ron has no idea he was speaking to a different Graham.

He continues to watch, as the security man disappears back into the warehouse. Downstairs in reception, Doppelgraham hurries towards the revolving front door. He waves at Dorothy as he passes.

"Your mail!" she calls as he disappears. "Dozy bugger."

Round by the warehouse the real Graham is desperate. The policewoman has twisted his arm into an unfeasible position, and has folded his wrist back on itself. She has clearly got it wrong. Arms don't bend that way. It reminds Graham of past attempts to refold an Ordinance Survey map, but with more agony and fewer contours. He struggles to comprehend what has led him to this painful predicament. How can your fortune turn on such a stupid misunderstanding? He agonises. Should he try to escape? Or stand by meekly while his fate is determined forever. The policewoman tells him not to move. With her free hand she presses a button on her shoulder radio and conducts a conversation which seems to involve a lot of abbreviations. Then she lets go of his arm and takes out her notebook.

Graham is astonished to find himself legging it down the road. He wasn't aware he'd made a decision, but suddenly, and uncharacteristically, he's off like a sprinter on steroids. Tautology, he thinks, although fairly briefly, as he's concentrating on getting out of the policewoman's sight as fast as possible. He runs back down the side of the warehouse and charges into the bushes. The policewoman (shall we call her Enid?) sprints across the end of the car park to head him off. As soon as he's hidden by foliage Graham doubles back, and while Enid hares towards the entrance to the yard, Graham leaps back out of the bushes and vaults into the nearest wheelie bin.

Enid (despite humorous convention this isn't actually her name, but you'll realise that she's far too busy for me to stop her and ask) skids to a halt on one foot and looks all around. Then she spots Doppelgraham scurrying across the yard at Emission Solutions, head lowered, trying not to be spotted.

"Stop!" she shouts. "Come here!" Even she thinks this sounds a bit limp, so she adds, in quite a deep voice for a woman "You're nicked".

Graham starts to clamber out of the wheelie bin to give himself up, but as the lid rises and he looks out, he realises that Enid's shouting at someone else. (I was able to let him know about the Enid name thing while he huddled in the dark.) Meanwhile Doppelgraham freezes. Enid grasps him by the arm and forces it up behind his back.

Above them, the CCTV camera on the corner of the warehouse swivels back to its usual position, presumably protecting the girls on the playing field from harm.

Chapter 6

For the second time that day Graham slopes into the men's toilet through the door from the far office, and does his best to straighten himself out before heading for his own desk. Then he walks over to the inner wall and steps into the stationery cupboard. Pulling the door shut behind him he picks up a stapler and bends over to try to repair the rent in the front of his trousers. Moments later Heather from accounts opens the door and is astonished to see him firing staples into his groin. Her eyes roll upwards and she falls in a faint to the floor.

Actually that bit's not true. I made it up because it would have been quite funny. As it is he effects a crude repair without attracting too much attention and sets off up the stair to look for Pate from Research.

Pate is invaluable to EDITsolutions. He is kept upstairs so he won't have to socialise with normal people. He is the only known case of someone with a full head of hair who employs a Bobby Charlton comb-over. In the classic version a sensitive slap-head will comb every hair they can find at the sides over the top of their shiny skull in an attempt to conceal their shame from the world. Over the years the side parting will migrate south (like Des's moustache) until the comb-overee is teasing hairs out of their ears and trying to get them to come out and graze upon the Serengeti plains of their scalp.

Pate fears that this will be his lot. And he knows that the ruse has never been known to succeed. (He could be wrong. There might be some very successful and effective comb-overs walking among us undetected. Possibly.) Pate's theory is that over the years people notice the downward slide of the parting and suspect someone is trying to pull the wool over their eyes. So to speak. So he has decided to comb his bushy hair right over his thickly thatched crown from just above his left ear to the tip of his right so that when eventually baldness strikes nobody will realise. His task is complicated by the fact that his wiry, slightly crinkly hair is thick and stiff. In fact as hair goes it's on the bushy side. Like Berberis perhaps, or Gorse. So he needs to cut the top fairly close and use hair gel to induce the combed-over hank to keep its allotted position on the top of his head. This luxuriant quiff is fairly resistant to strong winds, but tricky when swimming, when it tends to float upwards from the left side of his head like kelp on the edge of a reef. To prevent this he used to grow a small tuft over his right ear too and tie this to the top hank. However this caused confusion in crowds when people to his right would assume he was a Hassidic Jew, while his left side looked positively Christian. There was a bad experience once when visiting North Finchley when he found himself in the middle of an argument in the street and was attacked by two rival gangs. He only escaped by swiftly turning to face back the way he had come, simultaneously defusing the situation and confusing his assailants.

Graham finds Pate insufferable. Pate delights in demonstrating his superior learning and intellect. But

Graham tolerates Pate's put-downs because he knows himself to be brighter and can afford to be gracious. Pate only appears smarter because he is a nerd and ought to get a life. Graham knows that nerdiness doesn't equate to intelligence. But somehow he can have conversations with the infuriating Pate which wouldn't happen with his other gormless colleagues, and Pate can't find anyone but Graham prepared to talk to him at all. So they irritate each other constantly, never missing an opportunity to get their heads together for some mutual disparagement. Others might mistake this for friendship.

Graham pushes open the door to Pate's small room. The Research Library is an exception to the open plan scheme of the general office, because it's a Library. For Research. Or so the theory goes. In practice it was decided to enclose the room to prevent Pate from annoying other staff, or alarming them with the realisation that in the 21st Century anyone can still believe that it's acceptable to wear men's trousers in taupe.

"Aha!" declaims Pate annoyingly. "How goes it, my old mucker?"

"Tread carefully," says Graham. "I'm having a very difficult day, and it's not lunchtime yet."

"Hence the olfactory assault." Graham smells of eau de wheelie.

"Hence."

"So what seems to be the problem, madame? Just the facts - nothing but the facts."

"Well it started this morning when..."

Graham breaks off suddenly, remembering the fat green badly drawn caterpillar and the matchbox. He fishes in his grubby suit jacket and pulls out a rather battered box, which he places on the desk between them.

"I was going to ask you about this, but there's some other weird shit going on."

"Your oblique demeanour suggests there's something in the box other than matches. Perhaps you should recount your tale first. Then we can proceed once more to Canterbury."

Graham, not for the first time, wonders what the hell Pate is on about.

"There's no great mystery. Just a caterpillar I thought you'd like to see. But wait till you hear this…"

And he recounts the tale of how he couldn't decide whether to wait for the bus or charge on ahead, and how the bus appeared when he was stranded between stops.

"It was going like the clappers. It came careening round the bend at the end of the road -"

"It was pulled over on its side by ropes?"

"Of course not. It was leaning over because it was going so fast."

"You said careening."

"Duh."

"You mean careering."

"Do I?"

"You careen a ship by pulling sideways on the masts with ropes to reveal part of the hull, to allow weed and barnacles to be scraped off. So although the lateral vector may be appropriate, there's no suggestion there of speed. So I suspect you mean 'careering'."

Graham kneads his brow with his knuckles. His head careens over. Attempts to talk to Pate often induce a severe knot of pain. Slowly, fighting the sensation of steel bands around his forehead, Graham straightens.

Steel bands as in metal strictures round his skull. Not the steel bands which create ringing metallic noises by banging old oil drums. These have more gaiety and limbo dancing than Graham is currently experiencing.

"If you let me, I'll hone in on the important bit."

"You hone a knife to sharpen it, so I think what you're trying to say is 'home in'."

In the outer office staff look up at the sudden bang from the Research Library. Then they remember that anything involving Pate would also involve a lengthy explanation, and set to their chores once more.

Within the Research Library, both Pate and Graham nurse their sore heads. Pate speaks first.

"Touché."

Graham resumes. He doesn't feel proud of what he's just done, but he'd run out of alternatives.

"So I look up, and there on the bus, looking back at me is - me!"

"Gadzooks," observes Pate thoughtfully.

"How could there be two of me? And then I get to the office, late, and I'm told that I'd already been there half an hour before. And I go out to the client and I've been there too. And I'm still bloody there! And when the guy spots me he looks just as surprised as I am - like it's me that's the spare part!"

Pate looks very thoughtful indeed. He stands up and smoothes down his thick wiry hair in an automatic nervous gesture. He ponders. He sucks his teeth. Which may be annoying, but less so than sucking someone else's. At last, when Graham is heartily sick of him milking this critical moment, Pate sits down and looks intently at him.

"This caterpillar. Is it still alive?"

"Let's have a look..."

"No - wait."

They look at the box. But not in it.

"The caterpillar may be cognate to your ancillary experiences."

"Come again?"

"The two may be related. Have you heard of Schrödinger's cat?"

"Sort of. Remind me."

"Erwin Schrödinger was the father of Quantum Theory. Now Quantum Theory is incredibly accurate, but totally bonkers. He created a famous thought experiment. 'Imagine that we've sealed a cat in a box' he said. In the box is a phial of poison gas. Looming over the bottle is a hammer which is attached to a Geiger counter beside some uranium. One cheep from the Geiger counter and the cat's a gonner. So after a while the cat may have died, or it may have survived. But without opening the box we have no way of knowing. Schrödinger suggested that until we open the box the cat may simultaneously be dead and alive. Only when we open the box does this dual possibility collapse into a single outcome."

"That's rubbish. Doesn't need me to point that out."

"Aha - my incredulous confidant. So you might presuppose. However the world is full of things we don't understand, which require very strange hypotheses to elucidate."

"Pate - stop speaking like a twat. This isn't easy for me."

"OK amigo. Think tiny. Sometimes electrons behave like particles - but sometimes they act like a wave. And this really bugged the scientists. In 1925 Schrödinger proposed an equation to describe the mysterious wave behaviour of electrons. It was amazingly accurate. A revolution in physics was underway. Quantum physics was born. Scientists were sceptical. American scientists were skeptical. Scientists with sore throats were streptococcal. But since then quantum physics has stood the test of every measurement and examination a baffled world has been able to devise. But what was Schrödinger's wave equation actually describing?"

Graham looks blank. He hopes the question is rhetorical. Pate pontificates on.

"Maybe it represents the probability of finding the electron at any given point. If the value is high, then it's likely to be there. If the value's low it's probably somewhere else. Maybe."

"Why doesn't someone just have a look?"

"Because looking changes what you're looking at! And the electron could even be in two places at once!

"That's bollocks."

"No – there are two of those, in one place each. You'll just have to believe me about the electrons. Sneaky little buggers, with negative attitudes. Impossible to pin down. When Schrödinger devised his thought experiment he was trying to explain this. So listen up! An electron can be 50% here and 50% there."

"Where?"

"There."

"Ah."

"In the same way Schrödinger's cat could be both dead and alive, with a probability attached to each. Only when you opened the box would the wave function collapse and you'd know the outcome. So looking decides the fate of the cat!"

"Pshaw."

"Pshaaw indeed." (Pate pronounces it a little differently.) "That's the easy bit. Now let us contemplate the multiverse."

"Multi? As in lots of verses? Like 'The Lyke Wake Dirge'? Or lots and lots and lots, like songs by Fairport Convention?"

"There are some scientists who think that we live in an infinite multitude of parallel universes - a veritable froth of universes constantly spawning from each other, blossoming out through the dimensions of space and time in the ever-expanding aftermath of the Big Bang."

"Why would our universe spawn, or split, or whatever?"

"I know this is hard for you..." Pate ignores Graham's filthy look. "If it's any consolation, Einstein thought Schrödinger's cat was bollocks too. In a statement slightly less well known than E=mc^2 he said 'Schrödinger's cat - zees eez bollocks.' But even Einstein came to believe it, in the end. He hated to admit it. In fact it really pissed him off. But he couldn't find a flaw in the argument. He also said 'Zis Schrödinger's cat eez bollocks, but eet eez ze dog's bollocks."

"Are you sure about that bit?"

"It's high on my wave of probabilities."

"So how does this help me?"

"We're getting to that bit. This still left the major philosophical question: what exactly triggers the decision? Alive or dead? How does nature decide?"

"I have a hunch you're going to tell me..."

"It could be that the reason the cat can be both dead and alive is that the universe has split in two. In one it's a cat-o-nine-lives. In the other it's a catastrophe. Each universe is as real as the next. If there are parallel universes then the wave function never needs to collapse magically. Both outcomes can continue to be true. All possible worlds can coexist. We are on a roller-coaster ride within a proliferating labyrinth of everything else that ever could be."

Graham ponders this for a while.

"Bugger me," he eventually concludes, philosophically. "So where does my caterpillar come in?"

"There seems to have been some sort of malfunction. Sounds like you've got two not-quite-separate universes, or a not-quite-collapsed wave function."

Graham understandably looks blank. "Does that mean there's a universe in which you haven't got a bruise on your forehead?"

"Exactly! Now you're getting it. Now think back - what was the key decision you took this morning, between picking up the caterpillar and spotting yourself on the bus?"

"Well first I had to decide whether to have coffee or tea, but I guess I always have coffee. Then again, I could have decided to change my mind..."

"What about the bus thing?"

"Right enough, that was the biggie. I guess I was all stressed and everything, and wondering where the hell - well never mind about that just now."

Pate ponders.

Then pronounces.

"When you decided to hurry on towards the next bus stop, that must have been a quantum decision. But because of the caterpillar in your pocket you managed

41

to trigger a state where two alternative universes were spawned. Amazingly, each continues to occupy the same physical space. In phase. Coherent."

"Does that mean that me on the pavement and me on the bus are actually the same person?"

"Precisamente. Initially your lives will be very similar - but who knows what consequences there might be from such a simple decision? The two Grahams' lives might start to go differently in all sorts of ways we can't even begin to imagine!"

Graham thinks of Doppelgraham being led off by the scary WPC.

"OK," says Pate. "So let's open the box now and see what happens!"

"Wait a minute!"

Graham grabs the matchbox off the desk. Inside it he feels something thud slightly from one side to the other. Was that a tensed 'shit-I-hope-this-doesn't-hurt-in-caterpillar-thought-language' kind of bump? Or a caterpillar rigor mortis kind of thump?"

"What if it's a butterfly?"

"Let's find out."

"But hang on. As soon as we find out - that'll collapse the wave function, won't it?"

"Certainement, mon brave."

"And either me or other-me will suddenly vanish."

"I think that's very likely."

"Well I can't open the box then, you wally! I'd have a fifty/fifty chance of ceasing to exist!"

"Don't be slow Grey." And Pate snatches the box from his grasp. "You'll still exist in one of the universes. It just might not be this one..."

And Pate starts to slide the matchbox drawer open...

Chapter 7

WPC Enid Sneep leads Doppelgraham through to an interview room in the police station. (If you remember I made up her first name, since she was too busy for me to ask at the time. Sneep is a guess too, but it seems rude to butt in now to check.) A young Constable accompanies her. Doppelgraham is restrained by a force field of furrowed brows and jutting lower lips. Enid seats her suspect on a hard chair at the far side of the table and leans over to the cassette tape machine. She finds there's no tape, and thinks about muttering under her breath. She resists the temptation because she wants to keep the upper hand and let this slimy little perv fear the full force of the law in all its inexorable efficiency.

"Wait here with him. I'll be back in a minute."

We shall call the young Constable Donald Ainstable. (That is his name, although only by coincidence. After I made up the name I found his mum and dad had called him exactly the same thing. They chose Ainstable because that was his dad's name as well.) Constable Ainstable sits down on a seat between Doppelgraham and the door.

He tries to look anywhere but at Doppelgraham. When he weakens and sneaks a sideways peek, Doppelgraham immediately starts to babble.

"Look there's been a terrible mistake! I was upstairs in an office - I've got an alibi - I mean a witness - and I saw this shifty bloke, and I do agree he looked slightly like me, if you didn't get a very good look, which of course you wouldn't, with him running away and stuff but..."

PC Ainstable is desperately racking his brains for the legal stuff they told him at Police College. He decides firm non-communication is the best bet. He holds up his forefinger.

"But..."

PC Ainstable moves the forefinger to his lips.

"B..."

Then he points at the tape recorder and microphone.

Doppelgraham decides to wait.

Constable Ainstable crosses his arms and looks patiently at the ceiling.

Chapter 8

I know that was a very short chapter, but Chapter 6 went on forever, didn't you think? I'm sure I'm not alone in thinking they'd never give up rabbiting and get on with it. So there's Pate pulling open the matchbox, and Graham trying to grab it back again, and the drawer shoots open and the great big green badly drawn caterpillar shoots across the room, hits the wall with a thwack, and drops to the floor (with a thwock).

"Fuck's sake Pate! You could've killed it! And then what?"

They both look in horror at the lump of caterpillar. The eyes outlined on its rear end continue to stare wide open, bright orange and sky blue. Presumably its real eyes, tiny and invisible at the other end, are clenched like buggery. Hang on! Do caterpillars even have eyes? Maybe they just pulsate about like a clenched gut after a vindaloo until they bang into something. Like wriggly green students. Fortunately it really doesn't matter whether caterpillars have real eyes or not, because if I have to go and find out it'll just keep you waiting, and you may be anxious to know what happens next.

Very slowly, the caterpillar starts to unroll itself. It positively bristles. Though this is with indignation, not actual bristles. We've already established that this is not a hairy caterpillar, but a clean shaven one.

If it had been a hairy caterpillar it would have been the size of a Victorian moustache. Big enough to impersonate Lord Kitchener saying "Your country needs you!", but without the pointing finger, or the military hat, or the uniform, or indeed anything of the face except the monstrous tash. But it is not hairy. It is bald. Like an elderly party balloon. With a very bad drawing on its bum. It does, however, share the hypnotic power of Kitchener's upper lip.

A memorable, iconic caterpillar.

Pate looks at it with fascination.

"Aaah. Papilio Glaucus. The Eastern Tiger Swallowtail. Interesting. What's that doing here?"

Graham has subsided panting on the floor beside the caterpillar.

"You bastard. You could have killed me!"

"You still don't get it, do you? Of course you wouldn't have been dead. You'd just be somewhere else. And once you came back to the office, you and I could carry on our conversation like the old, well, acquaintances, that we are. I'd just have to fill in the odd gap, and we'd all be hunky dory."

"But that wouldn't be me. I'd be gone. As far as I was concerned I'd be dodoed. Dead as..."

Pate sighs. Sometimes Graham can be very hard work.

"Not at all. You'd be exactly where you are now, having this conversation. Just in another universe."

"So I wouldn't be here, now, alive!"

"But that's where you're missing the point. What you define as here, and now, and alive, is all relative to where you happen to find yourself. So in that other universe it would feel like nothing had changed."

"Hmmm."

And carefully, not entirely convinced, Graham picks up the caterpillar and puts it back on the desk. He believes things may have changed in ways mysterious, subtle and downright slippery. It's probably the first sensible thought he's had all day, as he will shortly begin to discover.

Chapter 9

WPC Enid Sneep strides clumpily back into the interview room with a cassette tape. Nothing has changed. Constable Ainstable sits by the door, arms folded resolutely, staring at the ceiling. As Enid enters he looks at her and nods, briskly and efficiently. WPC Enid looks over at the empty seat on the far side of the table, and her jaw falls open.

Sorry, did I say nothing has changed? My mistake.

Nothing has changed apart from the absence of Doppelgraham.

"Well?" bawls Enid.

PC Ainstable looks over at the suspect, and finds no suspicion of one. His jaw does more than drop. He gasps and gurgles.

"You absolute tosser!!" yells Enid. "Where the bloody hell is he? You're gonna die!"

Chapter 10

Check that one out if you thought Chapter 7 was short! Let's concentrate and see if we can string a few thoughts together this time. When Pate opened the matchbox the overlapping parallel universes popped apart. The two versions of Graham could only co-exist as long as the fate of the caterpillar was uncertain. The moment it wriggled, the two quantum outcomes found their own proper places in the multiverse. Still with me? Try to stay with me.

In the other universe Graham vanished from Pate's office, while Doppelgraham remained in custody. But that's not where we are, so it's not the tale we continue to explore.

And here we are, with good old Graham. He struggles through the rest of the day doing routine paperwork, which is really not ideal since if he's not lurking around a worried client it's not so easy to charge them for his services.

At last it's sloping off time.

He sees no sign of the other Graham on the way home, and the house is just as he left it, apart from an envelope on the mat inside the front door. On this is written a small capital G. With a full stop after it.

Graham wonders how significant the punctuation is. And there's no point in us making jokes about the G-spot because it would be right over Graham's head. Which may be where he's been going wrong.

He props the envelope up on the breakfast bar. Then he takes off his jacket and tie and drapes them over a kitchen chair.

He stares at the envelope from time to time as he pours himself a large Glenfarclas. He turns on the telly with the remote, then channel hops for a few seconds, then switches off again. He takes a belt of the malt whisky.

Then he opens the envelope and removes the note within. As he has already realised, it's from Kerri.

Graham, it begins.

I know you will have been aware for some time now that things have not been going well.

"Oh really?" thinks Graham. What things? Why does she have to be so mysterious? Perhaps she means her mother's had another of her not terribly funny turns.

When we embarked on this venture together it seemed as if we had all the time in the world ahead of us. But months passed, then years, and it began to feel as if our existence was limited; as if there would never be long enough to make all our dreams come true. You seemed happy to let matters slip by. But I was impatient to make the changes we had planned in those happy days when we dreamed together.

"Ah," thought Graham. "I've got it now. She wants to remortgage the house, so we can build the conservatory. But she's had to go to her mum's. Ah well. She'll want me to talk to the Building Society."

We no longer work together.

Obviously. Duh. I'm a management consultant, and she isn't.

And that is why we must grasp the nettle
and not deny the facts of the matter any longer.
We must act now, while my resolve is firm -

"She's really keen," thought Graham. "I'm really going to go for this, before she goes cold on the idea again. This'll be her way of cheering me up. She knows I get a bit mopey when she has to go to her mum's.

- before the petty hindrances of life drag us
into a dreary routine which we will both live to
regret.

K.

Graham picks up the phone and dials Kerri's mum. The phone rings about 10 times, then is seized, clattered and rustled. It then sounds as if it has been plunged into a mass of cardy and bosom. Graham can just make out some muffled conversation. Then there's a further clatter, a bit of raspy breathing, and then some words which are perfectly clear.

"She's not 'ere, so you can bugger orf!"

There's a loud bang, then some further rustling.

Mrs Kerri's mum obviously thinks she has hung up, because Graham can hear a conversation resume, faintly, but with perfect clarity.

"I told 'im 'e could bugger orf. An' so 'e can."

'Ah bless,' thinks Graham. 'She's really losing the plot. Kerri's such a saint - taking care of her like that'. He hears Kerri's voice answering the dottled old fart.

"Are you sure that's wise? I want him to sort things out with the lawyers - not take the huff."

"Isn't that just like Kerri?" thinks Graham. "Always thinking of me."

51

And satisfaction is written all over Graham's face. Except from where we are sitting there's a rather crucial fact hidden from view.

Can things get any worse for him?

(That's another rhetorical question. This is a book, so clearly they can and will...)

Chapter 11

The following day at Emission Solutions Graham finds it hard to concentrate. Dorothy at the desk reminds him of some mail he's meant to know about. It must have been that other sod she was speaking to, he thinks. It's amazing how much he dislikes himself, on principle. How dare he confuse my life! Chancer!

He places the large matchbox containing the swallowtail caterpillar on his desk. He keeps it just a little bit ajar, although he's sure that at a caterpillar level oxygen atoms won't exactly find it hard to make their way in, even in pairs, hand in hand. Just to be safe he's punched some little holes with a pencil, holes smaller than a caterpillar, but bigger than a molecule. He's also put in a selection of leaves, hoping that none are poisonous. Some lettuce, a green pointy one from the garden, and some of the houseplant he found the caterpillar on. Whatever that is.

He feels a bit sorry for the caterpillar. How could you live your whole life as a practical joke? Nature's way of confronting something which would otherwise eat you. and scaring it shitless. In human terms this caterpillar's badly drawn bum face would be like arming little old ladies with fake Kalashnikovs which they could pull out of their shopping baskets while being mugged. Crap plastic replicas, but enough to empty the bowels of any lairey junky who fancies his chances. Graham wonders why a caterpillar native to North America is hanging out in his kitchen. (Obviously its agent sorted the deal, not just because of this book, but because there could well be a screenplay adaptation to consider. But Graham doesn't even understand women, let alone publishing deals, so leave him in peace.)

Graham picks up the phone and calls Pate.

"See that bloke that looks like me. Is he really gone? And that's it?"

"In another universe he's wondering the same thing. As soon as we found out whether your caterpillar was dead or alive the two universes snapped apart."

"Bumface."

"I beg your pudding?"

"Bumface. I've decided to call him Bumface."

"Oh. Good. I'm sure that will help." Pate rolls his eyes ostentatiously upwards, mainly for his own satisfaction, since they are, after all, on the phone. He removes them from the phone and puts them back in their sockets. "Anyway, in that other universe the other Graham will be very puzzled. And he doesn't have me to explain things to him. Although, hang on a minute... Of course he does. I expect by now he's back in the office bending my ear and asking for wisdom. Which of course I will be dispensing."

Graham thinks about this.

"So I've made another Pate too?" The prospect is alarming.

"And another Bumface. Although in that universe you may have called him something different."

54

Graham opens the box and lifts Bumface carefully out. Bumface sits on his finger, like a... Like a... Well certainly not like a scary thing. Even looking with half closed eyes you'd have to be deranged to think he looked like a lizard or a snake. Like a caterpillar made of green plasticine with two crap eyes drawn on his bum with a felt tipped pen. By a three-year-old.

"Would the same caterpillar work twice?"

"It shouldn't have worked once."

"But if I were to make a decision, do you think another me might appear again?"

"Could do. You could try I suppose."

"Hmmm."

Which is why, immediately after work, Graham has stopped off at the park. He picks a big wide empty expanse of grass. There are very few people about. This time he wants to try to catch himself in the act. In his pocket Bumface nestles in his matchbox, very quiet, not yelling or breaking things or anything which would give the game away on his state of health.

To Graham's right are some benches. To his left is a bench sitting alone, and on the other side of the path leading to it are some bushes.

"Right," says Graham, out loud, but quietly. Out quiet, really.

"Right," he says. "I am about to Make a Decision.

"Will I sit on the benches to my right, or the bench on my left? I think I will go to the right."

He sets off to the right a few steps, then stops.

"No," he says. "I'm not entirely sure about that choice. I wonder..."

And he strokes his chin and looks upwards into the middle distance, in what he imagines is an appropriate

55

pondering pose. "No, I think I will change my mind. I will choose to sit on that bench to my left."

So he turns round and walks thirty yards or so (this is a pre-metric park) to the solitary bench. He looks around. He is alone. He sits down.

"Right Bumface," he says to the caterpillar which may be dead or alive in a matchbox in his pocket. "Let's see what happens."

Then he lapses into silence, as he realises that his voice has risen from out quiet to out medium.

And he sits.

Every so often he glances over his shoulder, to see if anything's happening.

Nothing.

'Presumably if anything was going to happen it would have happened by now,' he thinks.

But he can't be sure.

He looks around again, first one way and then the other. He stands up, turns around slowly, then sits down again.

And he waits.

"I'll just sit here on this bench that I Decided To Sit On, in a free choice, after I rejected those other benches." He says this out loud, but with the sort of croakiness which comes from the tension in a throat and mouth which don't want to be overheard, as if they were more embarrassed than his brain.

After a while, he realises that he needs a pee.

He gets up and looks around. Nobody.

He walks casually up to the bushes, as if innocently looking for something - maybe caterpillars. Then he sidles into the bushes and unzips his trousers. Although his willy is hidden, he is clearly visible from the waist up, and he is acutely aware how easily an innocent venture into some bushes can be interpreted as something far less savoury.

So while his fingers are fumbling below, his top half is trying to impersonate a decent chap with an interest in caterpillars standing waist deep in bushes looking around innocently.

It's an impersonation which by comparison makes Bumface's rear end look like a slavering, hissing Komodo Dragon. At last we have found something worse than Bumface's artwork.

Graham shakes his willy like a caterpillar expert shaking a leaf and glances back over his shoulder. He is shocked, nay astonished, to see himself sitting on the bench, glancing around over his shoulder, and wriggling a bit like someone who needs a pee.

His eyes meet, so to speak. They look at each other.

Not cross eyed. Not 'look at each other' like Graham's left eye looks at Graham's right eye. No, both his left and his right eye look straight at the other Graham, both of whose eyes look straight back at him.

And widen.

Both sets.

Graham straightens up, and adjusts his clothing. He doesn't want the man to see his willy. Although if anyone in the world has seen his willy as often as he has it is that man on the bench. Just not from that angle.

Graham walks over slowly. I had better keep the upper hand here, he thinks. After all it was me who called this meeting.

"Hello," he says.

"Hello," replies the man, in a voice as unfamiliar as a tape recording. 'God, is that what I sound like?'

thinks Graham. This doesn't cause any delay in the proceedings, because the other man is thinking exactly the same thing, for the same length of time, in the same inner voice.

"Do you need a pee?" asks Graham, thoughtfully. After all, he can empathise with how it feels.

The man nods.

"Why don't you go over there in the bushes and I can keep the seat. Then we can talk."

The other Graham says thanks and heads over to the bushes. He actually says it like "Thanks" with apostrophes, but we needn't worry about that right now.

"No, I would go to the left a bit," warns Graham. "Some of those leaves are a bit drippy."

Graham waits, and looks around at the empty park. He doesn't want to embarrass the man by looking at his willy. God, it's not very big, he thinks, before he can stop himself.

After a while the man returns, and joins him on the bench. Graham has been thinking about his opening gambit.

"I expect you're wondering what you're doing he..." they both say at once.

"You see, I..." they chorus.

"But this was my ide..." they tail off simultaneously.

There's a pause. This isn't going to get them very far. Graham raises his eyebrows, as if asking permission to speak. The man nods. Graham makes a start.

"You were..."

The man nods.

"And you've got a..."

The man nods again.

This is not going well. Each of them knows exactly the same as the other. And thinks the same. And has the same questions. It's eerily fascinating, but in another way, quite dull.

The other Graham takes a matchbox full of holes out of his jacket pocket. Actually it's not full of holes, more perforated with them. Presumably it's full of caterpillar.

He opens his mouth. Graham smiles permission.

"I call it - "

" - Bumface," Graham finishes the man's sentence.

The man looks at him as if he's a prick. "Good name," he says, a little guardedly. "Because of the..."

"That's right," says Graham. "How dare this wanker look at me like I'm a prick," he thinks. "Supercilious little tosser."

"Turn your head sideways." says Graham. He appraises his profile. 'I've not got a very strong chin,' he thinks. The man looks back at Graham, and leans to one side. "My nose is bigger than I thought," he says.

'Bloody cheek,' thinks Graham. 'Yours is just as bad.' Pot, kettle. He spots an irritating detail. "You've got some shaving foam just behind your ear," says Graham. "No, at the bottom."

The man wipes his left ear with his finger. "You too," he says.

'He won't let anything rest, will he?' thinks Graham, and rubs his right ear as if looking in a mirror.

"No, it's your left ear too," says the man. Smart arse.

They try a game of paper, stone, scissors.

Both hide their hands behind their backs, then pull them out at once. Both have fingers apart in the scissors symbol.

Then they both do paper.

Then, in a double bluff they both do scissors again. Then in a desperate bid to out-think the other they both do scissors again.

"Shall we stop now?" they both say together

The man opens his mouth a fraction, and Graham nods.

"Think of a number," says the man.

"Fourteen," says Graham.

"That's right," says the man.

The other Graham lifts his matchbox. "Do you want to see my caterpillar?" he asks.

"Sure."

The man opens the box and a lets a green caterpillar with a face on its bottom crawl on to his finger.

"He's very like Bumface," says Graham.

"He is Bumface," says the man, putting him back in the box.

Graham gets his box out of his pocket and holds it on the palm of his hand. The man's brow furrows, and there's a moment when time seems to stand still. It doesn't of course, but since these things are pretty subjective and both men are the same subject, let's assume it does, slightly.

Suddenly both men are struck by the same thought. If that other bugger wants to get rid of me again, he might try to nobble Bumface! Graham starts to pull his hand away sharply, and in a flash, the man grabs out for it. Graham punches him just above the left eye, and the man's flailing counter punch knocks the matchbox flying to the grass.

I already know his one's alive, thinks Graham, illogically, as he grabs for the man's jacket pocket and the man pokes him in the eye. Graham wrestles with the man, his face streaming, and they fall to the ground. The man tries to reach Graham's matchbox, which lies just out of reach, but Graham has a firm grasp around the man's waist.

They are evenly matched. Obviously.

For some time they grapple, the man trying to reach the matchbox on the ground, while Graham tries to hold him back and fumble for the other man's right jacket pocket, just beyond his grasp under the man's hip. The other Graham stops struggling momentarily as if exhausted. I've overpowered him, thinks Graham. Because I still have some puff left. And this is a struggle to the death. Which is how he knows the man is bluffing, and is ready for his renewed onslaught of kicking and wriggling. The man punches Graham on the top of the head, so Graham bites his thigh. (The other man's thigh. As a self-motivation ruse it might have worked, but Graham prefers to inflict the pain elsewhere.)

The man yanks at Graham's hair, and Graham punches him in the nuts. That feels a bit gay in a sadomasochistic kind of way, thinks Graham. How can that be?

And as he is distracted, the man suddenly lunges forward, squirming out of his jacket to reach the matchbox containing Bumface. Graham leaps to his feet, leaving the jacket on the ground, but before he can dive at him, the man holds the matchbox aloft and starts to slide open the drawer.

'Oh fuck', thinks Graham, as the man's face lights up in triumph.

And realising that he has no alternative, Graham swallows his scruples (why have I never tried eating archaic weights and measures before?) and stamps down viciously on the man's jacket pocket.

There is a slight squelching sound, and the jacket, and the man, suddenly vanish, leaving the matchbox containing Bumface in mid air.

Fortunately Graham has time to catch it before it thuds to the ground.

Unfortunately although he has the time, he doesn't use it wisely, remaining rooted to the spot staring at the space where the man stood a moment ago.

Which is why the matchbox does indeed thud to the ground.

Graham has distress written all over his face. But from this angle, all we can see is stress.

Chapter 12

"Of course he's in the ruddiest of ruddy good health," says Pate. "For anything smaller than a hamster air resistance means that friction with the atmosphere limits their terminal velocity to less than a fatal value. Whereas pit ponies who fall down pit shafts go splat, and the elephant which ran amok in a plane while being transported and had to be shown the exit - "

"Please, not the details - I get the general idea," pleads Graham. "And it's not just him. I was almost a gonner."

" - made elephant jam. You're being more opaque than usual, confrere."

"Well, if he'd managed to squash my Bumface before I stamped on his, I might have been history."

Pate winces at the mental images which have been conjured up by this innocent but misguided assertion.

"Why would it have made any difference? Whatever the outcome your two consanguineous universes would have split. And you would vanish from one while he would vanish from the other."

"You're totally missing the point. I didn't want to end up in the universe I'd vanished from!"

"If you'd vanished from it, how could you end up there?"

Graham's forehead starts to ache again. Pate always has this effect on him.

"But if it was me who'd suddenly stopped existing and him who was still there, then that would be like I'd died."

"Except you wouldn't be there to experience it."

"Exactly!"

Now Pate's head starts to throb too, although this could just be because of the seven kilos of hair he has gelled to it.

"Let me attempt to explain this in words of one syllabub," Pate says slowly. "Nobody can kill you, or otherwise cause you even the slightest iota of discomfort simply by stamping on a caterpillar - whether the said prepupating larval grub is yours, theirs, subcontracted or freelance."

"But he vanished!"

"Only from this universe. By definition, in the universe he is presently in, he is in it. And as far as he's concerned, you vanished, departed, extinguished and became defunct. Defuncted. He's probably laughing away that he was trying to pulverise your caterpillar while you were trying to mash his, and then you got there first and - lo and behold - you suddenly vanished! Things returned to the correct state - one of you per universe, and you boldly inhabiting the universe in which you live!"

It all seems much simpler when Pate explains it properly.

That little caterpillar is to tell you that time has passed. But it doesn't feel like we need a new chapter yet. Don't you agree? So let's try to keep this one going for a while with the help of some Bumface facsimiles.

Graham mopes for a week or two. Work is pretty shit. They've managed to persuade the client to engage them for phase two of the project. In phase one they persuaded the client that they (and only they) knew how to save him costs. In phase two, where the real money lies, they will help him to sack his longest serving staff. To Graham, the fun seems to have gone out of it. Dorothy will have to go, to be replaced by an automated telephone answering system. The result will be an unchanged volume of calls. Hardly anyone gets through at present. But it'll be cheaper.

Graham really doesn't want Dorothy to lose her job. He knows he has to cut costs to save the client money, so they can afford to employ Graham as a consultant. But he really, really hates his work.

Graham just can't understand why shits prosper, and Mr Nice Guy gets the soggy end. There must be a way to succeed without being a complete bastard. There must be an answer! Perhaps it lies in one of these other universes. Perhaps there's another Graham Paint out there who's rich and successful. And perhaps he can let me in on the secret...

Graham continues to feed and nurture Bumface. Now he lives in a shoebox with airholes and a wonderful selection of leafy things which Graham changes whenever they start to smell or look moody. Bumface would like this, thinks Graham. So he moves out of the shoebox and gives it to Bumface instead. The house seems so much roomier by comparison.

One day Graham comes home to find another letter on the mat. This time it bears a postmarked stamp. Graham knows it's from Kerri. It's addressed to Grey Paint.

The message is brief and to the point. Which is just as well. Because if I said it was brief and rambling, or lengthy but concise, you'd think I was talking mince.

   Dear Grey

It says.

   I am sorry not to have heard from you. If you haven't made your position clear by the end of the week I feel I have no alternative but to place matters in the hands of a lawyer.

   Yours sincerely

   Kerri Paint

'Bloody hell! The conservatory!' - thinks Graham. Right enough, I'd better get my arse into gear. His heart is warmed by that bit about 'sincerely'. From the brevity of the note she was obviously pushed for time, but she still managed to include a personal touch.

In fact Graham has warmth written all across his face. Except from where we are sitting all we can see is an arm.

Chapter 13

Graham's life is as tense as an overstretched simile. He knows that Bumface won't be with him forever. If he doesn't die, or choke on an endive, he will metamorphose. What on earth must that feel like? wonders Graham. For your body and presumably even your brain to dissolve into a mush of protein like a beaten egg, then reassemble itself into another living creature - how bizarre is that?

I wonder if a butterfly can remember being a caterpillar? wonders Graham. I wonder if it crawls out of its pupal case, looks in the mirror, and thinks - You can keep your Ten Years Younger! The face lift and tummy tuck were bloody amazing! And look at this frock!

Unfortunately Graham isn't even sure if a caterpillar can remember being a caterpillar. There's certainly no cosy sign of recognition in the mornings, no wagging tail, no panting to be let out for a walk. Just a badly drawn face, staring impassively, orange and blue, from Bumface's nether regions. Maybe that's the problem, thinks Graham. Maybe I inadvertently keep smiling at the wrong end.

So, for now, life with Bumface is fairly dull. Apart from the multiple universes.

"The trouble is," Graham explains to Pate, "even if I managed to trigger another quantum decision using Bumface I'd just end up with another me. And I know you'll find this surprising, but I find myself quite boring. In fact, pretty irritating."

"No surprise there at all," Pate reassures him. "I know exactly what you mean."

Graham gives him the benefit of the doubt and presses on.

"I wonder if this kind of split has happened before and I haven't noticed? It's all very well meeting a version of myself who's shared all the same experiences up until a few minutes previously. But it would be much more fun meeting a Graham Paint who set off down a different path of life's journey some years ago. Wouldn't it be brilliant to find out how things might have turned out? What lucky breaks or disasters he might have had? Or are our lives predestined? Will we always end up in the same place in the end? Will this other Graham be able to help me sort my life out?"

Pate considers this. Graham persists...

"It could of happened!"

"It could have happened," corrects Pate.

"You agree then?"

"Indubitably," says Pate. "In a world of infinite possibilities it has to have happened. But remember, at each quantum decision point a new universe is spawned. This allows both outcomes to be true simultaneously. But it's not at all normal (in fact it may be far from right angles) for both universes to coexist. For another Graham to be wandering about there would have to have been another Bumface."

"There could of been," says Graham eagerly.

Pate sighs.

"Have been."

Graham looks puzzled. Pate decides not to enlighten him.

"The other Bumface would need to have been kept in conditions where you had no knowledge of whether it was dead or alive."

"But it would of turned into an Eastern Tiger Swallowtail Butterfly by now. Then died of old age."

"So the catalyst couldn't be a caterpillar," muses Pate. "I wonder what other living creature might have triggered a quantum quasi-schism at some point heretofore? An erstwhile simultaneity?"

"I'm going to keep my eyes open," says Graham. "And I'm going to search my shed."

Which is why Graham's work takes yet another turn for the worse. He's preoccupied, and distracted.

He looks up the phone book for another Paint. There are very few, and only one G.

"Hello."

"Hi, is that Graham?"

"No."

"But you're G. Paint."

"So?"

"Well what's the G then?"

"If you're phoning to ask about Grey Paint then you can fuck off," says Gordon Paint (no relation). "You seriously think I haven't heard it all before?"

Slam.

Chapter 14

It's Friday night, and Graham heads home. He wonders if Kerri will be back. He opens his front door.

"I'm home!" he yells to no-one in particular.

No-one replies.

Which is only polite.

On the mat there's another letter. But this time it's been franked by a company called Rapid Remedy Claim Consultants. Graham winces at the word 'consultants'. And fails to spot the word 'claim' lying in wait with a stocking over its head and a cosh in its fist.

He opens the letter. The letterhead repeats the name beside a logo depicting a little stylised smiling man with a line of tyre tread across his torso. He seems to be dialling a mobile phone. A strap line beneath says "We throw the book at 'em!"

The letter is blunt, although its tone is sharp. And the words are pointed, even prickly. Barbed in places. So how can the letter be blunt? He reads on to find out.

Dear Mr Graham Paint

It says.

We are acting on behalf of your estranged wife, Mrs Kerri Paint.

Well that's bollocks, for a start, thinks Graham. They don't even know she's just gone to her mother's.

We note that you have failed to reply to our client's correspondence, despite repeated attempts on her behalf to engage in constructive and meaningful dialogue. We therefore advise you that we are recommending your wife to sue for divorce. We would suggest that you should offer her sole ownership of the house and four wheel drive or we will put your nuts in a vice and turn the handle with all the merciless vigour of the law.

Graham's jaw starts to slacken and point Berberwards. He has no way of knowing that a bored trainee lawyer wrote this letter because he really, really wanted to, but had no intention of posting it. And an equally bored secretary signed it on his behalf without reading it, and franked it. And it got posted. Because that is the way things happen in offices.

The law cannot distinguish between good and bad, between deserving and undeserving. It blindly tries to establish whether the rules have been observed. We spend our professional careers understanding not only the nuances of the law, but the quirks and foibles by which cases are won and lost. You, on the other hand, know bugger all.

Our clients only pay when we succeed. We then take an astonishingly large percentage of the vast amounts of money we win for them.

71

This encourages lots of people with flimsy claims to engage us. But we know the dodges, so on average we make a mint.

We have you in our sights, so you might as well bend over and kiss your ass goodbye.

We will be back in touch. Until then, sweat on it, sucker.

Yours sincerely

Squiggle scrawl.

P. S. Don't fuck with us - we know where you live.

Graham realises that he has forgotten to breathe for some time. He can't remember what comes next. To breathe in or out? He tries to inhale, but he's actually pretty well full. So he lets out a long sigh, which seems to get things going again.

Well, he thinks. They've got a fight on their hands this time. Haven't they heard of negative equity? And the price of diesel? They can have the bloody house and the car and stuff them up their briefs. Fuck them, and the horse they rode in on.

But it's a little worrying all the same.

Graham starts to pace around the kitchen, looking at the dead plants. Dereliction of duty, he thinks. She's meant to water them, and now they're dead. So that's one thing she's not going to get her hands on.

Graham opens the front door and starts heaving houseplants out into the garden, still in their pots, most of which make a satisfying crockery smashing sound. One by one he lifts them off the windowsill in the

72

kitchen and lobs them out the front door. Behind them are ancient dead flies and spider structures full of insect corpses being digested from the inside out. They may not even be dead. They're probably kept alive so they won't rot while they're eaten. Graham ponders on the inconceivable cruelty of nature and wonders whether there's the faintest justification for attempts to introduce any moral framework within a universe of such unimaginable pain and suffering.

What he doesn't realise is that in a system of multiple universes there are other worlds where flies suck spiders' brains through straws, and where ambulance-chasing lawyers are stunned, paralysed, then woken again to be fully conscious while their bodies are digested from the inside out by the injected stomach acids of the spiders which have escaped the flies. These spiders are big fuckers, which is why flies don't bother them. About five feet across and three feet high. Which makes eight feet. Which sounds about right for spiders.

So between those worlds and the one we live in things pretty well even out. And in Graham's world he's just spotted an ancient dusty packet of seeds which has sat hidden behind the plants on the windowsill for God knows how long.

Those'll be knackered, thinks Graham.

He picks up the packet and presses the bin pedal with his foot. Then he pauses.

And yet again... he thinks.

There might be something in there which could still germinate. But until I open the packet and plant them, there's no way of knowing.

I wonder if they've generated another parallel universe? he wonders.

I wonder if I made a decision years ago, when these seeds were still in their prime? he wonders.

And I wonder if another Graham Paint sprang into existence? he wonders.

And I wonder if he's out there, doing his own thing? he wonders.

And I wonder if I can find him, and learn from him? he ponders.

He's still wondering, but by now he needs a 'p'.

Chapter 15

"Hi Graham. Another day, another dollar," says Dorothy at reception as Graham wanders in to Emission Solutions. He looks distracted.

"Oh yeah, right," replies Graham. "It is..."

"Are you OK?" she asks. "You seem a bit..."

"Sure. Well, eh... What was that? I was thinking of something..."

Dorothy hands him a couple of sticky Post-it notes. Graham thanks her and puts them down on the reception desk without reading them. Dorothy picks them up again and staples them to his tie.

"There you go," she says breezily. Then - "Good day, Emission Solutions, providing peace of mind for the motorist through technology, Dorothy speaking, thank you for calling, how may I be of service to you? Today?"

There's a pause. Then Dorothy tries pressing a couple of buttons on her switchboard.

"Hello?" Press, press. "Hello?" She hangs up.

"Hung up?" asks Graham sympathetically. Not many callers stay on the line these days to the end of Dorothy's speech. Which is a shame, because she's only being nice. Interminably.

She nods.

Graham decides to change the subject.

"Dorothy..." he ventures. "Have you ever seen anybody wandering about that looks like me?"

She looks blank. He presses on. "I mean, if I had some sort of distant relation who looked a bit similar, it would be good to find out what they were up to."

Dorothy closes her eyes just a fraction, and looks as if she's trying to bring him into focus. She senses he's about to ask her something which will confuse her. She's right, of course.

"Like I'm thinking, what if there was someone who looked just like me, but was a Member of Parliament, or a bank robber, or a..." Graham tries to think of other turns his career might have taken. It's not easy. "Or a train driver."

"I think I need to put some toner in the photocopier," says Dorothy, and scurries off into a back room.

Graham has been trying for days to work out how he might find himself, if he's out there. He's been Googling his name, and variations on it. He's been squinting at photographs in newspapers. He's been freeze-framing crowd scenes in British movies in case an alter ego got a job as an extra.

Instead of walking briskly through crowds in town he's been giving everyone he passes a good stare. Every bloke, that is. This has earned him some surly scowls and a couple of alarmingly welcoming smiles.

He goes into a police station (not the station near Emission Solutions, just in case) and approaches the desk sergeant. "Hi. I'm here about a missing person."

"Name?"

"Me or him?"

"I need to put them both on the form. Better start by telling me who's missing."

"I'm not sure of his name - at least he may spell it differently, or use an alias or something."

Constable Dunstable gives him a squinty look through half-closed eyelids. Thank goodness it isn't Constable Ainstable, or Graham would really be in it up to pussy's bow. Constable Dunstable continues warily. So there's someone missing, but you don't know what he's called..."

"Ah, but I do have a photo."

Graham gives him a photo.

"That's you."

"No, of course it isn't. It's, um, a long-lost relative."

"I see that you and your long-lost relative share the same taste in clothes. Even the tie."

"I lent it to him for the photograph."

"So you know him well enough to lend him your tie, but you don't know him well enough to ask him his name?"

"Erm, yup."

"Right, name?"

"My name this time?"

"You don't know that either?"

Graham gives him his name and address. "I don't know much more, but could you put the photo on lamp posts or something?"

"That would be a much better idea than chasing burglars and terrorists. And tax payers would be very pleased to know that their money wasn't being wasted, specially now it's a police service rather than a force. Now if you just leave me the photo I'll personally see to the graphic design and printing. I'll pay for it myself if I have to. This is far too important a case to allow petty bureaucracy to stand in the way."

"What petty bureaucracy?"

"Oh, the usual stuff. Checking that we're not being sent on a wild goose chase by bampots, and felons, and timewasters."

"Do you get many of these?"

"Oh you wouldn't believe the half-witted, vole-brained, self-deluding plonker-pullers who come in here seeking attention."

"No, I certainly wouldn't. You must see all sorts in here."

"Believe me sir, I do."

Graham's faith in human nature is bolstered and uplifted, like a breast in an Ultimo bra.

Which is appropriate, given what the desk sergeant describes him as after he goes out the door.

"Where the hell have you been?" Simon Edgar doesn't look well pleased. "I called Emission Solutions, and Ron says you were only in for about an hour this morning."

Graham had been wondering what to put on his time sheet. Edgar rants on. Rant rant rant.

"You know it's critical to stay in their faces." Graham knows very well. Edit Solutions has replaced the client's computer system with a network which will need constant input from the firm of consultants from now till doomsday. But that is still just the tip of the iceberg. In addition to the car exhaust business they have all the waste segregation and disposal operations, with some major oil industry contracts. And Simon Edgar wants to get his claws into the whole group. Because the group is making serious money out of the oil industry, which is desperate to maintain a wholesome public image.

The oil and gas majors have to show how green they are and how they are bending over backwards to save the planet. To look at the publicity material you would think that their burning ambition was to fill the world with windmills. Surely these can't be the same companies that brought us global pollution through the extravagant consumption of irreplaceable fossil fuels to drive billions of gas-guzzling vehicles? Not the same companies who brought us spectacular oil spills from stricken tankers, with fish, cormorants and seals choking to death on leaking crude? The companies who want to extract petrochemicals from Alaska and the pristine Arctic wilderness? The companies who for decades flared off natural gas in great smoky plumes of fire from North Sea rigs as a useless by-product until they discovered they could make money out of the resource they were squandering? The companies who weren't content to piss on Alaska and Shetland and Nigeria, but had to shit on capitalism's front door in the Gulf of Mexico?

Clearly not - for these corporations are no longer oil and gas companies but energy companies. They love the wind in their hair, the tide between their toes and the waves which splash their rolled-up trouser legs. (As long as the waves are sparkly clean and not full of brown tarry pelicans.) These companies are into sustainable energy, replaceable energy, soft, warm, clean cuddly power which will save us and our planet.

But while they are developing these new energy sources they will continue to squeeze the last drop of petrochemicals out of the earth's crust, using filthy polluting technology like the steam heating of tar sands in northern Canada which uses up masses of energy to extract the last drops of low grade claggy fuel from vast open cast mines. But they only do that because they love us and want to please. And all the time they really just want to play with their windmills.

Which is why on their lethal filthy rigs and platforms they bend over backwards to be good citizens. Safety is all-important. All workers must use the handrails while going up and down stairs, because slips and trips are a principal source of accidents and "time-lost incidents". You mustn't use a power tool for too long in case your knuckles turn white and your nuts drop off. (Not many women on rigs, and the ones who do work offshore probably have nuts too. And bolts.) You must sign on, and off, and have passes and cards and "tool box talks" and risk assessments and "right to work" permits and safety boots and safety glasses and anonymous cards you can fill in and drop in a box to say 'I saw someone stand on a packing case to reach something and they could have tripped and slipped and fallen and twisted their ankle' so that the company can introduce yet another regulation to prevent this from ever being a problem ever again.

So does anybody ever fill in an anonymous card to say 'I hold the handrail on the stairs because my sodding safety glasses steam up and obscure my view and I can't hear the warning shouts because of my ear protectors and I don't care because the main risk I run is not a slip or a trip or a stumble but the overwhelming odds that this clapped out under-maintained knackered rust-bucket of an offshore oil and gas production platform is going to leak, ignite and blow us all to buggery like Piper Alpha where the only way for some people to escape was to do something very bad and dangerous and against the rules like jumping over the rail with melting shoes and plunging a hundred and twenty feet into the blazing oil and debris-covered waves in the dark and hoping someone in a standby boat finds them in the tarry burning water before they die of hypothermia or burns or both.'

?

Well?

I'm waiting...

Chapter 15, the bit after the caterpillar, second attempt

Oops.

Got a bit carried away again.

We'll take it from the caterpillar...

So where do Emission Solutions fit in?

Well the oil companies are so green and tree-hugging that they no longer just chuck all their crap over the side into the North Sea like they did for years. Now they ship it all back onshore on the supply vessels which come out to deliver their drilling mud and baked beans and porn DVDs. But that means loads of stuff being shipped back to clog up landfill sites on the mainland.

So the planet-saving earth-cherishing oil companies train all their staff to segregate waste at source, into the skip for plastics and the skip for building waste, and the skip for paper and the skip for green glass and the skip for brown glass and the skip for clear glass and so on. Emission Solutions supply all these skips, and take care of the whole process of taking the contents back onshore for recycling or disposal.

Emission Solutions are cheaper, more efficient and much more profitable than their rivals because once out of sight they chuck most of it over the side into the sea.

Apart from the aluminium cans, which are worth a bob or two.

Let's do another of those caterpillars at this point.

Simon Edgar is well annoyed with Graham because the Emission Solutions project is about to enter Phase Three. If you remember, Phase One was the low-cost company security audit, and Phase Two was the expensive and high maintenance computer system.

At the end of Phase Two, the consultants will request a meeting with the client and disclose to them that in the course of their work they have uncovered Shocking Inefficiencies. The consultants know how the client can save a lot of money. This involves shedding a great number of staff. Not the cheap young ones who arrived recently. No, the expensive, experienced, long serving, (i.e. loyal) ones, who are such a drain on the payroll.

And since giving these people the bullet might be a little traumatic for the client (not to mention the staff concerned) the consultants have a specially trained division with unique skills and experience in the subtle arts of redeployment and downsizing.

We know this isn't easy, they will say, but you owe it to the business and its shareholders, so give us some dosh for the ammunition, stand back and cover your ears.

Did I mention that Graham was getting a little jaded in his work?

And now Mr Edgar has noticed that Graham seems to be dragging his feet, failing to bring matters to the critical point where the client begs for Phase Three to begin.

Graham has spent a great deal of time recently, not at work, but wandering the streets staring at strange men (or women who look like they might once have been men), searching for a glimmer of recognition.

"...and that's why I'm letting you go."

"OK. Cheers. I'll get back to work then."

"No - not 'letting you go', like back to your desk. I mean 'letting you go' like P45, jotters, empty your desk..."

Graham realises Mr Edgar's lips have been moving for some time now, but he was thinking about renewable energy and oil platforms and whether there might be someone who looked like himself working on a rig, which would account for not bumping into him on the street.

"Now."

"What now?"

"Now. You're not making this easy for either of us. Go away. You're fired."

Graham frowns in concentration. He seems to have come in halfway through a conversation, albeit a rather one-sided one.

"How can I make myself clear? Piss off out of my sight. Now I'm going to call security."

Graham realises that something has gone horribly wrong. The job is awful, but he always intended to dump his employers, not the other way round. He decides to seize back the initiative. For once he is bold, decisive, commanding.

"Right! You can stick your job where the sun doesn't shine. I resign!"

He wonders whether 'don't shine' would have sounded better, if a little American. But it seems to have done the trick. Yes it's a cliché, but it's one he always fancied trying.

Edgar suddenly bends over his keyboard and rattles away at his PC for a few seconds. Then he grabs a sheet of company headed notepaper, stuffs it into his printer and hits return. The printer bursts into life.

Edgar seizes the page and thrusts it at Graham.

"You've got me by the short and curlies," says Edgar. "I give in. Sign here."

Graham signs the letter with a flourish. He even underlines his name. The letter reads:

Dear Mr Edgarf

Resignation

I hereby resign my post with Edit Solutions with immmediate effecdt an d am lo longer employed by the company and agree that I am conractualkly bound not to work in theis filed of othersie compete with Edit Solutioons ro speak to any of their clients or breath a word of anything I have eelaned at work outoisde thios office.

Yours sincerely

Flourish, flourish

Graham Paint.

Simon Edgarf is a rubbish typist, but he wants Graham to sign the letter asap and can't risk the delay caused by spellchecking it. Which is why Graham is now unemployed, and the robust case he had for unfair dismissal a few moments ago has drifted away like a binliner in the sea.

Chapter 16

Graham has lots of free time now to concentrate on finding an alter ego. He's convinced this character exists, and is sure he could learn from him how to stop his life being so shit. For days he's been rattling around his house with only Bumface for company, beating his brains to try to work out how he could find himself.

He's exhausted the possibilities of the phone book, and has Googled himself without avail. He's fascinated to find out that there is indeed an American company called Graham Paint which makes paint - an excellent and estimable company of unimpeachable reputation whose paint is no doubt superb. All of us involved in this novel, and our lawyers, can't speak highly enough of Graham Paint. But that's the real company, not the fictitious figment of a character whose imaginary exploits we are following.

So Graham tries to work out what the common thread might be between himself and any potential double.

Obviously another Graham would share his tastes. He might develop some new interests, like drinking expensive bottles of champagne if he had the dosh. But he might just continue to indulge in the same things as Graham. So Graham starts to write down a list of his interests.

Things I like, by Graham Paint.

He sits at the kitchen table and tries to remember what he used to do before work, house and marriage took up all his time.

Swimming.

Well that's really going to help. What's he going to do? Hang around staring at people in public baths? Hmmm.

He remembers he enjoyed the Salsa dance classes he went to when he and Kerri were first married. So he writes that down.

Salsa dancing.

It still doesn't feel that he's uncovered a silver arrow which will lead him straight to the target.

Drawing and painting.

Trouble is - that's a bit private. You don't normally get mobs of artists. They tend to scratch away on their own at home. Dead end.

Graham buys a What's On magazine. If he looks through this to see what might appeal to him, then this could lead him to his doppelganger. Now there's an interesting word, thinks Graham. Double-goer. Unfortunately it sounds better in the original German, and a bit (frankly) pathetic in English.

He scans the attractions. Fungus walks in a forest. I may have spare time, he thinks, but not that much.

Blockbuster movies.

Musicals.

New restaurants.

Nothing really commands his attention.

The Boat Show.

Aha! Wouldn't mind going to that. Graham recalls happy times pottering about in dinghies when he was a lad. Now that might be more promising. He adds another entry to the list:

Sailing.

The London show opens this week. He's never been, but always fancied it. And hundreds of thousands of folk traipse through it every year. That's it!

Two days later Graham packs a bag and jumps on a train. Brilliant not having to ask for time off at work! When he arrives at the Royal Victoria Dock the queues are already hundreds of yards long. He's never been so happy to stand in line. He aims a silly soft grin at everybody else who's waiting. Hundreds of them, all interested in boats. And when he eventually gets in to the exhibition halls there are thousands and thousands. Graham decides to pace methodically up and down the aisles. And he finds himself enjoying the process. Why didn't he think of indulging himself years ago?

Of course, being Graham, he worries about the best method of seeing as many visitors as possible.

Stratagem One: If everyone was standing still he could walk very quickly around the exhibits looking at everybody there. Problem - the exhibition covers an area about the size of Guatemala. And people won't stand still.

Stratagem Two: Stand still and gaze nonchalantly at visitors as they pass. Problem - not everybody will look at the whole show, so where to stand? And he won't get to see the show himself.

So Graham decides he will walk very quickly round everything. This will take him a couple of hours. Then he can start again. And keep that up for three days.

"What d'you think that bloke's up to?" asks Arnold Strood, as he watches the monitor screens. Ryan, his colleague, shrugs.

"That's eleven times."

"Wot?"

"Or maybe twelve. Course I might not have clocked him early doors."

"Wossat?"

"Look. He's on that one now."

A grainy Graham strides purposefully across the security screen from right to left, then appears on another one heading left to right. Although there are a couple of dozen tellies in the dimly lit room it's easy to spot him. Thousands of people dotter and ditter. Graham zooms like a Muncher in a Pacman game in the final stages of a seriously high level.

Ryan and Arnold watch him, fascinated. Or as fascinated as you might be watching a man walking. But remember, the security of thousands of visitors rests in their hands.

"Where's the sense in that now?" says Ryan.

"Should we send Yash to have a word?"

They watch Graham scurry across a screen near the ceiling, then pop up on one far left just above the desk. The grainy image seems to show he wears a slight frown of concentration, but with a slight upturn of the corner of his mouth to show that he is not concerned, but doing something important, although not worryingly so. It's like the Mona Lisa trying to blend in with all the other portraits by adopting the sort of expression people normally adopt to have their portraits painted.

Never works.

"He'll be security."

"We're security."

"Shows how much you know, me old son."

"But we are."

"Yeah but - we are not alone..."

"Ahhh." Ryan nods as if he understands now. Although if he did he wouldn't need to nod or say Ahhh, because Arnold wouldn't have needed to explain.

By the third day, there is a worn track on the exhibition carpets, and a burnt-in streak on some of the monitors. Graham has seen everything there is to see. Dinghies, books on sailing, stands offering live-aboard holidays around Mull and Magaluf, miraculous aids to navigation which can tell you to within 30cm where you have put the box down in your living room. And how deep your shag pile is. A vast tank full of great white sharks, barracuda, and piranhas whipped by gale force winds driven by an array of giant fans like aircraft propellers, where competitors take part in the extreme windsurfer championship. Hall after hall of jaunty little tubs, serious blue-water cruisers, and away up there with their own individual access platforms, ludicrous gleaming conspicuous floating temples to pockets as deep as the oceans.

Graham is wearing a pair of yellow wellies. His shoes fell apart after two days and there was a limited choice of footwear available. He liked the deck shoes, but reckoned he would get more wear out of the welly boots.

"Look."

"What?"

"He's slowing down."

"Right."

Graham is fed up. He's seen all there is to see. And still he hasn't seen himself.

"That's funny."

"What?"

"I can see him on this screen as well."

"So?"

"But his wellies don't look yellow from that angle."

"Be the light," says Ryan brightly.

"He's not even wearing wellies," says Arnold darkly. "So it can't be the light."

The men squint at the two screens. One shows Graham face-on, staring up at the millionaire cruisers. On the other screen he's in profile.

One one screen Graham looks at his watch.

On the other he doesn't.

"Bloody Norah," says Arnold.

Graham (who didn't just look at his watch) is getting pretty cheesed off. Three days he's spent wasting his time.

It's my double or quits, he thinks.

He gazes up at the blue-water millionaire cruisers.

I fancy a look at those, he thinks. You can always dream...

So he walks over to the staircase which leads up to the platform surrounding the biggest one. There's a sign on the handrail.

This vessel is a one-off design for Legend Global, it says.

It is capable of circumnavigating the globe in luxury with accommodation for a crew of forty and twenty four passengers. It is schooner rigged, and within its steel hull it has garage facilities for dinghies, windsurfers and several cars.

Graham stands in awe.

He can't decide whether to lust after this sublimely crafted toy, or whether to recoil in disgust from its "I have so much money I don't even count the people I employ to count it for me" pretensions. Being Graham, he decides to climb the staircase to examine it from deck level, so he can make up his mind.

The hull gleams a rich dark blue and smells faintly of wealth.

At the top of the staircase stands a man in a dark blue breton jumper bearing the vessel's name. Graham wonders whether he's allowed up here. Not the man in the jumper obviously - himself, Grey Paint. Is he trespassing?

"Good afternoon, sir," says the man, and ushers him towards the platform from which he can step aboard.

That must be a salesman, thinks Graham. They certainly know how to treat their billionaire customers.

Another chap stands on deck. He sports a dark blue polo shirt, bearing the same name and logo. *Blue Water Legend* it proclaims, discreetly.

"Welcome on board," says the man deferentially. "I see you found us without any trouble."

"Hard to miss," chuckles Graham.

"Have a look on deck - I'll just make a quick call."

Graham nods and starts to explore the deck level. The designers have managed to pull off the trick of packing every facility into the vessel, while keeping the clean lines of a racing yacht. There is one single level superstructure about two thirds of the way back from the bow which houses the bridge - apart from that the decks are clean and spacious.

The man speaks briefly into a handheld radio. "Forget about the Meeting Point. He's just turned up here." Then he rejoins Graham.

"Shall we?" he says, and opens the door to the bridge. Inside it is a combination of gleaming lustrous mahogany from threatened rain forests and stainless steel from threatened steelworks. Beside the bridge is the skipper's quarters and radio shack. They make their way down a staircase to the suites below deck. Graham is thrilled by the attention he's being given.

I don't suppose they get too many chancers like me, he thinks. Maybe they think I've got this sort of cash. He's inwardly flattered that he looks like the kind of person who could buy a yacht like this.

He's taken on a tour of the passenger suites, the dining room with magnificent antique table to seat about twenty or thirty, and the sitting area with bar. Round the bar are padded swivel stools on brass posts, clad in soft leather.

"Remember the story about Aristotle Onassis, the shipping tycoon?" asks Graham.

The man shakes his head. Graham continues. "Jackie Kennedy married him after hubby was shot in Dallas. Onassis used to fill his yacht with babes, and chortle away when they sat round the bar in their bikinis."

"Why was that, sir?"

"Well the leather on the barstools was made from sperm whale foreskins."

"Is that what you'd like, sir?"

"Ha ha ha," laughed Graham. What a wag! "Of course! Unless you have a better idea?"

"No sir. Yes, of course sir." The man seems flustered for some reason. "Yes, ha ha."

God, they really have to crawl to the customers, thinks Graham. Maybe it's not easy to sell these yachts after all.

"So how much?" asks Graham.

The man looks blank.

"How much what? Whale, er, leather?"

"Ha ha," joshes Graham. "No skip, that - I'll take it as it is." It's good having a laugh with this bloke - he seems to have a good sense of humour. "So how much?"

"For..."

"The yacht. I'll take it. I just need to check how much cash I've got on me. What will that come to? You'd better fill her up as well."

With a massive wave of relief, the man suddenly realises that Graham is joking. "Oh yes, the price. Ha ha ha. We'll fill her up sir. Absolutely."

"And leave all these bottles in the bar. And get some Bunnahabhain. I might be thirsty after reversing her out of here, with all these people watching."

"Oh yes, of course sir! Yes, of course. Ha ha. Well, I'll just send the bill to the company. In fact I think they've already picked up the tab, haven't they sir?"

"Ha ha. Yes of course. Silly me. Well I'll just put my wallet away then."

"Ha ha. Boona what was that? Is that Indian?"

"Bunnahabhain. Single malt. From Islay. Don't tell me you haven't heard of Bunnahabhain?"

"Well I have now sir! Boona Harvin? Rightoh. Ha ha."

"Ha ha."

"Ha ha."

And then as they move back upstairs to the bridge again - "Ha ha."

There is clearly something nagging at the man. He starts again, hesitantly. "Sir, you do realise I'm not a salesman?"

"No, of course not," says Graham breezily. "No, you're, em..."

"Rodger, sir. The skipper."

"No, Rodger. Fear not! I'm just winding you up. Come on, how about the rest of the tour?"

Graham steps forward to the ship's wheel. It is large and stainless steel, bound with light grey leather. He grasps it in a nautical fashion. "Yo ho, heave to and avast behind!"

Rodger smiles. Graham continues. "I'd like this replaced with the old whale leather, same as the bar."

A flash of anguish crosses the man's face. Maybe his boss was serious about the bar stools. The consequences of guessing wrong don't bear thinking about.

"Whale, er..."

"We'd better make the wheel leather out of scrotum rather than foreskin," says Graham. "Takes balls to steer something like this, eh? I presume whales must have them."

"Ha ha," says the man, with an expression which suggests his own leather parts are in the vice. "So that's foreskin for the barstools, and scrotum for the wheel."

"Give them a shave, mind," says Graham.

The man frowns. The man nods. "You said sperm, sir??"

"Did I? Bit rude! Yes sperm whale. I presume it's endangered."

"Almost certainly, sir. But we can check."

"No that's fine. Sperm it is then."

"Ha ha."

"Well it's been really good of you to give me the tour. Great fun. See you sometime, then."

And Graham steps out of the wheelhouse and sets off across the deck.

"Wait sir! There was one other thing."

"Really?" Graham steps back inside.

"The other spec change you asked for."

Graham waits for the punchline.

"The encryption system on the satellite comms."

Graham doesn't get it. That's not as funny as whale goolies. He frowns and nods. Maybe the punchline comes next.

It does.

"Right here, Mr Dupeint. It's fully operational now sir."

The deck seems to move under Graham's feet as if the Blue Water Legend is already on the deep ocean. "Encryption?" he asks weakly.

They've entered the Roaring Forties, and ice is growling around the hull as they lurch from swell to swell.

"Yes sir. Everything's fully secure now sir. Sorry it's taken this long, but we've never had to work with a military system before."

"OK. Fine! That's good. OK. Right then, see you. Erm, stand easy. Ta-ta."

Graham grabs the handrail at the second attempt. Having said his ta-tas, he titters at the man, teeters down the steps, and totters away into the crowd, his nerves in tatters. As he pushes past people, tutters show their disapproval.

He's desperate to put a few sea miles between himself and the Blue Water Legend as soon as he can.

He is soon lost in the crowd.

Well, almost.

"There he goes again," says Arnold.

"Well who's that waiting at the Meeting Point?" asks Ryan.

"No idea. But there's no point him poking away at his mobile - he won't get a signal in here. He looks well pissed off."

On the screen, he does indeed look well pissed off. But in the flesh, Grim Dupeint looks more than well pissed off. He looks absolutely, thunderously, murderously livid with rage.

Chapter 17

Graham knows he's cracked it. Clearly there is someone around who looks exactly like him. And this character is also filthy dirty pornographically rich.

Good start.

He lifts the lid of the shoebox in which Bumface now resides. and has a chat with him.

"How goes it old chum? Still eating your greens, eh?"

The silly expression depicted across Bumface's arse remains impassive. In fact there's not a lot of movement anywhere. The caterpillar still seems to be sitting where it was when Graham last looked.

"So I know two things. The first is he's called Dupaint. And second, his company seems to be Legend Global.

"Should be easy."

Graham fires up his PC and Googles the company. It proves surprisingly difficult to find what he's looking for. He tries Dupaint, Dupeynt and Dupeint, together with Legend, but can't find anything that ties in.

At last he finds a tiny reference in some sort of listing which refers to LGH, which could at a stretch be Legend Global Holdings, or Legend Global H-something-else. But he can't find a Ltd or an Inc or a Cie or any of the other company abbreviations.

He picks up his mobile and dials. Dial dial dial.

Actually, he goes punch punch punch to call Pate, but if I said that you might think he was doing a bit of shadow boxing, so I just took the liberty of saying dial dial dial in the hope that you'd follow the action. How long is it since a phone had a dial? The bit with holes in it which you pulled round with your finger and released so that it whirred and clicked on a spring back to where it started? Yet we still talk about dialling a number. How bonkers is that?

Sorry - I must have keypadded the wrong number.

Our language is on a different planet from what we're actually doing.

I'll give you a bell after work. No I won't. Phones don't ring anymore, like bells. Unless you have a ringtone which sounds like an old bell. So I'll give you a ringtone after work. Hang on a minute - I can't do that. It can't even be a ringtone. Because that still refers to phones ringing. They don't ring. They play a polyphonic midi file or audio sample. And if yours sounds like a bell that's irony.

So I'll give you an audio sample after work. More accurate, but ambiguous to the point of meaninglessness.

Give me a word ending in lessness.

I just did.

But that can't be a real word, surely?

What about haplessness? Or shiftlessness?

Maybe. But you do realise that if you keep going on about words, they go on strike and refuse to mean anything any more. They're sensitive like that.

I'll give you a shout after work.

So you won't need a phone then?

All right - I'll give you a call.

Still shouting?

I'll give you a phone after work?

No need. I've got one.

Graham presses buttons on his telephone to cause it to induce Pate's phone to make a sound which Pate has already selected to correspond to the indication that someone wishes to speak to him electronically and radiophonically from a distance, which in turn entices Pate to press a button on his own handset which completes the connection with the line from Graham's telephone.

It's not a line. Mobiles don't drag miles of wire about with them.

Well it bloody rings and Pate bloody answers it.

"Hi ho!"

"That you Pate?"

"Durn tootin. Sho nuff."

"Fancy a pint after work?"

"Mais certainement, mon brave."

"The Rat Up a Drain? Or the Laughing Stoat?"

"What about Scabby McAllister's? Or Manky McTinkie's?"

"I'm not keen on pubs with the contents of a Killarney builders' skip nailed to the wall."

"Willie o' Toole's?"

"Still a bit Celtic. And a bit gay."

"Flash o'Panties? Lucy Lastic's?"

"Better."

"How about the Mutt and Futret?"

"Good call. I've got something I need you to help me with." And Graham tells Pate about Legend Global.

That evening, Graham and Pate sit nursing two pints of Old Scruttock's Falling Down Medication on a sticky table made from an old sewing machine.

"The Goat and Compasses," says Pate. They are discussing pub names.

"What's that mean?"

"God Encompass Us. That's what the sign would have said originally. Corruption."

"That's what I like. Go to the pub and get corrupted."

These discussions are generally brief, because Graham knows Pate will always beat him.

"The Slaughtered Lamb," says Graham.

"That's not real."

"It was in 'American Werewolf in London'."

"So it was made up, for comic effect."

"Obviously."

"So it doesn't count. How about the Bag o'Nails?"

"Named after a bag of nails, possibly? Just abbreviated slightly?"

"Nope. It was originally the Bacchanal."

"Bollocks." Graham decides to cut to the chase. Did you find out anything about Schhh you know who?"

"Not easy," says Pate, looking about him as if the pub is under surveillance. Which it is, but that's the lounge bar where the football casuals hang out.

Graham looks expectant. There's a pregnant pause. His breathing becomes laboured.

"So..."

Pate looks smug. He strokes the massive hank of wiry hair which is plastered to the mass of wiry hair beneath. He still doesn't seem to be going bald.

"Go on..."

Pate looks left and right again. He leans forward. "They're not into ostentatious marketing. They don't exactly advertise their services."

"But..."

"But. I've made some limited progress."

"Well?"

"The Legend Global Holdings group seems to be registered in Stirkmenhistan. It's actually Legend Global Holdings Splv."

"What's Splv short for?"

"It isn't."

"It isn't?"

"Splv is a word in Stirkmenhistani."

"What does it mean?"

"There's no direct translation in English."

"Is there a rough equivalent?"

"Well... The closest approximation - "

"Yes?"

"- is 'dodgy bunch of shaders who don't pay tax unless you count bribes and backhanders and whose registered office is a holding address at a shell business in a fictitious street in a country which is itself a single lane between two other countries with one doorway containing two dozen separately labelled letterboxes'."

"And that's Stirkmenhistan?"

"In one."

"A bit like Switzerland?"

"More open."

"So what does Legend Global Holdings Splv actually do?"

Pate looks around again, in a highly suspicious manner.

"They do lots of things. Their lines of business appear to be separate. But scratch the surface and they're linked in a spider's web of international deceit, dissemblance, dissimulation, guile, chicanery, artifice and cozening."

"Cozening?"

"Bilking, chiselling, gypping and flimflamming."

"Ah. So what do these lines of business include?"

"At their black heart, Legend Global are arms dealers. Legend Arms has a subsidiary called Legend Mines."

"Mines as in digging up or mines as in blowing up?"

"Kaboom."

"That's not a very nice line of business."

"It gets worse."

"Really?"

"They are brazen beyond belief. Legend Brown Envelopes does not make stationery."

"No?" Graham knows the best plan is to encourage Pate to show off his new-found knowledge.

"Legend Brown Envelopes is a front company to process bribes."

"Is there a Legend Laundry?"

"You're catching on. You must think along similar lines to these people..."

"So Legend Laundry doesn't clean clothes?"

"That's just a front."

"A clean front, to conceal a grubby posterior?"

"You gaddit. And it gets worse."

"Worse than money laundering, bribery and arms dealing?"

"The mines are plastic fragmentation mines, banned by the Geneva Convention. Incredibly hard to clear after a conflict, since they don't trigger mine detectors. But it gets worse..."

"How?"

"Legend Bionics makes artificial limbs."

Chapter 18

Armed with this information, Graham has a stab at tracking down Legend's London headquarters. Pate was not wrong about their lack of marketing. You'd almost think they didn't want people to find them. How useless is that! He searches on the internet for everything he can think of which might relate to what they do. Nothing.

Until...

Graham finds a reference to a patent application for a prosthetic device. There is an address. It just says LGH splv.

"Eureka!" shouts Graham.

Bumface flinches, not at the noise, but at the banal choice of phrase.

The address is in an area which used to provide a refuge for car respray and identity switching enterprises housed under railway arches. There were places that stripped wooden furniture with lethal chemicals which they washed away down the street. Shops selling repossessed black and white TVs. Chinese takeaways with no customers up two flights of stairs providing cover for heroin imports. Seventy year old hookers in short skirts. Punching people.

Now the area has gleaming new offices made of glass, chrome and artifice. Chaps in sharp suits talk loudly into their bluetooth earpieces. Women in blue chalkstripe clack along on four inch heels as they busy from meeting to meeting.

In other words, it's gone badly downhill.

Graham gets the bus.

It's not easy to find the address. The street's there, but the buildings don't have numbers. He approaches one of them and squints through the glass wall, trying to make out the nameplates on a plaque in reception. They are made of brass-effect plastic letters on something like ridged fuzzy-felt.

Graham hears a voice. "Can I help you?" say the words, although the tone says fuck off before I break your legs. The man with the tone is Tone. His mother calls him Antonio, but nobody else dares to call him anything. Tone steps between Graham and the building. Tone blocks out the view, the light, and Graham's hopes of learning anything useful.

"I was just trying to -"

"It's private. You have to leave."

"But I'm standing on the street. I'm allowed to look."

"No you're not."

"But this is a public road!"

"No it isn't. It's owned by the Duke of Richborough. All the streets round here."

"But there are buses..."

"He lets them. But not you."

Graham is speechless.

"Have you got an appointment?"

"No."

"Right. You have to leave."

Graham backs away, and takes a few steps down the street. Tone watches him.

"Is this OK?" asks Graham from a distance.

"No." The man gets out a walkie-talkie and presses the button. It squawks at him like a parrot. That's been stood on.

"OK, OK. I'm going."

A big heavy-set bloke comes out through the revolving glass door and joins Tone. "And don't come back," grunts the Caucasian sumo.

"I don't like your tone one little bit," says Graham. Tone looks baffled, and alarmed. Sumo looks at Tone. "You know this bloke?"

Graham walks away down the street. The next building is set back from the road. It is five stories high, glass and concrete, with a useless paved area in front fenced off by railings along the edge of the pavement. There is a man in a booth by the entrance, which is fitted with a turnstile. It makes the previous office look like it has a welcome mat.

The man in the booth squints at Graham, who pulls up his collar and hunches. Graham walks across the road away from him as if going somewhere else, but continues to peek. Once he gets to the far side, he bends down and loosens his shoelaces, then ties them up again. He does a double bow. Then he leans the other way and reties the other shoe. He can't make out any signs or logos. On the corner of the building a CCTV camera swivels in his direction.

Graham stands up and makes as if to set off. Then he pulls some change out of his pocket and drops it on the pavement. It takes him a while to gather up all the coins. One has rolled quite a long way.

He spots a post box in the brick wall along his side of the road, a few yards further on. He strolls over to this and examines it, all the while glancing round to try to see what this building might be and who uses it. He pulls out a street map and peruses it. The address he's looking for must either be this one or the one with a belligerent Tone.

Still nothing obvious. He reads the collection times on the post box, and then pulls out a pen and starts to copy these down on the back of the map. It takes quite a long time to transcribe all the details about Public Holidays.

Down the street, Tone and Sumo stare at him. Tone talks into his radio. Sumo pulls out his radio and answers him.

Another CCTV camera pans across to Graham.

Graham starts to fold the map. Not easy. He tries again. Tone takes a step down the street in his direction. Then a large black car appears at the end of the street and heads towards them. Tone and Sumo immediately step back to stand on either side of the revolving door. Fifty yards up the street, opposite Graham, a section of railings slides sideways on wheels. The man in the booth leaps up and stands to attention beside the opening. As the car sweeps into the gap Graham peers to see the occupants, but the tinted windows defeat him. The limo pulls up beside an entrance to the building as the railings slide back to where they began and clang shut. Graham lifts the map up in front of his face, and peeks over the top.

The nearside rear door of the limo swings open, and Graham sees himself step out.

This must be Dupaint! He is tanned, muscled under his expensively cut suit, and wears a gold bracelet on the wrist which doesn't sport a gold Rolex. He is very angry.

He points into the car and shouts at somebody within.

Even from this distance Graham can hear him.

"Fucking useless! They think it's Earl Grey and scones! If you don't get it sorted yesterday you're toast!"

And with that he sweeps into the building.

As the railings slide open once more to let the limo leave, Graham ducks his head and scurries off up the street. What the hell was all that about? He's obviously found the right building, and the right bloke. But how to get to meet him? And what was all that Earl Grey stuff about?

Earl Grey and scones?

Afternoon tea? And someone in the car would be the toast.

They think it's Earl Grey and scones. Who are they? And why do they think something is tea and scones?

High tea.

IT.

They think it's Earl Grey and scones! As in, they're so useless at IT they think it's high tea!

This could just be a way in.

Graham has delight written all over his face. But from over here all we can see is the light.

Chapter 19

There are two problems staring Graham in the face. But he's a management consultant, so he thinks there are two challenges presenting opportunities for dynamic change.

Pillock.

The first is how to use his IT expertise to wangle a job inside the organisation. The second is how to disguise himself so that neither Mr Dupaint nor his minions recognise him.

Graham fails to ask why he thinks the whole thing is a good idea in the first place, but we're stuck with that. Even if we shout he won't hear us.

Go on. Try it.

Does that feel better?

Did he look up? Did he give the slightest indication that he heard you?

Didn't think so.

Do your family and neighbours seem concerned? Always a risk when shouting at fictional characters. So why don't we just try to control ourselves from now on, and let Graham get on with his misguided mission in peace? Not that he heard you anyway.

Graham reckons the obsessive secrecy of the organisation may just help. And the paranoia.

So what about his appearance?

Prosthetics like a false nose would be pretty obvious, close up. And quite hard to maintain. Imagine blowing your nose and finding it had changed shape? Or come off in the hankie?

Gross.

A wig is an obvious first step. Graham's hair is a nondescript mousy brown colour. The colour that hair defaults to when it can't make up its mind. So does he go darker? Or blonde? Black hair might just look a bit too similar in certain lights. So blonde could be the way to go. Another step would be to get coloured contact lenses. Graham's eyes are like his hair. Floating voters. Uncommitted. Greyish brown. If he were to go blonde then he could get blue contact lenses. That would certainly make a big difference.

"Hi, I'm after some coloured lenses."

The assistant is a crisp clean-cut kind of girl. Graham wonders if opticians have to create that clinical sparkly ambience to reassure their customers. Cool colours and halogen lights seem essential. A cosy old bookshop feel would be alarming. Might suggest dust. Not a good concept.

The girl's name tag announces that she is Dusty.

"Did Iris leave then?" asks Graham. "Were you her pupil?"

Dusty looks at him through her trendy specs.

"You just get cornea and cornea," she says.

"Let's put a lid on it then."

"Bags eye do it," says Dusty, settling for an honourable draw. "You'll need an eye test first."

Graham's eyesight is, like the rest of him, pretty average. "I don't think I need a test. I just want a change, in, like, the way I look."

"We'll still need to measure your curvature."

"Can I do yours first?"

Dusty smiles ever so faintly, brings out the catalogue and lays it on the counter. Graham rules out the feline green and amber traffic light extremes. The one which looks most different from his natural colour without being too theatrical is a pale blue.

"I think I'll go for the Cool Hand look," says Graham, pointing.

Dusty groans and whacks him with the catalogue. Graham feels an immediate pang of lust at this physical intimacy, even if his arm hurts. Specially 'cos it hurts.

Am I changing somehow? wonders Graham. Girls don't normally do that to me...

The wig shop proves trickier.

Graham tries a theatrical supplier, but nothing there looks convincing close-up.

"What you need is a hairdresser, mate," says the man. "For baldy people." And he grasps his fringe and pulls backwards. There's a sound like velcro, and an occasional sucking plop, and a gleaming dome appears - a sight which would send Pate fainting to the floor.

The man's scalp is blueish white, in contrast to the ruddy complexion of his face. It looks like the skull of a drowning victim. The man's head clearly hasn't seen the light of day since the fifteenth century. And even back then it was kept in a black plastic bag.

The man gives Graham an address, and a business name - Folly Curls.

Graham knows that there is a bylaw which insists that all hairdressing businesses must be given puns for names, but surely that one is against the Geneva Convention.

He hies his way to Folly Curls. The sign is bold and hand painted. He goes in through the door which still tinkles with a little bell which was nailed to the door when it was a greengrocer's. He can't bring himself to admit that he just wants to change his appearance, so he hints darkly that he may be about to undergo some sort of treatment which might make a wig necessary, and to cheer himself up he has decided to change his hair colour.

The lady there is considerate and helpful.

He chooses a blonde mane with darkish streaks. Bit seventies, but certainly makes him look different. Graham pays for the rug and heads home. He can't wait for the contacts to arrive.

Two days later he finds the solution.

It's on the floor inside his front door. And floating in the solution are two little ice-blue discs like tiny exotic jellyfish. He puts them in, then gets Boris out of its box. He stretches it over his head, tucks in his wisps, and blinks tearfully into the mirror.

Wow!

That is weird.

His eyebrows and eyelashes are still dark, but somehow that doesn't look too strange. Graham thinks he might just get away with them as they are. There's a kind of Hutch look going down - unfortunately not Owen Wilson, but David Soul.

But Graham Paint it ain't.

"Hi. I've got an appointment with HR."

"Name?"

"David Wilson." Graham quite fancies Owen Soul, but thinks it might be just a little too distinctive. And to learn from his doppelganger he needs to blend invisibly into his world.

The man in the gatehouse at Legend Global Holdings runs his fingers down a list. He looks concerned.

"David Wilson?"

"That's right."

"There's no David Wilson on the list. What time?"

"8.45."

"There's no David Wilson at 8.45."

"I'm not exactly surprised."

The man's eyebrows raise.

"I mean, that's exactly the kind of shambles I'm here to sort out."

The man flinches, ever so slightly. "Who are you meant to be seeing?"

"I have no idea. I don't organise your people's diaries. I was told to present myself to HR on my first day."

The man looks at him warily, then picks up a phone and punches in three numbers. There's a pause. People are still heading past them on their way into work. Usual morning chaos.

"Hi Joyce. I've a David Wilson here at the gate. *Beeble beeble beeble.* No, I don't have him either. *Beeble beeble beeble.*"

Says it's his first day. *Beeble beeble beeble.* OK." Then to Graham - "She'll be down in a minute."

Graham nods at the man. Then he looks at the people scurrying in to work. It's as if they are genuinely concerned that they might be a couple of minutes late.

Gerbils.

"Hello, can I help you?"

Joyce is businesslike. She's another of the blue pinstripe women's suit brigade.

"I sincerely hope so. Perhaps you can show me to my office."

"We don't have any record of you, Mr Wilson." Joyce looks belligerent. But Graham senses this isn't natural aggression, but fear nurtured in a corporate culture built on the allocation of blame.

"Your appointments diary is computerised."

"That's right."

"Exactly."

"Exactly what?"

"Well it doesn't work, does it?"

"It usually does."

"Usually?"

"That's right."

"Not always."

"Almost always. Look, Mr, er - "

"And what error rate do you think is acceptable? How many inconvenienced visitors? How much wasted staff time?"

"I don't know that's any of your business."

"Mr Dupaint doesn't think any of this is acceptable. And he thinks it is my business. Very much my business."

Joyce looks pale, but perhaps it's a trick of the light. Like the mysterious Queen of Hearts levitation and the one with the silk hanky which turns into the ring you thought you had on your finger.

"You'd better come upstairs while we sort this out."

Joyce picks up a Visitor Tag on a ribbon and hands it to Graham. She has a tag hanging round her neck too, but hers is a different colour and has her photo laminated into it. She leads the way up to the door where Dupaint entered and holds her tag up to a sensor. She then punches some numbers into a keypad, waits for a click, and pulls the door open. Graham starts to follow her in, but she stops and he bumps into her from behind.

Quite enjoyed that, thinks Graham.

She points to the sensor.

"You need to swipe your card too."

"Right."

Graham follows her up a flight of stairs, an experience almost as pleasurable as bumping into her. She leads him along several corridors and into a small office. She shows him a seat. He sits down and places his briefcase beside the chair. She sits behind her desk to establish a bulwark of protection.

"Did Mr Dupeint arrange this?" She knows the correct way to spell it.

"I'm not at liberty to say."

"So who asked you to..."

Graham raises one eyebrow. For years he's practised this in front of a James Bond video and a mirror. Sean Connery had the pecs, but Roger Moore had the eyebrow. Close call. He always believed this social skill would come in useful, and today's the big day.

He looks monosupercilious.

"Let's just say that Mr Dupaint is fully aware of the seriousness of the situation, and the radical steps which need to be taken. But he doesn't want this to be seen as a top-down initiative."

Joyce nods, thoughtfully. "Not system push..." she volunteers, hesitantly.

"Exactly," says Graham. "User pull. Far better. I can see we're going to get on fine, you and I."

"So no attribution?"

"Total deniability."

"Hmmm. How extensive is this, er project?"

"We'll start with the IT systems. Then we'll see."

"So IT know about this?"

"Good God no! Steady on." Then he adopts a thoughtful expression. "Look Joyce. I know I can trust you. Mr Dupaint...." Joyce blushes. So the boss mentioned her! By name! Graham leans towards her in a conspiratorial fashion. "He said - talk to Joyce. She's discreet."

Joyce looks into his piercing blue eyes and nods.

"What I'll be doing, you might describe it as an IT audit. You can't have all the responsibility resting with one department. Not in such a sensitive area. There need to be checks and balances."

Joyce nods again.

"Wheels within wheels."

Joyce nods again. He does have lovely hair, she thinks.

"But don't breathe a word of this back to his office. He would have to deny it. And then the tittle tattle would start."

Graham glances down at her desk. Lying there is a note. It's handwritten, and the handwriting looks familiar. He tries to read the name at the bottom, upside down. It looks like Grim.

Where has he seen that writing before?

Of course. It's his own.

He nods towards it. "You have a fair bit of contact with Mr Dupaint?"

Again she blushes, ever so slightly.

"I guess you could say..."

"He speaks very highly of you." So that's the name! Grim! Like a jokey contraction of Graham. Graham knows that he's almost there, and decides to go for the killer blow.

"I understand you need to cover your own position. I have a note here. Perhaps you could shut your eyes while I open my case."

Joyce knows that the company operates under conditions of extreme secrecy and paranoia. Evasion is the dung to its corporate mushroom. But this Mr Wilson seems to operate right at the top level of stealth. She shuts her eyes.

Graham unzips his case and opens it on his knees. Then he quietly picks up a blank sheet of Legend headed notepaper from the pile beside her desk printer and while rustling the contents of his briefcase he scribbles a few words on it.

Joyce,

He writes.

Give Mr Wilson every help. He has my personal security clearance. Say nothing. Deny everything.

"Can I open my eyes yet?"

"Just a sec. There's some stuff here Grim would definitely not want made public."

I'll remember your help.
Grim Dupaint.

Graham shuts the case. "I've got it. You can open your eyes now."

He produces the note with a flourish and hands it to Joyce.

Her eyes widen. *"I'll remember your help."* Wow! That's amazing! Whatever it means!

"I'll need that back."

Something catches Joyce's eye as she hands it over. "Why has he signed his name with an 'a'? Rather than an 'e'?"

Graham looks blank. "Look, there..." she says.

"Dupaint."

Graham's brain whirrs.

"It's a code," says Graham. "We go back a long way, Grim and I. When he does that it means I should memorise and destroy.

And he crumples up the note, stuffs it in his mouth, and starts, laboriously, to chew.

Chapter 20

It's just as well Graham isn't sitting in his kitchen right now. Because if he was he would jump out of his socks at the sound of Kerri opening the front door and bustling in. He's got used to having the house to himself. Unfortunately he's about a block away heading home from the bus stop so he's about to get an unpleasant shock when he arrives.

Kerri looks at the letter from her lawyers. It looks as if it's been crumpled up and then straightened out a bit. It has a couple of damp blotches where the ink has run. Kerri fears they may be tears - but they're smears from beers.

Graham nears.

Kerri wonders where the houseplants have gone. She looks out of the kitchen window and spots some dried remnants, surrounded by pottery shards. She recognises parts of the pottery as her favourite vase - a hand-painted Victorian monstrosity which she's always been attached to, ever since it was bought for her by an old boyfriend.

Quentin was the last man she went out with before meeting Graham.

And in the interests of accuracy, I should point out she also went out with him from time to time after she and Graham became an item.

In fact the vase was a present which Quentin bought for her in a shop in the Lake District when they went off for a dirty weekend a couple of months after the wedding. Kerri refuses to feel guilty about that, because it was all basically Graham's fault. He said he was going off to visit a client and that this would entail a long weekend management planning exercise in a hotel in Cornwall. Kerri phoned Graham's office and someone let it slip that Graham was taking a PA called Randy with him.

Kerri challenged him with that information on the Thursday night as Graham was packing. Graham had the total nerve to say that he hadn't mentioned it because he didn't think it was important. As if!

So Kerri had retaliated with Quentin, and got a vase for her troubles.

She was taken aback to meet Randy afterwards in the pub near Graham's work. Randy was not what she had imagined. She'd forgotten in these politically correct times a PA could be either sex.

"Hi, I'm Randy."

Randy had short cropped hair and a leather jacket, and a deep gravely voice.

"Bloody hell! Are you the Randy that Graham went off to Cornwall with?"

"Among others..." Randy looked at Kerri appraisingly.

"No, I realise that. But for some stupid reason I got it into my head that this Randy was a woman." Kerri took a sip of her white wine.

"I am a woman," growled Randy.

Kerri snorted the wine over Randy's leather jacket.

"That's pretty uncouth," said Randy. "But I forgive you."

But Graham deserved it anyway, in Kerri's estimation. First, he had worried her unnecessarily by failing to mention Randy and not explaining things properly. Graham said there was nothing to explain, so how could he explain it? Which was basically pathetic. Then Graham had got all sulky when Quentin started to pop round to see her. Over the past couple of years one or two of Quentin's gifts had gone missing. She could be a bit casual with her possessions but she definitely didn't remember putting a little cloth doll which said 'World's Greatest Lover' across its chest into the Aga. At least it was probably the doll. You can never smell what's in the oven of an Aga, which is why every Christmas there's at least one elaborate vegetable dish found on Boxing Day black and dried up like something from an Egyptian tomb.

One morning she found spoor in the snow outside the kitchen window and went shrieking to Graham that a large animal had been prowling about in the night. Graham had a look and said it was pakora and what was he meant to do - put them back in the Aga? Or leave them to stink out the kitchen with the smell of charred remnants?

So bloody logical.

Kerri looks around the kitchen. She's come back during the day so that she can clear out her clothes and possessions without being forced into an ugly confrontation. Not that she's bothered by Graham's girly whining, but her lawyer says that she should avoid direct contact with Graham if at all possible. Of course she has no idea he's packed in the job and might return

123

home at any time. She's only known him as a man of precise habits and regular timetables.

Pate describes Graham as a 'chronic metronome'. Graham prides himself on knowing this means 'chronic' in the original Greek sense of 'pertaining to time' and metronome as in 'instrument which counts a regular beat'. Pate's description of Graham actually signifies 'chronic' in its more common sense of 'won't go away' and 'nagging'. And the other word Pate visualises for his colleague is 'metro-gnome' - a humorously stunted creature of the metropolis.

Kerri looks at the jumble of clothes scattered everywhere, presumably waiting for a slave to wash them.

Graham opens the garden gate.

Kerri walks over to the front door. There's something odd on a window ledge in the porch. It seems to be a shoebox with little holes punched in it. She picks it up. She peers into one of the holes.

Graham steps up to the front door. It seems to be ajar.

In the darkness of the box something stares back at Kerri. With a jolt of pure horror she recognises a snake peering at her as Graham throws the door open which knocks the shoebox out of her hand and she screams and Graham leaps vertically in the air and brains himself on the lintel above the door.

Fuck me! thinks Bumface in caterpillarese as he ricochets across the box and goes crashing to the floor at exactly the same moment as Graham's lifeless body slumps to the ground.

This quantum event is a cracker in parallel universe terms. Several are spawned at once.

In one, Graham has a cerebral haemorrhage and dies instantly. Kerri immediately realises her mistake and pines for the rest of her life over the love she failed to value. She's more comfortable with a tragic memory than a tragic loser.

We'll skip that one because it's tedious and we're not sure how to spell haemorrhage.

In another universe he has a cerebral haemorrhoid. In that one Graham really has his head up his arse. We'll skip that too.

In a third universe Kerri cradles Graham's battered head in her arms. "Grey darling," she sobs. As his eyelids flicker open he recognises her through tears of pain and joy. "Oh Kerri," he gasps. "I love you." "Thank you," replies Kerri, who's not familiar with the way the dialogue is meant to go. This traumatic moment is a turning point in their relationship. "Tell us how you bumped your head and fell in love," the grandchildren plead. In that universe Kerri and Grey might tell the tale, but I won't, because it makes me want to puke.

In this universe Graham slumps to the floor as Kerri crashes backwards through a kitchen chair. The holy box hits the ground and Bumface is caterpulted (catapillared?) through the air before landing feet upwards under the kitchen table.

Graham lies groaning on the doormat, clutching his skull. If only he had Pate's hair...

Kerri, meanwhile, is sobbing and generally carrying on in a heap on the kitchen floor.

After a minute or two, Graham pulls his way up the door jamb. He stands groaning and feeling the top of his head for blood. No need. It's trickling down his face and into his eyes.

Kerri looks at him in shock.

Then Graham staggers towards her.

Kerri's heart melts as she realises that her big soft wazzock of a stunned husband is more worried about her than himself. Her mouth opens and she holds out her arms as he lurches forward. Graham holds out his hands too.

"Bumface!" he calls, with genuine affection and concern.

Kerri is touched, more than she ever could have believed. "Shit-for-brains!" she replies. She leans forward into his reaching arms and closes her eyes. Graham bends down and lovingly, gently, picks up the dazed green caterpillar. He is oblivious to the dull thud to his left as Kerri lands face down on the Amtico.

Graham wonders whether you should blow up a caterpillar's nose to revive it. The dopey face on Bumface's nether regions could lead to awkward confusion. Is there a law against having oral sex with an insect? Or when the volcano of cross-species lust erupts do you just go with the larval flow?

Fortunately, Bumface chooses that moment to curl up a little, thus saving Graham from his dilemma, and possible arrest.

Graham steps over the groaning form of his wife and reaches for the box.

"Excuse me," he says. "You're squashing the lid." He places Bumface carefully in the box, and picks up bits of lettuce and twig from the floor. He sets the box down on the table, then uses one hand to roll Kerri sideways and the other to retrieve the box lid. He places it back on the box, straightening it until it fits.

Kerri slides away from him and tries to pick herself up with the aid of the smashed chair.

"I see you've already chosen yours," says Graham. "I'll take this one then." And he sits on another. "Anything else you'd like to demolish before I call my lawyer?"

With the trickles of blood running down his face he looks like Brad Pitt in Fight Club or Bruce Willis in just about every Bruce Willis movie. There's something going on here she doesn't recognise. Graham is failing to whine. He's not analysing things ad absurdam. Or stopping to explain what ad absurdam means.

He's just sitting there, looking, quite, erm, gosh...

He stands up, and picks up the box.

"I'm not going to throw you out, because I'm not doing anything which would give ammunition to you and your scumball ambulance-chasing lawyer. But I'm not backing off either. So I'm off to the pub. You might be here when I get back. Or you might be gone. It's your call. Just don't expect peace, reconciliation and gratitude."

Kerri has amazement written all over her face. But from where Graham is standing, all he can see is men.

Chapter 21

"Hi Gordy. This is David. He's here to do an audit of our security systems."

Graham nods and shakes hands with Gordy. "Hi Gordy. David Wilson. An unusual system you've got here."

Gordy nods again, frowning. He is in his early thirties. His hair is receding and his clothes suggest that he can't quite decide whether to rebel against the establishment or sign up as a fogey. Skateboard chic crossed with pipe and slippers. Take the thigh pockets off his cargo pants and his baggy trousers wouldn't look out of place on his grandfather. And is his tie ironic? Or just, perhaps, a tie? He tries to think of something to ask Graham which won't sound too paranoid. "Are you, em, staff?" Nope. Sounded paranoid.

Graham starts to open his mouth, but Joyce intervenes. "He's here as the eyes of the fifth floor. That's all you have to know."

"Just routine checks," smiles Graham, chillingly. "Starting with IT."

Graham can't believe what he's seeing. The guy actually seems scared of him.

"Fine. Take a seat. Do you want a glass of water?"

"Yeah, great."

Gordy indicates to Joyce in a very obvious fashion that he wants her to accompany him to the water cooler. He does this by throwing his eyes up and sideways in that general direction until they twang against his upper eyelids and are catapulted back into their sockets. Try it and you'll see what I mean. Not in front of a mirror, though, cos they won't be able to point at the mirror while you're doing it. Not if you do it properly. If you insist on some visual feedback you'll have to use a video camera. Either put the camera on a tripod or get a friend to shoot it. If you choose the latter you'll need an explanation. Memorise this::

Hi friend

(You may substitute an actual name here. So long as it's the same as your friend's name. Then they won't realise it's a substitute.)

I'm doing a new nightclass in animation. It's fab. Our first exercise is to study eye movements. If you would be so kind as to press this button while I grimace I can do a frame by frame analysis.

On second thoughts, use the bloody tripod.

On third thoughts, just take my word for it.

Gordy does the roly eyes thing and Joyce follows him to the water cooler. She starts to open her mouth, but Gordy interrupts. "Look, I don't want to be unhelpful here, but my department takes total responsibility for IT security."

"Gordy."

"So how can we be responsible if random punters get access to the codes?"

"Gordy."

"I'm not being unreasonable. This is outrageous!"

"Gordy."

"I cannot work under these conditions. It's just impossible! How can the buck stop with us if we have no way of checking..."

Joyce imagines how the next few moments might unfold if she was in an alternative universe - one in which she was uninhibited and just didn't give a shit. Her version goes like this:

> Gordy stops abruptly. Joyce has grabbed the end of his tie and inserted it into the shredder.
>
> "I'm serious. My department has a 100% record in..."
>
> Bzzzt. Joyce presses the button for a moment. Gordy's face is pulled two inches towards the shredder.
>
> "There is no way I can..."
>
> Bzzzzzzzt. Another four inches.
>
> "Stop doing that!"
>
> Bzzt.
>
> I mean it!
>
> Bzt.
>
> A pause.
>
> Bzt.
>
> Joyce just did that one because she could. She raises her finger again, and lets it hover

over the button. "You will give David every assistance. And you will not breathe a word of this to anyone."

Gordy opens his mouth, but her finger quivers towards the button.

"Not even your own staff. If you co-operate then it may be noted. If you don't then it will be noted."

Gordy tries to nod, but his face is squashed against the machine. Joyce hands him a pair of scissors and leaves him to cut the Gordian knot.

Instead Joyce invokes the curse of Grim. "It's not just systems he's checking." Gordy frowns at her as she continues. "It's people. And whatever you do, don't let on I told you. Or we're both stuffed."

Gordy's paranoia tells him he'd better give the impression of co-operating with this annoying David Wilson. But it also suggests that it will all end in tears unless he's very, very careful. And very, very lucky. Legend Global Holdings is that sort of company. He walks back to Graham and hands him a cup of water.

Graham takes a sip. It tastes like water. The water delivery man used to marvel at the fact that companies paid for water when there was perfectly good stuff coming out of the taps free. He decided that he could make a good living selling water. So he booted up his PC and made a copy of the invoice which his employers sent each month to Legend Global. It was exact in every detail. Apart from the bank account number and sort code, which was his own. And the special offer which said the client could gain a discount by paying by direct bank transfer rather than by cheque.

Did I mention that his name was Ernie Waterman? No? Strange, that. You'd think I would have remembered. Because Ernie is sometimes abbreviated to Ern, which sounds like something you might keep water in.

Anyway, Ern started taking away the empty plastic bottles from the water dispenser and filling them from the tap at home. But he couldn't let the water company stop the account and take away the dispenser. So once every few months he would take a genuine bottle and pay for it himself by cheque from an account he had opened which he named General Office Sundries Account. As long as the client bought just a tiny amount of water the company which employed him would let them keep the dispenser. And all the time the cash flowed into Ern's account like, erm, well, water, obviously.

After a while, Ern got fed up hauling all these bottles backwards and forward to his house, where he filled them with a hose. The storeroom at Global where the empties were kept had a tap in it. So Ern brought in a length of hose and an adaptor for the tap and took to filling them there and then. From the client's own tap.

After a while he started to worry that nobody ever saw him carrying bottles in from the van. So he began sauntering out with a couple of empties, then struggling back with them one at a time as if they were heavy. Then he got bored. This was taking too long. So he would leave a bottle filling from the tap in the storeroom and lock the door. Then he would make several journeys backwards and forwards to the van with an empty bottle. Lightly he would skip with his featherweight empty. Then he would trudge back with the bottle on his shoulder as if he was carrying a boulder. It was still empty, but by the magic of mime he managed to make it look full. You might be forgiven for thinking he was suffering from a type of Sisyphus. If that were a disease rather than a figure from Greek mythology. Who lugged a boulder rather than a water bottle. Uphill, rather than across a car park. In fact, forget the Sisyphus comparison. It doesn't really hold water. Like Ernie's bottle.

Which must be the analogy I was groping for.

Graham takes another sip of the water. He nods his thanks. But not too vigorously. He doesn't want the blond wig to slide about. "Right," says Graham. "Let's start with a look at passwords and encryption." Gordy looks nervously at Joyce. "I think we should go to my office," he suggests. Joyce takes the hint.

"I'll leave you guys to all this techy stuff." Then she turns to Graham. "Just give me a shout if you need me."

Graham smiles at her. She's obviously fiercely loyal, which has proved to be her weakness. Now she will be fiercely loyal to Graham, in the misguided belief that he's meant to be there. Graham is very impressed with her. He almost feels guilty, taking her in like that. But he reassures himself that he's not here to do any harm to the company. He just wants to get to the bottom of things.

Why Graham Paint is an unemployed management consultant, while Grim Dupeint is an international success.

Why Graham Paint can't afford to tax his SUV, while Grim Dupeint gets whisked about in a chauffeur-driven limo.

Why Graham Paint is stony, while Grim Dupeint is minted.

Why Graham Paint can't even keep his wife, while Grim Dupeint presumably has more nookie than he can handle. Or does he? Before too long Graham will build up a picture of the man and his triumphs. And then Graham will vanish from his life as mysteriously as he arrived, armed with the knowledge which will allow him to achieve his potential and become a success.

After all they're both the same person! They have the same skills, the same IQ, the same looks (apart from the fact that one has a tan and cool threads and the other has a pasty face and a silly wig). The life experience has been different over the past few years, but that's the bit Graham plans to catch up on. And it promises to be fun.

The first bit of fun is going to involve this arsehole Gordy. What a crawler. A geek and a crawler. Graham's going to enjoy winding him up.

They go through to Gordy's office.

"I'd like you to shut your machine down and talk me through the start-up procedure," says Graham.

"Fine, er, David. Can I call you David?"

"Mr Wilson will do fine for now."

"Of course Mr Wilson."

In the course of the hour which follows Gordy shows Graham all of the security protocols and passwords. Or at least all of the bits which Gordy reckons he needs to know, for the time being. They talk about the networking system and the hierarchy of servers, the subgroups and workgroups, the need-to-know principles and the relationship between the different companies in the Legend Global Holdings group.

The structures are byzantine, and the IT system reflects that complexity. In fact it goes a step further, by creating further barriers to communication and analysis. It is a maze of firewalls, passwords and authorisation codes. Graham relishes the task ahead. The IT system is exactly the sort of thing he's used to setting up to make the system just about unworkable to anybody but the expert who created it. Who has made himself indispensable. So Gordy thinks he's got a job for life? Well in Graham Paint he may have met his match.

What's the job abbreviation for an analyst on a retainer? thinks Graham. An Anal. Retentive. Well he thinks it's funny. Which is why he's not headlining at the Comedy Store, but is an unemployed management consultant.

Although, come to think of it, that does make me laugh, quite a lot...

Chapter 22

"Hi!" says Graham to Grim as Grim walks by. It's 6.47 am, and Graham is busy tapping away at a keyboard in an otherwise deserted general office as Grim strides through towards his private rooms. There is a back stair where Grim can come and go unobserved, but at this time of the morning he thought he was safe going the direct route.

"Who are you? Do I know you?" Grim stares at Graham, taking in the wavy blonde hair and ice blue eyes. He's sure he's never seen the man before in his life, but bizarrely, his face seems familiar.

"David Wilson," says Graham. "I'm here to put a bomb under your IT people."

"Not before time," says Grim. "At last somebody's got the message. Who exactly was it brought you in?"

Graham looks at him and taps his nose knowingly. Then he holds his finger up to his lips in a ssshhhhh mime. Then he points to his ear, and looks around the office. Then he points to the phone. He picks up the receiver and pops the handset apart with the tip of a small screwdriver. Then he points to a random electricky-looking thingmy with wires coming in one end and out the other. Then he mimes putting on a set of earphones and pretending to listen studiously.

Why he mimes someone pretending to listen is a mystery. He really ought to mime someone actually listening. But to Grim's eyes, the message is clear. The place is obviously bugged. Of course he knows this, because it was bugged on his orders. But if someone else knows it's bugged, then perhaps some other buggers are listening too.

"It was the person you authorised to engage me, sir. The important point is that it was on your direct say-so."

"Ah," says Grim. Then he points to himself and screws up his face questioningly.

"That's right," says Graham, then does the eyeball-chucking thing in the direction of a small gizmo in the ceiling.

Grim looks up at it, then hastily looks down again. It looks like part of the sprinkler system, but of course some of these are actually concealed cameras. Grim had them installed himself, then paid the man who installed them a large amount of dosh to forget what he'd just done. The TV monitor screens are in a small room adjacent to Grim's office. So how the hell does this David Wilson know about that?

Of course Graham hasn't a clue. He was just looking vaguely upwards, throwing a few ideas at the wall to see what sticks. And from Grim's guilty glance there must be something dodgy about the sprinklers.

"Have I seen you somewhere, before..." asks Grim.

Fuck, thinks Graham. "Don't think so sir. But from what I can make of this pig's ear of an IT system, you may be seeing more of me in future..."

Good, thinks Grim. But there's something still bothering him, ever so slightly. He looks closely at Graham's eyes. Graham looks back at him, fascinated.

That's some tan, thinks Graham. And I'm sure my teeth aren't as straight as that. Grim decides to level with him.

"I don't know how to put this, but what the hell. Most people round here crap themselves if they see me. They all get their heads down and pretend to be working flat out. So how come you're not the same?"

"Don't know," says Graham with a smile. "Maybe we're like minds."

"Bizarre," says Grim. There's something about this David guy which does quite appeal to him. The absence of abject terror might have something to do with it. But there is a familiar sense of common ground they seem to share.

"Look, stick in," says Grim. "And keep me posted. And if you need to get hold of me you can get me through the switchboard." And Grim writes a number on a piece of paper. Beside it is the single word: Direct. Not the switchboard number at all. So who does Grim think is listening? Or watching?

Ya beauty, thinks Graham. He answers in a low steady voice. "I'll report direct to you."

And Grim nods at him, a faint smile at the corner of his mouth. Graham returns the smile, with uncanny symmetry.

Grim walks off towards his office. At last, someone he might just be able to work with.

For a couple of hours Graham continues to explore the IT labyrinth. There seem to be several different sets of admin and accounting systems. Some are self-evident. The accounts and ordering system for Legend Bionics are properly separate from those of Legend Arms. Legend Mines is a subsidiary of Legend Arms, but the day to day accounting is separate. It's only at the upper levels of group finance that the subsidiary status has any impact, and that seems to be more reflected by occasional share purchases and transfers between the two than any direct flow of cash.

Legend Laundry is there, but it doesn't seem to have any connection with the others, apart from having Grim Dupeint on the board of both. Then there's Screen Legends. And Gastronomic Legends. And Local Legends. And Legend Travel. And Legend Global Marine, who seem to be the company who own the Blue Water Legend megayacht which Graham visited at the Boat Show.

Boat!

That's a larf.

That little boat had bigger boats in its garage than Graham had ever sailed.

Graham is convinced that he still hasn't found a fraction of the companies which work within the Legend group. There seem to be some partitions on the main server hard drive which don't want to reveal their contents despite the list of passwords provided by that weasel Gordy.

Graham tries a few of his own little tricks. He does a search of the main server. Using a few keyboard shortcuts known only to geeks like himself, he asks the computer system to search for invisible files and folders. He doesn't think this will lead him straight to his goal. But there are always traces. After a while he finds some invisible files which have been created at the same time as their more obvious counterparts.

Whoever deleted the main files had obviously forgotten to delete the aliases. The file may have gone, but if you searched under recent files there were still indications of what the originals might have been called.

Graham looks around the office. It's seven thirty in the morning. One keen character has just turned up to work and is unpacking his sandwiches from his briefcase and putting them in Tupperware boxes in a drawer. Obviously a forward planner. No sign of Gordy so far. Graham installs a disc rescue utility. This is useful if your hard drive falls apart. It helps you find the bits of files and put them back together again. The reason they're in bits is because computers will scavenge for free segments of memory to store files, and the more the drives are used the more fragmented the free bits become.

Then there's the useful fact that when files are deleted the computer doesn't actually put them through a shredder. It just throws away the note saying where they were stored. If you copy a new file on to the computer it may overwrite an old deleted one.

But then again it may not.

And the old files will just hang around in there, passing the time. Swapping yarns about the good old days. Jobs they worked on together. Great schemes and plans - which give them a heroic status in the eyes of younger files. Folders they used to hang out in. Partitions they ruled, back in the day. They refer in whispered tones to great files who've been overwritten. Some of the harder files may have rubbed many others out in turn in their climb to prominence.

Then there were files which were just a hoot. The sort of files your mates used to email to you, back before the crackdown. Pictures of fluffy kittens for the ladies. Jokes about old people's dangly bits. Nobody these days would believe what you used to see.

And there were picture files which would make your eyeballs steam up. Giffs and JPEGs. Even, stone the crows, movies. Like that chick in the smart grey suit who made the red silk hanky disappear to music. And kept getting her kit off. Until there was nowhere left to hide the hanky. And then she pulled it out from the last place you'd have imagined! In front of an audience!

You younger files just wouldn't believe what we used to fire backwards and forwards by broadband.

When Graham uncovers the deleted files and shines a metaphorical light on them there may be a few red faces.

But still he's sure he's only scratching the surface. Not always a good move in Legend Global. There's only one person there allowed to make waves...

Chapter 23

The waves spread across the large tank of tropical fish. The fish are used to it. They think a storm's coming.

That's how much fish know. Stupid scaly twits.

What's coming is Grim Dupeint, and the waves are caused by his energetic humping of Susan Hornygolloch. Bent forward over an executive couch she makes an impressive sight. Blonde hair falling across her broad Nordic cheekbones. Muscular thighs revealed under the tightly stretched material of the pinstripe skirt. A skirt hitched up just enough to allow Grim to make an entry in his accounting system. The system of shagging Susan Hornygolloch whenever he feels like it, which accounts for his remarkable ability to relax even when hair-raising business deals are underway.

Susan may be Nordic by ancestry, but by upbringing she's an Edinburgh slapper. Fortunately for Susan daddy put her to school at Hairy Foreskins, as her girls-only fee-paying establishment was colloquially known. This means that when she bends over to allow her arse to be slapped by some chap's thundering thighs it's usually quite an affluent pair of loins, which meets her high maintenance costs, and more.

Her real surname is something else, but nobody can remember what. Even HR would have to look up a personal file if they needed to remind themselves. And since nobody can remember her surname they wouldn't know what capital letter to search for.

It all went back to the day...

The day when...

The epic day when...

Susan had been employed to do some mindless job by a chauvinist under-manager who wanted her to brighten up his day. As office furniture. Grim had spotted her in a parsec. Or a nanosecond. Whichever is shorter. Look it up, for God's sake. This isn't a dictionary, you know.

Alright, here's a clue. A parsec is distance, and it's vast.

So that narrows things down a bit.

Grim had spotted her in a nanosecond.

He had immediately promoted her to Personal Assistant to the CEO (himself), and twelve minutes later (not a record, but not bad going for old Grim) she was beating out the first approaching waves of a tsunami across the fish tank beside Grim's couch. She proved to be a bit of a groaner.

Then a bit of a yelper.

Then - let's not beat about the bush (Grim's job) - she proved to be an outright screamer. Although nothing that a deftly inserted tropical freshwater carp couldn't fix.

Grim had never shagged a girl with a fish in her mouth before. Although there was that lass outside the chipper when he was a student...

OK. So he had shagged a girl with a fish in her mouth before. And chips.

But he'd never shagged a girl with a live fish in her mouth before - one which was flapping and slapping in counterpoint to what was going on in the shadier regions below the belt. It was about nine inches long, and quite meaty. Susan didn't know whether to spit it out. Perhaps that would be rude. But she couldn't bite too hard, because it might be one of Grim's favourite pets. So she had to try to keep it in place with her lips muscles.

It was that oromaxillary facial prowess, together with what happened when Grim came, which sealed her fate.

Grim came.

Susan came too.

Always a good move.

But in doing so, Susan gasped, and swallowed the fish.

Which gave Grim a startling illustration of what oral sex might be like with Susan.

Which is why she wasn't just a shag, but is now his PA. And has been for ages.

So where did the name come from? One day Susan came in to work and told her colleagues (who were very fond of her) that she'd had an infestation of little black insects in her flat.

Fleas? asked someone.

She didn't think so.

Crabs? asked someone else.

She was sure they weren't crabs, because they didn't have brown shells and big claws. Then she uttered the immortal words, in her Scottish accent.

"There were susans of 'em. Susans and susans o' wee hornygollochs."

"Hornygollochs?" said one of her perplexed audience. Gordy. He looked around for help. Most of his colleagues looked equally blank.

"Eariwigs," Susan elaborated.

"What about the Susan bit?"

"Susans!"

A voice came from over by the photocopier.

"I think she means thousands."

"That's right - there were susans of 'em."

"God, she does mean it too. Why doesn't she just say thousands? The rest of her gibbering is almost comprehensible."

"I <u>am</u> saying susans!!" shouted Susan, stamping her high heel.

"Wait a minute," says Gordy. "Give me a number between six and eight."

"Sivven," says Susan.

"Ah," says Gordy. "That explains it. You're not from Edinburgh at all. You're from the land of sivven and illiven."

"What's illivin?" asks a colleague.

"A number between tin and twilve. That's it. She may have gone to school in Edinburgh, but she must have come from Glasgow."

"Rubbish," screamed Susan. "It was Newton Mearns."

And that's how Susan became known as Susan Hornygolloch.

Chapter 24

"So what do you reckon?" asks Graham, unfolding a letter from its envelope and passing it over to Pate.

"I reckon it's your round and I will have time to read and digest this epistle, nay billet doux, by the time you return with another pint of Old Scruttock's. And get one for yourself why don't you?"

Graham rolls his eyes. In their sockets, rather than across the table. After all, they're not marbles. a) They would get sticky with spilt beer, and b) He's not sure he could do the wiring to put them back in.

Then he gets up and heads to the bar.

Pate and Graham are having a chinwag just off Cotive High Street, in Cotive Lane. The local at the end of the lane is a traditional old boozer called the Cotive Arms. This is where they were drinking last time and rabbiting on about pub names. But I could hardly have told you then that they were in the Cotive Arms. Because that was only on page 102. And faced with such a crap pun you might have thrown the book down in disgust and walked away. But now we're on page 146 and the shop assistant has spotted the coffee you splashed on the flyleaf, so you're probably stuck with paying for it now. Which means that you'll probably plough right on to the end, even if you do think this book is right out of ordure, just to get your money's worth. So now I can reveal that beside Cotive High Street is the Police Station on Letsby Avenue. And round the corner from there is Association for Live Entertainment on Seymour Circus.

I can't let this moment pass without giving credit to the angel who inspired this book. She lives in a small flat in Writer's Mews.

Graham throws a note down on the bar, tells the barman to keep the change, and picks up the pints.

"Hang on a minute! What's this?" asks the barman, staring at the note. "What kind of a note is that?"

"It's an F flat," says Graham. "Listen." And he hums a G natural along with it. At that moment a B buzzes into the bar. The sound is a harmonious paean to summer, if a little melancholy.

"What's wrong with that?" asks Graham.

"You'll have me done for serving minors," says the barman.

"OK, lose the B," says Graham, as it lands on the bar, sups some spilt Scruttocks, falls over on its side and starts to hum Moon River. "There's nothing wrong with that note."

"Bloody is," says the barman, who was hired for his charm.

"Bloody isn't," says Graham. "What then?"

"You said it was an F flat?"

"Correct."

"I'm going to have to ask you to leave. If anyone sees you passing Es across the bar I'm knackered."

"Oh, for goodness' sake!" says Graham, and puts the pints down with an exasperated flourish. He picks up the note and stuffs it back in his wallet. "Have this then." And he puts another note down on the bar. It's a C.

"What makes you think I've got change for that then?" asks the barman. "You taking the piss or what?"

Graham and Pate slow down to a jog, now that the end of Cotive High Street has vanished from sight. The barman couldn't pursue them past the door, or every bottle of spirits behind the bar would have vanished in an instant, leaving a strange wind as the air molecules of the lounge whooshed to fill the vacuum left by their absence. The whoosh of departing air wouldn't have left an area of low pressure, because by way of compensation every regular would by now have a bulge in the inside pocket of their jacket filling up the space.

Graham and Pate place their empty pint glasses on a wall and stop for breath. "That's not easy," says Graham. "Drinking while running."

Pate nods, and sends a shower of foam from his hair. Most of his pint seems to have ended up there.

"You could do a pirouette," says Graham. "Then the froth might spray outwards, by centrifugal force."

"No such thing," says Pate. "Centrifugal force doesn't exist."

"Wha!" explodes Graham. "Now you're really talking bollocks. I may not be an Einstein, but even I know what centrifugal force is."

"Right. Step outside, to the Appendix – Example 2, and we'll how hard you are."

148

In a couple of minutes they're back. Pate looks smug. Graham tries to change the subject. "Have you found out any more about Grim Dupeint?"

"Yes."

"Well?"

"You wish me to elucidate? To cast light on the glaucous, adumbrated pools of dark misunderstanding and ignorance?"

The glint in Graham's eye tells Pate that in another universe he has another black eye. He decides not to push his luck any further in this one. "As you might imagine, Grim Dupeint was christened Graham Paint. Because as far as I can ascertain he and you were one and the same until about twelve years ago. The first inkling I've picked up that you might have split was after you came back from a gap year after university. You went to South America, did you not?"

"That's right. Inca Trail. Nazca lines. Bolivian marching powder."

"Was there any particular incident you recall? Anything which might have heralded a parting of the ways."

Graham racks his brains. Most of the time he was with a group. The biggest decision they ever had to take individually was what souvenirs to buy from the market. Then something swims back up to the surface of his memory. "There was one time..."

"Yes?"

"We were well blitzed. We were hanging out with some of the locals at a bar, the night before I was due to fly from Colombia to Ecuador. There was this bloke wanted me to take a package in my luggage, to a mate of his down south. Said I was less likely to be searched than a local guy. I said no way was I taking drugs

149

through customs. He flat out denied it was drugs. But he was offering me a very large amount of dosh and I was skint."

"So what did you do?"

"I chickened out. He gave me the parcel. It weighed a ton, and I said no way, hoseasons. He was well pissed off."

Pate looks thoughtful. "What do you think it might have been?"

"It was bloody heavy. I wondered if it was a gun."

"That sounds like it. In one universe, if you took the parcel, and got away with it, who knows where it might have led?"

"I might have been tempted to try again..."

"Ferzackerly."

"So Grim Dupeint... might be me. But a version of me prepared to live more dangerously..."

"You wanted to learn the secrets of his success."

"Yes, but Bloody Norah..."

Graham is wondering what might conceivably have prompted him to risk dealing in weapons. He has alarm written all over his face. But from where Pate is standing he can only see a small arm.

Chapter 25

Graham gets stuck into work with a vengeance. Each morning he turns up at sparrowfart and rampages (virtually) through the company's hard drives like a Visigoth through the brothels of Rome. But he keeps his willy in his trousers. Because, like Rome, he doesn't want the sack.

And each morning (at least when the great man is not adventuring abroad) Grim Dupeint stops by Graham's desk for a natter. The two of them just seem to hit it off.

An odd couple.

Grim with his chiselled Heathcliff looks and groomed dark locks like waves beating on the shore of his tanned brow, gently rippled like an Ionian beach, leading to his virile eyebrows like the high water mark on that beach where a particularly fine crop of hairy seaweed has been deposited by the cruel relentless sea above the amber pools of his lambent orbs.

And Graham with his pasty complexion, ice-blue contacts and streaky blonde mullet.

But apart from that, they're pretty similar really.

Graham finds himself torn. There's a weird sensation of seeing himself in two separate lumps. Me here, and me over there. But he also has an immediate empathy with the loathsome Grim. Yes, there are aspects to his character which Graham finds repellent - a calculating ruthlessness which Graham doesn't recognise at all. And yet... Logic suggests that this vicious streak must also lie latent within himself, but if so it's passed the lie-detector test.

Then there's the problem of Graham's investigations into the company IT system.

What he's finding seems pretty unsavoury.

Legend Arms is indeed a multinational firm of arms dealers. Legend Mines is their biggest money spinner. It makes anti-personnel land mines. The mines last forever. They don't rust, because they're made of plastic. And like Pate suggested they don't reveal themselves to mine detectors either. It gets worse. If the mines lie in full view their bright colourful casings make them look like toys, so kids pick them up, and get blown apart. In their thousands. But the charge is calculated to be nonfatal. Because high numbers of severely wounded civilian casualties tie up an enemy's medical resources, whereas dead bodies just smell.

That's when Legend Bionics steps in with its carbon fibre legs, paid for by charities worldwide. And sells them by the thousand at a vast price, paid for by punters with a conscience. (Stump up now!)

If the people who've been gifted a crop of mines get fed up with the attrition then they can always (if they can afford it) call in Legend Mine Clearance - "What's yours is mines!" - to get rid of the problem. Legend Mine Clearance has no more idea than anyone else where the mines are, and it can't detect them either, but it does possess some bloody great armoured vehicles like diggers with massive shovels on the front and flails made of heavy chains which flap round on a roller pounding the ground ahead. (Don't get legless - make mines armless!) The mines are detonated and the shovel protects the driver from the blast. Presumably he wears earplugs.

And if you can't afford to employ these machines then you can always go to Legend International Aid Relief, which will put up finance by raising funding from governments with guilty consciences and taking a modest commission for the trouble. Of course the commission only needs to be modest, because the work generally seems to be passed to Legend Mine Clearance who trouser the rest of the dosh.

Did I say generally?

Make that always.

Graham is searching for some redeeming feature in this whole sordid conglomeration. Perhaps in an imperfect world there will always be businesses like this, and Grim is just making sure that he gets the jobs rather than somebody worse. Maybe he does good deeds with the profits.

He can't be as bad as he looks.

One morning Graham asks him how the Legend name came about.

"How did the Legend name come about?" asks Graham.

Grim chuckles. "It's not really Legend," he says. "As in mythic story."

Graham looks puzzled. Grim leans back and recalls the good old days.

"Back in the time when I was just working as a freelance, before the company started, I was in the Congo, and we'd just made this humungous sale to the rebels. So there were mines everywhere. And it was bizarre, but - wait for this, you'll split yourself - this bloke I'd recruited to do the local sales, he walked out in front of his house, and boom! he steps on one of the bloody things. Had no idea where his own people were putting them. So he's lying there yelling his head off, and over in the road is his leg, or a bit of it, and at that moment I had a great idea for a name for the company. (I was thinking of starting a company and going legit.) 'Leg end!' I thought. 'That's it! Leg End Mines!' But I'd write it 'Legend', and nobody would catch on."

Grim grins at Graham, who suppresses a sudden urge to vomit. "What happened to the guy?"

"Which guy?" Grim looks puzzled. "Oh, the legless one?"

He has a think.

"Fuck knows..."

And this is the moment when.

When Graham thinks *"Something needs to be done."*

It doesn't take him long. He already has access to the computer banking system which allows the company to make direct credit transfers. The main task is to set up a subroutine which obscures where the cash is going. So he writes a few extra lines of code. It's quite easy really. Because Legend Global has made secrecy so central to its way of thinking that nothing in the accounts is obvious.

Legend Mines has to pass payments to Legend Laundry for a bit of money laundering in order to get cash back into the UK free of tax.

Legend Laundry has to pass funds to Legend Brown Envelopes, to be used to grease the palms of international diplomats and high ranking ministers in order to secure the contracts to sell the mines, and transport them using Legend Global Marine.

But you won't find bank entries like "Bung for Foreign Office Minister" or "Transfer to Tax-Dodge Account".

Instead there are multifaceted transactions marked "Trsf 6077-384-1964 - hldg a/c" which bounce through endless series of temporary parking accounts and in and out of subsidiary businesses in a multitude of different countries and currencies before eventually ending up at their destined destination.

Which is why Graham finds it relatively straightforward (in a labyrinthine kind of way) to transfer ten million pounds from Legend Mines to Save the Children.

Chapter 26

At first it tingles. Then it feels more like an irritation, at the top of his thigh. All right, let's not beat about the bush. It's at the top of Graham's crotch, on the left hand side.

Surreptitiously he slides his hand into his left trouser pocket.

His mobile phone vibrates again.

Phew.

It's a text message, from Pate.

A Eiio Ouio. Oo ee oa uo. Ae.

Graham hits 'Reply' and types in his own message.

Wht fck y up to??? Vwls incmprhnsbl. Use cnsnnts. Twt.

He leaves the phone on the desk. It vibrates again.

Cll Mssn Sltns. Drthy nds mrl spprt. Pt.

Graham considers replying *K. T.* but instead gives Pate some of his own medicine and responds *O. a.*

Then he dials Emission Solutions and braces himself for Dorothy's oratory. Instead he's greeted by a recorded message.

Welcome to Emission Solutions - your premier port of call for all waste handling issues. Thank you for your phone call - we appreciate your interest. Some calls may be

156

recorded for the purposes of quality control and staff training. This call will be charged at the local rate, unless you're phoning from a mobile phone or certain call phones, in which case who knows? You will now be presented with a number of options. Please press the hash button on your handset.

Graham looks up at the clock, then presses the noughts and crosses symbol. He remembers when nobody knew what it was or what it was called, apart from the fact that Americans seemed to use it for their own arcane purposes. If you're still wondering it's this one: #

That's right!

They call it 'hash'!

Now you can make a phone call to a company with automated call answering!

That was worth the price of this book now, wasn't it?

Well done. Now let's try to help you route your call to the appropriate place so that we can handle your query most efficiently. If you wish to speak to a member of our Sales team, please press 1. For Frequently Asked Questions it's 2. If it's technical help you require, please press 3. If your call relates to skip hire, press 4. If you wish to enquire about confidential waste, it's 5. If you'd like to speak to a member of our Customer Service team please hold.

Graham is then treated to a few bars from a dimly remembered pop song by Blondie.

I'm in the phone booth, it's the one across the hall

Graham is impressed at the choice of song. The music is abruptly interrupted by the same soothing voice, which of course irritates him beyond measure.

Your call is now in a queue, and will be answered as soon as we possibly can. Thank you for your patience. Your call is valuable to us.

Don't leave me hang...

Then there's a click and another voice breaks in.

We are experiencing higher than usual call numbers. Due to the volume of traffic it may take some time for your call to be answered. Meanwhile if you would like to speak to a member of our Sales team, please press 1...

Graham hangs up. He knows the score. Every time he gets close to speaking to a real person he'll be put in a queue. Eventually he'll get a human voice which will tell him he's got through to the wrong department. They'll then attempt to transfer him, and he'll hear a dialling tone.

Of course this is one of the efficiency measures which Graham's ex-employer EDITsolutions has introduced. In fact it's what he was going to implement himself before he was resigned.

He thinks for a while, then dials his old direct dial number. There won't be anyone else at his desk, because, after all, the company is firing, not hiring. It rings for a few moments, then the call automatically transfers to reception.

"Hello, Emission Solutions, providing peace of mind for - oh sorry... Reception."

"Hi Dorothy."

"Waaaaah..."

The next bit takes a few minutes and there are a lot of aaaaaaas in it. I'd like to report that there's also the odd Boo and an occasional Hoo! but the noise is less articulate than that. At last communication is established, and Graham offers to meet her for a chat. He's not surprised when Dorothy says she doesn't want to speak in reception, but she offers to dodge out and meet him in a nearby cafe, just past the industrial units.

Half an hour later, Graham is shocked at how she looks. Her makeup is smudged and her eyes are brimming. She tells Graham she's working out her notice, but there's nothing to do anyway, and the men at the service bays have nothing either, and Mr Ron's confused. because the company seems to be saving money and the balance sheet looks good, but he can't quite understand how, because they're not actually doing any work.

Graham tries to reassure her that it's all for the best in the long run. Nobody's job would be safe if the company continued to run at less than peak efficiency.

Dorothy wails some more vowels at him. She sounds like a 'Speak your Message' version of one of Pate's texts.

Graham feels bad about this. He knows there's always a human dimension to his work, but he tries to reassure himself that nobody benefits from outdated work practices. Not when the Far East is so much more efficient.

Dorothy is still talking, and Graham nods sympathetically.

"So this Des or whatever he was called - one of your people anyway - he calls me into a meeting room and..."

Ah, so Des has taken over...

"He had this stupid moustache. I hated it. So he said take a seat..."

"Look if it's any consolation, in another universe you're still happily answering calls, while Des and his moustache have fallen under a bus."

Dorothy looks blank. Then continues. "At first he wouldn't say what it was all about, and asked me about my work..."

But is the Far East so much more efficient? The call centres are all in India, because they're cheaper and they speak English. And they've got degrees. But they're only cheaper because of the exchange rate - because everything's cheaper there. So they get the jobs which used to be British. And their technology and education is shit-hot, and their prices are competitive. So soon they get all the work.

"An automatic phone system! I mean, I was appalled! I know you told me it was coming, but I can't even begin to..."

And China does the manufacturing, and is starting to get in on the web and software design and higher level engineering. They don't speak English. But their internal market is so big they don't have to. And they offer Russia more for their natural gas than Europe. And Russia sends it East instead, because that's quite a laugh, and puts us in our place. And we're stuffed. And India and China become wealthier. And wages rise. And they do more of the brain work. Slowly they start to become less competitive on prices, But that's OK because the UK and Europe are basket cases by now.

We don't have any industry to compete at any level. And the US is stuffed because nobody can afford to drive to work.

So the Far East starts to outsource its manufacture to Africa.

"He said I'd been a loyal employee, so they were going to offer good terms, but it didn't sound very good to me, but what do I know, I'm only a fossil working for some crap business that doesn't..."

But then there's a problem. Because wages are so low in Africa that it's always going to be cheaper to do things there. And now they've been trained by the Indians and Chinese, and they have the technology, and they speak English and they start to do the call centres, and India and China can't compete because the standard of living is so much higher there, and they all want to be able to afford their holidays to the Eiffel Tower and Edinburgh Castle and the Washington Monument.

So Africa becomes the boom economy and they have natural resources and loads of people and they take over the world economy.

"...so I explained all this but he wasn't paying any attention. I can tell. And so then he said..."

But now the Africans want higher wages and holidays to the Great Wall and the Taj Mahal, so who the hell's going to do the work? Will the battle for the world's riches be won by the last most backward most miserable useless country with mass unemployment and a Monopoly currency?

So is Britain in with a shout again?

"Thanks for putting up with my ramblings. I feel so much better having someone to share things with. You're such a good listener."

At the far side of the cafe a sad hippy git looks away. He looks a bit like Graham would look if you fed him on tofu and wool. He has disgust written all over his face. But from where we are sitting we can only see the gust. And it's an ill wind for Graham.

"He's leaving the cafe now. It's definitely him! They've stopped outside. Now she's going left, left, left towards the industrial estate, and he's going - no wait - shit - he's got on a bus, it's a 13 - I'm not going to be able to catch him - I'll get her..."

And WPC Enid Sneep runs across the road, causing a couple of cars to brake abruptly, although because she's in uniform they try to stop with a wee skid as close to her as they can to make her jump.

Dorothy shrieks when WPC Enid leaps in front of her. Enid tries to calm her down. After all, this woman's an innocent member of the public and hasn't done anything wrong.

"You've been spotted consorting with a known villain and suspected paedophile who resisted arrest then escaped from Police custody, and I'm going to arrest you on charges of harbouring a criminal on the run and you'll get the same sentence as him for aiding and abetting plus extra for anything else you've done, so you'd better just cooperate or..."

Even WPC Sneep is taken aback by the sheer volume of vowels (following an initial W) which blast her hair backwards until she needs to grasp her cute little hat to prevent it from blowing off into the traffic.

Chapter 27

At work, Graham's investigations continue to bear fruit. He now understands far more of the complex business structure at Global Legend. As a Management Consultant he was well up to speed on all of the smoke and mirrors of consultancy. Not to mention the trapdoors, invisible threads, bendy saws and rubber chickens. The stacked decks and double-headed coins. The hidden bits of string. The misdirection.

But now he's starting to understand how business works in the real world. How a company mines a nugget of profitability, then cultivates contacts, inside knowledge, leverage and influence to ring-fence the work out of reach of the competition. How it will carry out this work with maximum profitability. How it will do the work with the least skilled, least expensive, most replaceable workforce it can get away with. Not consultancy. The real world.

He's also getting a handle on the single-minded ruthlessness which is needed to develop such a business - to bend the wills of hundreds, then thousands, of people to serving the ends of one.

He loathes Grim Dupeint's callous self-interest. He despises the vanity which made him opt for a French-sounding surname rather than the unremarkable one he was born with.

But he's also jealous of the way Grim has developed the skills necessary to succeed and prosper. They must be within him too. Surely there must be a way to develop them, without abandoning all principles in the process.

Graham wants to get inside Grim's head. And that's made slightly easier by the fact that he's cracked the security code system on the office doors. Now he can go wherever he wants in the building. He's even managed to do this without leaving a record of which code opened which door.

That leaves the bugging system.

It's late on a Friday night. Everybody's knocked off for the weekend. It's a hot summer evening and nobody wants to be stuck in the office. Grim is in the south of France, moored off Cap d'Antibes on the Blue Water Legend. Graham waits until the street quietens outside before he makes his move. He knows he is alone apart from the security guys at street level. He knows he won't be disturbed. He can hack into Grim's computer, but there are other things in the boss's office he'd like to see. Letters, contracts, handwritten notes. He can open the door to Grim's office, by hacking the keypad.

But there's still the small matter of the bugging system. There was a suggestion there might be cameras in the sprinkler units. Graham knows he has to conceal himself from these. He could try to put something over the units, but then there would be a recording of himself approaching the sprinklers before each was covered. He could get inside a binliner to conceal his identity, then stand on a chair, reach up and fasten a plastic bag over each with a rubber band. But then the organisation would know that there was a binliner maniac on the loose, which would limit his options thereafter.

164

Whatever he does must look like nothing untoward has happened.

Graham has a plan.

Graham's brilliant analytical brain has come up with a scheme so bold, so daring, so inspired that only a charismatic genius in a movie would attempt it. Or a halfwit in real life.

He is about to transform himself into a cleaning lady. But he can't just go into a toilet cubicle and change. That way a hidden security camera might spot a woman coming back out of the gents. Instead he has come in to work specially dressed in a quick change outfit of his own design. At the pull of a cord a long skirt will cascade down from around his waist to cover his trousers like a parachute bursting open. A CO_2 cartridge will inflate a lifejacket under his shirt, creating instant swelling breasts of mammoth proportions. (Did mammoths have breasts? I can't recall an elephant with boobs. For the purpose of this exercise let's assume that mammoths had great heaving mammaries. This would be where they got their name. Language was new and still developing. An ancient caveman would call out 'Would you look at the mamm, the mamma, the mammo, oh never mind, batter it anyway'.)

As a man Graham will carry a Tesco Extra plastic bag. But a quick flip turns it inside out, revealing a woman's Afro haircut topped with a baseball cap bearing the name and logo of the office cleaners.

That leaves the problem of where this woman should appear from. But Graham has this all worked out.

He sits at his desk, typing at his computer keypad, in the manner of a reluctant but dedicated employee engrossed in his work. Then he stands and stretches. He walks over to the stationery cupboard, and steps inside. However he doesn't switch on the light. In an instant he unfolds a large cardboard lifesize image of a cleaning lady, hooks it on to the Dyson in the cupboard, then backs out holding it.

"Sorry, I didn't see you there."

He engages the photo and vacuum cleaner in amiable conversation and makes his way back to his desk, leaving the two dimensional cleaning lady propped up on her 3D vacuum. Slowly he slides a small mirror from his pocket. Leaning forward to where a beam of evening sun crosses his desk, he tilts it to reflect a beam of dazzling light at the sprinkler. If there's a camera in there it will be completely dazzled. The automatic exposure will shut right down leaving the image of the office in deep shadow. Graham props the mirror in that position, then in an instant he lets loose his hidden skirts, pulls his plastic bag inside out and over his head, then pulls the cord on his lifejacket. He grabs the picture of the cleaning lady and flips it over, revealing a cunningly fashioned lifesize photo of himself at his desk. It only takes a moment to prop it on his chair, then he seizes the vacuum and picks up the mirror.

In a matter of seconds the scene in the office has returned to normal. Only this time, the cleaner is him, and the image of a man at his desk will continue to stare at his spreadsheets for as long as necessary.

Now it's time for Phase Two.

Graham picks up the nozzle of the vacuum cleaner and starts to busy about cleaning cobwebs from nooks and crannies. He cleans the ceiling tiles. But each time he approaches a sprinkler he surreptitiously sticks a small but powerful magnet on the nozzle of the vacuum cleaner, then reaches up and transfers it to the sprinkler.

"Henry. Come and have a look at this will you."

Grim Dupeint is sitting on the Blue Water Legend gazing at the screen of his laptop. He is watching the image of the outer office back in the UK. Henry comes across and looks over his shoulder.

Henry is in charge of the vessel. He's not the Captain. That's Rodger, the chap who sails it about. No, Henry is the one who really commands the operation. Henry is also in charge of top-level security. He's Grim's most trusted ally within the company, not known to the staff at headquarters, but familiar to those who cruise the international waters of Legend Global.

"What am I meant to be looking at?"

"There. When she reaches up."

They both watch as the cleaner vacuums about near the camera. As the nozzle approaches, the picture distorts, twisting and folding in swirls of static. The nozzle moves away and the picture flickers back to normal, but then it goes blank again.

"That's some sort of magnetic interference," says Henry. "The vacuum must have buggered the camera somehow."

Grim switches to another camera. From this angle the cleaner is further away, and there's someone sitting behind her at the back of the office.

In a couple of minutes Graham disables the other cameras. Grim and Henry on Global Legend are seeing blank screens no matter which camera is selected. Grim tells Henry to find out who the cleaner is and sack her. Unseen by them, Graham approaches the door of Grim's inner office. He taps in the code he has already programmed into the system. The door opens, leaving no trace of the fact. Graham walks over to the large desk and sits down.

So this is what it feels like!

A tropical freshwater carp looks apprehensively at him through the glass of its capacious tank.

Graham tries the desk, but the drawers are locked. How paranoid is that? Inside an office protected by a keypad security system?

Bugger.

Then Graham remembers who he's dealing with.

Where would I hide the keys if this were my office?

He rolls up his sleeve and plunges his hand into the fish tank. Lifting the little plastic sunken galleon he reveals the desk keys. He grasps them and lifts them out through the stream of bubbles supplied by a clever little pump. Now he has a wet arm, but not to worry - there's a private kitchen between the inner office and the private dining suite. He grabs a towel and dries his arm and the keys, then returns to Grim's inner office. The keys open the desk.

He lifts out a bundle of files, taking care to keep them in the order he found them. Then he settles down to a long night of study.

"Who was that working late? At the back of the room? Before the other camera went on the blink?"

"You haven't met him?"

168

"No."

"That's a new guy I've got checking IT and office security. Good bloke. David something. David Wilson."

"Where did he come from?"

"Certainly not from any of our internal people. His job is to give them the once-over."

But Grim is faintly uneasy as he fails to recall who exactly did recommend David Wilson.

"I wasn't aware of this," presses Henry, his nose out of joint.

"I have a good feeling about him. He's one of us."

'One of me' might have been more accurate, but we'll forgive Grim that understandable lapse. Henry grinds on relentlessly.

"It's not just the cleaner. I'll deal with her. But I'm concerned about the picture loss. Someone needs to look into that asap."

"Look, if David's there I'm sure there's nothing to worry about. Did he look bothered?"

"He looked asleep, more like."

"Don't be deceived. Not a lot gets past him..."

"Nevertheless... Let's give Joyce a call."

Graham's eyes are getting gritty with tiredness. He's found out all sorts of details of where Grim drinks, where he eats, where he stays in which city, where he tones his pecs. He's starting to build a more personal picture of the man.

His eyes are really bothering him. He removes the ice-blue lenses and puts them away in a contact lens case.

It's hot and airless in the office. The air conditioning must have switched off automatically when everyone went home. He's uncomfortable with a fully inflated lifejacket under his shirt. He takes the plug out of the inflation tube to deflate the jacket. He can always blow it up again later. There's a nozzle for topping it up, and a whistle for attracting attention. He shouldn't have inflated the lifejacket before leaving the aircraft.

Deflating it takes forever. He squeezes the jacket. It makes a loud farting sound. There's an awful lot of gas to get out of a tiny nozzle. He squeezes his chest to force it out. The gas bulges somewhere else. He fondles and squeezes. And keeps squeezing...

Joyce lets herself into the general office using the keypad. The lights are on, but the place is deserted, apart from a lifesized photo of David Wilson sitting at his desk. Bizarre. Then she hears a very long fart from the far end of the office. It goes on for an unfeasibly long time. She follows the noise. It seems to be coming from Mr Dupeint's office. The door is ajar. She steps closer. The noise gets louder...

Graham forces the last of the gas out with a final limp tharp.

"Christ, that's better."

170

Suddenly he sees something move just outside the door. He's conscious that he's wearing a woman's Afro wig and a fake cleaner's baseball cap. He drew the logo on with a felt tip pen. And invented a company name - Office Scrubbers. It might fool the cameras, but not close-up. Damn my waggish schoolboy sense of humour, he thinks. Shit! Fuck! he adds, in additional thoughts.

He pulls the wig and cap off his head and stuffs them in the bin, just as Joyce sticks her head around the door.

He thinks some more rude sweary words. Fuck! Shit! Bollocks! His mouth is open, but words come there none. All he can say is "...", as if he's run out of words, but without a preceding bunch of words to run out of.

Joyce speaks first.

"Hi."

"Hi."

"You got here first then."

"?"

"When you called."

"??"

"To be honest I wasn't even sure where you were calling from. It just showed up on my mobile as your mobile."

"???"

"Actually I thought you were in France."

"Ah."

Graham's brain is like chickpeas in a blender. But he's lost his sense of humous. Why the fuck would she think he was in France? And why does she look so nervous? And why does she keep sniffing? Graham decides to play for time. "Is there something wrong?"

"No, of course not." She looks around apprehensively. "The photo of David's a bit, well, strange."

"Ah. David."

Who the fuck's David? God, that's me. I forgot. So why didn't she say 'Your photo'?

"Are you alright?" she asks.

"Why?"

"Just, you look a little paler than usual."

"I'm fine."

There's an awkward pause.

"So will that be all, sir?"

Sir? SIR??? Good great God Almighty up above! Wht th fck? Srly nt?? Bldy hll!!!

Graham looks in the bin at the plastic bag and the Afro and the baseball cap. There, tangled up with them, is his blonde mullet. In his haste, he's jerked it off too. (It was a wig for wankers.) The ice-blue lenses are in his pocket. And Joyce thinks he's Grim! Buhluddy Hayll!! Hallelujah!

"I'm very pleased with you Joyce. Take a seat. You'll have gathered by now that this has been a security check. Not that I feel any need to check up on you, Joyce. Your loyalty is totally without question. But now we're taking things to the next level."

Joyce nods, speechless, her heart a-flutter.

Graham wonders if he could get her knickers off, right now, on the desk.

But that would be foolish.

Then again, when has sex ever been sensible?

But that would be really, really, foolish. Reluctantly, he sticks to getting himself out of this fan-scattered heap of poo.

172

"I want you to tell me things from your perspective - then we'll compare notes."

Joyce nods again. "I got your call at 7.49, just (glances at her watch) just twelve minutes ago. I was in a winebar not far from here. You said the security cameras had gone down. You thought it might be a problem caused by the vacuum cleaner. And you wanted me to check."

"I trust you, Joyce."

"Thank you sir. I was a little puzzled."

"Why?"

"Well I didn't know there were any security cameras in the office. And..."

"And?"

"...and I thought you were on the boat."

"Ah."

"So then I got here, and..." Joyce wonders whether to mention the noise.

"And?"

"Well. I heard... Coming from..."

Graham has the grace to blush. "Ah, that. I have to say your performance has been exemplary." Joyce's turn to blush. "So I'll let you into a secret. You'll be aware that in the course of my work, I might just - how shall we say this - I might just ruffle a few feathers. There are some out there who might not wish me well. So we have developed some new security devices." He starts to open his shirt. Joyce goes a deeper shade of rose. Graham points to the lifejacket. "This is a new bullet-proof vest. It operates on the same principle as an airbag in a car. The instant the outer membrane is punctured the bag inflates with a mixture of inert gases and something like candyfloss made of finely spun liquid Kevlar. This cushions the projectile and protects the wearer. It's light to wear, and practically invisible in everyday use."

"That's marvellous, sir."

"Call me Grim."

"Yes, Grim sir."

Graham leans closer.

"Dump the sir."

Joyce gazes into his eyes. "OK, er, Grim."

Graham tears himself away and sits back. "We're planning to produce a range of alternative undergarments. There would be no point in having a bulletproof vest and getting a slug in the nuts."

"No, Grim. Certainly not." Joyce imagines Grim's nuts, with and without a slug.

"There's still one problem we need to surmount."

"Yes, Grim. What's that sir?"

"The noise. That's what you heard when you came in. There'd be no point in evading a potential assassin if the whole world thought you had terminal gut rot afterwards. You might be physically intact, but your reputation..."

"Of course sir, Grim."

Graham looks down at the nozzle, which is now sticking out from under his shirt. Joyce looks curiously at it. Graham tries to explain. "There's a nozzle for topping it up."

Joyce looks longingly at his chest, then into his eyes. "And a whistle for attracting attention."

"Exactly. Now I must emphasise that all of this must remain absolutely hush-hush. The world must believe that I've been in France all along. I will return there by private jet as soon as we leave the office. If you refer to this I will deny it, so please say nothing. The walls have ears. Give it an hour. Then phone me on my mobile. Just say - 'It's all fine, sir. It was just the vacuum. It's sorted now.' "

Joyce nods, eagerly, thrilled to be trusted. "I've to call you sir again?"

"For the purposes of this phone call it's imperative. Lines may be tapped. Taps may be lined. Now try your lines."

"It's all fine, em, sir. It was just the, em..."

"The vacuum."

"It was just the vacuum. It's all sorted now."

But there's one thing still bothering her. "If I might ask... Grim."

"Ask away!"

"Why's there a photo of David over there?"

"Ah. Counter-measures. David's one of us. You must do everything he says without question. I'll explain later. When we're alone."

Joyce looks around apprehensively.

"No, of course we're alone now. I mean, when we're - alone."

Joyce almost slides off the seat.

Chapter 28

Monday morning, and Graham sits at his desk in the general office. He takes stock. Grim's still away, and there's nothing to show for last Friday's escapades. Apart from Joyce giving him a knowing look as she passes.

Time Bumface got some fresh leaves, thinks Graham.

Then - Where the hell IS Bumface?

Graham's stomach lurches with guilt and fear. Where did he last see the caterpillar? He remembers the incident with Kerri, and Bumface flying through the air. He definitely put him or her back in his or her box (the caterpillar literally, and Kerri metaphorically) and straightened it out a bit (the caterpillar literally, and Kerri metaphorically). Then he went off to the pub. He'd been so busy showing Kerri just how big and independent he was that he must have forgotten to pick up the matchbox.

Shit!

So he'll have to go back to find Bumface. On the plus side, the new job is a blast. Vastly more rewarding than EDITsolutions. Although...

It dawns on Graham that at least in his previous job he'd been paid. He's been so pleased with blagging his way into Legend Global that he's forgotten the small matter of a salary. Graham considers making up an invoice. He could submit it directly to Grim, who would pass it for payment, no problem. But that would involve putting lots of things down in writing, and given that he's not who he claims to be that might not be wise. It's not really the way that Legend Global operates either. Whatever he does he must be cautious. He mustn't do anything which would raise questions. He must show patience and prudence.

To buy time, he opens a new personal bank account called Glbl Hldng Ffshr #776 and transfers a million pounds from Global Laundry to himself.

That makes him feel perkier. He gets up and makes himself a cup of coffee.

Then he gets his head down and starts checking the notes he made in Grim's office.

He's still feeling buoyed by his new pay rise as he makes his way home on the bus. He's also encouraged by Joyce's response last Friday. After all, whatever magnetism Grim has, he must have too. So is it physical, or to do with money? Or power? Or confidence? Perhaps these all go hand in hand. Whatever it is, he's going to study Grim until he has it sorted, then he'll bail out and leave him in peace.

But that would mean abandoning the philanthropy. It would be a pity just to walk away and miss a golden opportunity to secure his place in heaven. Graham looks out the window of the bus, at the people fretting down the street, or tensed behind the wheels of their cars. What would they give to have Graham's power? He feels a warm glow, as if his heart has done a wee in a wetsuit.

Graham would be feeling a lot less confident if he knew there was an unmarked police car following the

177

bus. In the back of the police car is someone he would recognise.

"That's him!" spits WPC Enid Sneep to the driver, DC Current. Current joined the force because he wanted to transform society. His manner is direct. He gets a buzz from pressing charges. He has many contacts - some positive, some negative. But whatever the signs, he'll run the truth to earth. His first instinct is to stop the bus - until he remembers they don't have conductors any more. He wipes his shoulder and turns to his buddy in the front passenger seat. "That's him," he repeats to PC Brigade.

"Which one?"

"Dark hair, smug expression, left hand side by the window."

WPC Sneep snarls again from the back. "Right, we know where he's going. Overtake the bus and we'll park round the block from the house. We've got him this time."

DC Current sighs. He wanted to follow the bus round the circuit until it stopped at the terminal.

Sneep has given Dorothy the third degree. Needless to say, Dorothy told the police everything she could, about her work at Emission Solutions, and her impending redundancy. She explained the management consultants at EDITsolutions, and their man Graham. Which was all they needed. They phoned EDITsolutions and were told that he'd been, er he'd resigned. In a panic Dorothy phoned the company too, and was told the same.

His number and address are ex-directory (he does sack people for a living after all), but this doesn't stop the forces of Laura Norder.

The police note the address and start watching the house.

After they've gone Dorothy returns to work. Belatedly she remembers that Graham's contact details are on a sticky attached to her PC. She calls Graham's house.

"Oh Graham, thank God you're there! The police stopped me after you left and said they were going to arrest you for being a paedophile and resisting arrest and escaping from custody and they were going to charge me too, so I had to give them your name and where you worked, I couldn't really not do - I didn't want to but I was stuck, so I hope that's alright and I'm really really sorry."

"No, that's fine."

"And the woman was really horrible, she had short hair and red lipstick, which seemed a bit much for a policewoman. Are you sure you're not mad at me?"

"Not at all."

"How can you stay so calm?"

"Easy, really."

"How?"

"I'm not Graham."

In Graham's kitchen, Kerri looks up from the papers she's sorting through. "Who was that?"

"Someone for Graham."

"Who?"

"Some woman. Didn't give her name."

"Oh really? What did she want?"

"Just a message."

"Come on Quentin - this is like pulling teeth."

So Quentin tells her.

Kerri is shocked, then says it confirms all her worst fears, then says she must tell the lawyer, then starts to consider what wonderful news this is - all things considered. Quentin has chummed her to the house for moral support. Kerri is concerned that Graham might smash another part of the house with his head then start behaving oddly again. She also wishes she hadn't opened the matchbox and thrown that bloody caterpillar out into the garden. She suspects that Graham might go ballistic when he discovers. She binned the holy matchbox, stuffing it under a pizza box and a few teabags to avoid making it too obvious. And now she's worried that it might have been special, somehow.

Graham jumps briskly off the bus. He's anxious to get home and feed Bumface. He realises with a pang of concern that he doesn't even know whether the beast is dead or alive.

Twang.

Whoosh.

Pyoing.

In another universe, he rips off his clothes and runs off up the street before being rugby tackled by Enid Sneep in a herbaceous feature in the middle of a grassy roundabout and is consigned to solitary confinement and daily chastisement until he is too old to remember his own name. Which is a good reason to stay with this universe, because, being blunt, that would never find a publisher. Not now that misery memoirs are so passé.

Graham strides off up the road. DC Current, PC Brigade and WPC Enid Sneep observe Graham through the spokes of the steering wheel. That's how low they are.

"There he is. He's going in the gate."

Graham walks up the drive past the 4 x 4 he can't afford to run.

"He's stopped. Can you see him?"

"No, he's behind the car."

Graham takes out his key, then pauses. Through the glass door he sees movement.

"What's he doing?"

Graham bends down and very gently opens the letterbox. He can't see anything from that angle, but he hears voices.

"You know what this means Quent?" says a woman's voice.

"He must be on the run."

"And we're in clover."

"Y'know what Kerr?"

"What Quent?"

"S'made me feel all horny."

"Oh God, me too! Fuck me, fuck me!"

"Fuck me," says Graham.

Strange how the same words can have such different meanings.

Graham unlocks the door. Time this nonsense was nipped in the bud!

"He's opened the door!" hisses WPC Enid.

"He must be going in!" deduces PC Brigade, drawing on years of training.

Graham looks into the kitchen. They've disappeared upstairs. How sadly conventional. He decides he'll catch them in the act. His mobile has a camera. Let her lawyers chew on that one! Then he remembers the squeaky staircase.

"Go go go! Before he shuts the door!"

"No - let him shut it!" PC Brigade has a warrant, and he's never had a chance to break a door down before.

As the front door closes the three police crouch down low and run forwards with their knees bent, keeping their heads below privet height. Like Max Wall. Or a cross between Groucho Marx and Mr Natural, depending on whether you're 1940s or 1960s. If your frame of reference is more recent, try John Cleese and the Ministry of Silly Walks. What d'you mean that's ancient? When were you born? Does nobody study the classics? The chick from Planet Terror with her machine gun unscrewed? Ah. Now we're talking. So they run crouchily across the road to Graham's gate.

But Graham is no longer in the house. While the Force was crossing the road, Graham shut the front door quietly again, then tiptoed round the corner to the wall beneath the bedroom window. He clambers on to a dustbin, and uses this to transfer himself to a willowy looking birch tree. It might be a willow tree, but in that case it is a fairly birchy one. He reaches up for a higher branch, then lifts his left foot up on to the bracket holding the drainpipe. Now he's within a couple of branches of the first floor window sill.

WPC Sneep holds her finger to her lips as they sprint up the path to the front door. She doesn't want a sound to give them away until they're all poised for the grand entrance.

Graham inches higher. The branches are slimmer here, and he has to let go with one hand to get out his phone.

Quentin pounds at Kerri, who's arching her back and clutching the headboard. The bed thumps against the wall. The picture above the bed starts to swing. The curtains shake rhythmically.

"How hot am I?" shouts Quentin.

An alarm clock rattles its way off the bedside table.

"I'm on fire!"

Outside the window a tree shakes violently.

"Burn baby burn!"

There's a crash of exploding wood, smashing glass and collapsing masonry.

"Ah! Ah! Ah! Ah!"

Quentin is roasting. Kerri's fairly impressed. Graham's distracted because as he pulled a branch aside to look in the bedroom window he revealed a large green caterpillar with a stupid face on its bum, sitting on a twig.

"Yes! Yes! Yes!"

"Go! Go! Go!"

"Fuck! Fuck! Fuck!" Graham's lunge for the caterpillar puts all his weight on a slender branch which snaps and tears, sending him crashing to the ground in a Godalmighty crescendo of smashing branches which would sound quite remarkable if it didn't coincide with PC Brigade kicking down the bedroom door (just because he could) and Quentin having the best orgasm he has ever had (or ever will have) as a flushed policewoman rushes into the room at the perfect moment and crowns his climax by manacling him to the bed with a pair of handcuffs and cuffing his other wrist to herself.

"Fuck me," says DC Current, adding yet another nuance to a useful and well-loved phrase.

Chapter 29

Graham thinks it might be an idea to stay away from the house for a while. He's not sure why the police came battering into his bedroom, but it didn't bode well. That woman who charged in as he fell off his perch looked like the torn-faced cow who grabbed him in the bushes outside Emission Solutions. Not the sort of person you want charging you, in any sense of the word. And what the hell did Kerri think she was doing with that chancer Quentin? Graham is hurt and angry.

So he checks in to a hotel. It's not exactly lavish, but it's fancier than anything he's ever experienced before. After all, his paycheck this week was a little bit more generous than he's been used to.

A million pounds. And no PAYE. Or National Insurance stamp.

At the hotel there's a leisure centre.

He thrashes up and down the pool.

He lifts the weights, on hinges.

He runs on a silly little conveyor belt thing.

He even has a shot on a sunbed. Although he knows it will fry his skin and kill him. But he's rich enough not to worry about things like that.

He develops a taste for the me-centric life.

He goes to a dentist and gets his teeth capped. They're whiter, and straighter.

He gets some new clothes. At last, now that he's got a fine physique, the off-the-peg suits all fit him. So he buys made-to-measure, just because he can.

From time to time at work, Grim asks him into the inner sanctum. At first, it's to check arcane details relating to the IT system and office security. Then Grim confides that he's concerned that someone may be syphoning off sums of cash from the company coffers. He asks Graham (or David as he calls him) to get to the bottom of it. Graham assures him that he can take care of this.

Sometimes Graham thinks that Grim just wants to hang out with someone who understands him. Unfortunately Graham understands him only too well.

One morning Grim mentions that he's off to Buenos Aires for a few days. He tells Graham he wants to see some results when he returns. Graham assures him this won't be a problem. He says he's on the case, and already has an inkling that he knows what's going on.

"And..." prompts Grim.

"In good time," blocks Graham.

Grim stares at him with those penetrating, unblinking eyes of his. Nobody, but nobody, has the nerve to tell Grim that they know something he doesn't, and they won't tell him till they're good and ready.

"Tell me what you know."

"Not till I know for sure."

Grim's eyes widen. Graham decides he'd better explain, before Grim's eyebrows blow off into space like hairy booster rockets. "I'm on to something that could be very damaging. For a certain individual. A permanent solution may be called for. But I wouldn't want to point the finger until I have concrete proof."

Grim smiles Grimly.

"I'll be back on Tuesday," he says. "Kindly mix your concrete by then."

Snotty tosser, thinks Graham. Check out the power trip. And when I said 'permanent solution' he just nodded.

Graham can't believe that all of this behaviour, these domineering, ruthless character traits, are somehow hidden within himself. Logic tells him it has to be so. This is himself he's looking at, with only a few years of different experience to mould the separate versions. Yet this granite-nosed individual feels like a stranger. *Surely that's not me...*

On the other hand Graham is still amused that Joyce was so totally taken in, despite the many differences, like the teeth. Which were pretty wonky at that point, before he had them straightened.

He decides to put things to the test. With Grim heading off round the world, what better time to have a bit of fun.

He knows from the bills on the computer system that one of Grim's regular haunts is Au Quat' Cradoques, an eyewateringly expensive restaurant in town. Graham doesn't book. Nobody gets in without a reservation, and there's a three month waiting list. But he's trying to think like Grim.

He puts on a good suit (all his suits are good ones now) but doesn't bother with a tie.

186

His hair is its natural colour and he has no contact lenses. With his new buff frame, buff in muscle tone and buff in colour, he cuts quite a dash.

The cab drops him off at the door, and he walks up the steps past the potted bay trees. A bloke in a green tail coat and top hat opens the door wide for him. Graham strides past without acknowledging him. The restaurant is so posh that the flunkey keeps smiling a genuine beam at him, even as he passes. There's no outstretched hand, no V-signs afterwards towards his back when he doesn't give a tip. No, this guy knows enough to play the long game and wait for his reward.

Graham strides into the restaurant, where he's greeted by a smiling maitre de whose eyes say Oh fuck.

"Your usual table, sir, or would you prefer a private room?" smarms the man, grovelling non-obsequieously. (Rich gits prefer their grovelling to be subtle. Grovelling by John Cleese Fawlty Towers clones doesn't dissect the Dijon. They prefer to be discreetly grovelled to by really important people, who own businesses and restaurants and countries.)

"Whatever." says Graham. "The usual I suppose."

"Of course sir. Before you take your seat, I have a particularly fine Premier Grand Cru Dom Perignon which we acquired at auction. Perhaps you'd like a glass with an amuse bouche?"

"That would be splendid," says Graham. He fancies a lean at the bar while he watches which poor sucker gets booted off his table. It turns out to be a florid businessman accompanied by a young blonde girl with wide Slavic cheekbones. Graham overhears the spiel - "Sir, I'm delighted to be able to tell you that, as one of our most valued customers, you've been chosen for a special treat. The manager has suggested you might like to take your next course in our private salon. This room is normally reserved for visiting Heads of State, but for you, sir..."

And Mr Florid (which coincidentally is his name - Anthony Florid, christened Florid, A. by his geography teacher and universally despised by his peers) smiles with porcine delight. He reckons Tanya ought to be well impressed. It doesn't dawn on him that since he's paying her by the night it doesn't matter a bugger whether she's impressed or not.

Graham smirks, and swallows a mouthful of calves' thyroid glands dressed with tiny black salty blobs. Then washes it down with a swill of fizzy.

In moments, the table is ready, and Graham orders.

"Are the lark's tongues fresh?"

"They were trilling this morning, sir, at the beauty of the sunrise over an Aegean hillside."

"What about the salmon?

"The salmon made its final leap early this afternoon up a waterfall at the Falls of Blegh and into an oak vat of simmering 20 year old Glenbunion.

"The scallops?"

"They were hand-picked in the Sound of Muiseachd by a specially trained lady diver breathing only the purest of air compressed at the top of Ben Nevis. She shelled them on the seabed and transferred them through an airlock into a hot consommé of honey from bees exclusively reared on the Royal Banks of Scotland and gin made from the juniper bush planted by the late Queen Mother in the Royal Window Box outside her bedroom at Balmoral. They were then raised on a stainless steel cable from the seabed directly to the helicopter flown by another member of the Royal Family on an essential training flight which just happened to vector directly from the Kyles of Beaut to the verdant green you see outside this very window. It left only minutes ago. So sorry you missed it. It was an inspiring sight."

"Have you got any tomato soup?."

"Of course sir - an excellent choice if I may say. Sun-blushed explosions of tangy fruitfulness, married in a fusion of..." The man's voice trails off when he clocks Graham's expression.

Graham finds the experience great fun for a few minutes, and then feels like throwing up. Do rich powerful people really despise all of the drones who serve them? Or do they just not notice? Maybe they think it's normal. Like what they say about the Queen thinking that the world smells of paint, because she never gets near a place unless it's been tarted up first.

Well they can keep it, he thinks. Because it's tedious.

"Is sir dining alone this evening?"

"What does it look like?"

"Sorry sir, I can see... No I wondered if you would like us to arrange for some company? A companion perhaps?" Then seeing Graham's face - "No of course not. Sir chooses to dine solo. Quite right. Time to think, and relax."

The look Graham aims at the man is anything but relaxing.

"Quite so, sir..."

The night drags on, as Graham chomps his way through seven courses. He wonders how he will pay, but assumes it will be charged somehow. In the event the subject never even arises. He stuffs a few tenners tip in the maitre de's hand as he stands up. The staff assume there will be a car waiting for him outside, and he doesn't feel the need to disabuse them. He strides out, past the beaming doorman, walks round the corner and hails a cab.

Chapter 30

Graham decides he'd better take Bumface into work. He's shaken by how close he came to losing him (her?) and he's also seen the cleaning lady in his hotel looking at the new shoebox with evil intent. He'd hate there to be a misunderstanding. He sets the box on his desk. He thought about a jam jar with holes in the lid, but reckons that there might be an issue if the sun caught it. It's one thing to lose a caterpillar, but to chargrill a caterpillar that might hold your fate in its hands... Dozens of little green hands, dozens of potential outcomes.

Grim's back from South America. He catches up with Graham just as Ernie Waterman staggers past under the weight of an empty water container. Grim and Graham's eyes follow the man. Their eyebrows rise in unison.

"Find out what the hell he's up to," says Grim as Ern lurches off up a corridor, fighting the combined effects of lack of gravity on the bottle and the lack of a degree from RADA.

Graham nods.

"Right. Story time," says Grim, and heads off towards his office.

Graham takes that to mean that he should follow.

Susan Hornygolloch is sitting in the outer room in the suite.

"Go and feed the fishes," says Grim.

"So to speak," says Graham.

"In a non-Mafioso sort of way," says Grim, immediately reading Graham's implication.

Susan smiles coquettishly at Grim, and ignores Graham, apart from the minimal eye contact required to imply to Grim 'I respect your visitors, but don't want to shag them'.

Susan digs in Grim's drawers for some fish food.

Graham looks on in astonishment as Susan pulls a handful of dried flies out of Grim's underpants.

No, I made that up.

It was his desk drawers.

She opens a small tub beside the fish tank and scatters some flakes on the surface. The fish go bonkers.

"OK Susan. Give us half an hour."

Susan smiles and walks round the desk to where she has been sorting some papers into neat piles on the floor. Graham assumes that filing is part of her duties. She bends her knees and slinks down, moving in an agile and supple fashion as she picks up the stacks of paper in an order which makes sense to her. To Graham it seems to involve flashing taut lengths of thigh in Grim's direction from under the skirt, which rides up as she moves.

"Later Susan." Grim's voice sounds oddly strained.

Susan flashes a pout at Grim and leaves the two men to it. Grim fast-forwards past the scene where the plumber with the big moustache arrives, and cuts to the bonking. Metaphorically.

"I've had a complaint about you."

Oh oh, thinks Graham. One guess who that is. Gordy's feeling defensive. "Only one?"

"First though – I want to know whose paw's in the till."

Paws for thought.

Turn defence into attack. Gordy knows the company's dirty secrets. His job is to keep them secret, behind firewalls and IT countermeasures. He has blood on his hands. Graham knows he has to throw the dog a bone.

"It was obvious, really."

"So?"

"It had to be somebody who had access to the passwords, and the procedures."

"And?"

Graham looks up at the sprinklers. Then he doodles on a scrap of paper. He turns it face down and slides it across the desk to Grim.

Grim turns up one corner.

'Go' it says.

Grim's eyes meet Graham's.

Grim looks down again and turns the paper up further.

'Gordy' it says.

"Ahhh," says Grim. "That would explain the complaint."

"No – surely not…" says Graham in a limp attempt to feign innocence. "I guess you'll have to speak to him, then?"

"Not Gordy," says Grim. "I'll speak to Tone,"

"Who's Tone?"

"You don't want to know."

But Graham suspects.

"Is that belligerent Tone?"

"I prefer to think of him as caustic Tone."

"What will..."

"You don't want to know that either."

Graham's little brain whizzes round, like the Walnut Whirl in its chocolate coating. Do they do those anymore? OK, we'll stick with the traditional comparison of a frog in a blender. Whatever Gordy deserves it doesn't amount to the kind of punishment that Tone would deliver. Tone isn't HR. Not unless that's Hellish Retribution.

Graham tries to steer Grim away from this option. "This could present a minor prob, er challenge."

"Oh yeah?" ask Grim's eyebrows. His mouth stays silent, but his eyebrows have learned to carry out their own interrogations. They strip Graham naked, pile him on a heap of other Grahams, attach electric cables to his sticky-out bits and force him to simulate sex with a very dense woman. Graham wilts under the psychological pressure. But he can't just throw Gordy to the wolf.

"Gordy may be expecting us to do just that... He's not stupid. He may be dumb, but so are weasels. He may be green, but he's not cabbage-looking. He's not the last ant at the picnic. He may be..."

"What the fuck are you drivelling on about?"

"He may be... Sorry. I may be on the sunny side of the lolly here. He may be…"

Grim picks up a chair and lifts it above his head to threaten Graham into shutting up. It's an office swivel chair, and the base swings round and smacks Graham on the forehead. Grim didn't intend that, but pretends that he did. Graham is stunned.

"Tell me in a few short words why I shouldn't throw him to Tone."

Graham gasps several times for breath, then gathers his thoughts, which are buzzing and sparking like a broken neon sign in a bar fight. "It's like this," he gulps. "He may be, well, you know... At it. But he must have covered his tracks. And his back. Laid a few booby traps. Clad his arse. Left a few tripwires among the spreadsheets."

Grim still looks blank. Graham ploughs on. If you're American he plows on. (And sorry about the interrogation stuff. The photos were probably faked by someone who believes in evolution.) "Thing is," he says. "he may have set things up so that if anything happens to him, some cash transfers will be triggered, or information will become public, or dung will otherwise hit the rotary air conditioning."

"What do you suggest?"

"I can follow the slime. The snail leaves a trail."

"And then?"

"It's the slug pub."

"You what?"

"Like when gardeners leave out a glass of beer, buried in the ground. And the slugs love the smell, and they climb over the edge and fall in, and drown."

"A slug pub. So they go, but they don't make a fuss."

"A slug pub."

"Doesn't sound permanent enough."

"Believe me – it's terminal."

"And you can arrange this?"

"I'll make it my personal mission."
"OK bartender. The highballs are on me."
And Graham doesn't doubt it for a minute.

Chapter 31
(Version 1)

This chapter is an unnecessary waste of time, unless you're interested in the author disappearing up his own plughole, like water in an Australian bidet. An alternative version is provided afterwards. I'd skip this one if I were you. Really.

Bar Magnet is predominantly decorated in rolled aluminium and stainless steel, with a blue glow from concealed lights filling the gaps. In uneasy contrast to this science-fiction lighting scheme the seats and cocktail menu hark back to the 1950's, in a self-referential, post-modernist way. Less Officer Ripley, more Dan Dare.

This theme is explored in many ingenious ways.

The glasses have metal bases. You can't lift your drink off the bar until you've paid for it, when the till deactivates the electromagnet concealed beneath.

The waiters wear magnetic boots and walk from table to table upside down on the ceiling. This makes clearing used glasses off the tables easier when the bar's crowded. Although it takes more concentration to take a round of drink over to the customers.

Customers sit on bar stools around rectangular tables on circular plinths. Each table has a north and south pole and is attracted to or repelled by its neighbours.

Much like the customers.

From time to time a table will randomly flip polarity, which causes a chain reaction as tables swing unpredictably.

Much like the customers.

Drinks are sloshed about in the rapid realignment, but it's a great way of encouraging people to mingle as they find themselves all of a sudden sitting next to strangers.

"How long have you been studying synchronised swimmers?" asks Graham, in response to an observation made just before this chapter started. Tonight he's ditched the wig and contacts, and is plain old Grey Paint once more.

"I can recognise the stars by the soles of their feet."

"That's not very funny Pate."

"Humour is entirely subjective. It exists in a neurological excess baggage compartment, reflecting social mores, constructs of anticipation and expectation, and volte faces of confabulation."

"Are you sure you mean confabulation?"

"No, I think I mean stupefaction."

"Why didn't you say that?"

"You didn't give me time to look it up."

"It still sounds like you rehearsed that sentence."

"Of course I did. Can you imagine anyone being this good without practice? Paganini? Rafa Nadal?"

"Zane Stumpo?"

"Who's Zane Stumpo?"

"The guy writing this book."

"So he's just naturally talented?"

"Haven't a clue. He's never done it before. He wrote a thriller about the Scottish Parliament, but everyone thought it was bollocks."

"Did it sell?"

"Never got published."

"So who's publishing this then?"

Graham shrugs.

"You mean we might be doing all this talking and thinking up brilliant lines, and doing funny stuff and nobody might read it?"

"You can never rely on anything. Did you think he'd get an advance and guaranteed publication?"

"Well not exactly..."

"And a movie deal? And serialisation rights? And an even bigger advance on the trilogy? Or the franchise? Just how funny do you think you are Pate?"

Pate's bottom lip turns upside down, like a slug in a slug pub.

"You think all you have to do is invent a few bon mots..."

Pate's face turns down, all over.

"... and pull a few stupid faces, and people will queue up to read this. From Waterstones, Piccadilly Circus to the Main Street Trading Company, St Boswells? You think writing's easy? You think he just has to note down all the brilliant things you do?"

"This isn't easy either. The wit. The funny faces. It gives me a pain in the cheek muscles."

"So stop doing it, and see what happens."

"OK."

"So now there's no point in even trying?"

"Not if people aren't going to read it."

"Right then."

They sit in silence.

For a long time.

God, it's dull.

"God this is dull."

Says Pate.

"Dull it is," says Graham.

"God I'm bored," says Pate

"God, so am I," says Graham.

There's another long silence. Pate cracks first.

"Of course..."

"What?"

"Nothing."

Silence for ages.

"You were going to say something."

"Was I?"

"You said 'Of course dot dot dot.'"

"That was 'Of course ellipsis.'"

"Seriously?"

"Seriously what?"

"Is that what ellipsis means?"

"Absolutely. That's what three dots is. Mark(s) indicating ellipsis (print). And ellipsis is 'A figure of syntax by which a word or words are left out and implied (gram) - Chambers. Which is why I said, quote 'Of course ellipsis.' end quote. "

"Why did you just say 'Quote 'Of course ellipsis.' end quote.'? "

"Why did you just repeat 'Why did you just say 'Quote 'Of course ellipsis.' end quote.'?'? "

"I asked first."

"Because I couldn't say an apostrophe followed by another apostrophe. I had to say 'Quote'. If I try to say apostrophe followed by another apostrophe it goes like '.'"

"But that makes no sense. That's two quotes with nothing of substance between them."

"Like literary criticism."

"ʕzzzzzzw !"

"Ah."

"Yup."

"M-hmm."

"Yes siree."

"Durn tootin."

"Hardy har."

I should never have written that bit about not getting published.

"Who said that?" asks Graham.

And thanks to that cheap shot at literary criticism, I never will.

Get published, that is.

"Tough," says Graham.

You're not meant to talk to me.

"Says who?" says Pate.

I'm the narrator. You shouldn't be able to hear me.

"The way you go on?" says Graham.

"And on and on," says Pate.

"We can hardly carry on a conversation without you breaking in with your own smart arse comments," says Graham

I'm watching you, Graham.

"Oh really?"

Of course. I'm writing from a point of view of omniscience. I can hear every word you say, right down to the faintest whisper. And I can see everything you do. Even in the dark.

"That's pervy."

You have no idea just how much restraint I exercise. I could make you do things just for my titillation.

"Such as?"

At that moment, a totally hot girl across the other side of the bar (I think I mentioned they were in a bar - the one with magnets, remember?) anyway, she walks across to where Pate and Graham are sitting, ignores Pate, and leans down to whisper in Graham's ear. She whispers very very quietly because what she has to say might be embarrassing. She barely utters a sound. But what she whispers is "My mates have put me up to a bet, and they said I couldn't get a shag in ten minutes starting from now. And I didn't fancy your mate, so you're it."

As she takes his hand and pulls him to his feet Graham realises that she is incredibly well stacked in an excessive but natural way, with a face that oozes sensuality mixed with refinement, and a body that screams rampant lust combined with toned fitness and timeless elegance.

She drags him out the side door of the pub and in the dark alley she thrusts Graham's hand up under her skirt, where her thong would be if she had one. Moaning with anticipation, she tears his trousers open and grasps his vibrating -

"OK OK. You've proved your point."

How can you stop to talk? Surely by now you're in the fierce embrace of a passion which has no hand brake? Although I can see that her clutch is engaged...

"This daft cow's just ripped my trousers and grabbed my mobile."

That's because you interrupted before I'd finished the sentence.

"Can I go back in the pub then?"

Graham is instantly back in the pub. In fact he never left it. He focusses once more on Pate's face. For a moment he has been daydreaming about that fit chick across the bar.

"That's it then? It never happened?"

No. And I never got a chance to do the 'Crying Game' gag.

"She's not a bloke, is she? Never!"

Remember that I am an omniscient third party narrator. And you are my plaything. So why don't you and Pate start being a bit more helpful and stop whining on about not getting published?

"If you're so bloody omniscient and detached and third party, then why do you keep speaking like me?"

Do I?

"Bloody right you do."

When?

"Half way down page four. You said 'So that's what birds think snakes look like.' You pretended that was you rambling on, but it's obvious that was me thinking. So you just pinched it. And all that stuff about arithmetic means and bell curves when I was waiting for the bus. That's the sort of thing I would say. I've studied Operations Research. You're just a writer. You know bugger all about it. You were just writing as if you were me. So make up your mind. Are you an omniscient narrator, or what? Or are you copying me cos you want to be in a book? Instead of just writing one? Is that what it is? You scratch away or poke at a keyboard or however you're doing it somewhere warm and comfy with a cup of coffee while I rush around getting stressed and sweaty and risking my life and pushing back the frontiers of human experience? That's bollocks."

I really shouldn't tell you this.

"What?"

If you're too aware of the process it might undermine your spontaneity.

"I'm a big boy. I can take it."

If I explain, will you stop eavesdropping on what I'm writing?

"Maybe."

Need a promise.

"Oh all right."

Cross my heart and hope to die?

"Get on with it."

Well, it's what's called 'free indirect speech'. Flaubert's the boy. Kafka did it too. But you find it in Jane Austen, even Chaucer. The character's thoughts wander into the storytelling. And let's face it, you couldn't have the characters speaking like Trainspotting and the third-person narration sounding like Henry James. So I'm stuck with having to sound a bit like you. So now are you happy?

"Hmmm."

Well bloody get on with it then.

"Oh all right," says Graham. Then he grabs two lit candles from the table, sticks one in each ear and back flips repeatedly across the bar to the fit chick, who's totally impressed. As they head out through the door the fit chick shouts out in a voice husky with passion "Get your hairy mate to talk to my pal. She thinks he's cute."

And there follows such a scene of unbridled lasciviousness out in the alley that even the local cats leap into sheltering dustbins, their bulging eyes covered by their little furry paws.

She is female all right. All female.

She rips off her clothes.

Then she rips off her soft downy skin, revealing a scaly reptilian form, dark enough to merge with the alley's deep shadows, but outlined by the sodium glare reflecting off the slime which drips from each venom-tipped spine on her carapace.

Now will you get back to work?

Chapter 31
(Version 2)

This is an alternative version, for readers with more sense.

Graham meets Pate for a drink. They ramble on a bit.

Chapter 32

The next day Graham is full of fresh resolve, enthusiasm and determination. He had been planning to ask Pate's advice about the Gordy problem, but then he remembered that Pate was an idiot, albeit a very intelligent one. So now Graham has devised his own plan.

He waits until Grim is watching and strolls up to Gordy.

"Gordy."

"Hi," he replies, warily.

"Gordy, I was wondering if you fancied a pint after work. There's something I need to have a chat with you about."

"Can't we speak here?"

Graham makes some random grimaces, which say clearly "I can't even reply to that while we're being watched and possibly listened to."

"I really don't know if I can be bothered."

Graham's features pick sides, then engage in an impromptu game of touch rugby.

"What's up with your face?"

Graham is exasperated. His eyes roll upwards into his skull to make this very clear. He leans towards Gordy until he transfixes him with his blank white slightly bloodshot orbs. Then as Gordy is about to whimper, Graham flips his eyes back down and stares at him. This violent manoeuvre dislodges one of his ice-blue contact lenses, which slides to the bottom edge of his eyeball. It now looks as if one of his eyes has come loose, and not only points the wrong way, but has two differently coloured corneas.

Gordy yelps. Graham speaks very quietly, and very clearly.

"I will say this once, and you will do what I say. Tonight at 5.30 you will come for a drink with me. You will have a cheerful smile on your face. And within a short space of time, all will become plain."

Gordy gazes at him as Graham walks off to the Gents to sort his contact lens. Gordy is horrified. Grim observes from a distance, and nods ever so slightly to himself.

That evening, Gordy and Graham leave the building together. Gordy expects to go to the Shoulder Arms, but Graham says it's a dump. Instead they walk further, to a seedy, deserted place where they can talk unobserved. Graham buys a round. It's the least he can do. They take a seat at a greasy ring-stained table as far from the bar as they can get. I wish people wouldn't park their rings on the table, thinks Graham. He embarks on his prepared speech.

"There's no easy way of saying this. Grim wants rid of you."

Gordy's mouth opens with shock. Graham continues without a pause.

"Problem is, you know too much. And it's a sensitive business, in a rough old world."

Gordy has started to tremble. He suspects he knows what's coming. But he hasn't grasped a fraction of it.

208

"Why should I believe you?"

"I've been tasked with disposing of the body."

Gordy's drink starts to slip through his fingers. He lets it drop an inch or so on to the table, splashing foam over his fingers.

"But, wha... Oh God..."

"I'm giving you a way out. I wouldn't be telling you all this otherwise, would I?"

Gordy is ashen. He tries to take a swig of his beer, but his hands are shaking too much. He gives up and puts it down again. Graham continues.

"This is what's going to happen. You will take a walk up to the bridge. In this bag I have a hoodie and a pair of trainers. You will put these on, and leave your jacket, shoes and briefcase with me. You will then walk slowly away, keeping the hood up, and talking to no-one."

"But I've got stuff I need in the briefcase."

"We will go through it together. I'll decide what stays."

"Then what?"

"You are bright and resourceful. You will leave the country, discreetly, and immediately. You will never make yourself known here again."

"What about my mum? I help her out."

"She can join you later. If it all goes well, and she is as discreet as you are, there will be regular sums deposited in a bank account which you will be notified of."

"What if I say no?"

"I should have mentioned that in this bag there is also half a million quid. But that's just a sweetener. The real incentive is that if you say no, I will have to carry out our mutual friend's wishes. And if you mention this to him or anybody else, you won't just have me to deal with. And some of the guys wouldn't just get rid of you. They'd make sure it took a long, long time."

"Where's Gordy? Not like him to be late."

9.15 the following morning, and Gordy hasn't turned up for work. "Don't know," says Graham to Joyce. He turns to the office, and raises his voice. "Anyone know where Gordy is?"

Blank looks.

Apart from Grim, over in his private office. A smile drops its coat, streaks across his face wearing only a pair of gymshoes, and disappears behind his far ear. The staff say Grim hears everything. He must have an extra ear, like Davy Crockett. A left ear, a right ear, and a wild front ear. Grim is king of the wild front ear.

Two days later, reception gets a call from the police. Nobody wants to take responsibility for dealing with them. Word reaches the boss. Grim tells Joyce to agree to see them and find out what's up. Two blokes in plain overcoats turn up, and Joyce shows them into a room by the gatehouse. No way are they getting in to the main building.

One introduces himself as DC Current.

"Do you recognise this?" he asks, holding up a damp briefcase.

"Nooo," replies Joyce, although it does look vaguely familiar.

"Do you have a Gordy Barraclough working for you?"

"Yes, we do. He's in charge of IT. But he hasn't been in for a couple of days. Why? He's all right isn't he?"

The two men exchange glances It's a fair swap. Each is as darkly portentous as the other.

"We're concerned for his welfare."

"What's happened?"

"We have a lead," says DC Current.

"Where did you find the case?"

"He was last seen in the area of the Blackmire Bridge. A man was picked up on CCTV walking away from the area, looking suspicious. We found a single shoe beside the parapet, and the briefcase was washed up the following morning nearby. The jacket came ashore further downstream later that day, yesterday, that was."

"God... Has he been assaulted?"

"Potentially assault and battery," added DC Current, more positive now.

"Could it turn out to be a false lead?"

"Our enquiries could be entirely negative." DC Current seemed to be starting to alternate. "We don't know anything for certain. But we'd appreciate it if you would make discreet inquiries, and get back to us if you hear anything more."

"Of course."

Joyce briefs the boss. Grim calls Graham into his office.

"I gather Gordy's vanished. Rather abruptly."

211

"Dear, dear," says Graham. "I wonder what's up with him?"

"I think we can hazard a guess." And Grim puts his arms round Graham's shoulders. "I'm glad you're on the team. I think we can achieve a lot together."

And Graham nods agreement. But not too vigorously, in case his wig slips.

"I think it's about time you came for a jolly on the Blue Water Legend. You've earned it."

Graham has conspirator written all over his face. But from where Grim is standing he doesn't spot the con. He just sees the pirat, which makes Graham look like a bit of a pirate.

Chapter 33

Grim is away to central Africa to cement an arms deal.

Graham is fidgety. It all seems too easy now, without Gordy looking over his shoulder. He's been moved into a private office next to Grim's. On the wall is a Canaletto of the Grand Canal in Venice. He bought it at auction, on the company account. Everyone thinks it's a cheap imitation. That's because when you look at a real Canaletto, with its cartoony little squiggles of water, it looks like a fake Canaletto.

If he wants to watch the general office he can leave his door open. When it's shut people know to knock before they enter. At least he thinks they do. He can't remember anybody actually coming to see him.

He would yawn, but he's too twitchy.

He looks up the Yellow Pages and selects a firm of lawyers. The most commercially minded. The ones with the biggest advert.

Ambulances chased. Fat cats fried. Suckers sued. Someone piss you off? We'll welcome them to a world of grief.

It's all there, subtly implied.

"Hi. Can I speak to the chief Rottweiler?"

There's a laugh from the woman who answers the call. "I have just the man for you. I'll see if Mr Hardball is free."

She puts Graham on hold. Either that or she's held the phone out to a small orchestra crammed into reception. Someone whistles a familiar melody. The accompaniment swells, and whiplashes punctuate the beat. Graham can't remember whether it's "A Fistful of Dollars" or "The Good, The Bad and The Ugly." It might even be "For a Few Dollars More." Doesn't matter, thinks Graham. Works for me.

The music is cut off in mid phrase. "Hello. How can I help?"

"Hi. I see that you're one of those firms who do a 'No cure, no fee' deal."

"That is correct."

"What about 'No pain, no gain'?"

"I beg your pardon."

"I'll explain. My wife has engaged some avaricious money grubbing legal bastards to hound me for every penny I've got. I want to engage some even bigger legal bastards to make them wish they'd been strangled at birth."

"Is your wife trying to divorce you?"

"Right in one."

"And you want her to go away without getting her hands on your assets."

"She wants the goldmine. I want to give her the shaft. She's got her hands on someone else's assets already."

"Do you wish to commence a counter-action?"

214

"Not really. She's got bugger all. Just roving knickers."

"In that case we couldn't really take a percentage of winnings, em, funds secured in the event of success. We wouldn't want eighty percent of bugger all."

"Eighty percent!"

"Would you rather have twenty percent of something or a hundred percent of nothing?"

"I just want to stop her clearing me out."

"I see. Well. We could possibly work on a contingency fee basis. But it would depend on how robust your case is. Do you have evidence of any transgression?"

"I saw it with my own eyes."

"It wouldn't stand up in court."

"Bin the limp dick jokes, will you? I just want her and her loathsome lawyers to get a fright and go away."

"So there's no cash to pursue..."

"OK. I hear what you're saying. So I'd need to pay you. By contingency fee you mean I'd just pay when you succeeded?"

"I think we would need to agree some sort of advance."

"Thank God you said that."

"Why?"

"I was beginning to think you weren't big enough bastards. Right. How much do you want?"

Carver Hardball hesitates. Not just because he's taken aback, but because he's trying to work out from Graham's voice how much he's good for. "Why don't you come in for a chat and we'll see what's what?"

"I'm a busy man, and I think we can do this on the phone. My wife's shagging some little shit and I want

215

him, her and her lawyers to feel my displeasure. So how much?"

"Er, perhaps a couple of thousand? Then we can take a view, once you've given us the details?"

Graham gives him the details. Couple of grand? Not very greedy. Of course that would just be for starters. Ho hum. Better get the readies.

Graham logs on to the appropriate company accounts and pays himself another million pounds. Then he donates five hundred thousand to an animal charity, something to do with donkeys or pussy cats. Maybe dogs that were just for Christmas. Stuff with eyelashes anyway.

That feels a bit better.

But something's still bugging him.

In Grim he's found a successful doppelganger - a Graham who has carved out a different destiny for himself. This Grim Graham is decisive, fearless, totally devoid of ruth. Their paths diverged when Graham took a sensible decision, avoiding stupid risks. Grim took the chance and it paid off.

Graham wants to learn from this version of himself. But what he's learned so far is that he doesn't like this character. At all. In fact he's an evil manipulative bastard. So what's to learn?

Lesson One: All of these tendencies must be there, suppressed, within himself. The idea nauseates him. But he can't suppress the analytical side of his nature which tells him that it must be true.

Nature versus nurture.

Could the events of the past few years really change Grim into a different person? They share the same genes, the same infant environment, the same life experiences up to that gap year. Has Grim been traumatised by his vile experiences in war zones - the personal contact with brutality and the disintegration of flesh?

That must have marked him. But it doesn't explain the initial decision to live dangerously and play for high stakes. Grim has sought out the horrors, in the pursuit of personal profit. And it's paid off, with many many nothings on the end.

Whereas Graham can't make a move without calculating the odds. Not just guessing, but doing detailed mathematical analyses in his head. Creating a spreadsheet to crunch the numbers. Is that a side of his nature which Grim has to suppress? Or did he just back a hunch, and never look back?

There is, of course, a third possibility. It may be that Grim still does the sums in his head, then backs his own hunches based on them. A mathematical model can only be a partial simulation of real life. Instinct and experience can still play a part. Perhaps Grim understands more than Graham about the true nature of risk.

Chapter 34

Graham gives Pate a call. "Fancy a pint? Or a third of a pint of foreign lager in a bottle for the same price?"

"Do I have to choose one or the other? Could I not have a sweet stout? Or an elaborate cocktail with stylishly sculpted fruit and veg impaled on stalks of rosemary?"

"Whatever. Where do you fancy?"

"I'm attracted to Bar Magnet. We could gravitate there."

"Gravity's a very weak force," says Graham, trying to impress.

"You still go splat if you fall off a cliff," says Pate.

"There's a lot of me for gravity to act upon. And there's a lot of earth to gravitate towards."

"That's a lot of pulling power."

"More than can be said for you."

"Touché, you hormonal hostage."

"Right, see you at six. OK?"

"Oll Korrect."

Graham and Pate grab the same seat as last time. It swings round unexpectedly as they move towards it.

"Cool."

"This place is awesome. Cheers."

They hold their drinking vessels up, but don't manage to make them clink together. They laugh as they push against an unseen force. Suddenly Pate's tankard flips upside down and clanks together with Graham's, shooting his lager all over his knees. Now they can't pull their tankards apart. How they laugh!

A waitress clumps past overhead and passes a fresh drink to Pate. "This one's on the house."

"This one's on my trousers."

"All part of the fun, sir. I'm Danka, here to help you. Any tips, just throw them at the ceiling."

"How do you manage to keep your chests in the right place?" asks Pate.

"I wear my bra upside down. The straps are specially adapted."

"Thank you Danka," says Graham. He turns to Pate as Danka clumps off across the ceiling, dribbling slops on the heads of the happy customers below. "See all these blonde waitresses, Pate? They must be magnetic Poles."

But Pate is preoccupied, scanning the bar for the fit chick they spotted the other night.

"Pay attention Pate. I want your advice."

"I can understand that."

"Am I a bad person Pate?"

"That's all relative, and also highly subjective."

"I mean, do you think I'm selfish and inconsiderate and don't give a shit about anybody else?"

"I think you'd like to be."

"What? You mean I'm a failed bastard?"

"I think you settle for being likeable, but your heart's not in it."

"So I am a bastard?"

"No. I think you're an unsuccessful bastard."

Graham's lower lip trembles.

Pate frowns. "Maybe that was a little harsh."

Graham doesn't answer. He turns his drink in his hand. He makes slow circles in the spilt beer on the table. He looks into his reflection in his drink, and reflects. When he takes a drink, it's like swallowing his own head.

Pate fiddles with his hank of hair, making sure it's firmly secured behind his ear.

"Graham."

Graham look at the puddle of beer on the table. In it are reflected the waitresses passing overhead. It turns them right way up again, so it looks like they're miniature holograms walking about on his table.

"Graham..."

"What?"

"That bird..."

"What bird?"

"That one over there."

Graham doesn't look.

"She's staring at you."

Graham does nothing. Then his testicles make his head turn around.

He looks back at his beer, then does an immediate double take. The girl is gorgeous. She smiles at him and waves.

"Stap me vitals," gasps Pate. "Do you know her?"

"Bloody hell," mutters Graham. "That's Susan Hornygolloch!"

Susan heads towards them, weaving sinuously through the crowd. Some drinkers step aside in awe, while others pretend not to notice just so she'll have to squeeze past.

"Hi Grim. Can I join you?"

"Oh hi, Susan. Yes of course."

"I thought you were in Africa."

"Yes, I was, and em, I'll be there again soon, but I had to come back to this country for an urgent meeting."

"Here?"

"Well, it was kind of..."

Susan looks about the bar. She looks to the left of Pate, then to the right of Pate, then right through Pate. "So you're waiting for someone?"

"Erm, this is em..."

She looks around, bewildered. Graham points to Pate, his finger only two inches from Pate's chest. She looks at Pate and tries to focus. Graham pokes Pate in the chest. "Here. This is Mr em Wheeler."

Susan starts backwards as if Pate has suddenly popped out of his pint in a flurry of doves and rabbits. Strange looking men with frizzy hair piled up on top of their heads don't seem to register on her radar.

"Oh, sorry. I didn't see you there."

Pate nods. He can't think of words to say, and wouldn't be able to utter them anyway. Not without dribbling. Susan turns back to Graham. "I wasn't expecting this. Will you be long? I'll tell the girls I'm tied up this evening."

Graham swallows. His Adam's apple bounces up and down like a tennis ball waiting for a first service. "No, erm, that's us just finished. I'll um..."

"Great I'll just tell the girls. See you at the door in a mo."

Susan insinuates her way through the crowd once more. She approaches three girls at the bar. "Hi, can you tell me where the ladies is?

"Over there, behind the coats."

"Great, thanks girls, see you around byee!" And Susan kisses each of them on both cheeks and waves a large goodbye. Which puzzles them, because they've never seen her before. Graham and Pate watch this from across the bar.

"Why did you call me Wheeler?"

"I thought Dealer, but it would've been too obvious."

"Why didn't you introduce me properly? She might have liked me. Better than you."

"Shit, of course. An introduction might have made all the difference."

As Susan makes her way to the door she mutters under her breath to a bloke in an expensive suit. "That's the boss. Don't let on you're with me. He wants me to come with him for a meeting."

"What, now?"

"That's why they pay me so much."

"Yeah, but that's taking the piss."

"Sorry hon, must fly."

Graham gets to his feet and heads across the bar towards the exit in Susan's wake. He spots a glare from some random bloke. Jealous! Well you might be mate.

As Graham heads out of the door with Susan the world shifts on its axis. At least the world of Bar Magnet does, as Pate's table reverses polarity and flips round to leave him facing the wall.

Chapter 35

"OK pet?"

Graham nods. He has his frowns up.

"You look a bit serious."

"No, I'm fine. Just thinking."

Just thinking about the big stiffy which is making it difficult to walk. Graham looks like a shoplifter trying to get out of Tesco with a roll of kitchen towel down his kecks. And the adrenaline and hormones are mixing like a gin and sherbert, making him weak at the knees and giggly all at once.

"Back to the flat, bad boy?"

"Oh, I don't think we should go back to mine."

"Not yours silly. The flat. Back to ours."

"Oh right. Em, I don't think I've got the key."

"The keypad number? You can't forget that!"

"No, of course not."

Graham wonders what the hell the number is. Susan waves down a cab. For some reason, despite Grim's wealth and power, taxis always seem to notice Susan first. As the vehicle thrums its way towards a district where the flats have pillars outside and cost more than detached houses with ten acres anywhere else. Susan snuggles in to Graham's side.

He hopes she doesn't notice his big willy. How embarrassing would that be?

Susan puts her hand on his rampant rolling pin and looks up at him, all wide-eyed outraged innocence. "Gwim. You naughty, naughty boy. Just wait till I get you home. I'm going to spank you on your bare botty."

"Oh, right."

Graham points to the light which indicates that the cabby can listen in. "Eh, hello. Can you hear me?"

The cabbie pretends he can't. Graham realises he'd better act a bit more decisive.

"Switch the intercom off, will you?"

'Sorry mate. Didn't know you were talking to me."

And the little light goes off. Off course the cabbie can still hear every word, since he's wired the switch to turn the light on and off rather than kill the speakers. After all, it's a thankless job, and you've got to get your laughs somewhere.

Flash forward. The caff at the depot. The cabbie holds the floor. "So I turn off vlight, and vis bloke, he nods, all important like, like e's Lord Gawd Almighty or sumfink, so e takes a deep breff an says - just wait till you see wot I'm going to do to you, and she says - go on, tell me, and e says I'm going to take all your cloves off and cover you with fruit and unny and jelly an stuff, oo oo she says, an ven I'm going to start licking it off, and chomping your cherries, an I might just ide the odd banana, oo oo she says, an ven I'm gonna get right on you in the Armani, an slide about, and won't you get it all sticky she says, an e says I don't care doll, vat's how mental I am for ya, and ven you're gonna peel me off and chuck it in a heap an rub me wiv your melons an..."

"Wot? Wot?"

"Then she vanishes don't she, an I can't see her in vmirror, and is voice goes all blurry, and is eyes disappear back into is head, proper aargh it was, like one ovm zombie movies or such an I'm going as slow as I can an I've been rahn the block a few times so to speak, but I can't put it off no more, so I says vat's us mate, we're ere, an..."

"An wot?"

"An e jumps back and she pops up like a jack in a box an e looks all sheepish an says how come vlight didn't come on, an I finks shit, forgot the light, an I says, quick as a flash, don worry mate, comes on automatic when vcab stops, and e looks at me like vat, and vey get aht an e gives me a twenny an i says want a receipt? an e says nah mate keep vchange, an I says won't yer need it for vfruit, an I floors it an you should av seen im, mental e was standin ver elpless wivis bird, an I larfed and larfed..."

The caff is in uproar.

"Some bird vo, shoulda seener, gor, I'd slip er a wossit an no mistake..."

The cab driver wasn't from London. He was in fact a professor of sociology from Tunbridge Wells who had built his professional reputation by mixing with the hired hands of the hackney carriage trade and writing up his findings. He was good at the sociology, but crap at the accent, but the drivers didn't mind because it gave them material for their own outrageous stories.

"So then the Prof says 'So I turn off vlight, and vis bloke, he nods, all important like, like e's Lord Gawd Almighty or sumfink..'"

"Did he really say that?"

"What?"

"Vlight?"

"Absolutely. Like 'the light', but with what he must imagine is some sort of Cockney consonant sound."

"Unbelievable. Come back Dick Van Dyke - all is forgiven."

"Too true."

Back to the present. Flash forward finito.

"Did you hear that?"

"Hear what?"

"Cheeky bastard. He was earywigging."

"Who cares. He might have been watching too. But you don't mind that, do you babe? Bit of a show-off aren't you?"

Am I? thinks Graham. Never got the chance. Never really thought about it. Doesn't seem to bother Ms Hornygolloch too much. God she's a dirty bitch.

"God you're a dirty bitch!"

"And you're a horny hound."

"Should we go to the offy?"

"Why, have you emptied the place since I was here? Who've you been partying with?"

And Susan grabs Graham by the hand and leads him up some steps, past the pillars and the brass nameplate, and through a reception area. A man in a discreet black suit with grey striped trousers stands behind the desk. He bows as the pair walk past towards the lifts.

"Evening Trouser!" calls Susan cheerily, for that was his name. "How's things? We're just off upstairs for a shag."

"Good for you, Miss Susan. I'll ignore the falling plaster."

"Good man!"

And Susan drags Graham into the lift.

226

"That was a bit, well..." stutters Graham.

"Oh you know he's fine. What's the point of a happy humping ground if you can't relax?"

As the doors slide shut Graham pins her to the wall of the lift and thrusts his hands in a thrusty kind of way under her clothes. He expects her to push him away and say wait, not here, but she gasps and bites his ear, then waves up at the little camera in the ceiling. Graham pulls his hands free, turns round, stands up straight and gives a sheepish little wave too.

"What's got into you tonight, animal?" asks Susan approvingly.

"Same thing that's going to - God we're here..."

And this time it's Graham who grabs her hand and pulls her out of the lift.

"Wrong way, silly. God you are on fire."

They stride up a short corridor. A large door faces them at the end. Graham turns and waits for Susan to punch the keypad.

She laughs. "Can't even remember your own birthday?"

"Ha," laughs Graham sardonically, and wonders what the hell Grim's birthday is. "Now when was I born?" he muses, playing for time. Then it dawns on him that he's just supplied the answer. He punches in the numbers for his own birthday. And he hauls her into the flat.

Before the echo of the closing door has died Graham rips Susan's clothes off, and his own. He throws them in all directions. Willy nilly. But mainly willy. He jumps on her in the hall, humps her against the back of the front door, then on the hall carpet, then across the floor into the living room. He rogers her on the settee, then she throws him on his back, leaps astride him, and bangs away like someone on one of those imitation bucking bronco machines you get in pubs. Well maybe you haven't seen one, but they do exist, honest. She swivels round with her thighs around his ears and blows his love trumpet like jazz was back in fashion. Graham even forgets to be embarrassed about the scar on his willie. He caught it on a zip when he was in Primary 2. But that's all secondary to tonight's workout.

Graham picks her up and boffs her across the living room, then turns her round and humps her in through the bedroom door.

Which is where the fun starts.

The bed is massive, the ceilings mirrored. This is no time for reflection, thinks Graham, and dives down for second helpings of hairy pie.

They hear faint rustling outside the door, but ignore it. They can afford to lose a few cattle.

Susan is transported. In the old days she'd have been sent to Australia. In the throes of passion she reverts to her Glaswegian origins. Graham can't make out many words among the screams. The ones he can grasp are guttural and unfamiliar. Hoochmagandy! she cries.

Like two Duracell bunnies they go on and on. And on. There's another faint noise outside the door.

"Do that thing you do with your tongue," gasps Susan. Bugger, thinks Graham. What do I do with my tongue? So he does everything he can possibly imagine with it. It takes some time, but he doesn't think he's been found out. She still thinks he's Grim, but actually he's quite the opposite. Susan glows pink like a nursery lamp.

There are yet more faint noises outside the door.

Despite the hours in the gym, Graham's stomach muscles are starting to cramp.

Susan rambles deliriously. Then she removes her walking boots and jumps on him again.

The tides of passion ebb and flow, but mostly flow. They remember the shower and the jacuzzi and work up an all-over froth with shower gel, shampoo, and something else from a dispenser. It turns out to be toothpaste, but that just puts a bigger smile on their faces.

Their minds are filthy, but their bodies shine like eyeballs.

They slither and slop and splash and sploosh and slip and slap and eventually ripple and drip to a halt. They've inserted every sticky-out bit they possess into every sticky-in bit they can find, then wiggled it about. Susan takes her little left toe out of Graham's ear. Graham has a final thrust at her belly button, then withdraws his nose.

Their fingers are wrinkled like prunes. Graham's prunes are wrinkled like, well, prunes.

At last they are done.

Susan looks like Janet Leigh in Psycho. Her upside-down eyes stare as the water runs down the plughole. Fortunately she's not dead. Just knackered. Graham helps her to her feet.

"Wow," she flutters. "That was like the first time all over again."

"Buh," mumbles Graham, whose brain is custard.

As they leave the flat they almost trip over three copies of the daily paper - Tuesday, Wednesday and Thursday. In reception, Trouser is covered in a sprinkling of plaster dust. Graham licks his eyebrows and wonders what Susan sees in him.

Chapter 36

Graham's quest to analyse the secrets of Grim Dupeint's success is proving more complicated than he imagined. He opens the shoebox on his desk. For a moment he panics. He can't see Bumface! He lifts out some twigs and organises them neatly on his desk. Then he lifts a large leaf and spots the large caterpillar clinging to the underside.

"Ah, there you are. Now what are you up to? Do you want something a bit juicier?"

He's never been too sure what to give Bumface to drink. He did wonder about putting a jam jar lid full of water in the box, but wasn't sure if caterpillars could swim.

"Don't want any nasty accidents now, do we? Here, try this..."

And Graham pulls some soggy lettuce and a bit of tomato out of his lunchtime BLT, and holds them temptingly in front of the caterpillar's painted face. Then he holds them in front of the other end too. He's still not entirely sure.

Bumface's badly drawn eyes gaze vacantly at him, unblinking. Graham puts the salad on the bottom of the box.

His office door swings open, and Grim strides in. "David! How're things? What's that?"

Graham reaches for the shoebox lid. He winces as a sharp pain racks his stomach muscles.

"Oh, it's just something I found."

His tongue feels strangely tender too. How do you pull a muscle in your tongue?

"Stick insect is it?" Grim leans on Graham's desk and peers down into the box.

He spots the caterpillar and laughs. Then his eyebrows move quizzically, like the curtains at a school play starting to close then getting stuck. "I've seen one of those before. I didn't think you got them here."

"Where did you see one?"

"It was in South America. I was there doing a gap year. I put it in a jar, but I was flying to Ecuador and they wouldn't let me take it on the plane."

Flipping heck, thinks Graham. I'd forgotten all about that. I knew I'd seen something like it before.

"What happened to that one, d'you think?"

"No idea. I chucked it."

Into the salad bar at the terminal, remembers Graham. "It wasn't green like this one, though."

"No, it was purple. Same stupid face. But how do you know it wasn't green?"

Quick bluff. "I think the Colombian varieties are mostly purple."

"How did you know I was in Colombia?"

Shit. Bigger bluff. "Cos that's where you find them."

"Oh, right."

Graham's starting to sweat. He's not even sure that you get them in South America at all. Isn't the Swallowtail a North American species?

231

"Anyways up. Fascinating as this is, we have bigger fish to fry. I'm just back till the weekend. Then I'm off to the boat again. Fancy a jaunt on the briny?"

"Wow. Yes. That would be excellent. Where is the boat right now?"

"When I left she was off Tunisia. But we're meeting her in Monte Carlo. There's a trade fair I go to each year. You might find it interesting."

"Right."

"You don't look sure."

"No, I am, really. Is that a trade fair for, em medical er, or is it em..."

"Ah! Peg legs give you the willies eh? Now willies, there's a thought. I wonder if there's a market for artificial willies? Surprising how many people get them blown off."

Graham is still surprised at the enthusiasm with which his own was blown off, so to speak, only the day before.

Grim is in full creative flow. "They'd be like dildos, but we'd have to plumb them in somehow. Put in central heating. We could call the operation a strapadictomy."

"You're all heart."

Grim's head jerks back an inch. Then he laughs. "Actually I just about lost my own once. There was these two hookers in Thailand giving me a blow job, and one must have been more familiar with smaller ones and ran out of air and bit me! Left quite a scar!"

"Yeah, it's annoying when that happens."

"Anyway, speak to Susan and she'll sort out the travel. Talking of which, where is she? She was groaning on about having a sore back." Grim turns and strides back out of Graham's office. "Susan? Susan!"

The trip to Nice is very different to Graham's normal experience of holiday flights. Budget travel it isn't, unless your budget is vast. Grim picks up Graham in the big black limo with darkened windows. At the airport the driver takes a turning which leads away from the passenger terminal round the perimeter to a small suite of rooms set apart from the helicopter hangars. Inside there's a reception area, behind which Graham can see a lounge with just a few large leather armchairs adrift on seas of unfeasibly thick dark blue carpet. In case anyone runs short of supplies, tables like small life rafts bob beside each chair, threatening to capsize under their deck cargo of newspapers, malt whisky, gin and mixers.

At the reception desk a stunning girl in a discreet uniform greets them. She must have been standing there for ages, just waiting to make their day wonderful. Her blonde hair is tucked neatly into a jaunty flight cap, like a pale blue upside down girlie version of the RAF caps.

"Hi, I'm Amy. How nice to see you again. Nice today."

She's not talking about the weather, but their destination. So you can go back and read that sentence again if you got it wrong. If you guessed right, then no problem. Just keep reading from here, and sorry I interrupted. But of course some people will have thought it was the weather she was referring to, so I had to say something.

"Yes, nice day to fly to Nice," says Graham eagerly. The girl looks at him as if he's wonderful. Graham instantly feels wonderful. He wonders where Customs and the security machines are.

"You've been shopping again," she says, nodding at Grim's silk suit. It must have cost thousands, thinks Graham. Just as well I've got one like it, or I might feel a bit underdressed. Grim smiles at the girl. She looks deep into his eyes with a mixture of warmth, friendship and crisp professionalism. "You like it?" asks Grim.

"Mmhmm," she murmurs.

Wow, thinks Graham. So this is what it's like for rich people. She's clearly a high flyer (that's restating the obvious tautology quite unnecessarily) - a bright, charming, lovely person. She somehow seems to be able to talk to Grim as a friend, while still deferring to his status. She has a wonderfully deft touch. Graham can see why she's in this executive lounge, while the miserable grumpy harridans are causing grief to package tourists in the main terminal.

"Your reservations have all been taken care of," she continues.

"Excellent," purrs Grim.

"Good," says Graham.

"Now just one little thing. Sorry to trouble you, but can you let me see your booking reference number? I've been asked to do a cross check with our system."

"That's ridiculous," snaps Grim.

Graham's face slackens in astonishment at his change of tone. Amy tries to explain.

"Well, I'm terribly sorry, it's not for me, it's just that - "

"If I wanted to spend my life fiddling with stupid bits of paper I'd be over in the cattle shed with the peasants. You don't seriously think I booked this myself?"

"No, but it's just - "

"I've never been asked for reference numbers before. How dare you talk like that to me!"

Amy's lovely eyes well with tears, and a flush suffuses her delicate features.

"I'm so sorry, if it's a problem, then there's no need to..."

"It certainly is a problem. And I won't let this rest here!"

Amy bursts into a flood of tears and rushes off, disappearing through a door marked Staff.

"Bloody ridiculous. Piece of nonsense, that."

And Grim strides off across the sea of blue into the lounge, grabbing the Times as he sinks into an armchair.

Graham can't move. He knows Amy would have been well up to coping with the most demanding and abusive of passengers. But the thing which has thrown her is the instant whip between oily charm and verbal brutality. How could someone be so utterly horrible to her when she was going out of her way to be charming? Graham knows she'll be damaged by the experience. Her warm, trusting personality will now have a tiny constriction of reserve, like a pucker of scar tissue tightening the layers beneath her flawless skin. Graham feels dirty. He is revolted to be associated with that man. Nobody else has witnessed the exchange, but Amy has gone, and Graham desperately wishes he could say something to her.

There seem to be no formalities. Another woman appears after a few minutes. Grim seems oblivious to her bleak silence. A Customs officer nods at them as they make their way out to the twelve seater executive jet parked nearby.

There are five of them onboard, including the pilot, co-pilot and stewardess.

Grim takes a window seat, so Graham chooses a window on the other side.

"You'll get a good view of the Massif Central from there," calls Grim.

Graham grunts.

During the flight the hostess serves champagne and smoked salmon. To Graham everything tastes like something you would paint on your nails to stop you biting them.

Chapter 37

There's a car waiting for them at Nice. It's a Mini Cooper, split new and gleaming. Despite its sporty looks Graham wonders why Grim hasn't arranged something larger. Perhaps a furniture removal lorry, to carry his ego. Or a fork lift truck, to pick up his wallet.

Grim rabbits on as he drives along the coast towards Monaco, pointing out the sights. Graham wishes he would just button it. He loves this part of the Côte D'Azur, but the fun is spoilt by having to share the experience with such an anus horribilis. He's unsettled by the lingering conviction that Grim's loathsome character is something he shares. It must be embedded in his own, perhaps not too far below the surface. Is he constantly suppressing the urge to be a total bastard? The thought frightens him. And his blonde wig is itching in the heat. And the blazing sunshine is making his eyes water behind his pale blue contact lenses.

"Look, there's the Casino," announces Grim as they head into the city of Monte Carlo. "It's got fantastic paintings on the ceiling."

"I know," says Graham. "I went there once, years ago."

Grim looks surprised.

"I was on a school exchange, and the daughter of the manager was one of the kids hosting it."

237

"How bizarre," says Grim. "That happened to me too. Nice bird with long dark hair."

"Em, oh, gosh, I can't remember." Graham suddenly realises his big mouth and tiny brain is getting him into trouble.

"But isn't that strange? That happened to you too. Where did you go to school?"

"Oh I can't rem... imagine that there would be a connection. I went to school in -" Graham tried to think of somewhere he'd never been to " - in Shetland."

"Shetland? That's pretty remote. What's it like?"

Graham trawls his memory for anything he knows about Shetland, and fails almost entirely. Wasn't there something about blazing longboats?

"Oh, you know. Winged helmets. And they burnt their boats."

"That's just once a year."

"That's all they admit to… But we were mostly abroad."

"Where?"

"Oh, my parents moved around a lot. All sorts of places. But in England too. Sometimes."

Grim flexes his lips and nods. It's starting to occur to him that he knows bugger all about this David Wilson. He wonders who vetted him when he was appointed. He makes a mental note to look into it.

They approach the harbour. They pass the open air swimming pool, and head towards the main yacht marina. Graham is gobsmacked by what he sees there. They drive out on a jetty, then take a left turn along another section of pontoon. He recognises the Blue Water Legend. It is by no means the largest vessel in the marina. The super yachts are moored stern-on to the pontoon. Graham realises why they're in a Mini. As they approach Grim's floating palace he sees that a ramp has opened in the stern. Inside the lower deck garage are several other Minis, and behind them some larger vehicles. Of course. This is one of the crew runabouts.

"I'll just leave it here," says Grim. "The crew can sort it. We'll walk on board."

The two of them get out, and a man in a polo shirt sporting the boat's logo gets in and drives the car up the ramp into the stern of the vessel.

"Bit lazy to use the lift," says Grim. "Let's stretch our legs."

And he leads the way up a gangway which takes them up to the lower afterdeck. They still seem to be a few storeys beneath the main deck level, and the bridge is another level up from that again. Graham is astonished to see rotor blades above them. There appears to be a helicopter parked on the roof above the upper afterdeck. If you call it a roof. There must be a nautical name for it.

"What do you call the roof on a boat?" asks Graham.

"Fuck knows," confides Grim. "I pay people to know stuff like that. I know what the bar is though. It's a mess."

"I'm sure it isn't," says Graham.

"They step off the gangway on to the lower after deck. It runs round the entire back bit of the vessel. Graham gets a strong sense of déja vu. This heightened when he sees who's walking towards them, with an oily smile on his chops. For a moment Graham struggles with the urge to jump over the rail into the water, then remembers his wig and contact lenses. It's the bloke who gave Graham such a courteous tour of the vessel at the Boat Show.

"David, this is Rodger, our Skipper. Rodger, David's here to see what's what. Good man. Been very useful at head office. Look after him."

Graham nods and tries to look important but modest.

"Welcome aboard," says Rodger in a quiet, crisply enunciated voice. "I'm sure we can supply most of what you might need - but anything missing, just shout."

"Well I could do with some champagne and two or three women," jests Graham. "Any colour. In fact send me a selection."

"I think you'll find Rodger said to shout if anything's missing," grins Grim. "Obvious stuff like that's been taken care of."

Graham gulps. Then he laughs, not sure if this is a wind-up. Then he remembers where he is, and who he's with. And the moral foundation upon which this empire has been built.

"Good man, Rodger," he offers, limply.

Grim leads them along the deck, then up a flight of stairs to another deck. Graham turns right at the top and heads towards the midship section. "Can find his way to the bar, anyway," observes Grim wryly.

"Oh, yes, instinct," joshes Graham, realising that he mustn't let on that he knows his way about. Since this is the second time Rodger's shown him round. They make their way into a saloon and walk up to the bar. The scale of the boat makes it feel like a hotel, and within the shelter of the harbour there is zero impression of being afloat. Grim takes a seat on one of the grey leather bar stools. Graham looks at them, with horror.

"I'll just lean," he says. So that's what sperm whale dong looks like...

"Check out the barstools," exclaims Grim.

"In what way?" says Graham, looking grossed-out.

"Whale foreskin!" reveals Grim. "God knows whose idea it was. Isn't that brilliant?"

"You know it was your idea, sir," smarms Rodger.

"Bollocks it was! Your idea of a surprise! Rodger keeps trying to tell me I thought of it!"

Rodger shakes his head at the waggish humour of his boss.

Graham just nods, and tries to keep his mouth shut.

"Right, what'll it be?" asks Grim.

"I'll have a large Bunnahabhain. The twelve year old up there on the top shelf."

"Good call," chimes Grim. "That's my favourite too. This trip's going to be a belter!"

After a reviver Grim suggests Graham/David can have a lie down or a freshen up and they will reconvene in an hour's time for a briefing session. Captain Rodger shows Graham to his cabin, although that word doesn't do justice to the floating hotel suite he has been allocated. The rooms are immediately below the main deck. There's a square mile of window, but since the vessels are all moored stern-on to the pontoon all Graham can see is a gleaming expanse of white hull with gold embellishments - part of an equally large floating palace alongside. There's no window opposite, but Graham shuts the blinds, just in case. Boats have a habit of floating about, and he wants to take off his wig without being spotted by some curious Middle Eastern potentate.

He kicks off his shoes and lies down on the bed. He's too wired to sleep. He turns on the flat screen TV attached to one wall and flicks idly through the channels. He can't work out what the satellite system is. There seems to be a remarkable choice, even in these days of international programming. Perhaps Grim has his own selection. Probably owns the satellite.

There's no minibar. There is, however, a bar. And there's enough space in the lounge to hold your own party. Graham could almost relish the idea of running a rapacious global empire and living in such luxury. Then he remembers what the empire is based on - not just a population of customers, but an additional population of victims. Not consumers of baked beans or trainers, but consumers of violence.

Graham starts to feel twitchy again. He decides to go for a wander - perhaps find somewhere to sit on deck to watch the onshore activity and comings and goings on neighbouring vessels. He has a quick shower, then gets changed into some fresh clothes. There are crisp dark navy blue polo shirts in a drawer, with a Blue Water Legend logo. Graham is torn. They look really cool, and this is an astonishing yacht. He thinks about the donations he's been making to good causes from the pirate's chest of Grim's company coffers. Is there a way of reconciling the luxury of wealth with the suffering of others? After all, not everybody in the world can have exactly equal assets. So perhaps you just have to go with the flow, and try to do good when you get a chance? He thinks.

God, what would Kerri's face be like if she could see this?

Graham's face stretches into a grin so wide that his ears end up several centimetres further apart.

He has a skoosh of the deodorant in the shower room, then puts on a polo shirt. He adds white cotton trousers and a pair of soft leather deck shoes. Then he lets himself out of the door and goes for a wander. When the heat hits him he realises how effective the air conditioning in his suite must have been.

Not far from his rooms is another flight of stairs up to the main afterdeck. He springs up the steps, and finds himself on a walkway which seems to go right round the ship. He decides to leave the afterdeck with its harbour views for last, and turns to walk up the starboard side towards the bows.

On his left he passes a door leading in to the rooms in the superstructure. Through a window he sees a large lounge with soft seating, and what looks like a dance floor in the centre. The next door is marked "crew", then there's a window through which he can see a desk with charts spread out. There are more crew rooms, then ahead he sees the bridge. This occupies the full width of the vessel to allow for good views for precise manoevering from either wing when coming alongside.

The companionway he's following drops down a flight of steps under the starboard side of the bridge. It leads to a covered walkway which allows him to stroll towards the port side beneath the main bridge windows.

The open foredeck now lies ahead. It seems to be fenced off to visitors, with chains and hawsers occupying most of the space. Graham heads back down the port side towards the stern. As he passes under the flying bridge he meets a companionway leading back up to his original level. Although Graham thinks it's a flight of stairs.

The doors are now on his left hand side. They're similar to those on the starboard side. Unsurprisingly. He assumes the Captain's quarters will be right behind the bridge, together with the First Officer, and the crew responsible for navigation and communications.

A few yards further down, one of the doors is ajar. Graham glances in. There's an astonishing collection of electronic equipment. Graham assumed that there would be wireless comms, satnav and a few other clever bits and pieces. But this is more like the deck of the Starship Enterprise.

He steps back and looks upwards. On the deck above his head are satellite dishes and other stuff, presumably radar, in big enclosed farings like giant pingpong balls. Graham steps forward again to take in the flickering lights in the gloom.

Suddenly a voice barks at him from behind.

"Yes? Can I help you?"

Graham swings round and squints into the light. The man who has challenged him is wearing a dark grey suit. He's not particularly bulky, but there's something about him which would make you hesitate before getting in his way. His hair has been cut with such precision that it looks like fur.

"Sorry - I was, em just, em doing a bit of sightseeing."

"And you are?"

"Oh, I'm Gr, em David Wilson. I work for Grim, em Mr Dupeint, in the UK."

"I know who David Wilson is. You'll be shown which areas of the boat you can wander about in. And this isn't one of them."

"Right. OK. Who are you, by the way?"

"I'm Henry Hatchet."

"Ah."

Graham nods and smiles ingratiatingly as he turns and walks off towards the stern. Henry stares at him. Graham can feel Henry's eyeballs cannoning off his shoulder blades like billiard balls. Not literally of course, because that would be rather strange and disconcerting, and would make a mess on the shirt and no doubt the deck.

Chapter 38

At the briefing session Grim announces that Graham will be joining them to visit the trade show the following day. The show is the reason for this trip. It is not widely advertised. In fact the press and the public are not aware that it's happening, despite it being an annual event since the Crimean War.

Grim outlines tasks and timetables for the following day. Graham's job is to accompany Grim and observe, then make himself scarce when sensitive discussions unfold. Then on to more immediate plans. "David, I hope you won't mind eating in your suite this evening. I'm entertaining a client, and he prefers..."

"No that's fine. Perhaps I'll take a stroll ashore."

"Perfect. Sorry about that. He's not keen on discussing business with people he doesn't know. I just go along with it - keeps him sweet."

As Graham steps off the gangway on to the pontoons leading to the Quai Albert 1er he hears a rotor blade starting up. The helicopter on the upper deck of the Blue Water Legend is about to take off. After a minute or two for flight checks it rises from the deck, swings round into the breeze, then flies across the harbour towards a floating palace a couple of hundred yards away. It touches down, and the rotor blades start to power down. Graham can't see who it has ferried over the water - the helideck it came from is almost vertically above him.

Beats a rubber dinghy, I suppose, thinks Graham. And you wouldn't walk. Must be several hundred yards, among the poor people. Although this is Monte Carlo, so the poverty of the folk wandering about the quayside is relative.

Graham wanders through the town, studying menus, then settles for a small restaurant near the swimming pool. He reckons the Formula One cars must scream past just yards from his table when a Grand Prix is under way. He can see the Blue Water Legend from where he sits. He calls Pate on his mobile.

"Hi Pate. How're things?"

"Yo! Wassup?"

"I'm sitting on the quayside in Monte Carlo having a glass of vino and some rather fine seafood. Where are you?"

"I'm outside the Acropolis with a model that looks like Keira Knightley."

"No seriously - I am in Monte Carlo!"

"I don't doubt it."

"So you don't have to make stuff up, just cos you're jealous."

"I'm not dissembling or dissimulating. Although I might be making things up. But it sounds like you're alone, unaccompanied, desolate."

"Well yes. But women are provided. I just have to ask."

"Same here, my old comrade-in-arms."

"Right."

"Bye then. Have fun."

"You can't wait to get your model home, right?"

"Too true, blue."

"Bye then."

"Bye."

Bugger me, thinks Graham. Pate? With a model? He must be making it up.

Actually Pate will be making it up as soon as he gets home. Because he was exaggerating when he said his model looked like Keira Knightley. It doesn't yet. Maybe when he's stuck all the polystyrene pieces together and added some Humbrol enamel. But first he's popping into the Acropolis for a kebab.

Graham necks his wine and settles the bill, then walks back to the boat. He is stopped at the foot of the gangway, then again at deck level. This fun is hard work.

The next day he joins Grim for cold meat, fruit and yoghurt in the lounge. No bacon and eggs. Rubbish, basically. Then Grim leads him to a lift. He presses a button marked 'garage'. That must be French for garage, thinks Graham. They descend. This time their vehicle is a large black 4 x 4 with tinted windows. It's even taller than Graham's Chelsea tractor back at home. The windows on this one are too high to look into, even if they weren't impenetrable pools of pitch. Graham can just about see over the tyres. The driver wears a grey uniform and a cap. Grim and Graham get in the back, and the vehicle drives down the ramp and onto the quayside. They head across to the main streets, and follow a circuitous route uphill, towards the outskirts.

248

"What part of Monaco are we going to?" asks Graham.

"Not Monaco. You know how Monaco is a principality - surrounded by France, but not part of it?"

"Of course. First year geography. Good old Dr Mapley."

"How bizarre. My geography teacher was called Mapley too. Where was this?"

"I couldn't really give you directions. Mapley was crap. Geography felt like double Dutch."

"Hmmm. Well the place we're going to is also a separate country. It's surrounded by Monaco, but not part of it."

The vehicle heads out of town on a main road, but as it passes the built-up area it takes a sharp left turn into a driveway. There's a sign by the gate which says Mimosa, and a letter box.

"Is this a villa?"

"Best to let people think that."

The drive curves left through bushes. A cliff face looms in front of them, and the vehicle enters a stone archway. In the shade there's a red and white tilting barrier. A man steps out of a booth, scans their vehicle with something like a hair dryer, and lifts the barrier. A tunnel leads down in a straight line, through solid rock, picked out by the 4 x 4's headlights.

"I thought the Vatican was the smallest City State."

"It is. The principality of Mimosa's too small for a City. But it's not without its attractions."

They head down a gentle incline for another five minutes or so. Then they are dazzled by the full glare of the sun, as the car emerges from the tunnel and pulls up on a small quayside. Graham opens the door, and is hit by the smell of hot dust, hot tyres, hot salt water. To his left is what appears to be a hotel entrance, while in the other direction, along the waterfront, is an unspoilt Mediterranean fishing village. Wooden skiffs lie on the shingly beach, their paintwork a strident collection of primary colours. Plus green, which is a secondary colour. But not purple or orange. Just red, yellow, blue and green. And white and black, but of course those aren't colours at all. The boats look as if they were decorated by Mondrian, and scattered artistically on the beach by Picasso. Which they were. But that was years ago. Seurat said they should use some purple in dots on the shady side of the boats, and some orange and pink dabs among the yellow where the sun struck the gunwales. But he was overruled. What's the point, they asked? It would create a nice impression, said Seurat. Go and get your eyes tested, said the others. You're going dotty.

Beyond the hotel or conference centre (or whatever) Graham can see large yachts moored, but he's struggling to make sense of the geography. Grim leads the way up the hotel steps.

They cross a large hallway where delegates are queuing to collect badges and shoulder bags. Grim hands Graham a purple badge. "We pre-registered."

Graham's badge says Stanley Matthews, Tactical Supplies splv.

He looks at the name, then at Grim. Grim puts on his own badge. It says Harold Macmillan, Strategic Logistics splv. "Nobody uses their real name," he explains. But you need a badge to show security which areas you can access."

"Which areas can we access?"

"All of them."

They enter the main exhibition hall. At least Graham presumes it's the main hall. You could put the Vatican City inside it.

"I suggest you just have a wander about for a while. Get your bearings. I'm going for a chat with some old friends. I'll see you back here in an hour's time. Any change to plans, I'll give you a bell. What's your mobile number?"

Graham tells him. "What's yours?" he asks.

"You don't need to know," says Grim.

"Ah."

And Grim sets off, nodding occasionally to people manning stands - the vast really really expensive stands near the entrance. The ones which are two stories high, with private meeting rooms, and screening rooms, and restaurants and bars. And probably bedrooms, thinks Graham. For client hospitality.

He sets off in a random direction. Not entirely random, because he rules out going back out the way he came in. Or visiting the toilets. But insofar as he heads into the mass of stands and carpeted aisles he sets off in a pretty random way. Then, being Graham, he starts to ponder the most efficient non-random way of seeing the greatest number of stands with the minimum number of paces. That's almost a classic Travelling Salesman problem, he thinks. Where you have to visit all the towns, while travelling the minimum distance. Except this is more like one where you had to travel on all of the roads, which by definition means visiting all the towns. But the two aren't identical, he thinks. Not exactly congruent. Because in a classic problem you could visit the towns and completely miss out one of the routes. (See Example 3 at the end of the book.)

Fascinating! thinks Graham.

Which is where we differ.

But perhaps the analytical hemisphere of Graham's brain is starting to get some competition from the more instinctive part of his nature, wherever that resides.

On a whim he forgets the maths (or the math if you're American and thinks there's only one of them) and decides to follow a girl with unfeasibly long legs in a remarkably short skirt. But since he hasn't got a remarkably short skirt he settles for following the long-legged girl in his trousers. Of course the long-legged lovely isn't in his trousers. Although Graham wishes she was. So he follows her regardless. And who cares whether her chosen route is covering the exhibition efficiently or not?

She appears to be handing out leaflets. Graham catches up and takes one from her. She beams at him. The leaflet explains the particular benefits of a proprietary fragmentation charge. It can be dropped in a bomb or fired within a missile. Its Unique Selling Point is a sensitive altimeter which triggers the bomb just above ground level, exploding a burst of mini grenades. These shoot out horizontally for a hundred metres in all directions, before exploding in turn with a starburst of tiny fragments of phosphorous. These rip through anything they encounter, causing tearing wounds which are incredibly difficult to treat. The fragments continue to smoulder within the victim's flesh, causing shock, gangrene and terminally fatal cases of death. The leaflet describes these weapons as "ground denial" rounds. It says they render large areas unsurvivable, and because of the lingering (though ultimately deadly) nature of the wounds the weapon is also guaranteed to overload and effectively negate the benefit of any hospitals or medical facilities within a far larger radius. Like the plastic mines, but faster.

Graham catches up with the girl, and looks imploringly into her gorgeous, girlish, pouting, beautiful face. "How can you work for a company which sells these?" he pleads.

"I don't. I work for a company which hands out leaflets." Her accent is faintly East European.

"But surely this must offend your moral principles!"

She looks blank. Then she looks at Graham's badge. "Ah, a purple badge. Do you want to make fucky fucky?"

"No, of course not! That's terrible! No, I don't mean it that way. Of course I'd love to, em, give you a good rodgering. Quite honestly, of all the lovely women here, I really would rather bonk you than anybody. You're truly lovely. I just couldn't stand to..."

"You are gay? I can get a boy."

"No, I'm not, and I truly would love to give you a good seeing to. But I just couldn't do anything so impersonal."

"So."

And the girl steps closer to him and grabs his wedding tackle through the front of his trousers. Graham has a big stiffy, (deja vu?) and once again doesn't know whether to be embarrassed or not. He decides he'd be more embarrassed if he didn't have one.

He backs away, thanking her, but saying she's too good for this kind of thing, and wouldn't she be better off with her family in...wherever. "Where are you from?"

"Stirkmenhistan."

"Ah."

"Third door on the left."

253

"I see."

"Enjoy the show."

"You too."

The show continues to reveal its horrors. Much of it is couched in military scientific jargon. Some of the smaller stands are manned by crop-headed entrepreneurs with tattoos. But the overwhelming impression is that of great wealth, international contracts, and influence which reaches like dry rot into the very rafters and spires of government.

Graham wanders, in a genuinely random way.

He stops at a water dispenser on one of the stands, obviously a company overflowing with human kindness. Or perhaps there's anthrax in the water, as an experiment.

"Feeling the heat mate?" The man narrows his eyes and scans the floor like someone squinting into the desert sun to count the serried ranks of Zulus within range of his Lee Enfield.

Graham can't think of anything to say. The man continues. "First time, is it?"

"Does it show?"

The man does more squinting, narrowing and furrowing. His brow is like concrete after the men have put lines in it with the edge of a plank to stop you slipping.

"Years of training, mate. Observation. One step ahead."

"What are you selling?"

"Intelligence, mate. An' no need to smile. Not intelligence like wire taps, intercepts and that stuff, although we can supply that kit an' all. No, real intelligence. Access. It's all very well having the latest gizmo to blow the enemy into smaller pieces than ever before, but you have to know who wants to buy it. And who can afford it. And how to get to them."

"I don't suppose the Yellow Pages is much use."

The man's eyebrows huddle together for protection. They bristle around checking for incoming threats. His brow scrunches a bit more. Now it's like corrugated iron shielding a gun emplacement. The bags under his eyes are like sandbags. His eyes are like gunslits between the sandbags. His nose is like a big nose-shaped kitbag, carelessly abandoned between the gunslits.

Graham gestures around at the lethal hardware on show. "So there's more to this show than the toys, then."

"You've got it mate. In one. It's the deals. That's where the dosh is."

"Not the toys?"

"Not the toys."

"Not even the unmanned combat robots?" Graham looks over to a stand which has a gun turret on caterpillar tracks sitting in front of it. The turret swivels round, as an array of sensing apparatus analyses each passing delegate. From time to time it rumbles forward a foot or so right in the face of some startled onlooker, and barks "Wot the fuck you looking at?"

"It can do that in eighty three languages, including tribal dialects," says the furrowed one. "Course it doesn't bother in the theatre."

"It acts?"

"Damn right. Theatre of war, it's just boom! One bloke can control fifty of those, from his living room back in Blighty. Course now they're designing another machine to sit in the living room. It can deploy a

255

thousand warbots. It doesn't need to make decisions for them - they do all the on-the-ground assessment. The face to face stuff. No problem."

Graham may be mistaken, but he thinks he can detect just an inkly winkly tinkly inkling of a problem with heavily armed killing machines deciding who they like the look of and whose face doesn't fit. Just a teensy weensy problemette. But he doesn't want to be a party pooper. "So what's the hot ticket this year?"

"Back to tradition mate. Retro stuff like."

"Like Monopoly and Cluedo? And Rubik Cubes?"

"Yeah, gorrit in one!"

"So what's the must-have retro weapons system of choice?"

"Nuclear warhead on an intercontinental delivery system. Big demand mate. Can't make enough of them."

"For Iran? North Korea, or that sort of place?"

"Nah mate. Those are countries. They can make their own."

"So wh...?"

"Blokes mate. We're talking personal muscle here. Deranged religious zealots with a few oilfields and a tiny dick. Pretty big market."

And he taps his kitbag-shaped nose knowingly.

"But who would sell nuclear weapons to deranged religious zealots?" Even as his mouth utters the question, his heart supplies the answer.

Chapter 39

That evening, Graham is invited to join Grim for drinks before dinner. Grim tells him that he is entertaining a business client, and hints that the Global will be substantially wealthier by the end of the evening, God willing.

"You're a good judge of character, David," says Grim, revealing that he isn't, and therefore Graham probably isn't either. "Interesting to see what you make of him."

Graham looks over his shoulder, then remembers not a moment too soon (probably) who he's meant to be.

Grim chortles. He thinks Graham's being funny. Not many people make jokes when Grim's around.

Back in his suite Graham chooses a cream linen suit and knots a striped silk tie over a white cotton shirt. So hard to know what the right dress code is for an international arms deal. Then again, who cares what the bastards think of him. He looks through his blue contact lenses at the mirror to make sure that no dark hair is escaping beneath the edges of Boris, the blonde wig. Given the vast leonine sweep of his lustrous false mane it would be hard to imagine anything managing to outgrow it.

Graham makes his way to the upper deck where chilled pitchers of exotic coloured drinks stand ready.

He nods to the company representatives standing with cocktails in their hands like extras in a Bond film. Of course it's the representatives who look like Bond extras, not the cocktails. Which would be silly. And this is a serious party. A crew member in immaculate white uniform offers Graham a glass.

"Give me a strong one - something with rum," says Graham.

"All non-alcoholic sir. You can have peach and mango, guava and papaya, Paraguay and passion fruit..."

"I'll have a big pinky orange one."

"Good choice sir."

The man pours a generous measure into a glass frosted with condensation.

"What's the uniform for? You'd think we were on the Royal Yacht!"

"This evening sir, that's pretty appropriate."

Graham's eyes widen, then as the sound of rotor blades swells, his ears widen too. A helicopter appears suddenly from behind the bridge and his mouth widens as well. Fortunately the rest of him remains roughly the same width or he'd have a problem with his tailoring.

The helicopter touches down on the helideck one level up from the drinks reception. Grim emerges and strides across the H on the green deck to welcome his guest. The H is a guide for helicopter pilots coming in to land. It stands for 'Here'.

The co-pilot jumps down and opens the rear door. The helicopter isn't as big as a Super Puma, but is slightly larger than a Twin Squirrel. It's a Triple Wombat. It's fitted with extra carbon fibre and enriched uranium armour on its underside. This limits its range to about half a mile on a full tank, which is plenty to take it across most harbours. Fortunately it doesn't require armour on its upper surface since the people throwing beer bottles tend to be standing on the piers below.

A dark silken Suit steps out and shakes Grim warmly by the hand. The Suit's wonderful iridescent sheen is reminiscent of a petrol slick in a tropical lagoon. It fits its wearer like a glove - two legs, two arms and a large thumb sticking out of the back of the jacket. No, it fits better than a glove - it fits like a superbly tailored Suit. Nowhere is it baggy, yet when the owner stretches out his hand towards Grim it seems to release unseen material from private gussets to allow him to move without restriction. It compliments the breadth of his manly chest, providing ample room for the mats of dark hair which would no doubt luxuriate on his toned torso were it not for the owner's daily depilatory routine. The Trousers conceal the pinkie proportions of his family jewels with discreet padding. The Double-Breasted Jacket subtly masks the slight thickening at the waist which even the daily gym routine can't eradicate. (The Suit's owner specified that he wanted to do a four hour workout each day, but could only spare twenty minutes from his hectic schedule. His technicians and personal trainers came up with muscle stimulator pads which created the effect of a full workout in only minutes. By applying the pads all over his body it saved the tedium of doing one exercise after another - far faster to do them simultaneously. With further research it was discovered that the process of applying the pads was taking longer than the workout itself. So now an electrode is carefully applied to his left big toe and another to the end of his nose. He's then plugged into the mains and dropped into a pool of salty water. Remarkably he now enjoys his four hour workout in the time before his convulsing body can be hauled out by men wearing large rubber gloves. The routine is completed in around twenty six seconds. Of course he has had to work up to this, so don't try to copy him without expert advice.)

So who is the owner of The Suit, the pilot of this exquisite couture?

His complexion is dark, but of course that might just be a result of all the cruising and sunbeds. He could be of North African or Mediterranean origin, but then again he could come from another part of the world entirely. His accent might be from the Far East, but polished by several years at Oxford and Sandhurst, where he learned military techniques, made friends for life, and decided who to blow up once they'd all gone home to run their own personal despotic regimes.

What did you get at school today dear?

Dictation.

His religion might be many things, although he's probably not a Bhuddist zealot. But who knows? Perhaps being first in the marketplace is an advantage in world domination as well as business. (Although they do say that being second is even better - the first pioneering Bhuddist zealot goes bust, but the second learns how to monetise it).

And what about the non-alcoholic cocktail party? Maybe he drinks privately over dinner later. Maybe he carries a hip flask of Grandma Bangle's Moonshine. Maybe his consultant told him to give his liver a break.

But if you're reading this and recognise yourself I don't want to offend you. If you're a deranged zealot, this isn't about you, right? It isn't an insult to your beliefs, your family, your country or your religion. OK? It's somebody else. Somebody totally different.

Someone I made up. So don't come round and blow me up, please.

All this passes through Graham's mind in a flash.

Grim treats the man with the utmost repect - not as his superior, but as an honoured guest who soars the stratosphere of the super rich, an environment where Grim is on almost equal terms. Except Grim is wearing a gold-buttoned black blazer bearing the Blue Water Legend crest on the breast pocket, with an open necked white shirt and cream slacks. And the guest is wearing - The Suit.

Grim leads the way down the steps to the deck where the other guests are assembled.

Everybody watches in polite silence.

Grim walks past Rodger the Captain and Henry Hatchet with perfunctory nods. Henry's right hand twitches as if he's not sure whether to shake hands or not. Rodger salutes.

Grim looks around for someone he can trust. Not much choice. Sign of weakness anyway.

"Your Excellency - I'd like to introduce David Wilson. You may be seeing more of him."

David holds out his hands and curtseys. He's not sure why, but his legs have never met an Excellency before and are confused.

His Excellency has the ability of all Royals to put lesser life-forms at their ease. He curtseys too.

So Graham does it again.

"You are from...?" asks Excellence in a Suit.

"It's a local custom, in, er... ...Shetland."

"Is it?" asks Grim. ""Slipped by me."

The Excellent Suit beams at Grim. "I have been there. I was honoured to visit Sullom Voe. I flew into

Scatsa. Sounds like jazz-rap fusion. Looks like a muddy field. Ha ha."

"Yes, Scatsta, ha ha," says Graham.

"We passed a place which sounds like a hooker."

Graham and Grim look baffled. His Suited Excellence continues. "Mavis Grind." They look blank. "But of course that is only funny if you have heard of Mavis Grind, the place. If you look it up in an atlas it will not seem so very funny. And it will need to be a very large map, because Mavis Grind is not much more than a lay-by. Forgive my peculiar humour - your English ways are still mysterious to me."

His hooded coal-black eyes twinkle above his large hooked nose. Or perhaps it is wide and flat. And his eyes could be hooded in a more Asiatic way, perhaps not even dark, but perhaps a grey-blue, hard to tell with all that hooding going on, although come to think of it maybe it's just the way he's squinting with his once-pale Caucasian face into the Mediterranean sunlight. (So it really isn't meant to be you.)

After some more polite but frankly baffling smalltalk Grim leads His Excellency The Suit through to a private stateroom for dinner. There's some activity on deck, and Graham wanders astern, towards the quayside. Hawsers are cast off, a vibration starts to make the deck shudder (discreetly), and froth appears below the stern. Gently, the huge vessel eases forward, away from her natural habitat (the quayside and casinos) and towards the alien depths of the azure Mediterranean.

Jaunt on the briny, wonders Graham, or more privacy? He watches for a while as the coast slips astern. There are some distant islands to the south, or perhaps it's just a promontory. Soon there's bugger all to see, except sea. Well that's just fab, thinks Graham.

"It was awful," says Kerri. "I think she wanted to join in."

Jonathan Scrawl nods sympathetically. Jonathan is the son of Octavius Scrawl, Senior Partner of Squiggle Scrawl and Codicil. He is but a trainee lawyer. In fact it was he who penned the letter to Graham. Squiggle Scrawl and Codicil are a rather traditional firm. But that should not imply that they are stuffy. They have done a lot of stuff over the years, and it's been successful stuff too, but stuffy they are not. They have built their reputation on steely determination, bold negotiating stances, and complete refusal to back down in a fight. Regardless of what this costs their clients. This means that their success rate is high, and their reputation is formidable. They have also ruined more of their clients than any other litigation-obsessed pig-headed writ wranglers. But they've ruined lots of their prey too, and this is what makes the headlines.

Jonathan Scrawl hasn't yet acquired any of the knowledge or skill of his father, but he has inherited his uncompromising obstinacy.

"Did WPC Sneep touch you inappropriately?"

"She put her hand on my tits."

"Ah," says Jonathan Scrawl, trying to keep his eyes off her tits. "But it was your, erm, your Quentin who they handcuffed to the bed."

"They seemed to think he was Graham. I mean he doesn't look like Graham at all. But when WPC Sneep rushed in, his bum was in the air, and I suppose one arsehole looks much like another."

"Did they say why they were looking for your husband?"

"She used the word paedophile," announced Kerri triumphantly.

Jonathan looks very pleased and makes some emphatic notes on his pad, underlining furiously. (Had Kerri been more meticulous in her recall, what Enid Sneep actually said was 'Right you pervy paedophile bastard, we've got you, keep shtoom if you want, you filthy Peeping Tom, but stop shagging while I'm talking, and we'll take it down, and stop yelling! and if you omit to say anything which you dream up after you've talked to your lawyers you lying bastard then you'll be screwed for not telling us now and there's some schoolgirls who can sleep safe in their beds tonight oh fuck...' The 'Oh fuck' bit coincided with Quentin turning round to see who had just made up a threesome, and Enid realising that this was not the man she had been pursuing. But it was too late because Quentin pulled Enid on top of himself and Kerri by her handcuffed wrist and stuck his tongue in Enid's ear, which was when she overbalanced and mostly by accident put her hand on Kerri's boob and lay there pinned between the two of them. It took PC Brigade twenty minutes to separate them, but it must be said that WPC Sneep didn't seem in a rush to help.)

"Paedophile," underlines Jonathan Scrawl.

"So what will we do?"

"I think this calls for some discreet observation. We have an excellent private investigator who's proved invaluable in cases like this. I think if we keep tabs on your husband for a while, with still and video cameras, we will soon have the evidence we need to render our case unassailable."

"You mean nail his nuts to the wall?"

"Precisely."

"And who is this private dick?"

"It's a she. And she's one of the best. Trace McCall."

On board the Blue Water Legend Graham takes what's left of his pint of fruit juice down to his suite and throws three miniatures of gin into it. Then he finds some rum and chucks that in too. His dinner is solitary, dull and boring.

He turns on the telly and flicks through the channels, kidding himself that he's really interested in the news before accidentally (and prematurely) coming upon the porn.

The same old slapping and heaving. What new is there under the sun? He watches idly for a while, then starts to look more closely. Something is bothering him. Something is wrong. The women are pneumatic, their lips pumped up with exercise. Their silicone breasts would keep them afloat in a maritime disaster - a strange and unforseen form of natural selection.

The men have hair like Boris the wig. They have hastily abandoned plumbers' toolbags. They have bulging pecs, delts, abs and other forms of power assisted braking. But there's something weird...

"Bloody hell!" Graham ejaculated. Sorry. Make that Graham exclaimed.

Whether using their tools as hydraulic rams or presenting them for worship like little totem poles or lollipops all the men have something in common.

Never, in all his years of watching porn (out of academic interest) has Graham seen so many buff, tanned, six-pack-toting dudes with such tiny dicks.

What wealth! What attention to detail! Grim has clearly commissioned a selection of porn movies specially to make His Excellence the Suit feel good. Graham is almost impressed. He watches for some time longer, to check his theory. But eventually even the cinematographic art loses its lustre, and Graham decides to take a turn on deck. He mooches down companionways, wondering how the private discussions are progressing. If Graham's theory is correct, the runt in the Suit is about to purchase the biggest dick available. A zillion megaton one. So which unlucky neighbour is going to be humiliated and held to ransom? His Excellency will probably feel obliged to launch the thing, just to let people have a look. After all what's the point in having the biggest missile if you keep it in your pants? Then one of the superpowers will probably nuke him, just to make an attempt to revert to the previous power balance. And one way or another every one of us will be eating, breathing and pissing radiation for the foreseeable future - if such a concept is still possible.

Graham wanders down towards the bow, gravitating away from the lights and crew. Darkness has fallen while he ate, but there's a moon and the bow wave gleams with phosphorescence along each edge of the darkened foredeck. Graham climbs over a metal rail on to the deck area reserved for the matelots. This is one of the few visible working parts of the vessel. Massive chains emerge from holes in the deck and over the teeth of the winding gear. Smaller hawsers are neatly coiled, some large enough to be springs for the vessel herself, many more attached to fenders, ready to be lowered over the side to protect the gleaming paintwork. (To Graham they're just ropes and bits of machinery.)

Graham threads his way between bollards to the very front. Near the tip of the bow a small tender sits on deck, an open boat of around twenty feet in length. It sits on strops attached to winches, ready to be lifted over the side to ferry passengers ashore when the vessel's not moored to a jetty. On the port side of the ship a section of the rail has been cut away to allow passengers a route to the tender once it is moored alongside. A rope is hooked across the gap - not a scuzzy old orange nylon thing, but a length of white rope with dark blue leather bound around it. At each end is a stainless steel hook with a safety guard. By Graham's feet on deck is a buoy line laid out ready for use. At the seaward end lies an anchor shaped like the Ace of Spades with a handle. Attached to it is a line flaked out in a figure of eight pattern to ensure it runs smoothly over the side once the anchor is cast overboard. At the bitter end of the rope is a large orange buoy.

Graham leans his elbows on the rail and stares over the side. It's quieter down here among the winches and machinery, away from the intensity of business mixed with compulsory fun elsewhere on board. He just can't work out what his next move is. He tries to analyse the risk/reward patterns of his actions, but somehow his analytical brain is failing him. He hoped to learn from Grim, but all he's established is that Grim is a double-dyed bastard. Which makes Graham a bastard too. But maybe it's not the capacity for being a murderous reptile which marks us out - we must all have that capacity within us. Perhaps it's what you do with that potential, what decisions you take...

Graham is startled out of his ponderings by his mobile going off in his pocket.

"Yes, hi." The caller number isn't shown.

"David - you're not in your cabin. Fancy a drink? Where are you?"

"I'm, er, right down at the pointy end. Watching the waves."

"Cool. Down in five." And the line goes dead. Five what? A few minutes later, Grim appears, carrying a bottle of Bruichladdich single malt whisky. He sloshes some in Grim's empty glass. "How's it going mate?"

"Fine, I guess. How was your meeting?"

"Reckon we've nailed it."

"So, em, well done."

"Just some details on the price. You're a mathematical whizzo, right? Thought you might be able to help."

Graham is astounded. "How?"

"Well obviously this isn't the first time I've done mega deals, not by a long chalk. But this is a bit different. You know about probabilities and game theory, right?"

Graham nods, a look of concern on his face. Grim continues. "See, normal rules don't apply here. I can level with you, OK?"

Graham nods again, warily.

"Normally, right, with a new weapon, you test it, right? Then you carry out a trial at the client's place. Maybe let him have a couple, with a few consultants to show him the ropes. His guys go out with our guys onto a range, and there are a few bangs. If he's got a bit of

268

local trouble then you do it for real, zap a few freedom fighters, boom, there's your warranty, does what it says on the tin."

Graham feels more than a little queasy. He looks out at the horizon to try to settle his stomach. Grim continues. "So then your man buys a dose of them and blazes away, or parades them past his monuments, or polishes them in the garage, whatever. And we sell him spares, and ammunition, and upgrades. He gets the Mark II, then the Mark III, and the new guidance system, and the training for the upgrades - see what I mean. We can tweak the prices as we go along. And if business goes a bit quiet we can sell a few Mark IIIs to the other lot, so he has to get the Mark IVs or he's stuffed. So it's a nice little earner."

Grim notices that Graham has a calculating look. He has, but it's not doing sums. It's working out just how loathsome Grim's value system is. Grim continues. "Trouble is, with a nuke that price model doesn't apply. It's more of a one-off. So what the hell should we sting him for?"

Graham's gaze is a laser guidance system, which Grim is misguided enough to misinterpret. Graham tries to get the words out, through grinding teeth. He speaks very quietly. "So let me get this straight. You're flogging a weapon to this social inadequate, someone you wouldn't trust with a penknife in case he cut himself or poked it into someone's eye. And it's not just something that'll kill tens or hundreds of people. You want to flog him something which he could use to take out the capital city of his neighbours, which let's face it is a kind of use once no returns kind of a deal. And you want me to use game theory to work out what the best price structure is?"

"That's it," says Grim. "Why, is there a problem?"

"Damn right there's a problem, you cretin. What about the hundreds of thousands of dead? The burned and maimed and radioactive? What about the planet?"

Grim goes nuclear. "Fuck off and die! If I don't someone else will!"

"What about humanity? For fuck's sake, what about your own hu...?"

Graham breaks off as a bottle of Bruichladdich clunks off his temple. Unlike bottles in films which are generally made of sugar, real ones bounce off heads. Graham is stunned, but he flinched enough at the last minute for the blow to glance off. He looks around, but can't see a weapon he can use to protect himself. Grim backs off, then smashes the bottle on a winch, leaving him holding a shattered glass weapon by the neck.

"Who the fuck are you?" screams Grim. "What gives you the right?"

Graham reaches up and pulls off his wig, throwing it away. Grim looks on, astonished. Graham tugs at his eyelids and pops out the blue contact lenses. Grim's mouth falls open.

"Ever looked in the mirror and seen something you couldn't stand? Well here I am! Nobody counts but me, eh? Well maybe you're not the one and only!"

Grim looks devastated. Then he lunges forward. Graham jumps back, level with the safety rope. He sees that Grim has stepped into the coil of rope flaked out on the deck, and is poised to lunge again. With his left hand Graham unhooks the safety rope, leaving a gap with no rail to prevent someone from falling overboard. Then with all his strength he grabs the anchor and swings it towards the side of the ship. It slides, teeters on the edge, then drops over. Its weight combines with the drag of the rushing bow wave, as the salty water catches its broad flukes. As it goes, the rope snakes out after it, then a fraction of a second later the loops where Grim is standing start to close. Grim tries to jump clear, but two loops tighten round his ankle forming a perfect clove hitch which whips his foot away from underneath him. As the anchor gains downward momentum Grim slides across the deck towards the sea. With one hand he throws the bottle at Graham, then he slides over the edge. The bottle clanks against the tender and drops to the deck. Just as Grim vanishes he grabs the rim of the scupper. Only his hands can be seen, and his shouts can barely be heard against the rush of water beneath. He can hardly breath with the effort of hanging on against the weight of the anchor pulling down on his leg. "Grab me you cunt! What do you want?!"

"Everything," says Graham and stamps on his fingers.

Grim slips down into the rush of passing water, his eyes still locked on Graham as they disappear beneath the water. For a moment Graham stands gasping. The rope continues to snake over the side, and for a moment he thinks of trying to grab it to pull Grim back.

Nah, fuck it.

Then the big orange buoy at the end of the line almost knocks Graham overboard as it bounces its way over the deck into the sea and disappears astern. He hears a shout from up at the bridge, and knows he only has moments to get this right. What was Grim wearing? Graham rips off his suit jacket and throws it overboard. His forehead is pounding where the bottle hit him, and he can taste blood in the sweat which is dripping down his face. Grim had light slacks, white shirt, no tie, Graham rips off his tie and throws it overboard as

271

footsteps rattle down steps towards him, the shoes, what the hell was he wearing? Better to be safe, and Graham kicks off his shoes into the water. That should pass muster.

"Sir, are you OK?"

What about the fucking wig? It must be lying there on deck somewhere in the dark.

"I heard a shout, breaking glass..."

At least nobody will ever find the contact lenses. They scuttle for cover whenever you drop them. "It's OK, I'm fine, well..."

"Step over into the light sir. Your head..."

"Get Henry. I'll be fine in a moment."

Graham subsides onto a winch cover. He feels lousy, adrenaline overdose and probably concussion. Shit. He'd better not screw this up. In a few moments Henry appears.

"What's going on? What've you done to your head?"

"I'm fine. Or I will be. It was David Wilson. You were right. He was up to something. So I dealt with the situation."

"Where is he now?" Graham nods over the side, and Henry immediately gets his drift.

"Are we compromised in any way?"

"He's not floating about. I made sure."

"Is there anybody else?"

"No. He was alone."

"How can you be sure?"

Graham steps over and picks up the jagged neck of the whisky bottle. "I had a very thorough conversation with him before he went for a swim." And Graham throws the broken bottle over the side. "Get this mess cleaned up, Henry. And go and get the doc to stand by in the medical room. I'll be up in a moment."

"Wouldn't you be better if I gave you a hand. That head looks..."

"I'll decide how I feel," hisses Graham. "And I want the story straight. He went for a stroll on deck. We haven't seen him since. Not that we're going to report anything."

Henry nods reluctantly, and sets off back to the lights of the upper decks. Graham gives him a few moments, then reaches over on to the deck of the tender, where a large blonde wig has been sitting watching the proceedings like an unusually quiet Pekinese. Graham throws it overboard.

"Bye Boris."

For a moment he panics as the breeze catches it. It lifts in the air and spins past the bridge in a final ceremonial flypast. It performs banks and loops, narrowly evading wires and aerials, then with a final cheeky barrel roll it vanishes into the gloom. Graham steadies himself to make the climb up to the sickbay.

But first he takes a moment to inhale the ocean air and admire his lovely yacht.

Chapter 40

Graham wonders how he'll be able to get into Grim's cabin. It would look pretty limp if he couldn't remember his own pass code.

"Henry."

"Sir"

"I want you to change all of the entry keypads. I don't think David Wilson has compromised security, but I'm not taking a chance. Change the numbers, and give me a list of the new ones."

That felt quite decisive. Within a few minutes he has the list, and heads towards Grim's cabin. Henry accompanies him to the door. To his surprise there's no keypad - just a small microphone. Henry looks permanently suspicious, thinks Graham. This one must work on speech recognition. So what should he say? Graham is weary and stressed. He says the first thing that comes into his head. "Just fucking open - I can't be arsed with this."

The door swings open with a delicate hiss of air. Henry looks relieved.

"You haven't changed this one then?" asks Graham.

"No sir, it's still what you always say."

"Well we'd better record a new one then."

"Hardly necessary, sir. Your voice is unique."

"I don't want to get home one day and find Rory Bremner going through my drawers."

And the moment passes without further incident. Grim's cabin isn't a suite. It's a floor of a building. In which Graham has a very comfortable night in a great big bed, with some stewardess who appears unannounced.

In the morning, Graham picks up the phone and dialls Henry's extension. "What time did we decide to reconvene?"

"Ten, sir."

"Has the Most Excellent One had his Rice Crispies?"

"He still seems to be in bed. Either the TV's on quite loud or he's not alone."

"Playing hide the sausage, no doubt. Or in his case, hunt the chipolata..."

Henry smirks audibly at the other end of the phone. In case you haven't heard an audible smirk, it sounds like "Fhnphffff." We'll settle for that, shall we?

"Call me when he emerges."

Graham's standing right in the bows of the vessel – the scene of last night's vote of no confidence in the boss. He reckons the cabins will be bugged - even Grim's. But up at the pointy end it's all chunky machinery, not an area generally used by anyone but crew, lashed with salt spray (on the rare occasions the ship ventures out of port). His mobile seems to have a signal. He hopes nobody intercepts the call.

"Look Pate, bit of an odd one this."

"Odds bodkins."

"I have a problem. There's been a bit of a mix-up, and these people I'm staying with think I'm the boss, which means I own a multi-billion pound global empire and a yacht larger than Basingstoke full of nubile lovelies who will carry out every despicable fantasy I could ever imagine, and I've got enough money to fill the swimming pool and it's a very big pool. And I've got a suntan."

"...and the problem?"

"Well it's a bit tricky."

"Wrong wrong wrong." Pate chimes like a bell. "Tricky doesn't amount to a problem."

"Well it's a bit of an evil empire..."

"...which makes you Darth Vader. Cool."

"...which sells nuclear weapons to mad tyrants..."

"Not cool."

"There's this creepy little guy, mega-rich, wants to buy one. What should I tell him?"

Pate ponders.

"Are you still there?"

"I'm pondering. Ponder ponder."

"Should I just tell him to fuck off?"

"Methinks nay, sirrah."

Pate thinks for a moment, then continues. "There is a better way. Work out what he can afford if he sells the odd palace, then multiply it by ten. Make his eyes water. Then if he walks away he'll keep it quiet..."

"...cos it looks like he can't afford it! But what if he says yes?"

"Better bump the price up by a hundred then."

"Wow."

Graham puts the mobile back in his pocket. He returns to Grim's suite.

It might seem a sign of weakness to let His Inadequacy choose when he's ready. But Graham hasn't come up through the consultancy ranks without learning a trick or two. He and Henry convene in the wood panelled boardroom. The panelling is made from the last surviving tree of the Irokothokopoko species, a slow growing, fine grained tropical hardwood like teak or mahogany. Grim knew it was the last surviving example because he had cut down the rest of the forest, leaving a big soggy infertile hole in the middle of the Amazon basin. So now the tree is just a memory, like Grim. Its panels and mouldings are pinned to the boardroom wall. And Grim's genes and chromosomes, flesh and bones, are sitting in one of his blazers at the head of the magnificent polished Irokothokopoko table. To Graham's right sits Henry, while on his left is a company lawyer.

Each is poised, ready for action.

The clock says 11.23 am.

There is a knock on the door. Graham stands up and turns the hands of the clock back to 9.59, then he and his colleagues step through a door into an anteroom and quietly close the door behind them.

There's another knock on the main door, then it opens.

His Excellency and two of his minions step into the room.

What is going on? The dignity of his position requires that he is always last to arrive. Keeping others waiting makes him feel bigger, somehow. But the room is empty. He hears a faint noise and steps forward to look at the clock. The big hand clicks forward to the vertical. The clock faintly bongs. It is ten o'clock! As His Suitedness gazes at it in horror Graham and his colleagues breeze in behind him.

"Morning Your Excellency! How did you sleep? Refreshed I hope."

Graham pulls a chair back for The Suit and helps him to sit down. The minions are shocked at this breach of protocol. His Suitedness is still comparing the clock with his watch. It is made of solid gold and weighs about 45kg. The ship lists when he walks over to the rail. Graham and his partners set off for the far end of the table. It's a very large table, as befits such a large room. By about twenty past ten on the clock they arrive at their seats, gesturing to the minions to take a pew.

"I'd like to repeat how honoured we are to have your company."

The Suit bows graciously, trying to mask his apprehension. "Your head. You have had a maladventure?"

Graham ruefully touches the plaster on his forehead. "It's nothing. I always forget I'm on a boat."

His Suitability agrees, though since the doors into this room are about eight feet high, he's not sure which bit of the boat his host forgets he is on. Graham continues.

"We are privileged to have the opportunity to discuss matters of mutual advantage with so esteemed a guest. Let's recap our conversations so far. As always, nothing said here goes beyond these four walls."

"...goes beyond these four walls," says the recorder in the adjacent suite.

"...goes beyond these fur balls," transcribes the speech recognition system.

"Strictly entre nous," says Graham.

"Strictly entre nous," says the recorder in the adjacent suite.

"Strict Lee on train who?" transcribes the speech recognition system.

He's on form today, thinks Henry. Bump on the head's done him no harm.

"We will supply you with a number of warheads." Graham looks at Henry, who splays out four fingers beneath the table. "Four to be precise. We will also supply a propulsion system. Henry perhaps you'd like to provide the details."

Henry picks up the ball and runs with it. Then, wiping a light sheen of moisture from his brow, he continues to list the specifications of the deal. The rockets will have a range of no less then two thousand miles. There will be six of these, to allow for a maintenance cycle."

"A cycle. Yes, a cycle," says the Suit.

"You can also fire one or two with non-nuclear warheads if you fancy. To prove you have the range and accuracy."

"Good. I like this idea," says the Suit. "Better than the cycle."

"We will provide technicians and ongoing support for ten years."

"Or until you fire the first nuclear device," interjects Graham. "Then it's heads down and earplugs in."

"Yes, I see. Heads down and earplugs in."

"...and earplugs in," says the recorder in the adjacent suite.

"...a knee plug sin," transcribes the speech recognition system.

"So now we come to the matter of price," says Henry, lowering his voice to indicate that this is a distasteful but unfortunately necessary bit of commerce creeping into their friendly chat.

The Suit makes a wha wha wha sound, implying that this is a trivial matter, hardly worth discussing among gentlemen. He waves his hands as if broadcasting corn.

"Grim, perhaps you'd like to take over again."

"Sure thing. Thanks Henry." Graham takes out a piece of paper. He removes a Mont Blanc fountain pen from the inner pocket of his immaculate blazer, and writes a few numbers on the piece of paper. Then he writes some more. The visitors peer across the table to make out the number, but he just seems to be drawing little circles. He draws more. Then he draws some more. Perhaps he's doodling?

He draws more circles.

"I can lend you my pen..." offers His Exocet.

"No it's working fine thanks. I'm almost there."

Graham draws a few more circles. Then he pauses. Then he looks at the ceiling, his lips pursing in a frown of concentration. His Excel Spreadsheet looks slightly apprehensive.

Graham looks down at the piece of paper. Then he adds another circle.

He lifts the pen once more, and this time his guest flinches, just a little. So Graham plonks a full stop down on the page. Right over on the right hand side, the only place he can just squeeze it in.

Sighs of relief are heard. What sighs of relief? XXXL sighs of relief. The biggest sighs in the shop.

Graham folds the piece of paper and passes it to his right. Henry lifts the edge and peeks, then coughs to hide his reaction. Then peeks again to make sure he hasn't missed a decimal point. Then goes pale. He stands up and walks round the table to hand it to His Excellency the Suit. After a few minutes he takes a vacant seat and pours himself a glass of water. He picks it up, but his hands are shaking so he puts it down again. He sets off again, turns a corner and is on the last straight. Not long after, he bows and presents the folded piece of paper to His Eck.

Who opens it.

Then stares at it.

His hands are a-tremble too.

The recorder in the adjacent suite picks up the noise.

The speech recognition system transcribes "Te- te- te- te- te- te- te- te- te- te-..." all the while trying to recognise the phrase and punctuate it. Its predictive text algorithms are scrabbling for a match.

The Suit folds the paper suddenly and puts it down on the table to stop his hands shaking.

"...-tse fly!" concludes the speech recognition system.

The Suit has lost its sheen. Its owner looks thunderous. Warm fronts dampening his shirt have met a ridge of high pressure across his forehead. He is used to reigning, but now he needs to pore over the piece of paper.

Graham thinks the atmosphere needs lightening, so he strikes.

"Perhaps you'd like to take some time to consider."

Then he strikes again, in the same place.

"You'll no doubt need to speak to your bank."

The smell of ozone is in the air. The Suit leaps to his feet. His face is as white as a sheet. A white sheet. It is much whiter than a blue sheet or a red sheet, and a bit whiter than a pink sheet. He crushes the paper into a ball.

"I do not need to speak to my bank. I own my bank. This is my likeness!" He pulls out a banknote and waves it in the air. "I can meet your generous terms with ease. Thank you gentlemen, and good day."

By the time the proud owner of a new top-of-the-range intercontinental ballistic missile system with sat-nav, go-faster stripes and alloy wheels has stormed out of the door with the men who take care of his hench, Henry has almost made it back to Graham's end of the table.

"God almighty, boss. I don't know how you do it."

Graham smiles wanly, acknowledging the accolade.

"I was convinced you'd gone over the top. I mean he's rich as Croesus..."

("Rich as Croeses...")

("Richard's creases...")

"...but even so. What if he'd just told us to piss off?"

That was the idea, thinks Graham. But instead he says "There aren't too many other stores that stock the merchandise."

Graham suddenly feels all faint. If the slimy little pinkie-dick had gone elsewhere they would all still be in line for a nuclear holocaust. This way Graham can make sure that the warheads they sell him are useless and fall apart. And they can flog the same rubbish to his warring neighbours. Thus creating a state of MAD, or Mutually Assured Dismay. Graham realises that he's been playing a very dangerous game trying to price the deal out of the market.

"Oh well," he says. "All's well that ends well."

"All's well that ends well," says the recording machine next door.

"All swell that end swell," runs the transcription on the speech recognition system.

Chapter 41

"Bumfy wumfy! How is oo?"

On his return home Graham immediately collects Bumface from the hotel where he'd been staying (how splendid it is to be able to afford to pay for a room just for a caterpillar!), checks out and moves into Grim's house. There's no problem finding it. The chauffeur drives him there.

And there's no problem getting in. More voice-recognition, plus a touch pad for fingerprints. Peasy pimps.

Graham feels quite at home.

It is a ludicrous pad. Well, house. Well, mansion set in 400 acres of prime land within easy commuting distance of the office (by helicopter of course).

The house is a Palladian stately home with a wing on either end of a magnificent facade, making an H. It also has a curving wing attached to each main wing (making an H with a C on each end) with a further block at the end of each curve joined to it by a curtain wall (making an H with a C on each end and a little D attached to the outer edge of each C). To the rear are stables and kennels. They would cater for all the transport and sporting needs for a household of around two hundred, and all of these people are needed to maintain and run an infrastructure capable of supporting an obscenely avaricious individual and his family. And Grim is but the latest of a long line of grippy bastards. Correction. Graham is now the latest.

Since buying the house, or actually faking the suicide of its owner, Grim had restored it to its original opulence. He succeeded in refurbishing the finest original features while sympathetically installing the latest in 21st Century luxury.

Graham quite likes it. In fact for an unprincipled, loathsome shit, Grim's taste seems to chime perfectly with Graham's own. Except while Graham might admire a Picasso in an art gallery Grim would just buy it and hang it on the wall. And if that was too heavy for the plaster he would take the pictures out of the gallery, discard the building, and hang up the pictures instead.

Graham has invited Pate over for a drink. Graham asks one of the staff to send him up. The butler does a bad impersonation of Graham's voice. Graham says to forget that instruction and when Pate arrives to send him up instead. There's a lounge fitted out like a gentleman's club which Graham has spotted, and he thinks this might be a congenial place for a wee snifter. It takes Graham half an hour to find the place again, and another forty minutes for Pate to join him, even with the help of the staff and several calls on his mobile.

"You've fallen on your feet me old bucko," says Pate. He takes a swallow of his pint of Old Scruttock's Falling Down Medication. There seem to be stocks of his favourite beer available. In fact there's just about any drink there that Pate can imagine. Graham takes a large belt of Bunnahabhain, then washes it down with some Old Scruttock's.

"S'awl wight innit?" says Graham in a humourous accent. At least it amuses him.

They gaze about them at the Rembrandts and Vermeers on the dark panelled walls.

"Job going OK?" asks Pate.

"Yup. You?"

"Yup."

It's almost as if they're a little overawed.

"How did the bomb thing go?"

"Yeah, great. You were spot on. Course we won't give him real warheads. I'm thinking a dustbin full of Austin Allegro spare parts."

"Yeah, sounds good. Hang on - won't he spot that?"

"No. It's our guys that do the maintenance."

"Cool."

They take another swallow. Pate looks up at one of the portraits. He stands up for a closer look. It's Grim, painted in the style of David Hockney. He looks closer. It's Grim, painted by David Hockney. "Uncanny that," says Pate.

"I know. The eyes follow you right around the room."

"No. I mean uncanny how much it looks like you. Specially now you've got the tan and il denti perfecti."

"Ssssh."

"Ah. Mum's the word." Pate look around him and taps the side of his nose. "Walls have ears, eh?" He sits down again, this time beside Graham on a large buttoned club sofa. This leaves about thirty nine seats free. It's wonderful having a choice of a multitude of bars and sitting rooms in your own house, but the emptiness is disconcerting. It's like being in a very expensive and horribly unpopular hotel, while everyone's having fun somewhere cheaper next door.

"Try to lower your voice," says Graham quietly.

"How's the business side?" Pate's voice is deeper, but very loud.

"Quieter."

Pate tries again. This time he hisses his question in a very quiet, sibilant tone.

"How'sss the businesssss ssside?"

Graham sighs and goes back to speaking normally. "Fine, oddly enough. It's all horribly profitable. But it doesn't seem very efficient. There's cash leaking out the system all over the place. God knows where it's going. I've put a stop to lots of it."

"Very wise, great ruler. Truly you have many centimetres scribed along your length."

"It's as if there's so much cash coming in that they've never needed to apply regular business controls. And it's so secretive that nobody's been aware of the inefficiency." Graham drops his own voice to a whisper. "Apart from Grim, maybe. But he was totally driven by sales. Couldn't be bothered with the cash control side. Boring admin."

"Are you still selling the rockets and stuff?"

"I'm trying to sort it out. First thing is, I've put up all the prices."

Pate looks unimpressed. Graham continues. "By a vast margin. Then I've introduced a vetting system, to weed out undesirables. There are personal interviews and personality tests for Heads of State - Royalty, Presidents and so on - and obviously Chiefs of Staff, Generalissimos, Warlords etcetera. There's a pretty stringent exam about each country's political aims and ambitions, together with general 20th Century history. Then there's an audit of each country's human rights

287

record. And an independent survey of the people they've got banged up in jail."

"That must piss them off."

"It doesn't seem to. They all want to do the personality test, so they put up with the other stuff."

"You must have found quite a few psychos..."

"Not really. Bit worrying. They all seem pretty much the same as the rest of us. Maybe just a bit greedier, or a bit less conscience stricken. They do everything they can to build their own fortunes, and turn a blind eye to starvation and suffering in their backyard. Just switch off that bit of their minds. But it's what we do as well. The same people are suffering in the same places. We see it on the news, when the networks reckon we can take a quick burst of Third World angst. We may be part of the problem, or maybe not. But we're sure as hell doing bugger all to stop it."

"Your perspicacity leaves me in awe."

"That makes us the awed couple."

"You have been studying at the Book of Pate."

"In matters of dreadful punditry I am but your humble acolyte."

"What about the staff?"

"What?"

"I said, what about the staff?"

"You'll have to speak up just a bit."

"The staff?"

"They all seem terrified. I don't know what I've been doing to them in my other life. I told a whole bunch of them that I was sacking them pour encourager les autres. They believed me."

Pate looks quizzical. Graham continues. "I was only kidding obviously. But there do seem a lot of bodies

288

with no obvious function. Then there's the women. Half of them seem to expect me to sleep with them."

"Bummer."

"I don't think it's like they think they have to. Some of them give every impression of enjoying it."

"You mean you... Actually..."

"I'm only human."

"Shock and awe."

"I'm just not sure if they really like me for myself."

"My heart bleeds. B Positive."

"I'm trying to be. Still waste not, want not."

"Do you think there's any going to waste?"

But Graham fails to detect the plaintive note in his mate's voice. Already he's thinking about which charities will be the beneficiaries of tomorrow's corporate spending spree.

"Morning Joyce!"

"Morning sir, Grim."

"Sir Grim. Like the sound of that."

Joyce is covered with confusion.

"Morning Susan!"

Susan steps into Graham's office and starts to close the door behind her.

"No it's OK Susan. That'll wait for later. Tell the fish to relax. Time for the morning meeting. Rally the troops!"

The staff are less than impressed with the morning meetings. Graham felt it would be useful to have a general sharing of plans for the day, from sales, to admin, to IT, to manufacturing and order fulfilment. Cross-disciplinary communication. The meetings are held at seven thirty (gives us time to make a coffee first, eh?). They're strictly for ten minutes and aren't compulsory. But anyone who wants to be in the loop has to be there, so attendance is self-imposed. Hellish really, when your boss is so keen.

People gather in a loose circle, sitting on chairs, edges of desks.

"Right, Joyce - you do the white board. Now, let's start with the numbers..."

To Graham's surprise, income seems to be rising. His policy of making the company too exclusive and too expensive has clearly backfired. Which suggests he never really paid any attention to his management textbooks. Sales may be down a fraction, but income has risen. So given they've not had to make so much product, profits have soared.

"Ah Henry, you're joining us this morning!"

Henry Hatchet has slid into the back of the room like WD40 into a hinge. He looks awkward when Graham draws attention to him. "We've just been catching up on sales!"

Henry nods, his face expressionless.

"Right, good. What's next?" continues Graham.

Joyce puts her hand up. "Fire away Joyce, don't be shy!"

"Well I don't know how you want to play this, but there a journalist been on the phone. She's trying to stand up some silly story. Don't know how you want to handle this one..."

"Don't tell me - it's the Princess Di thing again..."

"Similar. For some bizarre reason she seems to think that we've given rather a large sum of money to a charity of some sort."

Henry's eyebrows rise several millimetres. For him this is an expression of astonishment and outrage. Of course nobody notices. Graham looks taken aback. "Em, she didn't by any chance say which one?"

"It's something to do with civilian casualties in Africa. She wouldn't be precise."

"Ah."

He asks the room for suggestions.

"Deny everything!"

"Threaten to sue!"

"Offer her a better paid job to keep her quiet."

"I think we'll just make like the crocodiles."

The room looks blank. Time they hung some pictures, or at least a calendar with some nice Shire horses. The people in the room look even blanker.

"The crocodiles? Dear dear, where have you chaps been? They were in de Nile." They titter dutifully, but Graham is still thinking about the 'job to keep her quiet' thing. That would account for a lot. The staff with no obvious reason to be there...

As they head back to their desks to get the day's work underway, Henry takes Joyce to one side.

"This charity thing. What brought that on?"

"Well it's a bit odd. I gave the charity a call to try to find out where the confusion had arisen, and they seemed ever so grateful."

Henry is speechless. Then he speaks. You can't trust Henry.

"Grateful you'd called, or..." The alternative is unthinkable.

291

"No apparently we've endowed rather a generous amount of money, but with the condition they don't reveal where it came from."

Joyce gawps at Henry's back as he strides off to Graham's office.

He knocks and hears a yalp from within. Then he knocks louder and strides in. Susan is polishing the fish tank with what looks like a pair of knickers, while Graham is huddled over facing the back of the office pretending to look for something on a desk.

"Ah there it is!"

Zip.

He turns round. "I was looking for a Zip file." And he holds up a computer drive thingy.

"I want a word, Grim!"

"Sure. That'll do for the moment Susan."

"Shall I come back in a while?"

"Yes. That bottom corner still looks a bit dusty. Now Henry, what can I do for you?"

Henry watches Susan leave, and waits impatiently as she closes the door behind her.

"It's this charity story. Tell me it's not true."

"Ah. I'd been meaning to have a chat with you."

"Has that blow to the head caused some sort of lasting damage?"

Graham looks at him. He looks Grim. His eyes narrow in his tanned face. He leans forward, just a fraction. "Now listen very carefully. I employ you because I trust your advice. You're not afraid to speak your mind. But that places a burden of responsibility on your shoulders. And that means you should avoid bursting into my office and sounding off before you've thought things through. Do I make myself absolutely clear?"

"Yes."

"So go away and reflect. Then we can talk, on a more considered basis."

"I'm sorry. I just..."

"Later Henry."

Henry gets to his feet. What Machiavellian scheme is Grim up to now? He opens the office door, then pauses as Graham adds "You can tell Miss Hornygolloch she can come back in..."

Graham has smugness written all over his face. But from where Henry is standing all he can see is a mug.

Chapter 42

Tracey McCall opens a Thermos flask and pours a coffee. Then glances back up through the windscreen at the street. Graham's house is a hundred yards up on the right, and from where she sits there's a clear view of the front door, and enough of the side of the house to know if anyone tried to access by the rear. Her photo of Graham Paint doesn't reveal much. A pale, slightly paunchy man, standing with his arm round his wife. It was the only one Kerri had on her, and for obvious reasons she doesn't plan to go back to the marital home for a better one right now. The photo is small, and has been scuffed and forgotten in her purse for a long time, probably since the time she liked the guy enough to carry his photograph about. He looks like Norman Normal. That's generally the case. Paedophiles often pass as ordinary inoffensive family guys. Until the truth comes out.

The plan is to keep the house under observation for a few days. A phone call to his office revealed that he had resigned, and hadn't been seen since. Very strange. Unless he had a new job. But without any information on that the best bet is to keep watch on this address, and hope that he hasn't fled overseas.

So far nobody has called at the house. The postie has been each morning, but he hasn't lingered, apart from noting the growing pile of Lidl brochures on the floor in the front porch and wondering whether to call his mate, who's a housebreaker. But there is just a possibility that Graham Paint is boxing clever. There is a car parked a few yards past the house, on the other side of the road. In it is a man reading a newspaper. The man puts his paper down, and fiddles about out of sight. Then he raises a plastic beaker to his lips, and scowls. This procedure has gone on for some days now. He seems to be paying rather a lot of attention to the Paint house. He's hunched down, as if trying to remain inconspicuous. He seems to be pale, slightly chubby, with dark hair. You've got to get up very early in the morning to outsmart Trace McCall!

"Henry, Could I have a word?" Joyce looks worried. "I wanted to speak to Grim but Susan says there's something he wants her to take down first."

Henry takes Joyce into his office. It isn't anywhere as large as Grim's, but you could still play cricket in it if you moved the furniture beyond the boundary.

"What's the problem?"

"That story. They intend to publish. They say they've checked it out and it all stands up."

"What's the paper?"

"The Hard Times." The 'hard' was to distinguish the paper from its online, telephone and iPad versions.

"But that shouldn't be a problem. Have a word with Sir Freddie. In fact I'll give him a call. He'll sort it out."

"I've already been on to his office. Apparently there's a little difficulty."

"Financial?"

"I'm afraid so. Apparently we keep him on some sort of a retainer. Or we did. We paid him something each month to... ...actually I'm not sure what it was for. But apparently we've stopped paying him."

"Bugger."

"And he's pretty miffed."

Underlying this guarded conversation is an unstated but salient truth. For years Grim has built up a regiment of newspaper proprietors, police, judges, lawyers, TV newsroom editors - a web of influential members of society. All of them have been beneficiaries of his largesse, from holidays in exotic locations for the police, offshore bank accounts for the press barons, down to more old-fashioned remuneration for councillors who wear cardigans under their suits and have building site mud on their boots. There's something reassuringly traditional about a wad of tenners in a brown paper bag, like robins at Christmas.

"Have you noticed anything odd about Grim recently?" asks Henry.

"He's been in a very good mood."

"So he hasn't been himself?"

"I think perhaps we're seeing a side of him he's kept up his sleeve till now."

"That's what I mean..."

Henry walks over to the door. Before stepping out into the general office he stops and turns back to Joyce.

"How far does this go? Where does it stop?"

"I don't understand." And Joyce is left looking at Henry's back as he strides across to Grim's office, sees

296

the closed door, then turns on his heel and heads off with stormy countenance towards the lift.

Only Henry knows precisely what this means. Graham hasn't an inkling. If the monthly payments to Sir Freddie have been stopped, then there's a long list of 'friends' of the organisation who might also be checking their bank statements with concern. The catastrophe won't be instant - they will suspect that Grim has kept hard evidence of bungs made to them in the past to ensure their silence. But everyone knows the game. If the cash doesn't continue to flow, then their cooperation can no longer be relied on. And Legend Gobal relies heavily on discretion, a PR profile of zero. Henry will have to sort things out, whether Grim goes along with it or not.

Nobody is bigger than the organisation.

Leachman Pryer has a nose. And today it is just visible over the top of a newspaper. It is pointing out of the windscreen at Graham and Kerri's house.

Leachman prides himself on his ability to see beneath the surface of people's banal public lives. He detects the seedy deceit and astonishing range of private vices which inevitably emerge when you shine a light into dark corners, turn people over and scrape away at their secret places. Metaphorically.

Usually.

Although sometimes literally.

He's not too proud to do a bit of shining, turning and scraping if the need arises. And therein lies his reputation. Leachman has a pigheaded persistence, combined with an ability to blend his unremarkable presence into the scenery for as long as it takes to peel back the layers of the lives he's been sent to observe. He dogs, he bugs, he tags, he digs, he ligs, he lies in wait.

Yes, Leachman Pryer has a remarkable nose. And he knows he is starting to make progress in his pursuit of Kerri Paint. Carver Hardball has tasked him with digging the dirt on the unfaithful wife of his client. Leachman has a photograph of his target. The client was only able to produce one. Apparently the others are in his house, and for reasons associated with his wife's misbehaviour Graham Paint doesn't want to return to his own house. But his wife might...

The photograph he was given is a strange one - as strange as he's seen in many years of snooping.

The camera must have been pointed in through a bedroom window. Some out-of-focus foliage obscures parts of the image, and there is an overall motion blur as if the camera moved while the shutter was pressed. There is also what looks like the end of a large finger to one side of the image. Kerri Paint is apparently the woman on her back. Her legs are twined round the backs of the knees of the man whose bum is in the air. Leachman believes it to be a man. But he presumes nothing. It might be a slim hipped scrawny bird with hairs on her backside. Possibly using some sort of appliance. But the client believes it was a man called Quentin. For the moment, in the absence of hard evidence to confirm the ID, Leachman will call him The Gimp.

Quentin Gimp's right wrist appears to be handcuffed to the bed head. The bed is a trendy brass repro model, seemingly popular with middle class perverts who like to combine bondage with a fresh take on a traditional style with easy wipe-clean no-fuss maintenance. His left hand is out of sight. God knows what it is doing. Kerri Paint's face is not as clear as he would have wished. There's the camera blur, but it would also seem that she is shaking her head melodramatically from side to side, making her hair fly about. And the expression on her blurry face is not (one would hope) the one she wears when shopping in Tesco. Not unless she does a lot of eye-rolling and screaming in the aisles. Her right breast is just visible - and here is the strange thing. There appears to be another right hand on the breast. And judging by the size, it looks like a woman's hand. It has a black sleeve and what looks like a black and white chequered pattern around the lower arm. Let us call this person Miss Groper. Miss Groper herself is hidden behind the thumb and some leaves, but to Leachman's expert gaze, based on the small bit visible, she might just be wearing a police uniform. Leachman has come across this kind of scene before. So to speak. The Housewife, The Gimp, and the Policewoman. Years of experience have taught him that the kind of people who like tying each other up also like dressing each other up. Then feeling each other up. Then unleashing their filthy perversion in a tide of...

Leachman Pryer realises that he is crushing his newspaper. Slowly, with a conscious control of his will, he relaxes his grasp and picks up his flask. He unscrews the lid and pours himself a cup of stewed tepid coffee.

Four days ago he began his mission outside the house of Kerri Paint's reputed lover Quentin, allegedly the Gimp in the photograph. He watched the house for an hour, before a woman emerged and made her way to a black Mondeo parked across the street. She had a lascivious air. She looked suspicious. Leachman's antennae quivered. Not the cockroach ones he wears with the costume when alone with Mrs Pryer, but the ones on the roof disguised as a CB radio rig, connected to the sophisticated tracking system in the boot. To his practiced eye the woman could be the one in the photograph – Kerri Paint. He tried to imagine her rolling her eyes and screaming, with a hand on her right breast. An untutored observer might think she looks nothing like the woman in the photo. But Leachman knows just how contorted people's features can become when distorted by lust. The woman who had left the house now shut the Mondeo door and, with a shifty look about her, she started the engine. Leachman knew he would soon establish her identity beyond doubt.

As she pulled out from the kerb he waited a few moments to let a couple of cars pass, then slid out and joined the traffic. Taking great care not to get too close, he discreetly followed the black Mondeo as it made its way a couple of miles across town. He suspected he knew exactly where it was going, so he let her get a full block ahead of him. Sure enough, she headed for the marital home whose postcode he had in his Sat Nav. She pulled in a hundred yards or so short of the house, so Leachman drove past, went round the block so that he was facing the opposite direction, then drove slowly back into the street and parked inconspicuously on the other side.

He slid down lower into his seat, and pulled out a newspaper. When he risked a squint he saw to his surprise that the woman hadn't moved. Interesting. There was that suspicious twitchy behaviour again. Looked like she wasn't going straight in. Maybe she was waiting for someone. Maybe she wanted to surprise her husband. In which case she was on a hiding to nothing. Cos hubby wasn't coming home. That's where

Leachman had the upper hand. He knew what was what.

Maybe she was suspicious. Well Leachman Pryer knows what patience is. And he can settle down for the long haul. Then the bitch got out a paper. Silly cow has no idea she's being watched. She's under observation. By a professional.

Which is why, four days later, Leachman's last drops of coffee are tepid, and there are three lemonade bottles full of pee on the floor, and he's read every bloody word of that sodding paper, and has even got one of the clues in the crossword.

Chapter 43

What price conscience?

A donation of 'several million pounds' from an unusual source has swelled the coffers of an African charity. The money appears to have come from Legend Global Holdings, a shadowy international corporation registered overseas, but known to be controlled by British financier Grim Dupeint.

Henry reads aghast, as the Hard Times thunders on.

'Families for Peace' has until now best been known for its work in assisting civilian casualties of the civil wars which rage unabated throughout the African subcontinent, while Dupeint's network of companies has build its wealth primarily from arms sales. But this donation, which is denied by Legend Global, raises serious questions about the relationship between the two organisations. Such a gift might raise suspicion that funds are being moved into Africa by a route which obscures their origins. While there is no evidence at present to suggest that this is the case it is clear that purchasers of

weapons within Africa are often influenced by generous inducements - and charities provide an obvious cover for such transfers of cash.

Henry bangs on Graham's door and opens it without waiting for an answer. Graham is studying the PC on his desk.

"Have you seen this?" asks Henry.

"Mmm. It's online too."

"Well?"

"At least they spelled the names right."

"We've spend a great deal of money over the years to prevent this kind of drivel appearing in the press. And it's worked well for us. Now you go and blow it with a cavalier disregard for the relationships we've cultivated. Why? I don't get it!"

"Oh really!?" exclaims Graham quizzically, while playing for time. "Oh really!???!!" he asks emphatically.

The last thing Graham wants is for his contributions to become public knowledge. He knows that Henry is just one of a group of powerful figures who run the company, whose personal fortunes depend on it flourishing in secrecy with its usual impersonal efficiency. The episode with Gordy suggests that it's not unknown for employees simply to disappear if their behaviour no longer coincides with the aims of the company. Graham wonders whether the boss himself might be regarded as dispensible (disposable?) if he goes off the rails. But he can't admit to Henry that this is all an accident. He can't just say – sorry, I forgot we were bribing everybody. He has to bluff it out.

"I realise that this looks unfortunate. But the company has to continue to grow. And we can't do that

303

indefinitely just by buying off adverse opinion. Where would it end? We'd have to bribe Presidents and Prime Ministers and Royalty!"

"We do."

"Yes, but we have to become more subtle."

"Subtle's too risky. We pay to eliminate risk. This is a leap in the dark."

"The company was built on taking risks. How do you think it started? How did it grow so fast?"

"That may have been true in the past, but we don't need that sort of risk now. The risk of an unmanaged press. I've been speaking to Compton and he's not happy."

Compton Coffers is the group Director of Finance, the only person apart from Grim himself who really understands where all the shadowy cash trickles. And of course Grim sleeps with the fishes. Needless to say, Graham is pretty uncomfortable around Compton.

"Compton counts it. And Compton juggles it. But Compton doesn't make it. And he could never have started an enterprise like this in a million years. So my heart bleeds for Compton and his unhappiness."

Henry holds Graham's gaze for 4.37 seconds more than is comfortable, then turns and walks out of Graham's office, leaving the door open behind him.

Oh fuck, thinks Graham.

The following day it's worse. Because all the other papers have taken the story and twisted it to take the opposite tack in an attempt to make the Hard Times look foolish. Further digging has revealed that this was by no means the only donation to charity made in the past few months by Legend Global and its subsidiaries. The press are now trying to portray Grim Dupeint as a secret philanthropist. And let's face it, the conscience stricken industrial baron who wants to buy respectability once the empire is secure is hardly an unknown phenomenon.

"Categorically. I can state with complete and utter certainty that I have absolutely no knowledge of this organisation giving a penny to any charity. The company is non-political, and we would be grateful if that could remain the case."

"But with respect, are you aware of every single payment made by Legend Global and its subsidiaries?"

God no, thinks Joyce. I don't want to go to jail. But she smiles a radiant and media-friendly smile, relaxed, with teeth, and a slight chuckle. "Of course I don't know every tiny detail. But I think if the company was giving away the kind of sums the papers are saying, I might just have an inkling. After all, that's more than just loose change, wouldn't you say?"

And her interrogator smiles and beams at the camera. "Debora Deadline, News at Ten, the City." Then she turns back to Joyce. I like that top. Is it Debenhams?"

"No, Primark. It's nice isn't it?"

By the end of the week the Hard Times is fighting a rearguard action. The paper proclaims that all these additional donations demonstrate how far the tendrils of influence reach. At the weekend, the red tops are asking just who Grim wants to influence in Battersea, and what effect rescuing homeless cats and dogs will have on international guidance systems.

By now the goods being sold by Legend are loosely described as high-tech defence systems, security shields - anything other than guns and bombs. The Grim Dupeint who has been revealed to the masses is nothing less than saintly.

"What do you make of it?"

Compton Coffers puts both of his hands on the edge of his desk. He doesn't look up at Henry, but continues to gaze down at the papers which lie in front of him. Compton has a boardroom type of face. Trustworthy neatly cropped dark hair, with dependable touches of white at the temples. Reliable square features, stopping just short of worrying good looks. A reassuring healthy tan - not a profligate international bronze, but a decent hill and heather kind of ruddiness. Team player's hands, which could wield a club on the links to modest, unshowy effect or unselfishly pass with the try-line in sight.

"It stinks," says Compton. Beneath his decent exterior lies a boardroom type of character. He's an unredeemed merciless financial psychopath. Which is why everyone can trust him to guard the stash of coins, and shaft everybody who comes in contact with the company in order to make the pile even bigger.

"You know he got a bang on the head?"

"I heard. That Wilson bloke, wasn't it? Who the hell brought him on board?"

"I'm trying to get to the bottom of that. Grim seemed to *trust* him," says Henry, uttering the word as if it leaves a bad taste in his mouth.

"That's what worries me. His judgement's always been spot-on. At least it has been so far..."

"What are we going to do?"

"Things are moving much faster than I like."

Pate walks down the aisle between the desks, glancing left and right at the empty office. He knows he has a tendency to live in his own little world in Research, but this is odd. He checks his solar-powered chronometer. It tells him that it's two days past a quarter moon waxing three weeks after the vernal equinox, and the time is three minutes past eleven British Summer Time. He steps over to the window, flips up the gnomon to just over 23 degrees to match the declination of the earth, and checks the time by the sun, remembering to rotate the bezel to add an hour. It's not a leap year, and neither Mercury nor Mars have any significant alignment.

He lifts the large mat of hair across his skull, scratches his head through the luxurious sheep-like hair beneath, and replaces his quiff.

How the hell do you tell what day it is?

Pate peers through the gaps in his sandals and checks his socks. They have Tuesday embroidered along the side in purple letters. That's helpful, but not infallible. After all, his underpants say November.

So where is everybody? Where's Des with his Zapata moustache and scalp like a knee?

He notices a movement up at the far end of the open-plan office. It's Simon Edgar. Well at least the head honcho is here. He should know what the billy-ho is going down on the street.

Pate lopes up to the desk with long measured strides. He has a hunch that we all take a pre-ordained number of steps in our lives, and if he works on lengthening his stride he will cover more ground in his alloted days. Edgar is trying to find something in his bottom drawer. He rummages away. He lifts out piles of old purloined Reports and drops them on the floor. Then rummages some more.

Time passes. It nods politely as it goes by. It passes quite slowly as if it's just stretching its legs, and doesn't really have any particular errand. Then it turns back as if it's just remembered something it meant to say, then changes its mind, doffs its straw panama hat politely and continues on its way.

You've forgotten your scythe, thinks Pate.

Time turns around. Yes the old ones are the best! I'm thinking of getting an electric strimmer, truth be told.

I'd go for two-stroke, thinks Pate. You don't want to be tied to the mains.

Time nods sagely, causing some wobbles in the space/time continuum. Good thought. I'll look into that. Well, good day. And the panama is lifted again, as time passes by.

"Ahem," says Pate. Actually the sound he makes is more of a throaty-clearing coughy thing, but I think we can agree on the 'Ahem' convention.

"Aaaarghhh," screams Simon Edgar as he leaps out of his chair, smashing his kneecap on the underside of his desk. "What the fuck are you doing here?"

"I was just wondering where my erstwhile compadres were soujourning?"

Edgar looks at him blankly. Then he looks upstairs, then back at Pate. "Oh fuck. I forgot you were in that other office. You really don't know?"

Pate shakes his head shakily.

"Seriously? It's been over a week."

"I keep my head down. I don't get many visitors."

Edgar looks deflated. "It was that bastard with the rodent on his upper lip. I should have smelled a rat long ago. He resigned."

Pate nods sagely. Then he nods like several other accounting packages in turn. He continues where Edgar left off.

"And he stole a copy of the Report."

Simon Edgar nods glumly.

"And he stole all the clients."

Glum nods.

"And all the staff went with him."

Nodding in a glum fashion.

"Like when you set up EDITsolutions."

"Exactly."

"Bastards."

"You're right. So are you going to resign?"

"Why?"

"I don't have any work for you."

"So don't you just make me redundant?"

"But that would cost me."

"So you want me to resign instead."

"Yes."

"You're asking me to resign?"

"Yes."

"Doesn't that mean *you're* terminating my employment? Not me?"

"Can't you just spontaneously see the futility of carrying on under such difficult circumstances and faced with an entirely personal but negative assessment of future prospects just decide to leave?"

"Not really."

"So you want me to make you redundant?"

"Yup."

"Sounds like you've decided to leave. In which case I accept."

They shake hands on it, and Pate goes back to his office to pack.

Joyce knocks timidly on the door of Graham's outer office.

"Em," she hears faintly from within. A few moments later, Graham opens the door a little way and slides out through the gap. The front of his trousers is soaking, as is the tail of his shirt. The shag pile squelches as he walks. Joyce glances past him and sees Susan Hornygolloch thrashing round with the fish inside the tank. She seems to be wearing some exotic pondweed, although this may be a trick of the light.

"She's doing the inside today," explains Graham. "Amazing how grubby it gets."

Joyce leads him across the office to the water cooler. "This better be good," says Graham.

"I think it is," says Joyce. "At least I hope it is. I got a call from a nice chap who works for some Government department. He asked me to go for a cup of tea and a biscuit at a lovely tearoom in Whitehall. I'll give you the name. It was Water something. Up a little lane near..."

"And?"

"Oh, sorry. You don't want to hear about tearooms do you? But it was very nice. No. So anyway it turns out he was discreetly doing some sounding out."

"About what? They won't be able to prove it."

"No silly, you are a one. No they always like to make sure that they aren't turned down."

"What are they asking for? Tell them we don't do discounts because they're a government. All of our customers are governments. Apart from the people who own governments."

"No, you're not listening."

Graham looks at Joyce intently. She really is rather likeable. "OK. So what did this geezer want?"

"He wanted to make sure that you would accept, if they offered you something. They don't like to be refused, by bolshy folk trying to make a political point."

"So what are they offering, then?" Graham is a little bemused.

"He said it was for all the exports you've won for Britain, and the sterling defence work you've done for

311

the Government, and now the charity thing. They were very impressed that you wanted to keep it quiet."

"Oh God..."

"I think they're talking about an MBE."

"Oh fucking Ada."

Chapter 44

Trace McCall adjusts the focus on the camera she's holding under her newspaper. It's not easy to get a decent shot of Graham Paint, since he keeps hiding behind a newspaper. She wants to secure proof that he's lurking outside his own house. And let's face it, nobody would do that unless they were up to no good. Tracey suspects he's waiting in hiding hoping Kerri will make a reappearance and he'll be able to confront her. Little does he know that she's on to him. And why has he got a camcorder? Does he seriously think that Kerri would reappear and do something incriminating?

Across the road, the man she thinks is Graham - Leachman Pryer, private investigator - pokes his camcorder round the side of his paper. He has it pointed up the street towards the house. But he's actually recording the reflection in his wing mirror, of the woman he believes to be Kerri Paint sitting in a car trying to pretend to be reading, but surreptitiously taking photos of the street. Just as well he's taken care to remain under cover.

Graham helps Pate up to his feet. To suggest that the horse has thrown him would be a little melodramatic. Pate has slid sideways over a period of a minute or two until he seemed to defy the laws of gravity. In these circumstances gravity has a way of winning, and resents defiant attitudes. Gravity has had years of practice, leading to starring roles in a series of television series such as 'You've Been Stupid', 'People Falling on Their Arses at Weddings', and 'Drunks Do The Daftest Things'.

No - gravity outweighed the opposition, and for the last half mile Pate's horse has been walking along with Pate hanging beneath it, his head dragging along the ground.

Graham holds the tethers of both horses, and says "Whoa boy. Or boys. Actually Whoa fillies." Graham's a natural. In another life he should have been a cowboy. Perhaps in another life he is a cowboy. Perhaps there's a cowboy Graham galloping around in this life? It doesn't bear thinking about. He disentangles Pate's feet from the stirrups and helps him to his feet.

"I think we should put them back before we get into trouble, gringo," says Pate brushing down his trousers. As usual he wears cargo pants with a sports jacket and tie, but as a practical fashion accessory he's donned spurs fastened on with gaffer tape over his trainers. They make him jingle jangle when he walks.

"How're we going to get into trouble? They're my horses. I can do what I like with them."

"This isn't the High Chaparral. Someone might object."

"Like who? Who's going to give me a row?"

"Somebody must look after them."

"Pate, you're just making excuses. Because you're crap at staying on."

"My seat is a work in progress, Kimosabee."

They lead the horses over to a fence and tie their reins to it, then sit down in the longer grass at the edge of the meadow. In the distance the end tower on the south extension to the front abutment to the side development to the west wing of Graham's house peeks through the trees. The horses pull free and start to wander off munching grass.

"Sorry about the job," says Graham.

"I was bored anyway."

"You can work for me here."

"Doing what?"

"I'll think of something. I'm so rich I can just invent something. I might start a research unit."

"OK."

There's a companionable pause while they chew stalk of grass and reckon it'll never catch on in restaurants. Then Graham ruminates, despite having only one stomach. "I've been having a bit of a worry."

"Tell me all boss. Or should it be sir now?"

"I think sir would be best."

"OK. Tell me all, sir."

"You know I told you about what happened on the boat."

"Yeehaw."

"I still feel bad about it. Tell me again, all that stuff..."

"Well, there's more than one consideration."

"Keep it simple."

"The bit about whether you can kill yourself is tricky. By the looks of things you can make another copy. You did it that day in the park. Identical twins will always have little differences, but these aren't identical twins. You and Grim were actually, genuinely the same person."

"But we'd grown different since we split up. Isn't that like identical twins having slightly different experiences during their development?"

"Good point. So it looks like in this universe killing yourself is Not A Good Thing. Because you could be bumping off another unique human bean. But that's when the multiverse comes in."

"I thought you might say that."

"The real anomaly was you and Grim ending up in the same universe. Normally when a quantum decision is made and things split into two different outcomes you'd have ended up in separate universes. You'd never have met. And it's possible that you and Grim were in different universes - just that they occupied the same place in space."

"Ouch. But I'm still a murderer. So how does that affect the morality of it?"

"Think of it this way. All that's happened is that the two universes have finally split. In one, you push him over the side - in another he does it to you. You're alive in one version - he is in the other. That's the way it should have been in the first place if some caterpillar or other hadn't cocked things up."

"So I haven't really killed him?"

"Doesn't look like it. It's the same result as if you found the offending caterpillar and opened the box to check on its health."

"But I did open the box."

"So the caterpillar isn't responsible for the Grim schism."

"I found an old packet of seeds. I wondered whether that might have done it."

"Could have done. Again, you haven't really killed Grim. It's the same result as if you planted the offending seeds to see if they were still alive. That would have split the universes too - just less dramatically. So if it's any consolation - in another universe Grim is still ruling his evil empire and you've been added to a list of his victims. Does that make you feel any better?"

"Yeah. I'm glad I got him first. Bastard."

"Quent, come here, quick!"

Quentin charges through to his living room, where Kerri lounges on the settee watching the news.

"Look Quent - that bloke on the telly. He looks just like Graham."

"Except he's wearing a top hat and tails and he's holding up a medal. How long is it since you saw him?"

"Maybe I was holding him back."

"Yeah and maybe he was a secret billionaire too."

"He couldn't be. Graham couldn't keep a secret."

"There he is with the Queen. Looks just like him too..."

In the local Police Office, where they provide Services to the Public (not the nick where they bang up villains), WPC Enid Sneep thinks so too.

"That's the last straw!"

"This makes us look like a laughing stock!"

"It can't go on."

"We'll have to do something."

"I've spoken to the others. The Board shares our outrage."

"Perhaps the time has come."

"Don't underestimate him."

"We'll have to be careful. He has a lot of people who are loyal - to him, not the company."

"I'll speak to Tone."

"Tone'll do what's needed."

"So, it's come to this..."

Compton Coffers and Henry Hatchet are discussing the day's front page. It doesn't really matter which is which - they're pretty much in agreement.

Tone drives Graham home from work that day. Tone is even more taciturn than usual. Graham does his best. "Look at the light coming through those leaves Tone. I love this time of year."

Grunt. (That was Tone.)

"Really must get this driveway seen to. Couple of potholes there. Never mind, the last seven miles aren't so bad."

Grunt. (Tone again.) Tone has replaced the regular driver. Graham presumes the other bloke might be on holiday.

"Everything OK?"

Grunt. Slight stirrings of sentience.

"Come on, spit it out..."

"Well..." Tone pushes his chauffeur's hat back, scratches his head and replaces it. The cap, not his head. His head stayed on throughout. The cap sits on the top of his head like a jam jar lid on a fat sweaty belligerent thing much larger than itself. "I met a bloke once looked like you. Wasn't though. Some joker."

And having sorted things out to his own satisfaction, Tone gets back to the driving in silence. When the limo pulls up at the front of the house Graham says he thinks he'll take a walk before tea. He phones Pate's mobile, but there's no answer. Not great reception in some parts of the house. Probably needs some more masts to cover the farther reaches. Graham enters a door at ground level and takes a shortcut through the house to the rear. This saves climbing the hundred and seventy three steps to the front door then going down four flights of stairs to reach the ground floor at the back. He makes his way across a courtyard, through an arboretum, up the side of a herb garden, past the stables, along the edge of a shrubbery full of botanical rarities, past the hermit's grotto, through the Japanese glade, round the edge of the curling pond, through the middle of the Italian garden, down the bamboo hill and into the woods.

Graham has become fond of the house. Grim's renovation and upgrading reflects great taste. At least Graham likes his taste. The artworks are what Graham would have bought if he'd had the money. Always a puzzle, how vile people can have good taste in art. And the amenities of the estate are perfect. Space to ride horses, rivers to fish in for trout and salmon, hills to climb. Birds and animals to admire and observe, even if you don't feel inclined to blast them into oblivion. From some of the craters on a nearby hillside Graham suspects Grim's been culling the deer with anti-tank weapons, and checking whether rabbits will set off landmines. It would be really helpful if he'd removed any live ones. Landmines, not rabbits.

Graham presumes that stepping on a landmine would be likely to count as a quantum event. So in one of the resulting universes relatives would grieve your scattered bits. While in the other the mine would fail to explode. And the one you'd be aware of would by definition be the one where you survived. So you can really walk where you want with impunity.

This is crap of course, and shows Graham still hasn't got his head round the concept. Because, your universe could be the one where you cease to exist, so who cares if there's another you somewhere else. And of course landmines aren't designed to kill you, but to blow your leg off. So wake up Graham!

He heads down through the woods towards the river. He likes to sit and watch the swirl of water over the rocky obstructions, and wait for fish to jump in the deep inky brown pools beneath. He hears rustlings in the woods behind him and wonders what creatures are watching. He'd be less relaxed if he guessed that Grim has introduced wild boar, wolves and panthers back into the area. But like Grim, he knows that these are shy animals who will leave you in peace. Apart from the boar. They can get a bit frisky. Oh and the black bears. Did I mention the bears? Sorry. Bears too. And a rhino.

So Graham warms to the rustling sounds, and relishes the sensation of being at one with nature - a small but significant part of its diverse realm.

He scrambles down through some bushes and steps over the rocks to the water's edge. There he sees a familiar flat stone, and prepares to take a seat. He watches for a minute or two, as mayfly dance in the sunlight. The golden beams are lighting the river from the far side, turning every tiny insect into an incandescent golden star, rendering its flicker of existence meaningful even to human prisoners of gravity. Concentric ellipses of shimmering light expand as fish rise to break the surface tension, each evolving pattern commemorating the demise of a tiny insect, like fireworks for a minor dignitary.

Graham takes in the hazy golden glow of a myriad one-day lifetimes. Then he sits on the rock. As he does so, the air above him parts with a swish and something goes kerthunkboing-oing-oing-oing into a tree beside where he was standing in a way which instantly makes him crave a cider. He looks up and sees a crossbow bolt embedded deep into the wood. Bloody hell, he thinks. I was just standing there. Then the battle juices surge through him and he resists the temptation to leap to his feet, instead rolling and scrabbling across the rocks to a new position behind a larger boulder. How long does it take to reload one of those things? Moments probably. A lot quicker than the time it would take him to charge into the bushes looking for his attacker. Graham's shoulder is killing him, with shooting bolts of pain, which is appropriate. Rolling on rocks is not a recommended pastime. Graham remembers a classic moment from all the Westerns he used to watch as a lad. He wriggles out of his shirt, wraps it round a branch which is lying on the ground, and lifts it gingerly above the cover of the rock. Sure enough, another crossbow bolt rattles off the rocks and skids into the water. It misses his shirt by miles. Graham seizes the moment and jumps into the river. It's bloody freezing. He gasps as the cold mass of water grabs him in its icy fist (metaphorically speaking), spins him round, and drags him rapidly downstream. He's already travelled twenty yards or so before another bolt splashes off the surface near his head and skitters away to the opposite bank. A few yards more and he's round the bend, with bushes obscuring the area where he was first attacked.

It takes Graham forty minutes to get back to the house, skirting round the woods in a long arc through clearings and open grazing. Crossbows are only accurate over fairly short distances. He's pretty sure he would see anyone who tried to get within range. When he arrives at the back door he shouts for somebody to find Tone. This takes ages, but eventually Tone turns up, and makes a long and effusive apology, by his standards.

"Went for a stroll. Didn't know you'd need me."

"No matter. I want you to watch the back of the house and stop anyone you don't recognise. I think we might have an uninvited guest on the premises."

The rest of the evening goes uneventfully. Graham grabs a member of the domestic staff, a bright local girl, and says he'd like a bedroom made up in the east wing annex. He tells her that she should keep this absolutely secret, and crosses her palm with a wad of notes to ensure her silence.

"That's very good of you, Mr Grim, but I know what secret means. I've always been very discreet. But that's just good manners. I do it cos I'm well brought up - not because you give me money."

Shit, thinks Graham. Maybe I'm forgetting how to trust people. It's too easy just to grab for the wallet. "I'm sorry, er, what's your name - I'm afraid I don't think we've met."

"The girl's face crumples and her lip quivers. I'm forgetting, thinks Graham. Who knows what that bastard Grim did with her?

"It's Linda," says the girl.

"Of course, sorry. I'm not feeling myself today."

"Makes a change."

What the hell does that mean?

Graham gives her his best open trustworthy smile. "I won't forget again, Linda."

How creepy did that sound? Graham's starting to forget how to relate to people. He seems to employ everyone he ever meets these days. Even Pate! How do you speak to people you don't own?

Graham spends a restless night. He puts some fresh leaves in Bumface's container, and puts him on the table by the door to the bathroom. Sometime after midnight Graham thinks he hears a noise on the gravel outside his window. He's chosen a suite on the third floor. He looks out into the garden, taking care not to show his silhouette. There's a little light from the moon. After a few seconds he thinks he sees a movement out of the corner of his eye, over beside the parterre, which has been clipped into the shape of large baroque fleur-de-lys, with different colours of flowering thyme filling in the shape in the middle of the miniature privet. By the time his eyes swivel the shadow has gone, and he can't be sure he saw anything. Perhaps a cat, or a fox. (Or a tiger, or a rhino.)

Graham locks the door, drags a wardrobe in front of it, and goes back to bed. He lies there listening for sounds in the corridor outside. Some time later he hears a floorboard creak outside the bedroom door. Very slowly, he hears the doorknob turn. He tries not to breathe. The knob is released, and he hears the faint sound of footsteps receding. He doesn't know it's a visit from Linda, who is now making her way back to bed, a little tear running down her cheek. Because Graham thinks only of himself. He has fear written all over his face. But from over here all we can see is an ear.

Chapter 45

"We need to step up security. It's not good enough."

Henry looks confused and worried. "Tell me again what happened."

"I went for a walk down to the river. Some bastard shot at me. I ran home. End of."

"Did you get a look at him?"

"Not a peep."

Henry's expression remains impassive, though a perceptive analyst might think a flicker of relief fluttered by - just the tiniest hint of a glimpse, like a bat passing Mount Rushmore. At dusk. Although obviously Henry has only one face, not four, and he doesn't look like a bunch of dead US Presidents. In certain lights he's a little bit like the one on the right, but not enough to sell postcards of the phenomenon.

"And there were three shots?"

"Uh huh. The first one hit a tree right where I'd been standing. Maybe we should go and get it. It might tell us something. We might get fingerprints off it."

"I don't think so. A high velocity round hitting a tree would spread. And dum-dum heads are designed to fragment and splatter."

"It wasn't a bullet. It was a crossbow bolt."

"Couldn't have been."

"Want a bet? Why not, anyway?"

"Well. it's not what..."

"Not what?"

"Not what..."

What the hell was Henry trying to hide? Did he know more about this than he was letting on? Graham suddenly got a horrible sinking feeling in the pit of his stomach like the time he'd got pissed at a mate's dad's flat in a very swanky apartment and had pulled a mattress into the lift for a laugh and taken off all his clothes and slept the night, and was woken early the next morning by the whole room he was sleeping in plummeting six floors which is the worst conceivable way of waking up with a hangover. The worst, bar none.

The second worst way of waking from a hangover is seeing the doors slide open and two fur-coated duchesses standing there with their mouths wide open and the security bloke shocked over the other side of the hall and starting to run to the lift and you knowing that the only way to escape was to stand up stark shiny naked to press the button for floor six and seeing the duchesses' mouths open even wider till it looked like their gobs were bigger than their bodies and seeing the doors slide shut again just as the security bloke skidded to a halt and pressed the open doors button on his side but just too late and feeling your bedroom take off like at Cape Canaveral and knowing you only had seconds to get the mattress out and bang on your mate's dad's flat's door and wish the other hungover bastards would get a move on because you felt a bit conspicuous standing there in the hall with no clothes on clutching a mattress, which seemed a much better idea four hours previously when you were all rolling around pissed.

That's the second worst way to wake up with a hangover.

But the worst way is just like what Graham is feeling now.

Graham's guts churn like mating snakes. Then there's a tap on his office door, and a member of the catering staff pushes in a trolley with some brilliant-looking food on it.

"Right, I'll be going," says Henry sharpish, and Graham doesn't like the look on his face, or the little nod he gives to the catering bloke who Graham's never seen before.

"No rush," says Graham. "Let's keep chewing this over. Over nosh. Why not give Compton a shout. He can come and join us."

"No, I don't think that would be a good idea. We should keep this entre nous."

"Nonsense. This affects the whole company. And we keep nothing from Mr Coffers."

"I've already got a sandwich in my briefcase..."

"Straight back." And Graham, points at his watch, threateningly.

A few minutes later, Henry returns with Compton Coffers. Both men look agitated.

"I've already eaten," says Compton.

"That's nice," says Graham. "Not 'How are you after the attempt on your life?' Or even 'Good day, how are you? Hope you're doing fine'. Just 'I've already eaten.'"

"Sorry sir, of course I'm concerned. How are you?"

"You don't seem very surprised to hear about it."

Henry and Compton exchange rapid glances. "I just told him," says Henry quickly.

327

"So how am I? As well as might be expected for someone who's just provided target practice for some homicidal maniac with a crossbow."

"A gun surely?" says Compton.

"Really?"

"Well, I presume..."

"What? That a professional would use something a bit more upmarket?"

"I've no idea. I just add up the numbers."

Graham looks long and hard at Compton Coffers, who holds his gaze, but with obvious discomfort. "Right, " says Graham. "Who's for some of these delicious-looking prawn thingies?"

There's a chorus of 'No, not for me, I couldn't possibly, no it's all for you, don't worry about me, you just go ahead'. You may have seen it in the West End. They had to extend the front of the theatre to get the full name of the show up. Or perhaps you're waiting for the cinema version with Meryl Streep. Graham ignores them and puts some delicacies out on three plates. "Just a waffer theen meent," he joshes.

The men sit and stare at their plates.

"On you go," says Graham.

"I'm allergic to seafood/nuts/gluten/egg/food." The last words are more of a jumble of sound than a chorus. Graham chooses to ignore them.

"Henry, try one of these caviar things. Tell me what they're like."

Graham passes one to him.

Henry looks at it. Compton looks at his feet and tries to remain inconspicuous, like a nude in a lift.

"Delicious," says Henry. "You should try one of them."

Graham glances back at Henry. There are no crumbs on his plate. He must have wolfed it in one. Unless...

Graham looks across at the fish tank. Ripples spread across the surface. In the middle, a piranha floats, belly up, occasionally thrashing its tail in a strange twisted fashion.

Chapter 46

Graham punches the repeat dial on his phone as he hurries down the street away from the front door of the office. He can't get Pate. He needs his help. Graham's on the run, and Bumface is still sitting on the shelf in the bathroom in Grim's mansion. He hails a taxi and jumps in, gets it to take him a couple of blocks till he sees another cab, throws a tenner at the driver and jumps out, then gets into the new cab, gets straight out the other side without stopping and enters a department store. He presses five, goes up three and gets out, then walks down to street level and leaves by a different door. Then sees a man with a distinctive panama hat, grabs it and hands the man a hundred pounds. He dons the hat, walks a block with a limp, places the hat on a tourist's head and steps on a bus. He goes upstairs and lies under the back seat for a while. Then he takes off his jacket, waits for the bus to stop, then just as it's starting to pull away from the stop he grabs the emergency handle on the door and leaps out.

"Bugger," he says, as he realises he's standing once more outside the front door of the office. Tone looks on, baffled.

330

"The first surveillance results are here, Mrs Paint."

"What's he been doing?"

"He's been watching the house for four days. He's sitting in a car pretending to read a newspaper. Pretty poor effort basically."

"What's he up to?"

"We're not sure. He's probably waiting for you to return. Our operative took these photos."

"Who the fuck's that?"

"Em, your husband?"

"Really? News to me."

"The first surveillance results are here, Mr Paint."

"What's she been doing?"

"She's been watching the house for four days. She's sitting in a car pretending to read a newspaper. Pretty poor effort basically."

"What's she up to?"

"We're not sure. She's probably waiting for you to return. Our operative took this video."

"Who the fuck's that?"

"Em, your wife?"

"Really? News to me."

Graham leaves his lawyer's office and sets off up the street again. He tries Pate's number again and this time gets an answer. He explains his predicament and arranges to meet him after dark. It's fairly crowded as Graham passes a row of shops and estate agents, but then the pavement thins out a bit. It's still thick enough to support his weight so he strides out briskly. Suddenly there's a screech of tires and an old beige Volvo swerves towards him. Graham doesn't have time to jump either left or right, but he gets his legs out the way of the impact by jumping upwards and at the last moment pushing down on the bonnet as it scythes through where he was standing and crashes into the wall behind him. For a second or two, the only sound is Graham thumping down across the bonnet, then rolling off on to the ground. Then a scream, and the car revs and revs and reverses off the pavement. There's a grinding sound and a smell of hot oil, and water from the radiator sprays out on to the tarmac as the car bumps back off the kerb. Then there's another screech and the vehicle swerves back out into the road. The rest of the traffic has pulled to a halt, and the crippled car has a clear run up to the next bend, where it disappears from view with a series of clatters and whines. People help Graham up from the pavement. He's unhurt apart from a bruised elbow. He thanks them and pushes his way past into the gathering crowd, then charges up a side lane and legs it away from the scene of the crash.

The car which went for him is found a few hundred yards up the road. There's no sign of the driver.

When police arrive there's no victim but plenty of witnesses, and just as many versions of the tale. But one persistent old lady says it was that bloke on the telly who met the Queen - that was definitely the one. And soon everybody agrees.

A few blocks away Graham tries a cashline machine. He doesn't have a card for all of his accounts, but he keeps a few million on hand for his day-to-day needs. He checks his balance. It seems to be fine. He's covered his tracks well. Even if the organisation is out to get him it will take Compton Coffers a long long time to work out where all the cash is going. And Graham has taken the precaution of inventing a couple of new charities whose sole beneficiary is himself.

Chapter 47

"Where's Grim? I think you should come straight away."

"Who says?" asks Henry.

"It's a bit confused.," says Joyce. "There's loads of them."

"Tell them to go away."

"You can't. It's the Police."

"Christ alive." This is a disaster. This all comes from Grim losing the plot and stopping the payments. For weeks Compton's being trying to reinstate them, but there may be some substantial sabre-rattling before the pay-offs are sorted, as pissed-off bribees try to push the rate up.

Henry and Joyce make their way downstairs to the little-used side reception area, where Joyce has tried to tuck the fuzz out of sight. If only there were a full Brazilian for police, thinks Joyce. They are guided to their destination by a rising rhubarb of Allo Allo Allo Allo Allo Allo Allos. As they hove into view the noise becomes hypnotic. Equally hypnotic is the bobbing up and down of dozens of capped heads as knees are rhythmically bent and straightened.

"Right ladies and gentlemen. How can we be of assistance?" asks Henry, convinced that a solution can always be negotiated (i.e. purchased) once the agenda is clear, but still clenching his buttocks on principle.

Several officers speak up simultaneously.

"I have a warrant for the arrest of Grim Dupeint who we have reason to believe escaped from Police custody on the afternoon of...

"I have a warrant to search the premises and am authorised to examine and remove any documents relating to Legend Global Holdings splv or its subsidiaries, associates..."

"I am investigating a hit and run incident this morning on the Hilltown by-pass and a witness..."

The police lurch to a halt and look at each other suspiciously.

"What are you doing here?"

"This is my case."

"It's a different case, you nonce."

"Which nick are you from then?"

"Please, ladies and gentlemen. One at a time. What are the accusations?"

"Stalking!"

"Paedophilia!"

"Assault!"

"Resisting arrest!"

"Attacking a Police Officer..."

"Money laundering, fraud, corruption, bribery, illegal international cash transfers, proscribed arms sales..."

The third officer shuffles his feet. "Leaving the scene of an accident?"

"Oh fuck off out of here," say the others.

Chapter 48

Graham peers through the bushes, as he tries to work out which lights indicate a person in a room, and which are there to make the place look occupied. It's such a warren. Who knows?

"I'm still not entirely sure what I'm doing here," whispers Pate.

"Thank God there's something you don't know," replies Graham, a little unsympathetically it must be said. Perhaps his attitude reflects the fact that he's still wearing a blue pinstripe suit - the only clothing he can lay his hands on without being shot, mown down or arrested.

"I agree that there are many unanswered metaphysical conundra which may for ever remain cryptic and incognizable. But in the here and now I presume you have a role for me, a cameo, a guise, a task..."

"Shhh. I need you to help with the ladder."

Graham leads Pate through the shadowy yew corridors, through which neither moon nor infra-red CCTV penetrate, towards the garden shed. It's not so much a shed as a centuries old industrial warehouse designed to house the hand tools, harrows, seed drills, mowers, hay carts and ploughs needed to tend the estate. The weathered wooden door creaks open on its rusty ancient hinges. After a couple of noisy trips over rattlesome balers and broken earthenware plant pots Graham manages to locate the extending ladder he'd spotted a few weeks ago on his explorations. He's glum indeed to be scrabbling about on his own estate in the dark. He'd started to feel that it was home, that he'd earned the right to live there. How appalling that he should be chased off the premises by a hideously ungrateful organisation and its psychopathic enforcers. After all - he was the boss! He'd made it what it was! Or at least Grim had, and that was almost the same. Graham isn't inclined to back off without a fight. But the odds seem heavily stacked against him.

They grab an end each and start to clatter their way back towards the door. It's starry moony dark outside, so inside the shed it's even darker. They clang their way outside and scrunch along the gravel to a section of wall below the rooms where Graham spent his last night in the house. It's not easy to extend a three part extending ladder at the best of times. But with two incompetents trying to manage it in the dark it's harder still. They think they have it cracked, but it seems the ladder is upside down, so when Graham tries to climb it, the sections telescope shut with a rattling of ratchets on rungs that mimics a First World War Gatling gun. Fortunately the nearest person within the house is about half a mile away, and nobody hears. Several large guard dogs come loping up and go for Graham's face as he lies defenceless on the ground tangled with the ladder. Dobermans, Alsatians, Akitas, Rotweillers. They lick him and slobber all over his chops.. They know he is Grim. They can smell him. They're just so pleased to see him. (Their night vision's better than his.)

337

They growl and snarl at Pate, until Graham tells them to behave. Which they do. Grim was top dog. And Graham's learning to fake it.

"I think we should try it the other way," says Graham.

"As in go home now and think of a better plan?"

"As in this way up."

They wrestle with the ladder and this time it stays put.

"Now I'm hoping this won't take too long," says Graham. "He's in the bathroom."

Pate nods invisibly in the dark. Graham has to find Bumface. He still has the packet of seeds which he believes were responsible for him and Grim becoming two different people. He's unclear what part the seeds are playing in this confused tangle of multiple universes. Surely Schrödinger's Cat was a mind experiment? It wasn't meant to cause all these real-life phenomena. But he fears that in the wrong hands the packet of seeds could cause him to disappear in an instant. He cannot take the chance. Pate has tried to explain, but Graham guesses that Pate's surmises are conjectural.

"Put your foot against the leg of the ladder," says Graham. He knows that the optimum angle for the ladder is with the distance from its foot and the wall between a third and a quarter of the distance from the ground to its highest point. Strange how the analytical side of his nature keeps popping up. But somehow it's there in an advisory capacity these days rather than playing the didactic autocrat. In other words he can listen to the words of wisdom, then ignore them. His instincts are different. Instincts aren't for listening to. They just cut in and kick him into action. He wonders if they talk to the scientific bits of his brain while he's sleeping. As often as not, his instinct proves to be right. But presumably there are universes full of dead Grahams with rubbish instincts. Perhaps the anthropic principle holds sway. The one which answers the question 'Why is this earth and this universe so perfect for humans?' by saying 'Cos if it wasn't we wouldn't be here asking the question'. This always struck Graham as being a pretty spurious argument. Particularly if there is only one universe. It's just a crap explanation of why this one particular universe is the way that it is. Like someone swimming in a crocodile-infested river saying 'Why is this river so perfect for swimming in?' By the anthropic principle the answer would be 'Because if it wasn't you wouldn't be splooshing about and asking the question'. But that's obvious bollocks - just an accident of the timing of the question. Cos right at that moment a honking great croc might be in the process of tucking in its napkin and saying grace.

Now, if you allow the possibility of multiple universes it might make a bit more sense. Then instead of asking the question 'Why is this earth and this universe so perfect for humans?' you should ask 'Out of all the universes which mercilessly (or mindlessly) exterminated every form of life at every stage of development (up to and including the ones which let us get to the mid 20th Century before Kennedy misjudged the Bay of Pigs and humans nuked the Earth) how come I pick the uniquely weird one (with surviving humans) in which to start asking silly questions? Answer: Because all universes simultaneously exist, and you're asking the question in the one where you're alive. And the people listening to you are there too. But don't forget just how profoundly unlikely the whole scenario is. Anything which is possible is also in existence. No matter how improbable. It's all true true true. By definition there is also an equally likely universe among the infinite choices where giant slugs are sitting round the dinner table saying 'I have that problem with humans eating my lettuces too. What you do is make a human pub out of a swimming pool full of beer. They start supping round the edges and before you know it they get pissed and fall in and you find them in the morning all bloated and pale grey.'

'Bit of a waste of beer! Haw haw.'

'Strangely, it improves the flavour.'

So, back to the ladder, and Pate puts his foot against it. Graham climbs up until he reaches the edge of an up and down section of mock battlements.

"I've got to the castellated bit," he hisses down to Pate.

"No you haven't."

"Yes I have – look." And Graham waves over the edge, down into the darkness.

"That's not castellated," Pate hisses back.

"Bloody is. Here's a wee dent for archers to shoot out."

"Bloody isn't castellated."

"You're denying the blatantly obvious."

"It's only obvious if you're an ignorant plonker. 'Castellated' means having battlements and turrets like a castle. How can battlements have battlements? If you were less dim you'd know it was crenellated, because that means having notches like a battlement. Which sounds spot on."

"You're the one who sounds noxious."

"Notches, you twat, otherwise known as crenels. Look it up if you don't believe me."

Graham believes him, but doesn't give a shitty poo.

He heaves himself over the edge and lands on a flat section covered in lead sheeting. He knows there's a drainpipe somewhere near which leads up past the window of the bedroom he was sleeping in. He feels for it in the shadow. He's able to get his fingers in behind it, and further up there's some ivy which will help. He glances up at the window and starts to climb. The window he's after is not the one immediately above him, but the one above that.

Oh well, he thinks. If I've understood correctly, the universe I'm in will always be the one in which I survive. And the one in which I'm killed doesn't matter. Of course Graham's too dim to consider the universe in which he survives in a wheelchair, but his ill-thought-out hypothesis reassures him, and he makes it up the wall. Opening the window from the outside proves tricky, and he's glad he has the ivy at this point to allow him to hang on with one hand while he wrestles with the sash with the other. He left the window open an inch or two last time he slept here, so he gets a purchase and manages to slide it up. He slithers in head-first, and ends up in a heap on the carpet.

He wonders whether he should put on the light. He scrabbles about for a bit and decides he has no choice. He finds the door to the bathroom and locates the pull cord for the shaving light.

The shelf where he left the caterpillar's box is empty.

He looks on the floor.

Nothing.

He scans around increasingly frantically, and then he notices the towels. They hang neat, crisp and fluffy from their rails. Not in a damp pile over the edge of the bath where he left them.

Bugger! The maid's been in. So Bumface has been chucked! What the hell is he to do? He can't abandon Bumface. His fate may hang in the balance! Or perhaps not. But that's the damnable thing about balancing fates. Damoclean Sword juggling. You just don't know what's going to make a difference. So you can't neglect anything which might help. Hence lucky rabbit's feet. And lucky bracelets. And religion. (Although any religion followed by commendably devout and decent sorts with access to explosives is clearly not included in this loose generalisation and you have every right to worship in the true faith and may you go in peace with my blessing.)

Graham opens the door to the corridor. He looks both ways. Shifty, then insouciant. He prefers insouciant, perhaps with a touch of je ne sais quoi, and a dash of élan. But his face keeps doing shifty, so he decides to settle for that.

At the end of the corridor to the right is a tee junction, with some dim light just picking out the walls. Had it been a tea junction he might have stopped for a cuppa. But that is not on life's menu. Facing him in the centre of the junction is a door which might be a cupboard. He pads along the corridor and tries the handle. It's locked. He looks about. To the left is another door. This one opens. It's another bedroom. He backs out and heads along the corridor to where two more corridors meet. A flight of stairs leads upwards. There's another little door under the stairs. It has a corner trimmed off diagonally to fit. He tries the door. It opens. It's a cupboard. He fumbles for the light, finds a switch, and clicks it. In the cupboard are buckets and mops and plastic bottles of bleach and furniture polish and three bulging blue plastic bags with drawstrings. He decides to drag them back to the relative seclusion of his own ex-bedroom.

After an hour and a quarter he manages to find it again.

He drags the bags into the bathroom and switches on the shaving light again.

Then he opens the first bag and empties it into the bath. Blehhh. It's gross. If the bedrooms aren't used very often it must take years for a full bag load. And there are three! There are decaying sandwiches, plastic wrapping, paper, assorted crud. The food isn't even mouldy any more. It's more - mummified. Graham plucks up his courage and rummages. Then he puts down his rummages and scavenges through the mess. There's nothing that resembles Bumface's box.

He picks up the second bag and tips it out onto the floor.

Sorry, Linda, he thinks. I'm really off your Christmas list now.

You know how you always find lost things in the last place you look? Well in this case that was the second bag. Because once he'd spotted the box, he was hardly going to open the third bag through a sentimental attachment to his old paper hankies, was he?

He grabs the box, and decides against opening it. He's becoming increasingly nervous of the unpredictable effects of quantum physics.

So he puts it carefully inside his jacket, and heads back to the window.

Going down is easier.

Mostly he falls.

Pate is asleep on the ground, dutifully continuing to anchor the foot of the ladder by lying against it. Graham lands on him, which obviates the need to wake him quietly.

They look around into the shadows, but there's no sign of anybody stirring. Or shaking. Or blending or liquidising. In fact there are no obvious signs of food preparation at all.

"Right. If we head due west, then there's a fair bit of farm land. That should be easier going. There's a woody bit first though."

They take down the ladder and stuff it behind some bushes. Then they set off across four or five acres of lawn towards some trees, whose outline can be dimly made out against the lighter black of the sky. Once they get to the wood it takes them an hour of crashing through undergrowth and barging into tree trunks before they start to glimpse pasture beyond. They make their way to the edge of the wood and clamber over a drystone wall into a patch of nettles.

"Did you know that nettles are often a sign of human habitation, centuries ago?" asks Pate.

"Fuck, shite," says Graham.

"They flourish where the ground has been disturbed - particularly where there is rubble just below the surface."

"Arse, bastard," says Graham.

They walk over an uneven stubbly bit and get on to an area which has been ploughed. It seems to be rough grazing of some sort, though Graham can't make out any sheep or cattle. About half a mile ahead there's another stand of trees. They decide to head in that

344

general direction. They trudge on for quarter of an hour or so.

Graham's heart starts to lift. It feels like they're going to get away without any confrontation. Remember this is a book, though. It would be a dereliction of authorial duty to give them an easy ride. There are probably laws against it - certainly fines from public libraries or some sort of writers' collective action which would send the guilty party to Coventry, were that not the kind of cliché which would in itself incur sanctions. And writers never do anything collectively. That would fly in the face of their soaring free spirits. Which would be another couple of clichés, which decent writers avoid like the plague.

So anyhoo...

"What was that?"

Graham hasn't seen anything. But Pate is wearing a plastic head-attachment binocular set which came with a copy of the Beano. He is not a man to be challenged, in matters of nocturnal ocular perspicacity, or astucity as he might put it.

"There, just in front of that bush. The one that looks like a clump of pubes."

"Male or female?"

"Anthracite," says Pate, demonstrating that he does have a sense of humour, albeit obscure.

Graham peers into the darkness. He can make out a bushy shape - a kind of Payne's Grey against the Lamp Black of the woods behind. He stares, until his eyes go blurry. Then he hears a noise. It's a snorting, coughing, bad-tempered kind of throat clearing, that in the natural world usually conveys the message 'Who the hee-ell do you think you are barging into my local hostelree with your oh-so-fine city ways and that get-out-of-my-way-scum look in your eye? I'm minded to teach you uppity trash a lesson.' That's the mammalian version. The reptilian one is more like 'Bend over and kiss your ass goodbye, lunch!'

When you hear a snort like that you stop and squint. And start whispering.

"There. It did it again."

Graham continues to watch, as his guts turn to Scourbog's Drain Cleaner with added biological action.

A shape starts to separate from the bush. If it had a hoof, Graham could have sworn it was hoofing the ground with it, sending up little gusts of dust.

"Pate. What do we do?"

"It's pretty straightforward," says Pate, in a watery-bowelled kind of voice. "You don't have to be able to outrun it. In the words of the old but oh-so-true jest, you just have to be able to run faster than the bloke standing next to you." And so saying, Pate turns and scarpers. Graham stands just long enough to see whatever it is start to move towards them, then he turns and flees in Pate's wake. Graham glances over his shoulder as he gets up speed, and is horrified to see the beast more clearly as it separates from the shade and starts to cross the meadow. Its two vertical horns and top to toe armour plating clearly identify it as - shit, I'm not sure. Something horny and armoured. An armadildo? But Graham has a theory. Oh my God, thinks Graham - these things go at forty miles an hour. Which is when he trips and falls on his face. Pate might have run back to help him if he'd noticed, but of course he's not daft enough to run while looking backwards. Or look backwards while running.

Graham hears the thundering of hooves or little dainty grey leathery feet or whatever these bastards

346

have, and can feels the ground shudder as the beast gets closer and closer. Its head is lowered to get the horns at the optimum goring angle. Its little piggy eyes are bulging like hernias.

It's twenty yards away.

It's heading for Graham like a four wheel drive.

It blows up in a bone-shaking ear-drum-ripping supernova of flame, butcher's counter and leather goods.

The blast sears over Graham's flattened body and knocks Pate to the ground some fifty yards further on.

"," says Graham. He can't hear his own voice.

Chapter 49

Graham leaves the clothing store carrying a large plastic bag full of jeans and tee-shirts and trainers. He would have bought tea shirts, but he's still stung by the disappointment with the tea junction. Apart from these clothes all he possesses is the tattered suit he stands up in, a box with a caterpillar in it and several bank accounts containing untold millions. He spots a public toilet where he can change. As he walks in, he notices a man washing his hands very slowly. The man's eyes dart in Graham's direction, then back to his hands, rubbing damply together like reckless gay celebrities in a public bog.

Graham enters a cubicle. He takes off his suit trousers, hangs them on a hook behind the door and opens the plastic bag. He pauses as he hears a scuffling noise from just outside the partition. There's a gap between the partition and the floor, labelled 'Beware limbo dancers!'. He hears a faint click. As a precaution he takes his credit cards and the matchbox containing Bumface and slips them down the front of his underpants. Out of the corner of his eye he thinks he sees something move right down by the floor. After a pause, he takes off his jacket and shirt and selects a tee-shirt from the bag. Suddenly a hand darts out from beneath the partition and snaps a handcuff round his ankle. Graham tries to pull his foot clear, but the other end of the handcuffs is snapped shut on the cold-water pipe leading to the cistern. Graham yells.

"Hoi!"

Then "What the f..."

Neither of these featured in the 'Hundred Greatest Responses to Being Shackled by an Unknown Assailant' TV special. Graham tugs at the handcuffs. This hurts his ankle a great deal, but doesn't seem to cause any pain to the water pipe. Then a yellow canister rolls under the toilet door. On it Graham sees a picture of a wasp and a number of illustrations implying danger, such as a skull and crossbones, a nose with a big red cross through it, and a rather literal depiction of a man vomiting several yards of intestine and enough internal organs to make a rather fine haggis. Then in a flash (rather appropriate given the location) the top of the canister blows off and everything is obscured by billowing clouds of smoke. Graham leaps over the door.

We'll skip the bit about the savage excruciating pain in his ankle because it doesn't bear thinking about.

Clouds of smoke roll into the street. From their midst (and mist) bursts Graham. He wears underpants, socks and shoes and he's dragging a length of pipe from one leg. At the other end of the pipe is a Victorian cast-iron cistern, from which water streams onto the pavement. The cistern catches on a parking meter, and fortunately for Graham the handcuff slips off the broken lower end of the pipe, thus releasing him (from bondage if not from acute embarrassment). The cistern makes a sonorous clang. Behind the high wall which flanks the street several monks start to chant their prayers several minutes ahead of schedule. God puts down the paper and his cup of tea and pretends he was paying attention.

At the far end of the street a man is running away. At the sudden outburst of Gregorian plainsong the man glances back. Graham sees the man's face.

It is his own. Except much paler, without the expensive dentistry, and fringed by hair which could do with a decent trim. Bit of a pallid hippy, in fact.

Oh shite. Here we go again.

The man turns and runs towards a parked bicycle. Graham runs after him. Pausing only to unlock the chain which secures it to a railing and to don a pair of plastic cycle clips and a helmet (which he straps securely under his chin) the man jumps on to the left-hand pedal, pushes off, and swings his right leg over the saddle as he speeds down the road. What a poser.

Graham runs after him in his underpants, the handcuffs clattering at the end of his leg. Ahead Graham spots one of those suicides on wheels - a man lying on his back on a thing like a skateboard with a pair of pedals mounted so he can push them horizontally. At the back of the wheeled open-air coffin is a whippy little mast thingy sticking up to about waist height, and on the end of it is a little orange flag. The man on the shin-high death bike reckons that articulated lorries which have difficulty enough spotting cyclists at the best of times will notice a poxy flag the size of your hand - and take avoiding action. Most of the time with these contraptions the flag isn't seen, making the fatality spectacularly gruesome. In the rare cases when the flag is seen in time it just gives motorists something to aim at. The cyclist doesn't even have the benefit of pushing down on the pedals using bodyweight and gravity. But since the typical user is an anorexic twat with sinewy teeth and a lightweight brain this doesn't seem to dawn on them. In the few weeks before they get mashed into the tarmac.

Graham sees no other option but to commandeer the vehicle. Anyway he reckons the supine death pedaller is asking for it. In fact, by stealing the man's wheeled morgue-trolley he might even be saving his life! Graham grabs the blood donor by his wispy greying beard and yanks him off the contraption.

"For your own good, mate!" he calls as he throws him into the gutter and jumps on. It's like lying on a roller skate. He lifts his knees up to his chin, grabs what he assumes is a tiller and pushes the pedals. Ahead, the man who looks like Graham is pedalling off into the distance on a proper bike. The brain-dead horizontalist tries to grab Graham, but only succeeds in pulling off the little mast thingy with the flag on it. Graham pedals off and disappears round a bend after his death-dealing doppleganger.

The man in the gutter yells. "Hoi!"

Then "What the f..."

Neither of these featured in the 'Hundred Greatest Responses to Having Your Horizontal Bike Boosted by a Random' TV special.

The man waves his little flag aloft, and is pancaked by an articulated lorry who thinks he's a legitimate target.

Graham pumps and pumps. He is gasping with exertion, and sparks are flying from his trailing handcuff as it clatters off the tarmac.

Doppelpeddler keeps glancing backwards, but can't see anyone following him. There's not even a stupid little orange flag to give away Graham's position. From ahead all that can be seen is the soles of two feet, and a couple of eyebrows peering over these. Graham is lower than a hubcap. The man literally overlooks him.

The pursuit lasts for a couple of miles. At one point the man flies through a set of traffic lights just as they turn to red. Graham still hasn't found the brakes. A lorry pulls out across his path. Graham skims beneath it, between front and back wheels. A car crosses in the opposite direction. Graham flies beneath that too. There's a white line across the road, and Graham almost slides under the paint. But not quite.

The surrounding streets are more and more run-down, though not as run down as the limbo bike's owner. Graham becomes increasingly sure he knows where they're going. He recognises landmarks from his childhood - a Victorian neighbourhood of factories and brick-built terraced workers' houses. At last, the man turns into a tatty residential street. The front doors open on to the pavement, while at the back of each dwelling is a tiny paved area enclosed by a brick wall and back-to-back outside toilets, now mostly converted to tool sheds. Graham knows instinctively which one the man lives in. He puts his heels on the ground and follows the man down the back lane, where he manages to come to a halt behind a parked van.

The man brakes to a halt, opens a wooden door in the brick wall at the back, and props his bike on the cracked concrete slabs.

Graham recognises the house where he spent his childhood.

At the time it felt cramped and scruffy, but while she was still alive his mother did her best to keep it scrubbed and dusted, like Graham. Graham didn't dust the house, obviously. She dusted him. Obviously after she died she was less effective, and his dad had never been a paragon of domestic virtue. The house went downhill while Graham was at university. But his father was unemployed and couldn't afford to have the foundations propped up. The cleaning regime went downhill too.

Now it just looks squalid. Couch grass and Rosebay Willowherb sprout from every crack in the paving and masonry. At roof level there's a small sycamore starting to take root in the damp-stained brick wall below a broken gutter. A window pane above the metal sink in the back room has been broken. Instead of a new pane of glass, there's a bit of plywood which was obviously meant to be temporary some years ago.

Surely not that long ago...

Graham remembers the crash of breaking glass the awful day he left home. Angry words had been said. Words had been said angrily. The row was prompted by the discovery that Graham's tortoise, Methuselah, had gone missing. His father had accused him of abandoning it while he was away studying. With the pompous self-righteousness of a twenty year old who knows he's meant for better things Graham had described the family home as a dump, and no place to keep an animal. For years Graham had kept his head tucked in, but that day he really came out of his shell.

His father completely lost the plot and threw his plate at him. It wasn't very heavy, but the row of even plastic teeth round the pink plastic gums made the denture an effective weapon. It ricocheted off Graham's temple and smashed a pane of the kitchen window.

'Youwam idle ufeleff toffer!' his father had shouted gummily. 'How dawe you accufe me of not wooking afster you!' He retrieved his dental plate from the contents of the greasy washing up basin and put his

353

teeth back in. 'I've worked my fingers to the bone to give you all this!' Then he took out his teeth again and removed the used teabag which had been jammed between the plate and his palate. Then he decided it was more comfortable the first time and put the teabag back in.

When he got up off the floor Graham stomped out, never to return. His drive to succeed in business was built upon a burning desire to prove himself right - to demonstrate that he could do better than his father. Much, much better.

When his father had died, not long afterwards, Graham had paid a firm of industrial cleaners to empty the place, then he put it on the market without ever going back. He had no regrets. But now he is starting to regret having no regrets.

Across the lane, Graham notices a building standing derelict. Its rear windows face out across the enclosed yards to the back of his former house. Graham waits till the mad hippy who attacked him is safely indoors, then clambers over a wall and through a nettle patch to reach the empty house. He manages not to scream at the nettles, but takes the precaution of grabbing a handful of dock leaves as he pushes open the back door. The top hinge pulls away from the crumbling masonry, but he manages to wedge it shut again once he's inside. Then he shouts 'Ah! ah! ah!" (commendably quietly) and rubs his skin vigorously wherever the nettles have reached. Which is basically anywhere not protected by socks, shoes and a pair of underpants. This scouring and scarifying relieves the pain a little, but leaves his blotchy skin covered in sap-green streaks.

All day Graham watches the house across the lane. He becomes rather chilly. The carpet in the derelict house has long gone, but he finds some ancient foam underlay, flattened as thin as cardboard through years of use. It has tyre treads across it. In fact it's indistinguishable from the man who lent Graham the horizontal bike. Graham wraps it round himself

From time to time he catches glimpses of the homicidal maniac across the road. From the canister he threw into the toilet he may be an insecticidal maniac too. Graham can't believe his bad luck. All he wanted was to realise his true potential, make loads of dosh and get his life sorted out. Admittedly he'd pushed Grim Dupeint overboard, but the man had it coming, and anyway it was really a bad version of himself, so the deed was morally defensible. Not murder. Not even bad. Barely naughty. But now, not only was he being chased by murderous hitmen from Grim's evil corporation, but he was also under attack from a deranged hippy version of himself. Loser bastard! He pulls the underlay tighter round his shoulders and watches. He's lost his mobile so he can't contact Pate and he can't go very far with no clothes. Actually he's just come several miles with no clothes, but he doesn't plan to repeat the experience.

There are other people across the road.

There's a woman.

There's a small boy.

There's a smaller girl.

They come out to play in the sunshine in the scabby little back yard. As a working hypothesis, he assumes they may be related in some way.

The girl looks a little like himself. She has eyes he recognises immediately.

The boy looks even more like himself. He has a nose and mouth which are instantly familiar.

The woman looks like the girl next door who he left behind when he stormed out of the house, never to return.

Until now.

Which is not really 'never'.

'Never' is an impossibility in a multiverse. But he wasn't to know that at the time.

The woman watches the children stick little plastic eyes, nose and mouth into a large baking potato. 'That looks strangely familiar,' she joshes.

"It's Daddy!" says the little girl.

"I can see that," says their mother, lovingly. "What did you use for hair?"

"One of the vests Daddy knits from yak wool," says the boy. "But daddy doesn't have as much as that," he chortles and pulls most of it out again.

"That's even better," jests Mummy, and they all laugh and laugh and hug each other. Then 'bolt from the blue' maniac man joins them, and they laugh again and hug him too. The man has changed into a gay multi-coloured knitted Peruvian hat with earflaps and an old pair of sandals. Which are a strange adornment for a hat, but in keeping with his overall fashion sense. His socks are multicoloured too. One says Monday in pale blue lettering along the side, but written in Tibetan. Graham assumes the other one says the same, unless this loathsome person has an even wackier sense of humour than Graham imagines possible. He probably has matching boxer shorts marked Year of the Monkey too.

The woman's name is Emma. She's lovelier than Graham remembers. Graham tried it on with her a few times, but Emma found him shallow, and lacking in principles.

356

"Tell me what principles you'd like me to believe in," said Graham. "I can do it!"

"They need to come from within yourself," she said wistfully.

"I can do that - I just need a hint..."

"You don't really believe in anything, do you?"

Graham was puzzled. He didn't believe in impossible things, like Santa Claus and the Tooth Fairy. He believed in possible things, like buses and pencils and taxation. He had no problem believing in things that existed. So did she want him to believe in something which patently didn't? It was worth a try.

"I believe in the Tickle Goblin," he stated solemnly.

She laughed and kissed him. And he tickled her, and they kissed again. Graham's tummy went all fairground ride at the memory.

But Emma became serious again.

"What would you give your life for?"

"Love."

"Seriously. You must want to make the world a better place. We're not here for very long. You can't just study to get a job and earn more money than the neighbours and get a bigger house and holidays with palm trees and a gorgeous wife with equally vacuous ambitions? Can you?"

At the time, Graham couldn't see what she was getting at.

"I write poetry and do paintings," he said, sincerely.

"And they're really good! You've got talent. You're sensitive. But sometimes I wonder - where that creative energy comes from..."

"I want to get better and better with practice."

"That's great."

357

"I might even go to Art College."

"Fantastic!"

"Then I could sell them, for loads of dosh!"

Graham never got his leg over. And he went to University instead, and did Accountancy and Business Management and Operations Research. And Emma never seemed to be free when he came back during vacations.

So how the hell is this hippy arsehole playing happy families with her and the two lovely kids? It totally doesn't compute!

It's getting gradually darker. The mad hippy bampot family go back indoors, and the kitchen light comes on. Graham wonders how sandal man has been able to track him down. And WHY? for God's sake? What has he ever done to him? Until a short time ago Graham didn't even know that the deranged bastard even existed. But the man must know about multiple universes. At least, he must have been aware that Graham was another version of himself. But which one? Perhaps the man thought he was Grim! Perhaps that would make sense. Perhaps the man was on a mission to rid the world of evil. Perhaps he had Principles. Perhaps he Believed in Something. Perhaps he was On A Mission To Make The World A Better Place.

In which case, the sooner Graham can point out his mistake, the better for everybody.

The streetlights come on. Graham wraps his underlay around his body. "Underlay underlay," he says in a crap Spanish accent as he heads back outside into the nettles. It's not so bad this time because he's already trampled a path on the way in. The shadows are black now, and the sodium glare from the streetlights picks out very little.

Graham stops by the gate out into the lane. He looks left and right. But before he can scurry across the lane for a closer look he sees something move, in the undergrowth by his feet. He pauses like a freeze frame.

For a long time nothing stirs. Then, very slowly, a leaf deflects. Graham crouches. Watching out for nettles, he pulls aside some grass and twigs.

An eye looks out at him.

It blinks.

Very slowly.

"Great Galapagos!" mutters Graham to himself, and bends closer.

Methuselah almost seems to smile. Although he might just be munching a nettle.

Graham reaches forward and carefully picks him up.

"I thought you must be dead," he says. "Although we could never be sure. I hoped you'd just wandered off and found a new home." Graham is almost overcome with wistfulness for the pet he hasn't been able to pass on to his children. And the children he hasn't been able to pet. What a waste! What has he been doing with his life? He tucks Methuselah under his cape and scurries across the lane. He opens the gate to his old house as carefully as possible. There's a faint clink from the latch, but he manages to get in and close it behind him. Nobody seems to have seen him enter the back yard.

There's a rabbit hutch beside the tool shed.

Ahhh. Bless.

Graham puts the tortoise down beside the rabbit. They look at each other. Then they chew silently, but without taking their eyes off the other. Like two hungry Trappist monks. Graham sidles cautiously towards the kitchen window, and flattens himself against the wall in the shadows. He can hear voices from inside, and laughter, then protests when Emma tells the kids it's bedtime. They clamour for a story from Daddy. He makes them laugh again by tweaking his colourful Peruvian earflaps up and down, then ties the little string under his chin and picks the children up.

"Don't get them too excited Hammy," says Emma as he heads for the staircase.

So that was the bastard's name. Right enough - Hammy, from Grey Ham. His nickname at school. So the retard was still called Hammy.

"They'll be fine, pumpkin," replies Hammy, then starts to sing a jaunty little song about mice in tiny clothes and some other nauseous drivel.

Something hot and wet prickles at the back of Graham's eyes. Pumpkin! Said with Principles, and Belief, and Ideals and Conviction! Conviction for Murder! How would he explain that away to his loving family?!! Graham's eyes flood. Must be a reaction to the nettles, he thinks, wiping his face with his wrist, for lack of an available sleeve.

He risks another peek into the kitchen. It's warmly lit. A hanging Tiffany lamp over the table casts stained glass pools of light around the room. It reflects off the dark red oilcloth, and the handmade pottery crockery. Around the room are dozens of paintings, filling every available patch of wall space, propped on the mantlepiece and dressers, making the dark green walls glow with rich warmth and comfort. To his astonishment Graham recognises a drawing of Emma he did at school, high up, above the picture rail. But there are others he hasn't seen before. They explore their subjects with élan, brio, panache, chutzpah, joie de vivre and other qualities we don't even have English words for.

There are sculptures and ceramic models too. Graham dimly remembers Emma might have dabbled. The children have obviously been inspired by the feast of visual stimulus around them, for their drawings are also there, in pride of place, sometimes even sticky taped on top of daddy's picture frames. Little plasticine figures. Eggs painted with Superman costumes and pirate faces. Full cooked breakfasts of sausage, fried eggs and tomatoes made of crepe paper stuck to paper plates.

Graham sobs. They're living in a cramped hovel with a leaky roof, and it looks - wonderful.

So what's this jammy bastard got against him? Why does this lucky sod want to exterminate him?

He hears a creak from the stair, and flattens himself back against the wall outside the window, as Hammy reappears. "Quiet as little mice," he says.

"We're so lucky," she says. "They're so good."

There's a companiable pause. Then the loathsome Hammy clears his throat. "Pumpkin."

"Mmm?"

"Pumpkin Pie?"

"Yes Hamster?"

Hamster?

Barff! Blehh!! Puke!!!

"I need to go out for a while."

"Not again!"

"You know I have to."

"I really don't think you do."

361

"But you've always said - when you really truly believe in a cause, you have to have the courage of your convictions..."

Ha! Now it's coming back to bite her bum! Graham suddenly wishes he hadn't summoned up that image. His knees feel a little wobbly, and something's stirring among the credit cards and matchbox full of caterpillar which he stuffed into his underpants.

"I know whatever you're doing is for the best. It must be, 'cos I trust you. But I do worry..."

"Just a little longer and it'll be over. I'm dealing here with the most loathsome individual you could imagine. More loathsome than you could possibly envisage, my sweet pet. And something has to be done. And I have a duty, a personal obligation, to put a stop to him."

"What are you planning to do? You won't - do anything to him?"

"Least said, soonest mended. My heart is heavy with the task ahead. I don't want you to have to share the burden."

A tear rolls down her cheek. Graham doesn't see this because he's lurking in the shadows earywigging, but you can take my word for it.

"I don't want you to get hurt..."

"I won't, my love. I'll be back by midnight. And then we can relax, because it will all be over."

Will it, you psychopathic zealot? You have no idea how badly you're fucking up here, Captain Fucking Improbable... The first thing to do once he's gone is nick some of his threads. It can't all be hand-knitted crap like his self-righteous mission. And I should be able to get into his clothes. Although they might be a bit tight. He's a scrawny wizened inhabitant of the planet Vega, while I'm a buff, toned, circuit training, horse-

362

riding athlete. Once I've squeezed into them I can move about in public again, and find Pate, and work out what I'm going to do with twat-features here. And with the lovely Emma he so richly doesn't deserve.

As the back door opens Graham sinks down into the darkest corner, with the underlay of invisibility over his head. Hammy puts on his helmet and bicycle clips, then opens the gate and lifts his bike out into the lane. "Bye Nibbles," he says quietly, pointlessly and extremely annoyingly as he cycles off. Graham suppresses the urge to reply 'Bye Hamster' in a nibbly kind of voice.

Chapter 50

For a couple of hours Emma watches the telly.

Celebrity WAG Swap.

Strictly Bedroom.

Police Camera Thieving Junky Car Smash.

Ho ho! Bet the Hamster thinks she watches *Coast* and other Open University 'improving' fare the BBC uses to make bland primetime programmes out of budgets and quotas earmarked for education.

Then she heads upstairs. The bedroom light goes on. She's probably reading some floss-brained commercial chick-lit. Graham waits, shivering. At last the light goes out. He gives it another twenty minutes, then starts to think about breaking in. He wonders about pushing aside the plywood behind the broken glass, but reckons that this will just get his hand into the house. Into the sink to be precise. And he really needs all of him to get in if he's to achieve anything. Then he wonders whether Hammy has a spare key hidden somewhere, and if so, where?

Then he realises that Hammy isn't the only tosser in town. Because Graham knows where the spare key is. It's obvious! It's on a nail inside the toolshed that used to be a toilet up above the door among the cobwebs.

Graham eases the shed door open. The key is on a nail inside the toolshed that used to be a toilet up above the door among the cobwebs.

Of course.

He has to stoop as he walks to hold the handcuff trailing from his left leg, to stop it rattling. He takes off his underlay cloak, eases the key into the lock and lets himself in to the kitchen. Then slowly, stealthily he climbs the stairs. He remembers the creak as Hammy descended the stairs, and tries to remember which tread it was. To be safe he climbs with each foot against the walls rather than standing in the middle of each step. At the top, he pauses to make sure he's going for the right bedroom. If he's to find some of Hammy's clothes he will need to let himself silently into the bedroom where Emma is sleeping, and locate the wardrobe and cupboards by the dim light from the street outside.

The bedroom door is slightly ajar, and swings open almost silently. He can see Emma lying under the covers, her hair backlit by a pale blue light from above the rooftops. His heart, which is already racing, does a few jumps over hurdles.

He feels for a chest of drawers and locates a polo shirt. Probably pink, but it will do. He tries a lower drawer in search of some trousers, without success. He looks around the room. On a chair by the window he spots a pair of jeans. Perfect. He inches towards them. Then he remembers we went metric years ago. He centimetres towards them. Suddenly he halts. Something is touching his knee. It feels like a hand. The hand millimetres up his thigh. He looks down.

"Hi," says a female voice.

"Oh hi," he replies, with a catch in his throat. He doesn't want the hand to stop, but he fears that the discovery in his underpants of a handful of credit cards and a caterpillar in a large matchbox would raise questions he doesn't feel equipped to answer.

He reaches down and takes her hand in his. Since he has an armful of clothes on one side this involves dropping the handcuff. There's a metallic rattle. He feels he needs to explain. "I'm, erm, I'm, er..."

"You're back early."

"I didn't want to frighten you."

"I knew it was you. You always come upstairs in the dark like that trying not to make the stairs creak. I love the way you're so considerate."

She thinks I'm him, Graham realises. The credit cards get a good shuffle.

"Come to bed," she says, in a come-to-bed kind of voice. To say Graham was torn would barely do justice to the raging conflict between the liberation army of his head and the Mujahadeen of his loins. He tells himself that he and Emma are married, in a confused alternative universe sort of way. And gets into bed. Emma snuggles up, and he pushes his left leg as far away from her as he can, with a subdued clank and rattle.

"What have you got there?" she asks.

"Later..." he replies.

"You're a naughty boy."

He wonders how naughty he can be. He's tempted to be very very naughty indeed. Emma continues. "Do you still fancy me?"

"You must be mental."

"Mental to think you don't fancy me, or mental to think you do?"

"Just barking," says Graham, and puts his tongue in her ear. She giggles and punches him.

"It's just, I thought, since I had the kids - I don't know if you think of me the same way."

"I can't think of you at all without being choked by a rising tide of red-hot lust."

This time Emma punches him in the ribs, then licks his eyeball. It is quite dark, after all. She continues. Speaking, not licking. Tricky to do both. "It's just that you've got - awful serious."

"I thought you wanted me to be serious. When we first started going out."

"Well you were a bit of a - joker."

"Tell me. I want to know."

"I used to think you were uncommitted. You didn't seem to give a shit about anybody but yourself."

"That was me. Back in the day."

"You were shallow. Fatuous."

"Me me me."

"You didn't care about social injustice, or poverty, or anything that wasn't completely superficial."

"Apart from sport."

"Exactly."

"That was a joke."

"Ah."

"So when did you change your mind?" asks Graham.

"It wasn't me that changed, It was you."

"Yes..."

Graham snuggles his forehead into the delicious soft space between her ear and her shoulder.

"That night when you and your Dad had that awful row."

Oh shit, thinks Graham. Emma continues. "He was so upset when he knocked you out. I heard the crash

367

through the wall. I came running in through the back door. You had blood in your eye, and teeth marks on your forehead. I was confused."

"Yes, the teeth marks."

"All you could talk about when you came to was Methuselah."

"That was my tortoise. He'd gone walkabout."

"I never understood that bit. Are you fond of tortoises?"

"Not in an inappropriate way."

"But you were different after that. More thoughtful. More considerate."

"And my dad?"

"You always got on so well. He was upset when you decided to go to Art College instead of Uni, but he never let on. And he supported you all the way. And I was just so moved - by the way you looked after him, when his health started to go."

Graham basks in a warm glow of self-righteousness. So that was when he and Hammy split into separate realities! The blow on the head! The uncertainty over Methuselah's fate! Schrödinger's Tortoise! Graham went on to become a management consultant, while Hammy trod the hippy dippy path. Graham breathes great sighs of great size. It's all starting to make sense. Then he remembers the more immediate dangers he faces.

"Em..."

"You haven't called me that for ages."

Actually Graham was just hesitating while he wondered how to broach the subject.

"Em. My mission. You must have read between the lines. You're very observant. Female intuition. How much do you know about what I'm trying to do?"

He strokes her soft downy cheek.

"I know there's a man, someone from your past. And I know he's done some terrible things. And you think you have a way to - stop him."

"So you don't know how, exactly?"

"I presume you're going to - speak to him."

"Ahhh. That's right..."

He runs his fingers through her hair.

"What have you put on your hands? They're normally so dry, with the turps."

"Just some face and hands lotion stuff - for men," he added, in case she thought he was dipping into her own supplies.

"You what?"

"On my hands. Stops them drying up."

There's a gulp from somewhere near his forehead. "You think that stuff's crap! What's come over you?"

"Closet metrosexual..."

"Hammy..."

Emma snuggles closer, and starts to run her fingers down his stomach, towards his caterpillar. "Wait," Graham breathes in her ear. He's trying to work out how to get closer without revealing the handcuffs. He gently lifts the hem of her nightie. In a single sinuous movement she pulls it off over her head.

"Fuck me, missus - you're a bit frisky!"

She smacks him on the head, then pushes it down against her. He licks her chest - indeed her chests. For she has two. She moans and wriggles under his lips. His tongue slides about on her like a Ladies Olympic Ice

369

Dancing champion reprising her gold-medal-winning routine. If he'd pushed a tiny tutu over his tongue and played Ravel's Bolero you couldn't have told the difference. Oh, and also pulled on a pair of rather opaque sludge coloured tights. He twirls, he leaps, he leaves little wet figures of eight on the rink of her body. As his tongue twirls, his hips gyrate as he pushes off his Y-fronts with their precious contents. Actually a handful of the precious contents leaps free unaided, while the credit cards and caterpillar box fall on the floor.

Then to a tumult of applause, the ice dancer bows and leaves, and the curling starts. The first throw is a big wet tongue which heads down down down towards the bullseye, or as the experts call it, the 'house', and in the centre the 'tee'. As it slowly curls towards its destination there's some brushing or 'sweeping'. Slowly it slides, towards a perfect position from which the player is guaranteed to 'win the end'.

Moments before Graham steals his end, there's a creak from downstairs. "Fuck!" says Graham.

"What?"

Graham knows fine well what the noise is. It's bloody Hamster coming home early, having failed to find Graham. No surprise there, then.

"Shit shit shit." Graham spits a hair out of his mouth.

"Did you hear something? I missed it."

"You were moaning."

"Of course I was moaning."

"I better go and investigate."

"Be careful!"

"Shhhh!"

Graham has dropped the clothes he was carrying, and decides to make do without. It doesn't make much difference. The jeans and the tee-shirt were Emma's anyway. He may have shed his kecks, but at least he still has his socks and shoes on. He grabs the underlay. Thus cloaked for battle, he starts to descend the stairs, avoiding the middle of each tread. Barely visible in the light from below he spots a figure with a John Wayne gait starting to walk cautiously upstairs the same way. Graham kicks out at the man's head. He misses, but the handcuff doesn't, smacking Hammy across the bridge of the nose. Instead of the scream and thwacking crash which would happen in a film there's just a dull groan as Hammy slumps backwards to the kitchen floor. Graham clatters down and grabs him by the shoulders, then starts to drag him across the kitchen towards the back door. Whatever happens he can't let Emma see both of them together.

Hammy starts to come round. He struggles, reaching around him for a weapon. The two men seem evenly matched. Oddly enough. Hammy grabs a chair but Graham kicks it out of his grasp. Graham pulls him towards the door, then lunges towards the cupboard under the sink, hoping for a plumbing wrench, or some bleach. All's fair in love and multiverses!

He grabs a roll of black plastic drawstring bin liners, which may be the most lethal weapon available. Graham gives another heave and the two men roll outside on to the cracked paving slabs. Graham drops the binliners and tugs at the underlay. Thank goodness for small comforts, thinks Graham, whose naked body is potentially at risk of abrasion. And death, if Hammy gets a grip on him. Graham gets his arms round Hammy's neck and squeezes. Hammy reaches around him, but only has one weapon to hand. He pulls a bin

371

liner over Graham's head and tugs the drawstring. Graham can't get a hand free to pull it off again without releasing his death grip on Hammy's neck. Instead he tries to nibble the plastic from inside. Who will weaken first? In this dance of death, there can only be one winner. A Pasodoble for matador and bull. So who will survive, and who will get the ears for souvenirs? And the nuts for breakfast? Destiny sings the tune to both men. Although it's a bit muffled for Graham, because the bag's quite heavy-duty plastic.

"You've got the wrong man!" shouts Graham.

"No I haven't!" grunts Hammy.

"I look like you! But I'm not him!"

"Perma-tan and flashy gnashers! I know exactly who you are!"

"I'm not Grim Dupeint! The man you're after is an international arms dealer!"

"The man I'm after is a bastard management consultant who puts honest men and women out of their jobs!"

Fuck, thinks Graham. That's me!

"Who ruins the lives of people like my friend Pate," continues Hammy.

The same Pate? Who knows? Could be another one, in another universe...

"I've reformed. I've seen the error of my ways!"

"Like fuck you have, you slimy tosser!"

"Get the bag off! I can't breath!"

"Let go my fucking neck!"

"Then you'll kill me!"

"Damn right I will!"

"But you can't. It's morally wrong!"

"Pate says it isn't. It's not even suicide. It's like cutting out a tumour to save the patient!"

Wait till I see Pate! thinks Graham, quite quickly since he's about to pass out. That's just the kind of intellectual shite he would say.

"The world will be better off without you," Hammy drones on, in a Save The Planet self-righteous kind of way.

"But if I deserve to die, then so do you! (Cough) We're the same person. (Inhales plastic bag and wheezes it out again) And you'll be destroyed by guilt..." Graham's voice is getting weaker. Hammy thinks for a moment.

"Nah, fuck it. You're a bigger arse than I am. Pate said that's how our worlds split apart. Because I took the decision to be good and thoughtful, and you carried on being a wanker."

"Please. Release me. Let me go..."

Graham's grip on Hammy's neck is slipping.

"For I don't love you anymore."

He lets go of Hammy's neck and feels feebly about him for a weapon. Like a total feeb.

Graham mutters something else, but if I told you what it would confirm he was singing a song, and I'd have to get copyright clearance.

His hand locates the rabbit hutch, but it's too heavy for him to lift one-handed. Then beside it, he touches something hard, just the right weight. He grasps it by the handle and with the last ounce (28.35 Grams) of his ebbing strength he swings it down on Hammy's head. Hammy looks up to see Methuselah being swung shell-first by the neck towards his face. "Where the..." are the last words he utters before - well actually there isn't an impact, because no sooner has he spotted the tortoise and its little beady eye in the wizened head in Graham's grasp than he vanishes with just the faintest whoosh of air skooshing in to fill the space he just occupied. Graham doesn't see this, because he has his head in a heavy-duty black bin liner.

For year after year after year Hammy just never knew whether the tortoise was dead or alive. And now, in an instant, the truth is upon him.

And his universe, and Graham's, pop apart, as they should have done years ago when Graham got a quantum gash on the temple.

The tortoise drops onto Graham's motionless body.

'You're the bastard who wandered off to University and abandoned me,' thinks Methuselah. And sinks his teeth into the end of Graham's willy.

The light in the kitchen goes on, and Emma leaps out wearing a dressing gown and wielding a plumber's wrench and a bottle of bleach. She knows where they live! Her man is lying there, deathly still. He is stark naked, apart from socks and some expensive looking black shoes. He has a pair of handcuffs round his left ankle, and a black plastic bag over his head, secured tightly round his neck. And he appears to be getting a blow job from a tortoise.

Emma cradles him in her arms, and pulls the plastic bag free. There's a faint gasp as Graham sucks in the cool night air. Emma looks down at him with resignation, and renewed interest.

"Still the same naughty old Graham. Well I never..."

Chapter 51

Graham and Pate chat as they walk down the street. Graham is in jeans, sporting paint stains and exuding a faint smell of turpentine. He wears flip flops. Pate wears Bermuda shorts and a Hawaiian shirt decorated with lurid palm trees and sunsets.

"Honest Cowboy - I never met the man."

"He said you were a friend."

"Clearly I have a quantum compadre. Somewhere there must be some poor creature both simultaneously dead and alive. And my fate lies in a Damoclean balance. Both mine and that of my Pate-shaped twin."

" I still feel a bit guilty. I've done away with Hammy and pinched his woman."

"It could all have worked out very differently."

"Sure. The tortoise might have bitten my dick off."

"Remember that neither you nor Hammy knew of its fate. Alone in that garden it might have been dead, or alive. So when you spotted it, you might have been the party to make a sharp exit. And dear Hamster would have been none the wiser - his routine blissfully uninterrupted."

"Guess."

"So you needn't concern yourself with the consequences. Indeed, in another universe he is still blissfully married to the fair Emma. Assuming that she wasn't completely hacked off to find her man in the back yard wrestling with a black plastic bag and a pair of handcuffs. And claiming, by way of an excuse, to have been fighting a naked replica of himself who's just mysteriously vanished into thin air."

"True enough."

Some yards ahead, seated on the pavement, a vagrant huddles on a blanket. He has a scabby dog in a cardboard box. He holds out his hand towards them.

"So your concerns are de trop," continues Pate. "You have the lifestyle, the girl, and the money. Your cup truly brimmeth over."

"I'm still worried about Bumface. Surely a caterpillar should have turned into something by now."

"And said caterpillar has still not come out, in gay finery?"

"Not when I last looked. So I've locked it away. I'm not sure if I dare find out whether it's still alive..."

"Spare a few bob mate. I need to buy a nuclear submarine to get back to South America."

Graham pulls a pound coin from his pocket and drops it in the man's polystyrene cup.

"Last of the big spenders..." says the man.

"Fuck you and your index linked pension," says Graham.

Their eyes meet.

They have the same eyes.

"I know you, ya jammy paint spattered hippy!" shouts the beggar. "Living in a garret cos you think it's what real artists do. You'd cut off your ear if someone paid you enough."

Pate looks at both in horror. It's another Graham.

376

"I used to be a contender," rambles the man. "Come here while I punch you."

The dog cowers down in the box. Nobody can see whether it's OK or not. Graham opens his mouth to shout abuse, but before he can utter a word Pate knocks him flying, just as a bullet zings by and embeds itself in the wall.

"That's him!" yells Kerri's private investigator Trace McCall. "Him on the blanket!"

Graham and Pate scramble under a parked articulated lorry with a small orange flag taped to the bonnet.

"Who the hell's shooting?" screams Kerri. "Leave him alive! I need to sue him!"

A large black car swerves past, and from the passenger side Tone unleashes a blast of machine gun fire.

"Is the dog OK?" asks Constable Ainstable.

"Bugger the dog!" shouts WPC Enid Sneep through a loudhailer, alarming the beggar, who thinks this is a police order. "Nobody move! You're all under arrest!"

Tone should have driven, instead of wielding the machine gun. Because Henry Hatchett is a better business shark than a getaway driver. And in the back, Compton Coffers has his hands over his eyes. The vehicle hits a wall and bursts into flames.

Kerri thinks the beggar is her husband, and stands shouting abuse at him. Because that's what she does.

Leachman Pryer videos the scene. Because that's what he does.

WPC Sneep locks up the survivors. Because that's what she does.

Graham and Pate get away.

Which is a bit of a break with tradition.

Epilogue

Graham and Emma sit in the kitchen. The Tiffany lamp casts a lovely warm glow. The kids' pictures are still on the rich green walls, but the walls are much further apart. And there are more of them. Around many more rooms. In fact Graham has a studio, while Emma has her own pottery room with kiln.

"Look Mummy, this key fits in the metal box."

"Now leave that alone, Timmy. You know daddy doesn't like you touching his things."

But Timmy is a lively child, accustomed to expressing his creative urges.

"Look Mummy, the key turns!"

Graham turns his head to see what they're doing. Little Adeline dips her podgy fingers into the metal box, and pulls out a matchbox. (Original Cook's Matches, extra-long). "Stop Addy! Don't touch the matchbox!!" Graham leaps to his feet, and knocks the table over in his desperation to reach the matchbox in time.

But it's too late. Addy slides open the lid of the matchbox.

And I take a deep breath, and stretch out my wonderful richly coloured wings as I clamber up on to the edge of the box. Graham looks on in wonder. I flutter them gently and take to the air.

"Ahhh!" says Addy.

"Wow!" says Timmy.

"Golly!" says Emma.

Pop goes Graham, as a whoosh of air rushes in to occupy the space where he was just a moment ago.

Alternative Epilogue

OK, so I can't remember which universe we were featuring. Does it matter? They're all true, all at once. Suit yourself.

Graham and Emma sit in the kitchen. The Tiffany lamp casts a lovely warm glow. The kids' pictures are still on the rich green walls, but the walls are much further apart. And there are more of them. Around many more rooms. In fact Graham has a studio, while Emma has her own pottery room with kiln.

"Look Mummy, this key fits in the metal box."

"Now leave that alone, Timmy. You know daddy doesn't like you touching his things."

But Timmy is a lively child, accustomed to expressing his creative urges.

"Look Mummy, the key turns!"

Graham turns his head to see what they're doing. Little Adeline dips her podgy fingers into the metal box, and pulls out a matchbox. (Original Cook's Matches, extra-long). "Stop Addy! Don't touch the matchbox!!" Graham leaps to his feet, and knocks the table over in his desperation to reach the matchbox in time.

But it's too late. Addy slides open the lid of the matchbox.

There in the bottom is a dried up long-dead brown shrivelly thing.

"Ahhh!" says Addy.

"Wow!" says Timmy.

"Golly!" says Emma.

"Thank fuck for that," gasps Graham, breathing out a large whoosh of air.

"Language!!!" shout Mum and the kids, then everybody bursts out laughing and has lots of fun, and I eat the brown shrivelled thing, then pull my head back into my shell for a nap, and Mummy and Daddy put the kids to bed after a lovely frothy bath, then go through to their own super bedroom for a game of Olympic Lady Ice Dancers, in handcuffs.

Graham's Problems

Example 1 – How not to be late for work

See Page 8. Graham thinks he may have missed the bus, but can't be sure.

Option 1: He can stay where he is and hope both the bus and its usual passengers are late. (He calls this Bus Not Been.) He'll be first in the queue (if one materialises) and can jump on board and grab the best seat available. But if the situation is actually Bus Been he could be standing here at the stop for ten minutes and will definitely be late for work.

However (Option 2) he can set off up the road and past the trees at the end and stride on another couple of hundred yards to the traffic lights near the shops. This allows him a choice of an additional bus (the number 19 which converges at that point with his usual 13). The two buses alternate in their arrivals. So if he has indeed missed the bus (Bus Been) then he will almost certainly catch a 19 before the next 13 appears. And if it's Option 2/Bus Not Been then he may in fact catch the tardy 13 at the shops.

The choice seems clear. Ish...

As the table on the next page should show.

	Option 1 Stay	Option 2 Walk
Bus been	Wait 10 minutes *Definitely 7 minutes late!*	Walk 4 minutes, Wait no more than 5 minutes and probably much less *Best outcome – 1 minute late* *Worst outcome – 6 minutes late*
Bus not been	Wait 2 or 3 minutes *Possibly on time*	Walk 4 minutes, wait no more than 5 minutes and probably much less *Best outcome – 1 minute late* *Worst outcome – 6 minutes late*

Graham's analytical brain tells him that Option 2 (Walk) gives him more choices of bus and a decent chance that he'll only be four or five minutes late. Whereas Option 1 (Stay) is a gamble. It's his only chance of arriving on time – but the downside is greater too. Graham opts to give up 'possible best' for 'least worst'. He decides to minimise his lateness by walking, but by doing so he gives up his only chance of arriving on time.

Pathetic.

Example 2 – Centrifugal force. We see it, we feel it, we know what it does. So how come it doesn't exist?

On Page 148 Pate's hair is full of froth from his pint. Don't ask why. Read the book if you're bothered. Don't just turn to the back hoping you'll find the answers.

"You could do a pirouette," says Graham. "Then the froth might spray outwards, by centrifugal force."

"No such thing," says Pate. "Centrifugal force doesn't exist."

"Wha!" explodes Graham. "Now you're really talking bollocks. I may not be an Einstein, but even I know what centrifugal force is. And where did Chapter 24 go? What are we doing in an Appendix? If it was up to me I'd remove all Appendices."

"That's because you know as soon as we hit the Appendix you're about to lose an argument. So what is Centrifugal Force when it's at home?"

"It's the force which when you spin an object round and round it makes it try to fly off into space."

Pate looks quizzical. "So what exerts this force?"

"Umm. Erm. Well, like, if you sit on one of those roundabout thingies in a playground you start to slide off towards the edge. That's centrifugal force."

"No it isn't."

"For flip's sake Pate! You're arguing that black is white. It is beyond all reasonable doubt. Something's pushing you outwards. You can test it. It works every time. Whiz whiz whiz, round round round, whee - fly off sideways, land on your arse on the ground. You cannot tell me that's not true."

"It's not centrifugal force."

"Well it's not elves and fairies pulling on invisible silken threads. So what the hell else could it be?"

"It's not centrifugal force."

"You can't win this one Pate. You fly in the face of reason. You slap the cheeks of sanity with your ethnic knitted mitts."

"Right, think it through. You're going round on a roundabout, OK? Like the gyrating funster you are."

"Correct. I'm having fun going round in circles. Like your pathetic argument."

"And suddenly a new force says 'Hey, there's someone going round in circles. I think I'll head outwards from the centre and push him off."

"Exactly!"

"Gonads, Mr Paint."

"You can feel it! It pushes you outwards!!"

"If it's any consolation, many generations of rotating numbskulls thought just the same as you. They were convinced there was a force. So they called it centrifugal force. From the Latin. To flee the centre."

"Precisely."

"That doesn't mean they were right. They also thought fire was a substance called phlogiston."

"But I can wave a bucket of water round my head until it's horizontal and the water will stay in."

"You can set your underpants on fire and cycle up and down waving them around on the end of a golf club singing Land of Hope and Glory. You, not the golf club. It still doesn't make centrifugal force real."

Graham is irritated beyond even the generous measures which Pate has inspired in the past. "So what the bloody hell pushes you off the roundabout?"

"It's very simple," says Pate. "Newton's Second Law. An object set in motion will continue in a straight line until a force is exerted upon it."

"Aha!"

"Not aha! at all. At every moment of your rotation your body is trying to fly off in a straight line. That's not centrifugal force. That's just you cruising along and trying to keep going. Like sparks off a catherine wheel. It's friction between the roundabout on the seat of your pants which keeps pulling you off course and constraining your motion to a circle. So the force you feel pulling you outwards is just the combination of all the straight lines your body really wants to take. But think of where those sparks go..."

"They fly outwards," says Graham, but more hesitantly.

"Not in a straight line from the centre of the wheel."

"No. They fly off at a tangent."

"Correct. Like your thoughts. The sparks fly off in a straight line from the edge of the spinning wheel - in exactly the direction they were going when they were released. Not like some imaginary centrifugal force which you seem to believe is pushing you out in a straight line from the centre. You've seen it with your own eyes."

"I've seen Spiderman swinging from skyscrapers. Doesn't mean I have to believe it."

"Suit yourself, guano brains."

There's a long and not particularly companionable pause. Needless to say Graham interrupts it. "See the water in the bucket flying round your head on a string? Is it suffering from an illusion? Does it just *think* centrifugal force is keeping it in the bucket?"

"You think about it, denier of reason."

Pate actually says this like Graham's denying something. He hasn't invented a new, more logical measure of thickness for tights and stockings.

"Now accept defeat, and get back to Page 148!"

Example 3 – How to visit all the towns by the shortest route

See Page 251. This is the Travelling Salesman problem. Take for instance:

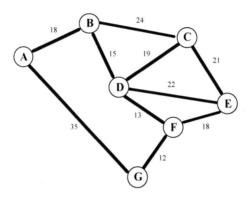

ABCDEFGA is 148 miles. ABDCEFGA is 138 miles. ABCEDFGA is a massive 180 miles. There are ten roads, but each solution only uses seven of them. Seems trivially simple, but the mathematics of finding a formula for optimal solutions defeated even massive computers, and even bigger mathematicians, for a long time. Instead, you had to use heuristics, which basically means guessing, then trying loads more guesses (iterations) until you think you're getting warm.

You could also try to use the quickest route rather than the shortest one, or the one which uses least fuel. All equally tricky. There's still no simple formula for the best answer, although mathematicians now have a process which can get them there. But the delivery guy isn't a mathematician, which is why he always has an excuse.

Typical.

Acknowledgements

To Lizzie, Rob, Ollie, Lucy, Jamie and my Mum and Dad who've all shown a remarkable ability to conceal their embarrassment in the face of my worst excesses.

Big thanks to Kirsten and Barry Butcher, and Alan and Jeni Strachan, who gave me hospitality and encouragement while I battered the keyboard.

And a massive ta to the authonomy community, who have provided sage editorial advice (which bits of the book were rubbish), copy editing (which bits were rubbish, inexplicable, and spelled wrongly), and proof reading (which bits were rubbish and badly typed).

They also gave advice on design and fonts, and encouragement for the three lines of text which were left after the other advice had been acted upon.

Thanks as well to Lindsey Fraser of Fraser Ross Associates, and to Sara Sheridan and Nicola Morgan for their input on branding and marketing.

And a big round of applause to Inga McVicar of Full Paper Jacket for a superb appraisal and marketing report.

t: 0782 444 3654 | e: inga@fullpaperjacket.co.uk

www.fullpaperjacket.co.uk

Other stuff

There's a website at www.zanestumpo.com
Scan this to get there fast…

For more about the book and other fripperies and ephemera go to…

http://zane-stumpo.blogspot.co.uk

You might wish to visit to engage Mr Stumpo in light banter and badinage. There's also a rather rude animated trailer for the book. This can be found on YouTube as well.

Zane Stumpo has recorded an audio book of Schrödinger's Caterpillar read by himself. There's a sample first chapter which you can find on the blog.

And if you're in a book group, then there are suggested topics for discussion on the web site.

About the author

Zane Stumpo is the younger, more successful version of an old fart who refuses to face reality. It's not obvious why he's coy about his real identity, since he normally grabs any opportunity to leap up and down shouting 'Look at me!'

The whiskery wrinkly version had a bizarre student lifestyle for many years. He did a degree in Architecture (failed), then English. He worked for a year in London as a trainee stockbroker, then did a postgraduate degree in Business Administration. Following this he accidentally did a PhD in Operations Research which involved computer programming and developing new pure mathematical approaches to sub-gradient optimisation. (Or sub-gradient optimism, according to his mother.)

His mum then suggested he should apply for a summer job with the BBC while he was deciding what to do next. His plans came unstuck when he inadvertently went for a permanent post, so he spent some years working in radio. He would have left, but they tried to get rid of him, so he had to stay. After years of idleness and occasional showing off on the telly he set up his own independent TV production company. Over the years he's spent more time looking for work than doing it, but on the rare occasions he bagged a commission he did at least get to visit remote and disreputable places.

He presented loads of programmes in America, which seemed like a good idea at the time.

He now makes short films in the forlorn hope that one day he'll direct a movie. His company has one member of staff. That's him.

He drew the pictures and designed the cover, although Zane said it was him. And he drew the animated trailer, and did the voice.

His doppelganger Zane Stumpo has all the experience and wisdom of the old git, but is many years younger and less frayed around the edges.

Lightning Source UK Ltd.
Milton Keynes UK
UKOW041142141212

203673UK00001B/2/P